PRINCESS IN AMBER

Other Books by Evelyn Wilde Mayerson

SANJO

BIRDS ARE FREE

NO ENEMY BUT TIME

PRINCESS IN AMBER

Evelyn Wilde Mayerson

DOUBLEDAY & COMPANY, INC.
GARDEN CITY, NEW YORK
1985

For Lilli and Joan

And for all who struggle with the
ethical dilemma of duty vs. self

Library of Congress Cataloging in Publication Data
Mayerson, Evelyn Wilde, 1934–
    Princess in amber.
    1. Beatrice, Princess, consort of Henry, Prince
of Battenberg, 1857–1944—Fiction. 2. Victoria, Queen
of Great Britain, 1819–1901—Fiction. I. Title.
PS3563.A9554P7   1985   813'.54
ISBN: 0-385-17995-2
Library of Congress Card Catalog Number 84–6039

ACKNOWLEDGMENTS

Setting a story in another time and place in which the major characters were historical figures demands ardent attention to detail and a concern for the dyes and fibers that fashion the weave of the time. It has been my happy experience to meet unfailing cooperation, sometimes downright enthusiasm, in my search. My grateful thanks are acknowledged to the staff of the London Library, the British Museum, the Wellcome Historical Medical Library, the New York Academy of Medicine Library, the Bodleian Library at Oxford, the Public Library of the City of New York, and the library at New York University. I am grateful to the skilled guides of the National Portrait Gallery, the Queen's Gallery at Buckingham Palace, Great Britain's National Army Museum, Windsor Castle, Balmoral, Carisbrooke Castle, Osborne, and the entire Isle of Wight, including the cabbie who drove me everywhere and refused a fare. For their searches in obtaining out-of-print and rare books I wish to thank Hatchard's Ltd., of London, Blackwell, Ltd. at Oxford, and the Royalty Book Shop of New York City. My most grateful thanks goes to my friend and colleague Lester Goran, who gave me insight into the special problems of researching historical fiction; and to Mildred Merrick, reference librarian at the University of Miami, which boasts an unusually fine collection of British local history and Victoriana, surprising when one considers that Coral Gables was not yet conceived at that time, much less the library.

AUTHOR'S NOTE

This is a novel whose central theme is the singular relationship between a queen and her youngest daughter. It is based on the author's examination of diaries, journals, letters, periodicals, works of history, philosophy, biography, medicine, military practice, dress, field sports, and deportment. While it is true to the spirit and events as they transpired, the author has taken the novelist's prerogative of reading between the lines to yield the richer stuff of motivation and desire.

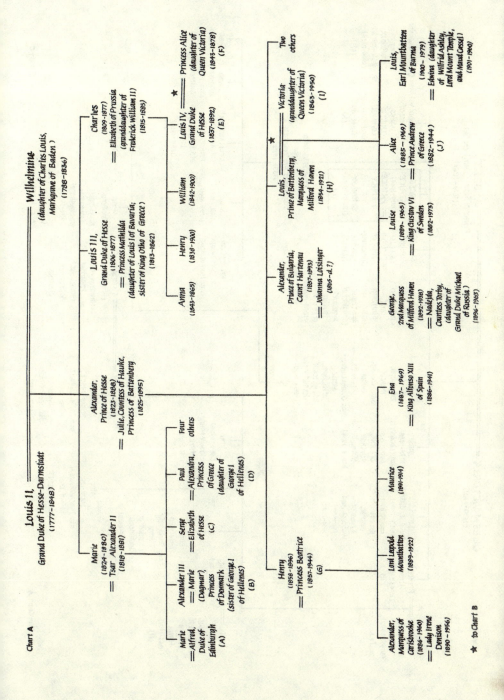

Chart A

Chart B

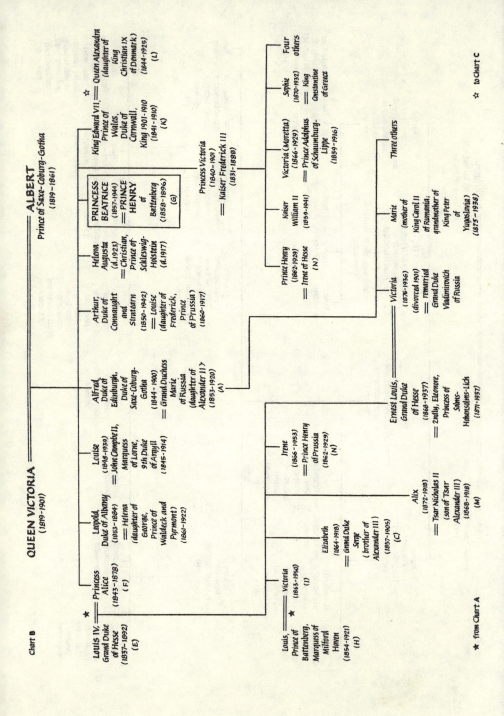

QUEEN VICTORIA
(1819-1901)
=
ALBERT
Prince of Saxe-Coburg-Gotha
(1819-1861)

★ from Chart A

☆ to Chart C

Chart C

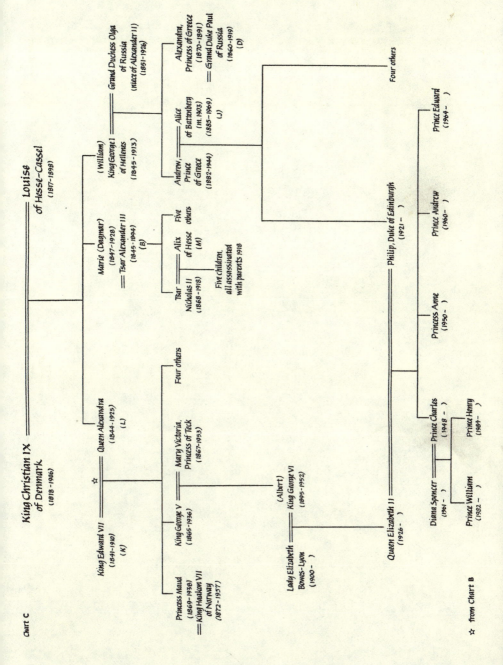

King Christian IX
of Denmark
(1818-1906)
══ Louise
of Hesse-Cassel
(1817-1898)

Princess Maud
(1869-1938)
══ King Haakon VII
of Norway
(1872-1957)

King Edward VII
(1841-1910)
(K)

Queen Alexandra
(1844-1925)
(L)

☆ King George V
(1865-1936)
══ Mary Victoria,
Princess of Teck
(1867-1953)

Four others

Marie (Dagmar)
(1847-1928)
══ Tsar Alexander III
(1845-1894)
(B)

(William)
King George I
of the Hellenes
(1845-1913)
══ Grand Duchess Olga
of Russia
(niece of Alexander II)
(1851-1926)

Tsar
Nicholas II
(1868-1918)
══ Alix
of Hesse
(M)

Five
others

Five children,
all assassinated
with parents 1918

Andrew,
Prince
of Greece
(1882-1944)
══ Alice
of Battenberg
(m. 1903)
(1885-1969)
(J)

Alexandra,
Princess of Greece
(1870-1891)
══ Grand Duke Paul
of Russia
(1860-1919)
(D)

Princess Maud ... King Edward VII ... King George V

Four others

Princess Anne
(1950-)

Philip, Duke of Edinburgh
(1921-)

Prince Andrew
(1960-)

Prince Edward
(1964-)

(Albert)
King George VI
(1895-1952)

Lady Elizabeth
Bowes-Lyon
(1900-)

Queen Elizabeth II
(1926-)

Diana Spencer
(1961-)
══ Prince Charles
(1948-)

Prince Henry
(1984-)

Prince William
(1982-)

☆ from Chart B

PRINCESS IN AMBER

CHAPTER ONE

The garden lay nestled high in the opalescent blue violet hills, one of many sequestered in the cliff of walls and barrel tile roofs, with steep narrow flights of steps, green shutters, and balconies, in the village of Menton. It overlooked the Mediterranean and the harbor below with its shifting screen of masts and ropes, patched bright orange sails of the fishing boats, and rust-streaked, faded emerald hulls that lay cradled on the rocky beach.

Shielded from the high winds by black cypresses, eucalyptus as high as elms, and fig trees with swelling buds, heliotrope and roses scratched for space with bougainvillea and sarsaparilla. Wild asparagus spilled over the rocks, minty gray-green sage and myrtle with dark fragrant berries poked between the crevices, and everything, even the graceful draping ferns, was scented with the sweet, sharp aroma of citrus from the lemon groves.

White-stockinged and powdered footmen wearing pink poplin breeches and tunics trimmed with silver epaulets entered the garden with lighted tapers. All had well-shaped calves; none, as in lesser houses, were uncouth, ill-favored louts dragged in hastily and stuffed into livery that was either too large or too small. Authentic footmen were always tall, something like the Prussian pages, who resembled geraniums, all stalk and no leaves but with better legs.

Seated at a small skirted table on which gleamed a silver tea service was a small, plump woman dressed in black foulard, a twilled silk that caught the fading afternoon light and lent to the folds of the long-sleeved, high-necked garment, as well as to her gray eyes, the same lavender hue of the deepening sky. She ignored the footmen, and they, in turn, like all well-trained servants, returned the courtesy. Unbuttoning her gloves with her customary deliberation, she slipped them off her small white dimpled hands and lay them in her lap, then untied her bonnet strings, flung them over her shoulders, and sipped from a royal blue and gilt Sèvres cup with the raised initials VR entwined in its medallion.

"The tea is especially good," she said to a kilted man with curly hair and beard who stood before her, holding a small tray. Her accent was Teutonic despite the fact that she was ruler of the British Empire, a nation that in 1882 was finding imperialism irresistible, less a brazen conceit than a worldwide trust to keep the peace, spread the wisdom of British institutions, and elevate the savage.

The man to whom she spoke, John Brown, was handsome, the angled planes of his face as sturdy as the crags of his native Scotland. "It should be, woman," he replied, his blue eyes steady. "It's got spurruts in it."

Victoria set down her steaming cup, undisturbed by her servant's crude familiarity, which had been the cause of scandalous rumors and had so enraged the Prince of Wales, her oldest son Bertie. "I might have guessed," she replied, glancing with irritation toward the villa, its gemlike windows divided by mullions into facets, now splashed with spray from the towering fountain that waved its water like a plume. "I am growing tired of sitting. I should like to be able to dance. As I used to. A wonderful Scottish reel where the ladies' skirts swing like great bells and the boots of the men tromp the floor like cannon."

"If it was a gillies' ball you were after, we should have stayed at Balmoral."

Victoria smiled, a cherubic smile that crinkled her eyes, curved her cheeks, and showed her teeth, and which photographers seldom caught, primarily because she found it tiresome to hold while they fiddled beneath their black tents. "You are angry with the Europeans because they laugh at your kilt. As it is, I find it impossible to see the sights with you looming before me like some Scottish colossus. All I can see of anything is your beard."

"There is good reason why I stand before you, ma'am," he replied, setting the tray before her and folding his arms across his chest.

She pursed her lips as she frequently did when she was not pleased with the turn a conversation took. "It is worth being shot at to see how much one is loved. I had no idea that I was so popular in other countries, although I do wish the foreign dailies would not draw me looking like a partridge."

"Popularity cannot protect you from the Fenians."

"The man was no Fenian. He was simply mad. Gladstone has told me that when an attempt is made on the life of the ruler in other countries, the motives are political, whereas in England it can only be insanity. It is one of the few statements he has made with which I agree," replied Victoria, who regarded her Prime Minister as being both disagreeable and boring, a combination without redemption. Worse, he was not Disraeli, a deficiency for which she could not forgive him. She began her dislike in earnest when it came to her attention that he had called her a small woman with a small mind.

"No matter. Fenians are about; you know that. Damned Irish, going about hamstringing defenseless cattle, murdering their landlords, just waiting for a chance to do you in. I'm bound to protect you even if you are not." He placed a black cashmere shawl over her shoulders.

"I do admit," she said, drawing the shawl closer about her, "that I feel safer knowing Parnell is in custody. I cannot believe that Chamberlain is negotiating for his release, despite my strong protests, and with the husband of Parnell's mistress. Let's see what sort of settlement that will bring. Parnell is English, you know, at least on his father's side. His family came from Cheshire. But his mother was an American. Which explains things."

"I admire the man's dedication," he said, "especially to a wee country with nothing much to it but peat bogs and blighted potatoes."

Victoria lifted her chin, aware that it was wanting and did not jut as far as she would have liked. "Parnell's passion is not love of Ireland, Brown; it is hatred of England. I cannot imagine what Gladstone can be thinking of when he pushes home rule. He made it his mission to pacify the Irish. Now the savages are chewing up the missionary. It serves him right."

The clatter of donkey's hooves and cartwheels rolling over cobblestones from somewhere beyond the garden walls caused her to frown, as did any noise, and sent a flock of blackbirds shrieking into the villa below. She tied her bonnet strings under her chin, curving her little fingers as she did so. "You must tell the new coachman that I am never to hear him jounce."

"I will speak to the lad. His father before him was a good man. You may remember. He was a groundskeeper at Osborne until his consumption. He used to shape the boxwood zoo you fancied."

"Well, then, why doesn't the boy become a groundskeeper? All people are not suited to all things. It seems to me that if groundskeeping was good enough for his father, it ought to be good enough for him. What are young people coming to? And especially with his father ill. It is his duty to continue in his place. I do not relish the heavy burden of sovereignty without my beloved Albert by my side, yet I persevere. Nothing is the same. President Garfield, Tsar Alexander, assassinated; it is too much. Of course, the Tsar brought it on himself by marrying his mistress. If he was bound to do it, he should have kept it a secret. I cannot imagine what Garfield could have done to make his people angry. Although in America it is difficult to tell why anybody does anything. They are an undisciplined lot, which furthers my point."

A chill wind swept past the eucalyptus into the garden, chasing the lengthening shadows before it into great pools of purple, as the newly lit torches flickered and the chattering flocks of birds, lighting in unison, shimmered onto shrubs and trees to claim them for the night.

"You best come indoors," he said. "You can attend to your dispatch boxes in the library." He leaned forward to help her from the chair, matching the pace of his long steps to hers as she hobbled toward the villa, leaning upon him, the hem of her gown swishing over the stone terrace and soaking up the evening dew.

She touched with a gloved fingertip a primrose trailing from an urn. "One by one, all the dear ones of my life are gone." She stopped, leaning more heavily on him than before. "If I did not have you, my faithful friend, and Princess Beatrice, I would have nothing. Baby lives only for me, you know. Of all my children, she alone keeps me alive. Leopold goes off like a streak of lightning for days at a time, racketing around with Bertie and Alix and that fast set and killing himself in the bargain. But Baby wants no one else. She has been, ever since her dear father died, the bright spot in my dead home. My right hand."

The garden doors were opened by a white-gloved butler, and they stepped inside the damp and chilly villa. At Brown's signal, a turbaned Indian servant in a long burgundy silk coat scurried down the carpeted hall, and a liveried footman who had been standing motionless against a mildewed and peeling red-flocked wall preceded them into the library to turn up the jets of the gas lamps. Within moments, the high-ceilinged room with all its furnishings, including a scenic panorama of Venice, a tiled fireplace, and a faded pastel-hued Tabriz silk rug, was bathed in a soft yellow glow.

Victoria sat heavily at a veneered desk. The marquetried top of tortoiseshell and brass was covered with bibelots: brass paperclips fashioned in the heads of ducks and hunting dogs, a papier-mâché box filled with steel nibs, a pair of brass tongs with coin-shaped ends for picking up red discs of sealing wax, miniatures in pearl-rimmed frames, a ram's-head rosewood paper knife, a string box shaped like a beehive, and a boar's-head pen wiper with a brush at its neck.

"How long can it take Ponsonby to give the local police their instructions? Really, this is impossible. How am I to know which has priority?"

She unlocked with a little key the red metal dispatch box handed to her by the white-trousered Indian servant and withdrew the papers, her habit twice daily, reading each message, then responding, dipping into the porcelain inkstand, shaped like a basket, to write while Brown leaned forward to blot each page.

"The idea of withdrawing troops from Egypt! They will all get letters. Every minister in my cabinet. Until they see reason. Especially Mr. Childers at the war office. Ponsonby must see that his are delivered hourly. It is stronger and more immediate measures that are needed, and Mr. Gladstone must remember how disastrous the situation became in South Africa when we withdrew troops. Our power in Egypt ought to be great and firm and the power of the Sultan reduced to a minimum. How can we build with such reluctant masons in the government? And with a pious hypocrite of a journeyman who, I have been told, has given a code sign to Lily Langtry so that her double-enveloped letters will not be opened by his private secretaries. Sanctimonious, boring old fool."

The wind rose and rattled the shutters, almost obscuring in its whine the sputtering, popping frosted glass globes of the lamps and the firm, light knock, a knuckled rap upon a wooden panel.

Brown strode to the double doors and cracked them open, revealing a tall, thin-faced lady-in-waiting, her graying black hair arranged in a low knot, wearing a gray-and-black-striped silk dress with panniers of deep purple zibeline draped upon her hips, standing in the hall.

"The Princess wishes to see Her Majesty," she said. Her voice was low, melodious, the words crisp and certain, spoken in the clear musical notes of women of the British ruling class, shaped by example, practice, and instruction, when girls, in elocution, a subject as seriously considered as the declension of Latin verbs was for boys.

Brown scanned her expression. "I dinna want her upsetting the Queen. She is attending to her dispatch boxes, she's comfortable, and I'm going to keep her that way. See to the lass yourself."

The woman drew herself up, elevating her shoulders out of the creaking casing of heavy stays and lacing that bound her torso. "Are you telling me, Mr. Brown, that I may not have access to the Queen?"

"I'm telling you, Lady Churchill, that neither you nor the girl are going in there and fretting the poor woman. Not now, at the end of the day, with her rheumatism paining her and that Colonel Arabi Pasha fellow heading a revolt. She needs a clear head."

"You cannot do that. You cannot decide who will be admitted and who will not."

"I've already done it," he replied.

Preparing to leave, Lady Churchill, aunt to the Chancellor of the Exchequer, Lord Randolph, lifted her narrow skirts with her fingertips, revealing silk embroidery on the ankles of her stockings. "I did not think, Mr. Brown, that your service to the Queen included discussion of matters of state with ladies-in-waiting. The Egyptian matter is a grave situation, and certainly not one to be on the lips of a servant, no matter how highly placed."

He closed the double doors firmly in her face, turned on his heel, causing his kilt to swing smartly about his knees, and entered the room.

"What was all that about?" asked Victoria. "Has my daughter returned?"

"Aye, and she's retired for the evening."

"I hope she's not brooding. I told her before that it is a habit suited only for chickens. If something is troubling her, she should come in and tell me, firmly, resolutely. I cannot abide timidity. It is unregal. I hope she is not going to affect that tasteless melancholy spectacle of young women flopping about on sofas." She picked up a millefiori paperweight, turning over the faceted dome in her hand. "Isn't that just like a child? Selfish, concerned only with herself. If she had a single thought for me, she would be in here, at the very least, to wish me good night. Was Prince Leopold about?"

"I dinna see him."

"I worry about him so, especially with all these stones and so many heights." She placed the paperweight on a sheaf of notes. "You cannot see when it happens, but you know it's there. That's the dreadful part." She sighed, thinking of the capricious, insidious bleeding that drained the color from Leo's face and caused his teeth to chatter. "I cannot abide the noise from these lamps. I want them replaced with candles. And where is the wax? Not these silly wafers. I need the other. The footman left no wax. How am I to seal anything official? This is becoming intolerable."

"What is intolerable, Mama? Brown, you are not doing your job."

They both turned to see a slender young man dressed in a dark blue worsted morning coat buttoned high to his silk cravat and narrow trousers cut over his pointed, black patent leather, buttoned boots. It was her youngest son Leopold, to whom she had recently granted the title of Duke of Albany, wearing a moustache and a small goatee augmenting his receding chin, his large blue eyes seeming to burn in his head.

Brown moved to block his entry. "The Queen is seeing to her dispatches," he said in a low throaty voice.

"Nonsense," replied Leopold, striding with a slight limp earned from a bump into an ottoman to stand before the desk, bow, and smile with an engaging charm. "Sorry to have missed tea, dear, but I was having such deuced good luck at the tables."

Victoria looked at him as she always did, with a mixture of fondness and sorrow, a combination of feelings, which, like threads in a woolen skein, she had never been able to separate.

"You spend too much time with Bertie," she replied in a tone that clearly indicated in what regard she held the Prince of Wales. "You even sound like him. All that was required of you, Leo, was a simple message to some person saying that you would be such and such a place and would return at such and such a time."

"Ah, but you see, Mama," he said, "that's the problem. I never know in advance where I will be, which is also part of the fun." He leaned forward to kiss her cheek, then stepped back, flipped his coat-tails behind him, and settled into a high-backed damask chair.

"Do tell your tailor to use more cloth," she said, composing, at the same time she looked with disfavor upon his fashionably tight trousers, a note to Victoria College, reminding them that under the terms of her agreement to permit them the use of her name, they were to have no rooms for vivisection, a subject that, she wrote, "caused her whole nature to boil over." She looked up. "You seem to find it amusing that I have been worried to distraction."

"If I smile, it is at your industry. I think no other head of state writes as many letters as you do. Don't fret on my account, dearest. I am going about. I am alive. I am relishing every minute. Believe me when I tell you there is no other subject in all your empire having such a jolly time or enjoying himself more." He reached into his coat and took out a cigarette case. "Do I have your leave to smoke?"

She nodded. Victoria's ban against smoking was usually relaxed for Leo. "Do not think you are so awfully modern with those things. I have smoked them myself at Balmoral to keep the midges away."

"I would have thought with all the balmorality in that dreary place such a thing was impossible. Where is Benjamina?"

"Baby is in her room, retired for the night, heaven only knows why."

Leopold struck a match and lit the dark Turkish cigarette. The smoke circled his head with a blue-gray haze. "Dear Mama, have you taken a keen look at Baby lately? She is five and twenty. And yet she looks and behaves as if she were sixteen. Much of the time she even dresses like a schoolgirl. One might say she has been held back."

"She has been held safe." Victoria continued to write, this time to the Prince of Wales, telling him that should an expeditionary force sail to Egypt, she could not grant him permission to join it, even as a spectator.

Leopold persisted. "Vicky was married at seventeen, Louise and

Helena had just lengthened their skirts when they tied the knot, and Alice colonized Darmstadt by the time she was Beatrice's age."

Victoria carefully dipped the pen into the porcelain inkstand. "Must you bring up what is painful for me to remember? How can you mention your dear dead sister Alice as if you were discussing the weather?"

Leopold recrossed his legs. "Forgive me, Mama. I have no wish to bring you painful memories."

She continued as if he had not spoken. "And further, Leo, I do not require you to remind me of the history of my own children. My recall of ages and occasions is excellent."

He made a tent of his hands. "Then surely you have only to compare."

"There is nothing to compare. They are not the same at all. The situations are quite different."

"What situation?"

Victoria placed her pen in its holder and narrowed her eyes. "You know how to skip to Cannes, driving your carriage, which is totally unsuited for these roads at breakneck speeds, and expose yourself to the worst riffraff of the Riviera, you know how to injure yourself needlessly and cause me untold grief, but of life you know nothing."

"Surely I am not as hopeless as all that."

Brown stepped forward to blot the page and glower.

"You know nothing of loneliness, Leo. Nothing at all." Her voice became dangerously small and thin, like ice about to crack, a warning not to press. Leo ignored it.

"Ah, but that is where you're wrong, Mama. I know all about loneliness. I was taught very early. Can you forget the weeks upon end when I was confined to bed? I surely never shall. My brothers and sisters shrieking through the halls, then tiptoeing when they passed my door, as if there was something outside my room waiting, some giant thing that would catch them in its fist."

"Nonsense! You describe loneliness," she said sharply, "as Mrs. Shelley's Frankenstein story. Loneliness is not some nighttime horror. Loneliness is emptiness without escape, minutes and hours of it, weeks and years, always there, a space, a void in one's life, a rend in one's heart. The subject is closed. I have no further wish to discuss it. Your cigarette has made it impossible to see."

She rang a porcelain hand bell, then signed the last of her messages with a flourish, while Brown leaned forward once more to blot the page, and the Indian servant, who had been standing before the scenic wallpaper, came noiselessly to remove the metal box, then walked backward out of the room. Leopold sprang to his feet, stubbing out his cigarette in a brass urn in which the royal initials had been stamped in sand. "Let me help you, Mama."

"Brown will do it," she said imperiously, her voice higher by half an octave. "Brown has been seeing to my comfort for a long time. He will not let me fall."

The Scottish servant placed a strong arm beneath hers, but not without first directing a menacing glance at the Duke of Albany. Victoria rose with difficulty. The rheumatism was worse. Nothing helped. Not the mustard plasters, spread and covered so carefully with woolen strips by her maids of honor, nor the nightly draft of potassium and opium prescribed by Dr. Reid that brought such heavy sleep, not even the red flannel petticoat that Bauer assured her was a certain cure.

"I expect you for supper," she said.

Leopold waited until the doors closed behind her, then followed, taking the marble steps two at a time despite the pain in his knee, passing two maids, who struggled beneath the weight of a tub of hot water, to where Lady Churchill stood issuing instructions to a bibbed servant from whose puffed cap fell streamers of ribbons.

Leo always liked this lady of the bedchamber better than the other servile, timid little shadows who fluttered about like sparrows or hissed behind the portieres. "Good evening, Lady Churchill. Has my little sister retired for the night?"

She curtsied gracefully despite her age, although, he thought, no one curtsied as well as Bertie's Alexandra, who always managed an effortless, lissome dip from the waist. "Certainly not, Your Royal Highness. Where did you get that idea?" Lady Churchill frowned, then looked down the hallway. Only two footmen standing on the black-and-white checkered marble floor, their gloved hands at their sides. "That horrid man," she said, turning back to him. "You will find Princess Beatrice in her sitting room, sir. She will be very glad to see you."

Leopold put his hands behind his back and limped to gilded doors, hand painted on their panels with plump and smiling naked cherubs, one of which reminded him of the red-haired doxy he had just left, who had been even plumper but whose smile, behind wanton, waving limbs, had been just as seraphic. He rapped once lightly, turned the crystal knobs, and entered the sitting room. A fire crackled in the fireplace before which Fräulein Bauer knelt, poking in her shirtwaist at sputtering logs with a long fork, even though such tasks were clearly beneath her station. A governess permuted by the age of her charge into a retainer of undetermined rank, she stood and dropped a curtsy at his approach.

At the window, her back to the door, stood a tall young woman wearing a bustled olive green cashmere dress nipped tightly at the waist. Her reddish blonde hair was drawn back with a ribbon and left to fall over a gold embroidered ruff that was supported by a wire frame. One pale hand caressed a fold of the velvet drapery.

"Benjamina," he said, "what can you possibly see out there?"

Beatrice, his youngest sister, turned slowly, her head high, her blue eyes steady, her long skirt draped to one side to display a pyramid of little flounces. The taut expression on her roses-and-cream face softened. "The wind is bending the pines right into the sea, Leo." Her voice was soft, low, toneless, the voice of one who does not wish to be heard.

"You can't possibly see that. It's as black as pitch outside."

"But I can hear them, twisting and sighing. I can hear their branches brush the water. I dislike it when it rains on the Riviera. It is not like our English mist. It is more like needles. The chill goes right to my bones."

"The chill you feel is only Mama's love of drafts. I daresay there is not a window fast in this entire villa. Come away from there and let me look at you." He took her hand. "Wonderful. Although you might have chosen a better color. One that makes you look less pale."

"Red cheeks are vulgar, Leo." The firelight gilded the planes of her brow and chin. "I saw that awful cartoon óf you and Bertie in *Punch*. I wanted to send Bauer out to rip it from every issue she could find."

"Actually I thought it rather amusing," he replied, "although I did not realize my eyes popped so. *Punch* can say anything they please, especially when they are correct. I do play second fiddle to Bertie. He is the Prince of Wales. Don't dwell on it. Think instead of my wedding. In one month, your brother Leo is going to be a married man. Settled. Stodgy. A Darby with his Joan, connubial and fat."

"Never you, Leo. You could never be like that."

"And why not?"

"You are endowed with too much life."

He thought of the blood seeping unchecked into his swollen knee. It would not do to challenge her remark. Even in jest. "So I am. Turn around. I see the bustle grows. Soon it will be a shelf upon which Fräulein Bauer may place your tea tray."

She brushed aside his hand and blushed. "Lady Churchill says the bustle is designed to give majesty to the carriage." Then she turned and touched the sleeve of his coat in a display of affection that was for her rare. "I shall miss you, Leo, terribly."

"Nonsense. I will see you just as often as I do now, and Helen will be a sister to you. She has already come to love you almost as much as I do." He paused and looked at her hard, as if he could bury himself in her thoughts. "I worry about you."

"Why?" she asked, sitting on the edge of a brocaded settee.

"What will happen to you?" Leopold reached behind him to a black-and-gold-lacquered commode decorated on its drawers with an Egyptian motif and poured claret from a crystal decanter.

"What do you mean, Leo? What is supposed to happen to me?"

"Nothing. That is what I am afraid of. Nothing is supposed to happen to you. Do you remember when we were little and Papa used to take out his collection of fossils and spread them over the table?"

"I think I do. That is, I'm not sure if I really remember it or if it has been described to me and I remember the description."

He sat beside her and sipped the ruby red wine, firelit and glimmering in its glass. "No matter. One of his treasures was a piece of amber with a fly embedded in it. Jurassic period, I believe."

"I don't think I ever saw it. I would remember something as awful as that."

"It wasn't awful so much," he said, "as immoral. You see, that little fly was meant to gad about, perhaps to irritate some prehistoric creature who thought he had the world by the tail; my apologies to Dr. Darwin. Instead, it was captured by time. Benjamina, I worry that you are to remain exactly as you are, just like that little ancient fly frozen in a piece of amber. Except in your case it is not by accident, some great convolution of earth, some freeze that turned molten lava into stone. It is by design."

"Whose design?" asked Beatrice, softly rubbing her hands.

"Whose do you think?"

She turned away. It was difficult for Leo to know whether or not she was crying. "I don't want to hear another word. If you are referring to Mama, that was a dreadfully wicked thing to say." She pushed aside the suggestion as one would bar a gate against an intruder, with all her strength, firmly and irrevocably.

"You know there's truth in what I say, or else you wouldn't defend against it so ferociously. Mama is determined that you will never leave her side; she has tossed you into a filial suttee in which you will never have what is a natural state for everyone. Marriage."

"But I don't wish to marry." She stood, clutching a brooch pinned below the ruff. "I wish to remain exactly as I've been, a dutiful, steadfast, loving daughter. Mama's right hand. She calls me so herself. She is so terribly burdened, and with you about to be married, Leo, I'm all she has."

He stood and set his glass upon the commode, keenly aware that he was treading dangerously but afraid that opportunities for private discussion were limited, if not diminishing. "All monarchs are burdened. But they have an entire nation at their disposal to help them shoulder it. And darling, how can you say in all seriousness that with the armies of people who attend Mama and the platoons of visiting royalty, most of them family, she is ever alone? Not to speak of the correspondence which keeps her united by post to legions."

Fräulein Bauer stepped closer to busy herself with a bouquet of silver, rock crystal, and precious stones that had not been properly dusted, not presuming to speak unless spoken to, yet determined to shield her charge, if only with her presence.

"As far as not wishing to marry," continued Leo, "you have just not met the right person. There are scores of suitable princelings and grand dukes, and if they are not so grand, Mama will make them so. When you meet the right person, you'll know instantly what I mean. It's my earnest hope, to use Browning's words, that someday very soon you will wake, remember, and understand."

"Don't quote that dreadful man to me. He shouts so, and he grabs your arm when he speaks and will not let go." The pain returned to her knuckles and fingers, palms and wrist, a dull, steady, intolerable ache, a sort of rheumatism. She drew her hands to her body, sheltering them against the warmth of her tightly corseted bodice as if they were a thing apart. "How can you say such an awful thing? How can you malign dear Mama, whose only concern is for me, who frets over every little thing I do?"

"Haven't you ever wondered?" he asked softly. "Aren't you at all curious why she has never allowed an eligible male within miles of you? Do you know that no one is allowed to even mention the subject of marriage in your presence? At supper only a few weeks ago, Secretary Ponsonby was foolish enough only to make reference to the engagement of an equerry, for which carelessness he was afterward severely rebuked by Mama."

"Perhaps Sir Henry was indiscreet in some other way. And Mama knows that strange men terrify me. Even men I've met make me uncomfortable."

"I have heard differently. What about Prince Louis of Battenberg? Louise thinks he looks like Papa. And don't tell me you didn't have some feeling for Louis Napoleon's son."

"It is not appropriate to speak that way of the dead. The Prince Imperial was my childhood friend. My very good friend. Nothing more. And Louis of Battenberg was much too forward. Further, he looks nothing like Papa." She thought of the tall Him, whose face, despite the scores of crepe-mantled portraits, she could not recall.

Leo was saying, "I heard Mama had him sent to sea. Could the fact that the Battenberg brothers are considered the handsomest men in Europe have had anything to do with it?" Then he threw fat into the fire. "There is still talk in France that Mama was seriously negligent in permitting the Prince Imperial to go to Zululand."

"His death was a terrible accident. Mama was as grieved as I. Whatever Mama does, she has my interests at heart."

"She has her own interests at heart." Leo moved closer. As he did so, Beatrice moved back. "She doesn't want to be left alone in her declining years, and so she has taken you, like one of her pet dogs. Only you will last longer, because your life expectancy is greater. I don't count Brown, because he is such a lummox. Don't you agree?"

Beatrice now stood with her back to the wall, both hands clenched at the ruff. "About what?"

"About Brown. Do you agree, yes or no? It is your opinion I want. I certainly won't repeat a word, since I can't abide the fellow."

"He is a capable servant."

"Is that all you have to say about him? I can't believe it. Whisper in my ear."

"There's nothing to whisper. I scarcely notice him."

Fräulein Bauer gave one last flick of her handkerchief to an opal camellia in the jeweled bouquet and moved between them. "It is time, Your Royal Highness," she said firmly, "to dress for supper."

Leo pulled out his pocket watch. "So it is, Fräulein." He felt suddenly sad, no longer the relentless terrier. He turned to his sister, who sat rubbing her hands. "You used to be the sunniest, most irrepressible little thing. You said adorable, funny things, and you got away with mischief that none of us ever did. Now you are deadly earnest. So serious. So guarded. Against what?"

Tears fell down her face. "Why are you bullying me?"

"Forgive me. The last thing I want to do is make you cry. Perhaps I'm afraid that when I leave, there is no one to champion your interests." He reached to take her hand, now cold in his own. "Why do you rub your hands?"

"The rain makes them hurt."

"Since when?"

"I don't remember."

"Look at this line. It goes all the way down into your wrist. It says that you will live to be a very old lady. I should like those years to be spent happily, with someone you love, perhaps even someone you can love deeply." She turned away. "Why not spend a day with Fräulein Bauer or Lady Churchill in Nice, do a little shopping, stroll the promenade, and perhaps visit the *Inflexible* on your return? The ship is quite new and rather splendid. At the very least, it will be a little diversion."

"I don't need diversion, Leo. I have enough to keep me content and occupied. I assist Sir Henry with some of the correspondence, Mama and I sketch in the garden, we go for carriage rides, I play the piano when I can, and sometimes I swim with Lady Churchill from the bathing machine while Mama watches from the bluff."

"The whole thing sounds tedious beyond belief."

Sounds of plucking strings were heard, then the monotonous wail of an A droning muffled and muted through the wall, at first a solitary note of a cello, then becoming a surge of whining violins, blaring horns, and reedy woodwinds.

Leopold had his hand at the door. "We're to be treated to Wagner this evening. I prefer the sugar and spice of Italian opera, but Mama is partial. Somehow a private performance doesn't have the dazzle of an opera house when the stalls are lit and everyone in attendance sticks on everything of personal adornment they possess, so that between the lights and the silks and the jewelry, the stalls are whipped to a thousand scintillations."

"I prefer the private performance," said Beatrice. "The tiers of boxes you speak of look like black gaping mouths."

A bleating tenor rose over the sounds of the tuning musicians. "Ah," said Leo, "that must be Herr Schott. Tannhäuser sounds like he might be a little under the weather. I can't wait to see him in his golden wig." He closed the doors behind him.

Minutes later, Fräulein Bauer, assisted by a maid, held in her hands a bustle made of white horsehair ruching while Beatrice stood waiting in turquoise satin slippers, white knickers, and a voluminous chemise cramped into wrinkles by her laced corset. Draped on a dark red velvet chaise longue with lion-shaped brass terminals atop the taller end lay a gown of turquoise faille with silver embroidery and sleeves and panniers of dahlia satin. Folded neatly beside it was a surah silk fan with a feather border.

"You must not be upset, Your Royal Highness. The Duke of Albany is a man, with a man's requirements, which are quite different from those of a young lady, especially a royal young lady." Fräulein Bauer signaled to the maid to lift the gown from the chaise longue, then circled her charge's waist with the bustle and prepared to fasten the tape. "Tonight, when you retire, I will rub your hands with quinine and castor oil. That is what Dr. Reid has suggested."

"There is nothing wrong with my hands. Why did you say anything to him at all? Who gave you leave to do so?"

Fräulein Bauer was injured. "You seemed to be in pain. I was only doing my duty."

"You really shouldn't take it upon yourself, Fräulein, to discuss matters regarding my person without first asking my permission. You are no longer governess. You must remember that."

"It is difficult, ma'am." Standing on stools, Fräulein Bauer and the maid slipped the gown above Benjamina's head, pulling down the low square neckline, then stepped down to close with tapes, strings, hooks, and buttons the myriad of closings. When the gown was settled and fastened, Fräulein Bauer knelt to slip her hands beneath the hem to close the row of tapes that hobbled the draped and pleated skirt, then stood with difficulty, grunting as she did so, to clasp a string of amber beads about her neck, while the maid fastened a detachable frisette of artificial bangs to the Princess's forehead and smoothed her upswept hair with a small yellow wax stick perfumed of lemon and lavender.

Fräulein Bauer stood back while Beatrice kicked aside the short quarter train with a lift of her foot. The princess was so sweet, so pretty, she thought, so *bescheiden.* But the Duke of Albany was wrong. As long as she did not have to marry, why should she not enjoy her life as a sheltered youngest daughter of the greatest monarch of the world instead of having to submit to the insatiable demands of some man? And what he said about the Queen—the whole thing was ridiculous. Widows, royal or not, customarily kept their youngest at their sides as a companion. Her own mother, God rest her soul, had done so. Fräulein Bauer followed solemnly close behind as Beatrice minced with six-inch steps.

Supper was served in a tapestry-hung dining room sparkling with crystal chandeliers to the sounds of coughs and the rattle of plates and conversation sputtering in fits and starts, like fires set with dampened wood. Footmen continued to roll in long buffet tables glittering with gold and silver epergnes and compotes, while others, bearing dishes held flat on the palms of their white-gloved hands, bent toward the guests, then at Brown's signal, quickly removed each plate, sometimes before the diner had finished.

Everyone smelled of lavender or rose, except for young Dr. Reid, who dressed his black moustache and beard with patchouli to cover the cloying scent of iodoform from which he could never seem to rid himself. Victoria, in black satin, had changed her earrings to long diamond pendants, and all of the men wore thin black bow ties over starched white shirtfronts. Only Leopold's shirt was studded with a diamond solitaire.

Victoria became annoyed when footmen rolled in a table, ornamented with a marzipan castle and knights, containing a dozen dishes of venison, all fashioned to resemble various animals, and one enormous platter on which was fixed a wild boar in aspic jelly, surrounded by piglets and garlanded with grasses and flowers. She turned to Brown, her face petulant. "Why do they continue to do this? I thought you explained to them that we are simple in our tastes?"

Sir Henry, Victoria's tall, dignified, gray-bearded private secretary, was speaking of the Savoy, the first theater in London to use electric lights. "It is the coming force," he said. "The day of the carbon and arc."

"But there is no flicker," said Lady Churchill, no doubt concerned, as are all women of a certain age, with the effects of harsh lighting. "It is too stark."

"It has other uses," said Dr. Reid, stroking his moustache. He had to speak up to be heard above the clatter of dishes and the clinking of glasses. "Someday soon, frozen beef from Australia will be revived by electricity; they will use it to power dirigibles, ships that will fly with deliberation, not drift like balloons. At the very least, it will be used to hatch Christmas turkeys."

"Why are you shouting so about turkeys, Dr. Reid?" asked Victoria, who disliked cross-conversation, believing that one should converse only with those at one's side, and then only in the most subdued tones. "There is nothing that cannot be said quietly."

"Beg pardon, ma'am."

Leopold was intrepid. "I'm all for a quiet discussion of Nellie Farren," he said.

Dr. Reid dabbed his lips with his napkin and cleared his throat. "Miss Farren is more than a clever burlesque actress," he said with a tentative look at his Queen. "She is an artiste, heart and soul in her work. When she sings, 'I'll tell your mother what you've done,' banging her little tambourine in that nasal twang, she is terribly infectious."

"Dreadfully shocking," said Victoria. "Nellie Farren dancing in tights. And she a grandmother."

"Beg pardon, ma'am," said Lady Churchill, "but if one may not dance in tights when one is a grandmother, I am sure I do not know when one may."

There was restrained laughter, then the censuring face of Victoria and silence, followed by the grimmer sound of plates and coughs as Brown signaled the footmen for the second remove.

The man behind Fräulein Bauer removed her service plate to set before her a freshly heated silver replacement. "I do not know why they bother," she whispered to Dr. Reid. "By the time the food gets to me, it is lukewarm."

Victoria fastened her gaze on Beatrice, who had been sitting primly silent, expressionless, demure, as if she would fade into the tapestries that hung behind her. "As long as you have decided to join us for supper, Beatrice, participate in the conversation. You are as animated as the aspic."

A prickly flush spread from Beatrice's silver-embroidered neckline to the frizzed fringe on her forehead. Why did Mama have any doubt about her coming to supper? It would not do to discuss this now before the others. Later, she thought, when they were alone. "Sorry, Mama." She reminded herself that she would have to remember to smile and look about more. That way, it would appear that she was contributing, attentive. It would lessen the ordeal.

Sir Henry sought to cover her distress. "It is the aesthetes I find so fascinating," he said, turning to Leopold. "They claim an appreciation superior to that of our common Philistine herd which they demonstrate with a certain posture."

"I know it well," said Leopold. "A sort of languid droop. One's head cannot be upright, like a flower too heavy for its stalk. The men's hair must be long, their clothing must drape and fall, flowing tie, baggy trousers, everything loose."

"Like their morals," said Fräulein Bauer.

"When I think of the aesthetes," said Lady Churchill, "I think of peacock feathers, Japanese fans, and Oscar Wilde."

"A colossally conceited fellow," said Sir Henry. "I met him only recently. He spent an entire evening gazing at a lily."

"He is a poseur," said Victoria, "and makes no effort to conceal it. Further, he is a friend of Gladstone."

The topic was ended. No one dared to pick up its threads, not even Leo. For a while there was silence. Beatrice was content. There was no stress in silence, no demand; no one expected her to comment, bringing down, as was so frequent, the disapproval of her mother or causing her tongue to tie itself in knots. Even though her stays dug deep, making breathing difficult, she could sit in safety, pat her lips from time to time with her damask napkin, and when she remembered, force a smile. It was not to last. Leopold was staring at her.

"Give us your opinion, Benjamina," he said, preparing to taste the sorbet, which would refresh his palate between the boar's head and the woodcock to come, "of the new women who want to play cricket and take up medicine."

Beatrice looked as if she might wish to reply. She put down her spoon and cleared her throat, blushing and stammering in the manner that had become her own. Before she was able to speak, Victoria interrupted. "Baby knows nothing about them," she said, "nor does she care to."

Sir Henry tried to lace enthusiasm into the faltering conversation, the way one might pour brandy into coffee. "There is in Scandinavia," he said, "a dramatist who encourages women to escape from their doll houses and live their own lives."

Nothing helped Beatrice's dismay, not Sir Henry's verve, neither Lady Churchill smiling in sympathy, not even Leopold leaning over the table to wink. Finding it too painful to pick up her spoon, she lay both hands in her lap and waited. There was silence once more while the salads were placed before them. Victoria spoke first.

"I'm sure I don't know what the world is coming to. Trust the Scandinavians to muck things up. It has something to do with their horrid winters. A woman's duty is quite clear. Her happiness is bound up in it. Her responsibility is always to her family. She is weaker and more dependent for a reason. It is the natural order of things."

"But Mama," said Leo, "you rule the British Empire, and you are a woman, one, I might add, neither dependent nor weak."

"I cannot believe the difference is unclear to you, Leo. It is a matter of duty. I did not seek to become queen. When it fell to me, I assumed it, as will Bertie, when, God help us all, I am no longer able to serve. When your dear papa was alive, I turned to him for everything, as it should be. A woman finds fulfillment in living for others. She simply submits herself to her duties and makes them habitual. She needs nothing more."

A clock struck the hour. Conversation had come to a standstill. Footmen rolled in a table of cheese and fruit, and another bearing a helmet made of ice cream. Those at the dining table eased shoulders aching from the stiff, unyielding chairs or wriggled toes grown numb, waiting for their Queen to rise.

After supper they withdrew to the music room where they sat again, this time on small gilt chairs, weary from dining, concealing polite yawns behind gloved hands while waiting for the concert, unlike the frantic musicales, thought Victoria, given at the German court for Herr Wagner. There the great man, wearing a frock coat and a black velvet skullcap, was besieged by everyone, including Empress Augusta in her ill-fitting russet wig, rushing around to get him rye bread, Limburger cheese, liver sausage, herring salad, black pudding, and raw smoked goose breast.

The orchestra was hidden behind screens and potted palms except for the grand piano, which was illuminated with candelabra so intricately carved with vines and leaves it would take an underbutler an entire morning to polish.

The diva, Madame Materna, entered, dipping low in a sweeping curtsy. She was dressed in peach and orange glacé silk adorned with a flight of stuffed swallows on her skirts and a pair of birds nestling on one plump shoulder and was followed by a bowing, bewigged Herr Schott and lesser members of the company. The audience applauded discreetly, correctly, one set of gloved fingers tapping lightly on the palm of the other hand.

"She's too stout to play Venus," whispered Leopold to Beatrice.

The singers bowed a second time and sang the Pilgrim's chorus, working up to a triumphal frenzy; then Herr Schott began Tannhäuser's hymn to Venus.

Beatrice leaned toward her brother. "I wouldn't know what to say to them without Mama."

"Who?"

"Anyone I should happen to meet. In Nice."

Leo restrained a smile and bent his head to gravely consider her question. "You say nothing," he replied. "Look sideways, or if you can manage it, a crooked little Mona Lisa smile. They will think you inscrutable."

"If they ask a question I can't answer?"

Victoria turned to frown, accompanied by Brown, who shushed them with a stubby finger to his lips. Leopold waited for his mother and her attendant to turn and for the pompous ceremonial march to conceal his words.

"The purpose of polite conversation," he whispered, "is not to exchange information, dearest. It is to flirt or promote oneself. When asked a question you can't answer, say, 'That is an interesting question. I need a moment to ponder it,' or, 'I would rather know what you think of it.' People are keen to talk about themselves. Actually, all a woman needs to succeed is to be able to speak French and to dance lightly so that she never steps upon her partner's toes."

Madame Materna began to sing in her powerful ringing voice Elisabeth's song to the evening star, and Beatrice put a gloved hand on the arm of her brother, closest to her own age, her lifelong dearest friend.

CHAPTER TWO

The matter was settled from behind a bathing machine, a hooded cabana on wheels that creaked as waves like tongues lapped against its sides. There, stiffly splashing, stood Beatrice and Lady Churchill, shielded from the eyes of other bathers by the rounded dome of the contraption's modesty hood, up to their knees in water, both wearing heavy dark blue serge bathing costumes, with collars and elbow-length sleeves, wide braid-trimmed drawers, red woolen sashes, soaked to a deep plum, straw-soled shoes with embroidered linen tops, and straw hats.

Beatrice was somber, a more or less ubiquitous state with which Lady Churchill, who spent three months yearly as a member of the royal household, was familiar. It was not quite a listless melancholy or a tear-edged sadness. Instead, the smothered moods of her malaise occupied a more meager palette. This day, they seemed quiescent and suspended, unlike the agitated seawater that trembled against the cabana.

Beatrice splashed her face with a delicate sprinkle. Strands of her long hair fell from beneath her straw hat and clung limply to her neck. "I promised to think about it," she replied, pulling back from the discussion of Nice the way one retracts a finger that has gone too near the flame.

She continued in the sort of apologia that one trots out to convince oneself that such and such is so. Lady Churchill was only half listening, primarily because she was finding the seawater especially soothing to her piles, which had been aggravated by the long nightly stands in attendance on the Queen, who permitted no one to sit in her presence. Her easement was interrupted by Beatrice, who was saying, "Mama thinks that it would be better if I remained here at Menton. She said that Leopold's interests and mine are not the same, nor are our abilities. That's very true, you know. Leo is easy with others, while I sometimes pray to be invisible. And that I must learn to stand up on my own feet and not let him talk me into things. Towel, please."

Lady Churchill signaled to a servant who had been standing in the darkened rear of the pitching wooden cabana. Crouching forward gingerly, the woman bent over the wooden steps in her long black dress and white apron to hand the Princess a white towel.

"I would be recognized and subjected to unwanted attention," continued Beatrice, as if she were reciting some sort of catechism, "from all sorts of impossible people. The only reason I abide crowds now is that the focus is on Mama, not me." She seemed to be waiting for an answer.

Lady Churchill suggested that if they brought no liveried servants to call attention to themselves, only Fräulein Bauer or one of the maids of honor to help carry packages, and instructed the officers of the *Cygnet* to follow at a discreet distance, they might go unrecognized. She added that she could be a formidable barrier should anyone dare to approach whom the Princess did not wish to greet.

Beatrice steadied her straw hat to keep it from tumbling into the water. "Is it so terribly crowded?" she asked.

"Nice is not so much crowded, Your Highness," replied Lady Churchill, "as it is alive, and beautiful, with sea foam breaking over red rocks, blue sky, and brilliant sunshine. Not like Menton where here the sun veils and unveils itself like a harem dancer. It is a city of carrara marble and villagers carrying huge white umbrellas, riding donkeys into the hills, and of course, the people. It has been called the drawing room of France."

"What does one do there?"

"One walks the promenade, nods to this one and that one, chats with some, ignores the rest, and shops. Nice has the most delightful shops in the world. There is one I recall that sells wicked sugared violets."

"Candy can't be wicked, Lady Jane. It is a word that can only apply to a person or a deed."

"I stand corrected, Your Highness," replied Lady Churchill.

"Nice is mainly a place in which one can be lighthearted, to throw one's cares to the winds, so to speak."

Beatrice turned large open blue eyes to her mother's lady-in-waiting. "I have no cares, Lady Jane."

"All the more reason, then, to go there. One of the shops carries a new fabric for bathing costumes, much lighter than the heavy goods we wear, that I am most anxious to see. It is called, I believe, stockinette, and is supposed to be something like the jersey that Lily Langtry has brought into fashion."

"I can't imagine what one does when it gets wet," said Beatrice. "It seems immodest." She turned to the sea and shielded her eyes with her hand to follow the gunboat *Cygnet* as it skimmed the coastline, then disappeared from sight of the cove. She would not believe the whispers that stopped at her approach, that Lily Langtry's child had been fathered by Louis of Battenberg. The thought made her blush.

"Your Highness is sunburned," said Lady Churchill. "We best get out."

The sun went behind a cloud, and the servant helped them climb the wooden steps, handing each a towel as two donkeys in harness began to haul the bathing machine out of the water and onto the rocky beach. Each bather stepped behind an ornamented silk screen, and with the help of the servant who rushed between them, pulling and tugging and dropping their sodden garments over her arms, stripped off their wet, heavy bathing costumes and tightly laced boned corsets, preparing to change into dry undergarments, corsets, stockings, gowns, and buttoned boots, the completion of which task would take them the better part of an hour.

"Bauer tells me, Your Royal Highness," said Lady Churchill through her screen, "that you are having some discomfort. I, too, have rheumatism, in my shoulder, for which a chemist gave me a wonderful remedy. One takes daily bicarbonate of soda, as much as will lay on a shilling in a half glass of water, and the juice of half a lemon. The relief lasts for hours. My chemise, if you please, Mayfair. This one belongs to the Princess."

"There is nothing wrong with me," said Beatrice evenly, in a small controlled voice, one that sounded like her mother's. "I don't require

bicarbonate of soda on a shilling or anything else, and I do wish
everyone would tend to his own affairs. Really I do."

Nice did not disappoint. One heard music everywhere, spilling
from windows and pavilions, Mozart performed by string ensembles,
the trill of a lonely Donizetti aria accompanied by a pianoforte, tubas
pumping Strauss, and plumed bands striking up sprightly martial airs.

The Promenade des Anglais followed the curve of the gray pebbly
coastline as it hugged the blue Mediterranean. On the other side of
its broad avenue were villas and hotels, with ladies holding domed silk
and lace parasols, standing in a graceful, carefully prescribed posture
that required them to thrust the upper part of their bodies forward,
head first, or perching on white wicker chairs, while young men, with
shiny hair and tight collars, sucking the knobsticks of their walking
sticks, sat in courtly, if not vacuous and solemn, attendance. Behind
the villas and hotels, a girdle of hills like an amphitheater enfolded
the town, and blue sailcloth stretched from house to house to protect
market stalls from the sun, while wagons chased women and children,
to scatter in their path like flocks of chickens.

The promenade was, as always in the season, movement, a rolling
tide of those who strolled in self-conscious, deliberate presentation,
their faces vapid and self-centered, everyone dressed in appropriate
promenade toilette for midday, the women's hips swathed and held
secure in rigid folds, the rear protuberances of their bustles wobbling
from side to side, the men in top hats and black or dark blue morning
coats, wearing spats over their patent leather boots and carrying umbrellas rolled into spindles. Moving in and out of the strollers were
English riders on splendid mounts, followed by their lackeys, and
carriages of every type, landaus carrying duchesses, phaetons with
men-about-town, victorias toting rouged fast women, barouches with
varnished panels and lacquered brasswork transporting dowager con-
tessas still in sausage curls twenty years out of fashion, stately carriages
with blazing escutcheons and coachmen in brilliant multicolored liv-
eries of the newly monied, Parisian cocottes in pony carriages, and
droshkies driven by bearded majordomos carrying haughty officers of
the Imperial Russian Guards wearing full drooping flaxen moustaches.

Beatrice, carrying an ecru crepe parasol lined with green silk, was
dressed in a modish seaside costume of violet velvet with an overdress

of ecru embroidered batiste and a hat of ecru straw covered with poppies and bows of velvet. Lady Churchill, in black bombazine and lavender crepon, was appropriately attired for a lady-in-waiting of middle age, to a court that still mourned the death of its Prince Consort.

Followed by a small entourage, they strolled slowly, holding their heads high, neither smiling, for a display of teeth would be inappropriate, nor appearing hot or uncomfortable, despite the fact that both were perspiring freely beneath their long-sleeved costumes, their sedate control originating in the same rigid rules of conduct that prohibited portrait painters from showing in either the eyes or mouth the soul of a subject. Behind them, carrying packages, were Fräulein Bauer and Miss Stopford, a prim, youngish woman, recently elevated from the position of maid of honor to that of lady of the bedchamber, and behind them, a third line, two officers of the *Cygnet*, one carrying a porcelain birdcage and canary.

Lady Churchill kept her word and stood between those who would advance without welcome. She did it with a stripping look, a downward sweep of her eyes that discouraged even the most blundering. "Money makes the mare to go," she said disdainfully when they were approached by a banker in a gray top hat who was said to own a controlling interest in the world's tin mines, "but it cannot make an English gentleman any more than the coat of arms purchased in Cranbourn Street for three and sixpence can give a man an ancestral tree."

They could scarcely avoid Louis of Bavaria, considered somewhat of a boulevardier, who would have followed them down the promenade had Lady Churchill not brushed him aside as one would a flea. Beatrice thought he was an ugly, horrid little man, primarily because he gave up his throne for Lola Montez, a woman of questionable reputation, and Beatrice had no respect for royalty who did not see their duty. They learned from the dapper Louis that they just missed seeing the King and Queen of Naples, which both Lady Churchill and Miss Stopford agreed was just as well, since the Queen had a reputation for hiring the hippodrome for an afternoon and there dressing up as a circus rider and galloping about the ring, an act that was enough out of the ordinary to mark her with suspicion.

Their brief encounter with Louis of Bavaria was followed with a protracted and dramatic chat with the Tsarevitch, Nicholas, riding with his mother, the Tsarina Marie Feodorovna, the sister of the Prince of Wales's wife, Alexandra. Beatrice had learned from her older sister, Vicky, the Crown Princess of Prussia, that the Tsarina's sitting room was pink velvet, pink marble, pink Venetian glass, with a white Aubusson rug with pink rose petals, but her own conclusions about the Tsarina's ostentation, a disgusting feature, it seemed, of all the Romanoffs, were drawn from the fifteen butterflies of precious stones she wore sprinkled about her skirt, their antennae of diamond dust, and this before evening. The Russians were accompanied by the Grand Duke Alexis, who bragged that he stocked the brooks of Gatchina with rainbow trout from California and who said *sotto voce* to Beatrice as he kissed her hand that he would rather do so without gloves. She regarded him with disapproval even before his untoward remark, as he wore no scent to mask the strong, unpleasant odor that permeated his clothes.

Fräulein Bauer recognized the elderly Victor Hugo in a wheelchair, pushed by an attendant, but Lady Churchill decided his infirmity prohibited any sort of exchange, if only for his fierce political sentiments, which, being so feeble, he might be unable to suppress.

The high point of the promenade for Beatrice was Madame Sarah Bernhardt. The French actress, in a white silk gown, with a large bow of tulle on its beaded collar, was quickly identified by her mass of curly, disheveled hair, red, as suggested by Fräulein Bauer, from Tricosia fluid from Bond Street. Madame Bernhardt was on the arm of a tall, handsome man with a large black moustache who was said to give oriental parties where his guests did unspeakable things like bathing nude in champagne. They were surrounded with a crowd of admirers who fell back, curtsying, at Beatrice's approach, as the actress made a sweeping drop to the ground. Beatrice asked what it was like to appear before so many people and so often. Madame Bernhardt replied that it was her life. What Beatrice really wondered, and what she could not ask, was what it was like to appear in public with one's hair undone. It seemed abandoned, immoral, free. Her hand began to ache, and she rubbed it.

Things appeared to be going well despite a few minor obstructions, such as their having to stop every few minutes for Miss Stopford, who was feeling faint, to sniff her salts. While it was true that Beatrice was painfully shy in all her limited encounters, even with her Russian cousins, she seemed to be enjoying herself, if her high color was any evidence, although Lady Churchill was quick to recognize that high color, the mark of the consumptive or the painted woman, was not necessarily a state to be desired.

In the late afternoon, it was decided that Miss Stopford and Fräulein Bauer would return to Menton with the packages and that Beatrice and Lady Churchill would be taken by the gunboat *Cygnet* to the flag-bedecked *Inflexible*, one of a fleet of ships anchored off the coast, more a floating pageant than a weapon of war.

After climbing the ship's ladder with some difficulty, the two women were piped aboard, and Beatrice was saluted while the band played "God Save the Queen." Almost the entire ship's complement of four hundred were on deck standing at attention, the officers in dark blue, gold-braided frock coats, with gold epaulets, the tassels of which twitched in the breeze, wearing swords buckled to their waists and carrying cocked hats under their arms, the men in serge frock coats and white duck trousers, some of them barefoot. The only activity during the band's playing of "God Save the Queen" was the frantic rush of seamen in white-and-navy-blue-collared jumpers to take down the bedding which lay airing on hammock nettings, a weekly housecleaning chore, the putting away of which someone had overlooked.

Then the captain, with heavy white moustache and a bulky cleft jaw that gave him the look of a walrus, and a handful of his officers escorted the Princess and her chaperone to the salon, where the ladies sat at a claw-footed round mahogany table, stripped off their gloves, and took tea. After Beatrice granted permission with an elegant sweep of her left hand, which was mercifully free of pain, the captain seated himself and asked Beatrice how she found Nice.

She tried to respond, but the tea went down her windpipe. Everyone waited in respectful silence as the gasping Princess, signaling with an upraised hand that she was all right, patted her lips and coughed. "Sometimes a quite nasty wind blows when it is least expected," she rasped.

"Yes," said the captain, "that would be the mistral. Did you have an opportunity to dine at the Regence, Your Highness? It is a favorite of mine."

Beatrice stirred her teacup, discomfited with one question so soon after another and with the junior officers standing over them, watching in respectful silence. It was then that she began to wish she had returned to Menton with Fräulein Bauer and Miss Stopford. On the promenade, one could indicate by the point of a toe that one wished to walk on. One or two brief exchanges and a conversation could be considered successful and closed. Here, in the ship's salon, she was trapped.

Lady Churchill rushed in. "The Regence is a favorite of mine as well, Captain. However, the Princess prefers the smaller *intime* cafés along the avenue. There is a confectioner's shop that makes the best chocolate. Didn't you find it so, Your Royal Highness?"

"The chocolate was very good," replied Benjamina, with none of the levity that marked the conversation of young ladies of breeding. "But the gnats were terrible. They crawled right over the rim of my cup and made it quite inedible."

"Yes, Your Highness," replied the captain, "the gnats are bad, and of course they're everywhere. And what news of London? My wife writes that there was a superb revival of *Romeo and Juliet* at the Lyceum. Did you see it perhaps, ma'am?" He turned to Lady Churchill. "I understand it was magnificent, although my wife writes that while Miss Terry's Juliet was satisfactory, her deliberate intensity had little of the warm impulsiveness we look for in one so young as Juliet."

"I'm afraid I shall have to disagree, Captain," said Lady Churchill. "I saw the performance, and I can report that when Romeo introduces himself, Terry is charmingly girlish."

There was an awkward silence. Obviously, the Princess was neither charmingly girlish nor warmly impulsive. The captain, considering that she would be more at ease with persons closer to her own age, nodded his head to his junior officers, who had been standing waiting. "Perhaps Your Royal Highness would enjoy a turn on deck?"

Beatrice glanced at Lady Churchill, who nodded imperceptibly. "If you wish," she replied.

Lady Churchill took a position at the rear of the party, with enough distance placed between her and the young people that her charge would feel free to speak her mind, yet close enough to let her know that help, should she need it, was there.

The young officers were gallant. They surrounded Beatrice, yet at a proper distance, escorting her past a silent cutlass drill, a detail of seamen in perfect synchrony flashing and twisting their weapons in the sunlight, hovering politely, expectantly, believing that the extreme shyness they saw was royal reserve.

The tallest one, a young lieutenant whose father was the provincial commissioner of the planting community of Ceylon, spoke first. "Are you enjoying the Riviera, Your Highness?"

"Thank you, yes," she replied.

The second tucked his cocked hat more firmly beneath his arm and gave it a go. "They say this season at Nice is the most brilliant in years. Do you find it so?"

"That is an interesting question," replied Beatrice. "I shall need a moment to ponder it."

They looked to one another. When nothing further was said, the third cleared his throat. "Did you hear Paganini, Your Royal Highness? We were told he gave a concert."

"We were in Nice only for the afternoon," interposed Lady Churchill.

The second officer smiled. "It is fortunate Paganini's talents lie in his hands. I heard his laryngitis is so bad he can speak only by forcing his nostrils together."

Beatrice found this objectionable, as she would any mention of a body part. She turned from him while his colleagues censured his indelicacy with a reproving look.

"I read in the *Times*," said the first officer, "that the government has sold Jumbo the elephant."

"We did?" asked the second officer. "Why ever would we want to do that? My little sister will be devastated."

"Why, indeed, ever," replied the first. "Money, of course. For the Exchequer. Jumbo was sold to a man from America by the name of Barnum. I believe he intends to put the lucky fellow in a circus."

"How dreadful," said the second officer.

"For the elephant?" asked Beatrice.

The young officer masked the expression that curled around his lips. "No, Your Royal Highness, for the ship that must transport it."

There was mild laughter. Beatrice was becoming more uncomfortable all the time. She had begun to twist the crystal handle of her parasol.

The tallest officer clasped his hands behind his back. "The *Inflexible* is one of Her Majesty's newest ships. Right, tight, ironclad, steam propelled, an eight-thousand-horsepower engine that can drive her at fourteen knots, the masts and sails purely ornamental. What do you think of it, ma'am?"

Beatrice, who was almost whispering, looked about her at the plated vessel and began to stammer. The desire to leave was strong, all the more frustrating since leave-taking would involve more ceremony, more stares, more conversation. "It seems unfinished."

"So it must to a civilian's eye, even the eye of a royal civilian. But I can assure Your Royal Highness the *Inflexible* is finished to the most demanding and innovative specifications. It is a splendid warship, protected by the thickest armor ever put afloat."

The second officer interrupted. "Our guns are encased in turrets on pivotal mountings."

There was silence. "Whatever for?" asked Lady Churchill.

"To cover a greater arc of fire, ma'am," replied the third. They continued to stroll, clacking across the deck, with Lady Churchill behind. Beatrice finally twisted off the crystal handle, and it fell to the deck where everyone scrambled for its recovery. Seamen on deck polishing the brightwork took the moment to glance covertly at their Princess and decided that as young ladies go, she set up very well indeed. Suddenly, in the midst of the confusion, she turned to the third officer, who was the least intimidating. "What are your hobbies?" she asked. There was embarrassed laughter while the young man in question made an effort to respond.

"I beg your pardon, Your Royal Highness. I was unprepared for your question."

"You should be placed on a pivotal mount, Jenkins," said the first officer, holding the crystal knob in his hand. "It might help you to think faster."

Beatrice turned to Lady Churchill. "I wish to return to Menton." Then she walked away as fast as she could in her hobbled skirts, once stumbling over the rim of a hatchway, then steadying herself on a polished wooden railing, with the perplexed officers trailing after her, at a loss for what they had done, or worse, had not done.

Beatrice said nothing in the *Cygnet*, even when the wind whipped her hat from her head. She faced the blackened sea before her, looking to Lady Churchill, who carried her dismembered parasol like a grim and lifeless figurehead. She continued her silence in the donkey cart that met them at the dock and carried them to the villa. The first words she spoke to Lady Churchill were in her dressing room as Fräulein Bauer helped her off with her basque. "I do not wish to speak of this afternoon, Lady Jane, ever again."

"Very well, Your Royal Highness, although I do wish you would tell me what has happened to upset you so."

"I am not upset," replied Beatrice.

The lady-in-waiting put her hand on a bell rope. "Let me ring for a tray, then, I beg you, a small supper. Surely you are hungry."

Beatrice looked out the window into the night. "This place is oppressive," she said. "The cliffs behind us. The sea before us. It is as if we sit upon an open shelf. There is no place to hide." Then, without warning, she gathered her skirts and bolted from the room to run to the Queen's study, where she rushed past Miss Stopford, broke open the double doors, and pushed, breathless, past a glowering Brown.

Victoria was attending to her dispatch boxes, this time with Sir Henry at her side, assisting her in decisions of priority.

"Is it true?" Beatrice demanded. "Is it true you sent Louis of Battenberg to sea?"

Victoria set her face as if into granite at this breach of court etiquette and filial consideration. "I did not send him to sea; he chose to be sent to sea. That is his career. He is an officer in the Royal Navy. Where else would you have him go?"

Beatrice was not mollified. "And you sent the Prince Imperial to Zululand where you hoped he would die."

"You are distraught," said Victoria. "I will call Dr. Reid."

"Don't call Dr. Reid," said Beatrice. "Just tell me: did you or did you not send him deliberately to get him out of the way because you knew he cared for me?"

"Where did you hear such nonsense?"

"I have my informants."

"Don't be absurd. Intrigue does not become you. Who was it, Leo?"

Beatrice's head dropped to her chest.

"I should have known. It's rot. Through and through. I will speak no more of it. The only excuse for your behavior is this wind. It is enough to unsettle anyone."

"Do not patronize me!" cried Beatrice. "I will speak of it. Now. Here. You sent the Prince Imperial to his death."

It was at this point that Brown moved before her. "Compose yourself, lass. You've become daft."

Victoria waved him aside. "Do you want to know," she asked, "why the Prince Imperial was sent to Zululand? This was not something to which I believed you should be privy, but you force my hand. He was sent because he demanded to be sent. He was pining for his friend Slade; he told his mother that if he was not reunited with Slade, he would die. He drove Eugénie to distraction. That is why he was sent. She knows it. I know it. Now you know it, too. And if you are interested, I have in my possession all of the letters you sent him. Eugénie kindly returned them to me. It would have been unfortunate had they fallen into the wrong hands."

Beatrice put her hands to her ears. "You have invented this."

"And you are trying my patience beyond all limits," said Victoria. "Dear child, I have never had a thought except for your happiness. You should be grateful that the Zulus behaved mercifully towards the Prince Imperial. He died without suffering. They even sewed up the cuts in his patrol jacket and destroyed nothing except his watch, and that was only to see what was inside."

"If you care about my happiness, then why do you push Parliament to allow a woman to marry her deceased sister's husband? Do you think I can't imagine why you press for this? It's so that I can marry Louis of Hesse and be mother to Alice's children. I will never do this. You can't ever make me do this, no matter what law is changed."

"I knew," said Victoria, "when Lady Jane and Leo urged so for you to visit Nice that it would be too much for you. You are so sheltered, my dearest baby. You know nothing of the world, nor should you be exposed without me to guide you. You should have stayed with me, and then all would have been well. As always."

Sir Henry placed certain letters into a courier bag and glanced at the trembling Princess. The long years of mourning, he thought sadly, a childhood spent in constant attendance upon a grieving mother, the ritual of sad anniversaries, of sheltering beyond that which was customary even for royalty, had taken their toll. This youngest daughter's spirit had been truncated, in the way the Japanese blunt their trees. It raised the question that he would take up in a letter to his wife of how a child becomes, or once become, is undone.

Beatrice began to cry. "I'm so sorry, Mama. I have been rude and selfish and ungrateful. Forgive me."

Victoria offered her one of her own handkerchiefs, a Belgian linen embroidered with black-and-white tears. Sir Henry was successful in leading her out of the room, and Brown was sent to inform Dr. Reid to prepare a sleeping draft. Victoria was in a rage at Leo and was quick to write him a hastily scribbled note that took precedence over the priority that Sir Henry had so carefully established, including a letter to Gladstone in which she would express her grave fear of losing suzerainty in the Transvaal and a personal note to Ferdinand de Lesseps, who was planning a visit to England in order to make arrangements with the P. and O. Steamship Company for improvements of sanitary conditions at the Suez Canal.

That night, Fräulein Bauer rubbed quinine and castor oil into the hands of the sleeping Princess, still wearing a white batiste combing sacque over her nightgown. The Princess was becoming too emotional. The Queen was entirely correct. It was the excitement that was responsible. Now, perhaps, her brother, the Duke of Albany, would not put such ideas in her head. It had something to do with a woman's private organs, which were well known to cause emotional disturbances of every sort. It was clear, reasoned Fräulein Bauer, that the private organs could not take the jouncing of carriages and gunboats and climbing up ships' ladders and whatever else they did that afternoon without her.

CHAPTER THREE

A mountain of trunks, satchels, portmanteaus, crates, and round cardboard boxes stood in plumes of mist in the courtyard of Balmoral Castle, all to be carried in and unpacked, only to be packed again within weeks when the royal entourage returned to Windsor.

Indoors it was no less chilly than the courtyard. Harriet Phipps, a maid of honor on her month's wait, her lips pursed in fury, clutched her braided cashmere mantle, picked up her skirts, and scurried through the drafty gallery past a cavalcade of antlered stagheads and Landseer paintings of dogs with sticks in their mouths.

Still in a pique over an encounter with the arrogant Brown, she was planning the precise words she would use to the Queen when she met Sir Henry in a rumpled herringbone morning coat and vest, his hands neatly and patiently placed behind his back, waiting in the corridor before the royal apartments. "You seem upset," he said.

"Brown is in his cups again," she replied.

"Good. He will not be around to pat me on the back. Heaven forbid he does that again to the Marquess. There will be an awful row. You must go in, Harriet, and hurry the Queen along."

"I have already told Her Majesty, Sir Henry, that you are anxious to begin the morning's work."

"Nevertheless, I would consider it a kindness if you did so again. They are clamoring for her to return to London, and we must make some response." He adjusted his heavily starched wing collar, which, he was convinced, was the only thing holding up his head after the long and sleepless night, and left to collect the telegrams that were being deciphered hourly by an undersecretary entrusted with the code.

Two blue-liveried pages opened the doors to the Queen's private apartments, allowing Miss Phipps to enter. The maid of honor, rehearsing her speech, tread her way carefully across the tartan carpet, avoiding the dogs as she moved into the tartan bedchamber, a mausoleum wallpapered in red with silver fleur-de-lis, the bedstead of which displayed a photograph of Prince Albert on his deathbed and was flanked by a glass case that contained casts of the Prince Consort's hands. She was uneasy being alone in this room and was glad to hear footsteps coming from the Queen's dressing room.

Followed by two dressers and her present lady of the bedchamber, Lady Southhampton, known to be dependable but tedious, Victoria entered slowly from her dressing room, wearing a crackling black silk gown. She shook her plump arms, and the elbow-length sleeves fluttered over the inner sleeves of white tulle, which the dressers were attempting to fasten in place.

"Have you learned, Harriet, why the gold plate has not yet been unpacked?" she asked.

"I was unable to have a satisfactory conversation with Mr. Brown, ma'am."

"Whyever not? Couldn't you find him? You probably didn't look well enough."

"I found him, ma'am, but he seemed to be under the weather."

"I hope he is not ill?"

Miss Phipps's hand went to the lace jabot at her throat. "Not ill, ma'am, confused."

"Confused? How so?"

The dressers looked to one another. Lady Southhampton tried to stifle her with a warning shake of her head. Confusion was a euphemism. It did not succeed. The Queen, who never took this message well, interpreted it correctly. Miss Phipps, who was forgetting her speech, began to pale. "He seems to have imbibed, ma'am, a bit too much."

"Nonsense. It is the way of Scots. I have known Mr. Brown for years as a man who holds his spirits well. He has been, and continues to be, a source of wisdom, strength, and truth. He is also courageous and handy. Hardly traits of a confused inebriate. It annoys me when others are so blind to his perfections."

Miss Phipps sighed. She told herself that in three weeks she would be home and away from Balmoral, which was to her as oppressive as any convent she could imagine. From somewhere outside came the reedy wail of bagpipes. "Sir Henry is anxious to see you, ma'am."

Victoria frowned. "I hope they do not continue to plead for my presence in London." A dresser placed a white widow's cap on Victoria's head. "There is nothing that I cannot do from Balmoral. I am not in Egypt, nor am I fighting this battle with my person. I have sent Sir Garnet Wolseley to do that. And my own son, my own dear Arthur, as well. Do they not consider my anxiety? My nerves are strained to a pitch. I am a mother, too. I cannot bear the burden of state and war in addition to the greatest worry a mother can have without the solace of Balmoral. Has Princess Beatrice been to breakfast?"

"Not yet, ma'am. She is still indisposed."

"Air is what she needs. Bracing and fresh and plenty of it. Please inform her that we require her assistance. The Crown Princess?"

"Dressing, ma'am."

Beatrice sat watching her oldest sister, whose clandestine visit to Scotland, with discretion and luck, would not have to be accounted for to her father-in-law, the Emperor, who had not given his permission for her to leave Germany. The Crown Princess of Prussia lay on a thistle-patterned sofa, loosely wrapped in a dressing gown tiered in cream lace ruffles. Beatrice thought how much like Mama Vicky looked, even though her face was coated with a paste of egg white, rose water, and alum to firm her skin.

"I don't see why that is necessary," said Beatrice.

"Because you are still young. Because my enemies rustle about the corridors of Berlin with bristling moustaches that have minutes before bent over my hand to kiss it and say that I am a spy and a traitor, adulterous with, of all people, dear faithful Count Seckendorff. The last thing I wish to add to their gossip is that I am getting wrinkled."

"Are you unhappy, Vicky?"

"Not unhappy, dear, wary. I have lived among them for over twenty years, and I still do not understand them. I thought they

would be like Papa. Imagine, can you, dinner parties at five, no flowers, no display of plate, no objets d'art in rooms that might as well be
in a hotel. Even at the palace on the Linden the only decorations are
silver dish covers surmounted with the Prussian eagle. Of fine living,
of fine feelings, they know nothing. I can't wait to see Leo. How is
he? Is she good to him?"

Beatrice looked down into her lap. The pain threatened to spark.
She had taught herself how to dampen the ember. She smothered it
by burying it deep. "Helen is a perfect wife."

"But?"

"Nothing. She is good to him, yes."

"But you must miss him. The two of you were so close as children,
the youngest two, the babies. We used to drag you about in a wagon."
At Vicky's signal, an elegant wave of her dimpled hand, a maid, who
had been silently preparing the Crown Princess's morning toilette,
came to wipe her face with a soft pad of lamb's wool.

"He is pale, Vicky, and very lame. I worry so for him."

"Yes. The hemophilia." Her eyes glistened as she thought of the
deficiency of epidermis that rendered her younger brother's veins and
arteries so vulnerable and which took the life of Alice's son, Frittie.
Vicky paused, grateful that her surviving sons had been spared, waiting for the maid to wipe off the final traces and remove the papillottes
that curled her hair into shiny, bouncing springs. "Bismarck is attempting to drive a wedge between Willy and Fritz and me. My son
is already acting as if he were Kaiser, only because of Bismarck's
encouragement. He is shown confidential dispatches. He gets hours of
briefing that his own father does not. Fritz has protested, but to no
avail." Vicky turned to her youngest sister, who sat before her, composed and bland faced, holding in her left hand, as though she were
sitting for a portrait, her swollen right. "Before you asked me if I were
unhappy. Are you?"

"I am content."

"So you continue to say in your letters. I do not believe you." The
maid began to brush her hair, hairdressing being one of the requirements of her position, arranging it into large coils that wound about
her hand.

"Why not? It is true."

"You are dedicated to Mama. That is a noble sentiment. An unselfish one, but it is also unnatural. You should be thinking of getting married."

Beatrice attempted to rise. "I do not think, Vicky, that it is for you to say what is natural and what is unnatural."

Vicky gently pulled her back. "Benjamina, don't leave. Sit here beside me." She dropped her voice. "Leo may not last among us, you know. One day he will suffer from an injury from which there will be no recovery."

"Don't say that. Don't make such pronouncements. You are not a doctor."

"That's true. I am no doctor, but I have seen much and lost much. If one prepares oneself, sometimes a loss isn't so brutal. There is another solution. You must plan an independent life."

"I know why they gossip about you, Vicky. You interfere." Beatrice stood and with her left hand arranged her skirts behind her so she could walk without impediment.

"Where are you going?" asked Vicky.

"To get my cloak and gloves and then outdoors to assist Mama. She needs me."

"But it is so chilly. My God, it is like the Tyrol in November out there. It can't be good for you." Vicky bent her head forward while her maid reached behind her to pin up her hair.

"Why not?"

"How can you pretend what is plain to see for anyone with eyes. Your hand is practically useless."

"I can manage. It's just a little stiff. It gets better as the day wears on."

The morning air had become dry and crisp, detailing with clarity the savage landscape. Behind were lonely glens and the dark, angry crags of Lochnagar, a fierce, forbidding, mist-shrouded mountain, the nesting place of golden eagles and peregrine falcons, skirted beneath its deep ravines with purple and lilac heather-covered hills. To one side was a dank and fecund forest of moss-covered pines; to the other, white poplars, through which was heard the whirring flight of grouse. A solitary lapwing rose from the marshy swamps near the river below, crying Pe Weet, to soar without effort from a dense mass of bullrushes.

Victoria, surrounded by Sir Henry, the Minister in Residence, the Marquess of Salisbury, the Secretary for War, Mr. Childers, their equerries and undersecretaries, sat at a table set on the sloping poplar-rimmed terrace, studying a map, the silver spectacles slipped down upon her nose.

"Here, ma'am," said Mr. Childers, pointing to the map. "Here is the Suez Canal."

"Which I can plainly see."

"Beg pardon, ma'am. And here, Ismailia. We have transferred our base of action from Alexandria to the Suez."

"The distance between Cairo and the Suez?"

"Eighty miles, ma'am. You can see that it is all desert."

"And Prince Arthur, where is Prince Arthur?"

"The Duke of Connaught is here, ma'am, in command of his Guard's Brigade at Ramleh, with a battery of forty-pounders. And Arabi Pasha is entrenched here, massing his forces at Tel el Kabir," replied Mr. Childers.

"Why isn't our cavalry being used?"

"Because, ma'am," replied the Marquess, "as I pointed out before, the horses, due to their overlong sea voyage, were out of condition."

Victoria held up a scrap of paper, which she shook. "And why this protest from de Lesseps?"

"De Lesseps had created a pact with Arabi Pasha. Granville informs me," said the Marquess, "that certain documents have come to his attention."

"Granville," said Victoria, "works with his wife and children in the same room. Very domestic but certainly not businesslike. It is difficult to believe that Eugénie's cousin could be such a whining coward. Does he really think that an unscrupulous adventurer like Arabi can guarantee the safety of the canal? Against lunatics who have declared a holy war against all Europeans? It must have something to do with a diet which provokes the blood. Releasing convicts upon a helpless population. The Khedive a prisoner in his palace. It is barbaric."

"We have reason to be optimistic," said Sir Henry. "The whole of Egypt, except for the coastline and Suez, was at his mercy until only a few weeks ago."

"Nevertheless," said the Marquess, "his powers of mischief are still immense. Although he no longer controls the railroad, he holds the highways."

"Our troops will give him the trouncing he deserves," said Victoria.

"Our troops, ma'am," said Mr. Childers, "fall from sunstroke and heat exhaustion. If we are to do it, it must be done quickly. And then, of course, as always in Egypt, there is the cholera."

Sir Henry watched his monarch set her face as hard as the polished granite of the castle behind her and thought how unfeeling was this minister not to be aware of Her Majesty's concern for her soldier son. "One must not overlook, ma'am, that we have on our side the most modern weaponry. Gatling guns, as I have explained, that have a crank-operated cluster of barrels from which to fire, not to mention the Gardiner and the Nordenfeldt and, of course, regimental spirit."

"And Right," said Victoria. "Never forget that."

Leo lay on the tartan plaid sofa, exhausted from his trip, pillows propped beneath his head and a tartan blanket draped over his legs. His skin was ashen; his eyes, once prominent, now lodged deeply in his head, like stones sunken in swale. Vicky, coiffed and gowned, smelling of roses and nutmeg, her cheeks and lips faintly rouged with Chinese leaves, sat beside him, stroking his hand.

"Can't someone stop that fellow? He has been bellowing since I arrived."

"Mama loves bagpipes," said Vicky. She stood to walk to the window, rustling across the carpet in her faille walking suit.

"Your train is much too long," said Leo. "And no one with taste wears the polonaise any longer. Dear Vicky, surely Prussian antagonisms toward the French do not extend to fashion."

"I have no antagonism toward the French. On the contrary, I have fond memories of Paris. You were too little to remember, but as a girl I visited with Napoleon and Eugénie at St. Cloud. I recall a little white satin door that opened on to a garden. But one mustn't dwell on the past. Have you heard anything more about the Egyptian situation?"

"Nothing. Not one word. No one speaks to me except to tell me how well I look, which has really begun to worry me. They are all outdoors, conducting the battle on the grounds. Mama is the only one without chilblains. The others keep coming in for whiskey. I would like to know how Arthur is faring. He always wanted to be a soldier, you know."

"He is in the thick of it," said Vicky. "I know that much."

"I would give anything," he said, drawing the blanket more closely to his neck, "to be in the thick of anything. Arthur is her favorite. If anything happens to him, I shudder at the thought."

"What makes you think he is her favorite?"

"She wore the Kohinoor diamond at his wedding. She did not wear it at mine. There are enough thistles on this wallpaper to choke a donkey. Why must this place be so deuced ugly?"

"I did hear someone mention," said Vicky gently, in the way one cozens a cranky child, "that the attack began at dawn. They are planning to rush the entrenchments. Apparently, the Turkish troops at the canal are unwelcome allies, but your British guns will be there to enforce their inactivity. I also heard that Louis of Battenberg is on board one of the battleships."

"I would say the less said about that the better."

Vicky turned to stand with her back to the tartan-draped window. "Leo, she suffers so. You must have noticed. One hand is practically useless. I see the way she favors it. She can't write or paint or play the pianoforte, yet it means nothing to her. She doesn't complain. She doesn't seem to mind at all. It's irrational."

"It's irrational to love someone and be totally unable to help her. I tried, but she is bound to stay with Mama. She will not even discuss going anywhere of significance without Mama, much less speak of marriage."

The doors swung open, and Beatrice, red cheeked, wearing gloves and a velvet bonnet, entered the drawing room. She glanced at her brother and sister and paused. She had hoped to find Leo alone. That they were talking about her was obvious in the way they both brightened at her approach, as if they were gas lamps and someone had turned up their jets. They would tell her what to do, coax her to leave Mama, most likely, trying to pluck her up roots and all, like some weed. She drew in her breath and felt her stays shift. If it became unpleasant, she would brave the cold again.

"What's happening, Benjamina?" asked Leo. "Tell us whatever news you know."

"The fighting continues," she replied. "We hold our ground against ten thousand of the enemy and have secured the freshwater canal which is vital to Ismailia."

"What about Alexandria?" asked Vicky.

"The second division under General Hamley was left to hold it."

"And Arthur?"

"Still no word." Beatrice turned to smile at her brother, pulling off her gloves finger by finger. "Are you comfortable?"

"As well as can be expected in this drafty castle."

"Where is Louischen?" she asked. "Mama has written her a note in which she assures her that our troops hold their own."

"Arthur's wife is with Helen. They are dandling Arthur's baby, who sleeps, as usual, very soundly from his dose of Godfrey's cordial. Thank God for opium. I plan to buy it by the crate when ours is born. Come, let me see your hand. Where does it hurt?"

"Here." Beatrice masked her face.

"Does it hurt here?" he asked.

"No. Only to here."

"You mean it stops at the wrist?" he asked. "In a clean line?"

"Shall I ring for another blanket?" she asked.

"If your plan is to smother me silent, it won't work," replied Leopold. "What have you done for it, your hand?"

Prying, digging, disturbing the layers like badgers. "Camphorated mercurial ointment." Her voice was tremulous and faint. She reclaimed her hand from his grasp and smoothed her face as well as her thoughts. It was as easy to do one as the other. She had had years of practice.

"Where are you going?" asked Leopold.

"To see that the note is delivered and then to help Mama."

"Why?" asked Vicky. "She has an army out there as big as the one in Egypt."

"Because she needs me. Because she wants me at her side. Brown is ill." Beatrice swept out of the room.

"That settles it," said Vicky. "I'm going to speak to Mama. This has gone far enough."

"I wouldn't," said Leo. "Not today."

"I am bound to do it before I leave. It can't be put off."

The day for Victoria had proved to be one of hastily read telegrams, whispers in the hallway, heartbeats that found their own erratic rhythm, the running steps of messengers, and trying to manage without Johnnie Brown, which was as much a trial as the battle.

She sat at the desk in her first-floor study, surrounded by card index boxes and family pictures, including a black-draped photograph of Alice and a large portrait of Albert mounted on an easel. Even though getting about was difficult, since no footman could support her as Brown did, she was feeling vigorous, alive, energized by the battle and by what Byron had called, when she was still a child and had not yet seen it, the steep frowning glories of Lochnagar. Balmoral always restored her. It was there in sight of glens so narrow they looked like slits in the rock that she felt Albert's presence, guiding her, protecting her, loving her as he had while he lived. It was there beside the rugged black gullied landscapes, despite rain clouds hanging like dripping blankets, that her veins coursed, rushing as the Dee, and the tingling air reached to the bottom of her lungs. If only she could persuade her children of the salutary effect on both body and soul of fresh natural air in every kind of weather.

The latest telegram, which informed her that General Wolseley's troops had cleared the trenches and were this moment charging home with their bayonets, prompted the Marquess to announce that he was going, with her permission, deer stalking. She, however, would relax her vigilance only when she learned that Arthur was safe. She thought of Gladstone, who at first had been opposed to military action. The memory made her sniff. Why couldn't he have been a Quaker like John Bright and have also resigned from the government in protest.

Vicky entered after a tentative, uncharacteristic knock. "I have heard the news is good, Mama. Is it too early for congratulations? May we chat?"

"About what? I am in the middle of a war."

"About Benjamina."

Victoria was annoyed at her eldest daughter. It was clear that since her years in the German court Vicky had changed for the worse. When she was a young girl, she was dutiful and obedient, Victoria's delight, and would never have dreamed of opposing her mother's wishes. Sir Henry made as if to go, but Victoria put up her hand, and he continued filing index cards. "What about her?"

"Frankly, Mama, I worry that no plans have been made for her marriage."

"Not everyone is meant to marry, Vicky. Benjamina remains with me to give me comfort, a fitting and quite satisfactory arrangement for all unfortunate widows and their last born, their babies. What's more, she fervently wishes it so, as do I. It is something which you will want to give much thought to. I have always told you, Vicky, that command is duty first and privilege second, but a privilege with a heavy price. You and I are not like other people. Royalty is never sure of those who serve. There is always that tiny reservation, that small caution that says, Beware, don't confide in this or that person, even if one desperately wants to do so with all one's heart. That is why I keep Baby at my side. She will be my dearest companion. You will want to do the same with your youngest."

The thought of turning her irrepressible youngest daughter into a spinster was appalling. "I could never do that to Mossy. I could never deprive her of her own life."

"That is because you still have Fritz. When he dies, what then?"

"How cruel you are, Mama."

"Not cruel, Vicky. Plain speaking. When Fritz dies, and since he is older, we will assume that he will do so before you, speak to me then of what you can and cannot do. Leaving home to marry is not always best for every girl, Vicky. Benjamina is timid and shy and can't stand up to others as you do. I do not want to happen to her what happened to you. I shudder to think of what would become of her had she been sent to the German court, or any place away from the people and things she loves best. I am determined to keep her safe."

Vicky, who knew better than to press, kissed her mother on the cheek and turned to leave.

"Your train is much too long," said Victoria. "Do, dear, have it shortened."

It was at tea that they deciphered the telegram from Sir Garnet Wolseley that said that the Egyptians were fleeing in disorder, that quantities of Egyptian supplies had fallen into their hands, that British troops were in pursuit of Arabi Pasha, and that although their own losses were very heavy, the battle, to all intents and purposes, was won. It was during the serving of haggis at dinner, a pudding made of the heart and lungs of a sheep minced with suet and oatmeal, that word was received that Arthur was safe and had behaved admirably while leading his brigade to the attack, that he was bringing home a trophy, a Turkish carpet from Arabi's tent, and that Sir Garnet was planning to ride in triumph through the streets of Cairo.

The Duchess of Connaught, Arthur's wife, Louischen, began to weep, prettily, delicately, in gentle freshets, as ladies learned to do when they were in the company of others. Lady Southhampton, who personally detested haggis, was glad for the opportunity to put down her fork, unnoticed by her jubilant Queen.

"It appears, Mama," said Leopold, "that you are the de facto ruler of Egypt." The pains in his leg were making it difficult to sit. He shifted to his side while he proposed a toast to the Duke of Connaught's continued health.

"Arthur has won his battle," exclaimed Victoria.

And I am losing mine, thought Leo, draining his glass.

"That is the death blow to military ascendancy in Egypt," said the Marquess, who had not gotten close to a stag all afternoon and was, as a consequence, miffed, "and a serious check on Islamic fanaticism."

The next telegram, which an equerry slipped first to Mr. Childers, came from Lord Granville, in which the Foreign Secretary said that France would propose joint occupation, which would be, in his opinion, very awkward. He added that Turkish occupation, under strict conditions, of course, would be preferable. This was followed by both a telegram of congratulation and a more detailed dispatch that had come on a special purple and gold train car from London from Gladstone, who agreed that further dual action of England and France be abolished, who said that he had ordered a gun salute in Hyde Park, who congratulated his Queen but who neglected, to his later regret, to mention anything about the Duke of Connaught's bravery. He concluded in his dispatch that he was averse to the establishment of Egyptian independence, not from love of Egypt, he wanted to make it clearly understood, but of fear of the general scramble for its spoils.

"The problem, ma'am," said the Marquess, "is what to do with Arabi once they catch him and how to square ourselves with France and Turkey."

"I have another problem, Lord Salisbury," said Victoria. "I must now invite Gladstone to Balmoral, and I do not want to do so. He will spend the entire visit trying to convince me that the *Iliad* and the *Odyssey* were written by the same person, as if I care."

Beatrice was weary again, overcome with a heavy fatigue that slowed her limbs, as if she were moving through molasses. She had said very little during the early dinner, lifting her shoulders close to her chin so that she would not have to converse with either Lady Southhampton or the Marquess. Now, as Victoria held court in the drawing room, sitting on a stiff-backed chair while others, except Leopold, who sat with his cane resting over his knees, stood in attendance, she was less ready to converse and asked to be allowed to rest before the victory bonfire. Victoria gave grudging acquiescence and reacted with tight-lipped displeasure at her youngest daughter's lack of fortitude, the special stamina so necessary to royalty, while Beatrice, her brocaded fan folded shut in her hand, kissed her mother dutifully on the cheek.

Victoria fastened her attention upon Miss Phipps and reprimanded her for the irritating habit of shifting from foot to foot. She did not have to turn to hear the Marquess whisper from behind her chair that Lord Rosebery had learned that the House of Lords would approve the bill allowing women to marry their dead sister's husbands. Victoria nodded. Of course, she told herself, she would only allow the marriage if Louis of Hesse agreed to leave Darmstadt and take up residence with her. Then she would have Alice's children, and Beatrice would have a ready-made family and a kind husband who, even if he was much older, was tractable.

When Brown suddenly appeared, dour and sullen in kilts and knee socks, to escort her to a window view of the bonfire, she visibly relaxed. A faint smile played over her lips. "It has been a very long day," she said. He took her arm. "You're getting heavy, woman," he said. "That and being stiff as you are makes getting you about no easy task."

Vicky watched them as they went, wondering how her mother was so blind to characteristics that she and Bertie and all the others found so abhorrent. She could never put up with a servant who displayed such familiarity. Perhaps it had something to do with Mama's age. Was she mellowing, like silver, or was she becoming, as many old and dotty women, overly dependent on a menial? She clutched her skirts, draping her train over her arm, and called after the Marquess.

"Lord Salisbury, what is it that Lord Rosebery says the House of Lords will approve?"

"You shouldn't trouble yourself, ma'am," he said, "with such matters."

"But I do, Lord Salisbury. I am very interested in the workings of government. I was well tutored by my father in that regard."

"And mother, ma'am. And mother."

The bonfires on the wooded hill of Craig Gowen illuminated the countless peaks around it, making them shine like muzzles, and could be seen from Beatrice's window. Shadowy outlines started up the hill from the castle. It would be like Halloween, she thought. The villagers would stream from their rude cottages for miles around, drinking into the night, and carry blazing pine torches, the gillies would be dancing reels, one after another, to the tunes of bagpipes, and some, with blacked faces, would drag a cart with a dummy witch, which they would set on fire. Beatrice, who hoped that her mother would not be very angry with her, stood watching the flames that seemed to lick the sky.

How distant they seemed, as if separated by years instead of meters, like a dim and formless memory that had no boundaries, far in the past, untouchable, elusive, like Papa. His pictures were everywhere; the footman brought nightly hot water and a clean towel to his dressing room. Did the man in the picture ever touch her? What did it feel like? Last night she dreamed of falling on her back through space. She hoped she would not have the same dream again. It had made her wake up with a start and a smothered cry. She would not have wanted Mama to hear. Nor did she want the other dream, the one of the wet and sodden nightshirt that smelled of cloves, that seemed to wrap her in a hollow embrace, from which she always woke trembling with fear. A feeling of panic tightened her throat.

If she hurried, she could catch the others. She ran to her dressing room and reached for a mantle trimmed in marten. It was easy to fasten, unlike the bonnet's velvet ribbons, which she could not tie. She called impatiently for Bauer and then angrily for the maid. Neither answered. She pulled the bell rope, then held aloft the hand

bell that lay beside her silver combs and brushes and rang it, shaking
its clapper furiously against the silver frame. Close to tears, she threw
it to the tartan carpet and left with the bonnet ribbons untied, fluttering around her quivering chin.

CHAPTER FOUR

Fall had come and gone, and winter was now roaring its last. The Thames was gorged, its flooded banks a shallow lake, its runnels seeping underground, worsening the noxious effluvia of the medieval drains and cesspools of Windsor Castle. Once a Norman fortress, the castle had been transformed through centuries and a succession of Plantagenets, Tudors, Stuarts, and Hanoverians into a palace equipped with opulent furnishings, a cumbersome staff of thousands, and a priceless collection of art. Icy winds and sleet howled through its towers and Gothic machicolated battlements, ruffling the ulsters of the yeoman guards making their rounds and diminishing their hoarse cries as they demanded the countersign from strangers.

The court was in mourning again, as it was every two or three months due to the web of royal relatives, woven back and forth across the continent of Europe, one of whom was almost certain to die, this time for the Grand Duke of Mecklenburg-Schwerin. Beatrice, wearing a black merino gown with long white weeper cuffs, could hear the tramp of sentinels on the battlements and the trooping of guards on the muddy ground of the quadrangle below.

Over the past few months, she had accommodated to her disability serenely, almost angelically, with the resignation, if not the relish, of a martyr and had even been able to paint and play the pianoforte despite the limited ability of the affected hand. She seemed to settle into the duties of royal life with some contentment, her edges worn smooth as she attended glittering receptions at Buckingham Palace, protected by a dais from the jammed and jeweled aristocracy who came to bow before her mother. She visited military hospitals, standing patiently in drafty wards and corridors to hold the medals that Victoria would select to pin on wounded heroes; she waited in an open victoria in the rain with an umbrella held over her head by a white-gloved footman in top hat and long box coat as the Queen granted new colors to a plumed and helmeted, dripping regiment. She even attended the theater without her mother, accompanied by only ladies of the royal household, as she had the week before, when she went to the Lyceum to see Henry Irving in *The Merchant of Venice.*

Her fears of separation from Leopold had not been realized. The Duke of Albany, now a father, was a frequent dinner guest at Windsor, and even though there were always others at the glittering table —visiting royalty, her pretty sister Louise, sometimes with her husband, the Marchioness of Lorne, her brother Affie, the Duke of Edinburgh and his wife Marie, sister to the Tsar, members of the government, of the diplomat corps, of the household, and celebrities, a nightly assembly as omnipresent as the flowers—there was always the chance afterward to talk to him, to hold his arm, to stand near him as he charmed everyone with his wit and made them laugh.

Now she sat composed and complacent, in attendance upon her mother, whose side she had not left since Victoria's fall down a flight of stairs. The lavish drawing room in which they sat overlooked the flat valley of the Thames, from where, in pleasant days, could be seen Runnymede meadow and always, as now, even through the sleet, the smoke of the city. Its walls and high-domed ceiling, spangled with crystal chandeliers, were of gilded cream, its gilt furniture upholstered in gold and crimson silk, and crimson silk draperies hung from gilt cornice poles. Beech-wood logs burned in the white marble fireplace.

Victoria, with a painful swollen knee, was settled in a heavily padded wheelchair. She looked bored. Gladstone stood before her, slightly stooped, suffering from an attack of lumbago. The pallor of the aging Prime Minister's skin was alabaster, his large bald head plastered with strands of white hair raked over the top, with wispy side whiskers clinging to his jowls. Behind them stood Brown, his arms crossed over his coarse tweed jacket. The staccato of a drum roll clattered from the triangle, followed by the clip clop of the royal cavalry.

"So you see, ma'am," Gladstone was saying, "Homer was responsible for the Greek religion. All the gods and goddesses who play such a large part in the *Iliad* were creations of Homer."

"If you continue, Prime Minister, along this line, I will go to Australia." It was one of two constant threats that she had used successfully over the years, the other being to abdicate.

"Beg pardon, ma'am," he replied. "Deference to Your Majesty's injury dictated that I ease in to matters of state."

"You do not ease in with Homer; instead, you make me wish to be with the wallaby."

"Get on with it, man," growled Brown.

"Certainly," said Gladstone with great dignity. "The Irish question —" he began.

"There is nothing you can say, Mr. Gladstone," interrupted Victoria, "which will make us believe that home rule is anything but an attempt to separate Ireland from the United Kingdom."

"Ma'am," said Gladstone, "free discussion and self-government are essential to man's dignity and self-respect. We cannot begin until we truly can agree on that basic premise."

"Anarchists who maim with bombs, slit the hindquarters of poor defenseless beasts, and murder landlords do not fall into that category. Lord Salisbury tells me that the arrears bill which you have introduced whereby tenants unable to pay do not have to do so is nothing short of robbery and confiscation. He calculates that you have reduced rents in Ireland by twenty percent."

"True, very true, ma'am, but in 1881, before the bill, there were 4,439 agrarian crimes in Ireland, and in the past year the number has been reduced to 870."

"I call that a pittance."

"Rome was not built in a day."

Victoria gave him a warning look, then turned to look for something. Beatrice was beginning to pride herself at being able to anticipate her mother's needs and moved to place a satin and lace pillow behind her back, but Brown sprang forward and reached Victoria first. Don't be angry, she thought. His touch is better. He has been caring for her longer. Don't be angry. Don't be. She clenched her hands in her lap.

"Under our present highly centralized system," continued Gladstone, "we cannot win. Every request, if granted, is a drain on the

British treasury, and if refused, a grievance. We need an Irish body competent to act for its own portion of the kingdom."

Victoria turned to Beatrice. "What do you think of all this?"

"We cannot yet trust the Irish," whispered Beatrice, "with popular local institutions."

"There, you see? Her Royal Highness has a perfect grasp. A girl with little concern and no practice to speak of in matters of state, to whom the issues are crystal clear."

Beatrice tried not to show her delight in her mother's approbation. She busied herself with smoothing her cuffs.

"Don't fidget," said Victoria.

"The perilous crisis," explained Gladstone patiently, "which we have not yet looked in the face, will arise when a united majority of Irish members demand fundamental change. I would like to avert such a crisis. Ireland forces upon us great social and religious questions. We must have the courage to recognize them and work them through."

"I am not an assembly, Mr. Gladstone; for pity's sake, stop looking over my head."

There was a rap on one of the polished ebony doors. Beatrice rose, unfolding herself, as she had learned to do one tedious summer, in one smooth, continuous movement, her back straight, her waist supple, her lower limbs a lever. When she was out of hearing, Gladstone continued, bent even farther toward the Queen, as if he were conspiring. "There is another matter, ma'am. It has to do with the contagious diseases act." He looked toward the door to make sure that the Princess was still out of earshot. "It is my belief that the government should support the resolution to condemn the system of licensed brothels which currently are in eighteen ports and garrison towns."

"I think you've said enough," said Brown.

Beatrice returned to announce that her eldest brother, the Prince of Wales, had arrived and would be waiting in Victoria's private apartments. It was soon after that, that a disheartened Gladstone waited to take his departure, while Brown, with Beatrice at his side, wheeled Victoria out of the white drawing room, past the halberd-carrying yeoman bodyguard in red knee breeches and flat-topped gold embroidered hat.

"Lord Beaconsfield knew how to explain things," complained Victoria, comparing her present Prime Minister to Disraeli. "Do you know Gladstone's wife ties knots in his nightshirt so that when she wakes, she will remember how many little things to tell him. She has the man tied in knots." This made her laugh.

Beatrice recalled that Leo had said something to her about waking and remembering. She must remember to ask him what it was. "How do you come to know such a thing, Mama?" she asked.

"A sovereign makes it her business to know everything."

The Prince of Wales was waiting in the Queen's private sitting room. His burly presence was in odd contrast to the litter of sofa cushions, photographs, bibelots, bric-a-brac, bowls, and baskets of flowers that were everywhere; even the grand piano was covered with china dogs and plaster statuettes.

Next in line to the throne of England, Bertie bowed to his mother, smiled at his sister, then glared at Brown, who returned his baleful look with matched hostility. Deciding that such an encounter was unbecoming to his station, Bertie came forward to kiss his mother on the cheek, then, in what seemed an afterthought, grabbed the wheelchair and wrenched it from Brown's grasp.

"You are no longer needed, Brown. We can manage without you."

"I take my orders from the Queen," said Brown. "I did not notice that you had been crowned."

"This is insufferable, Mama," protested Bertie. "The man has really gone too far. I will not stay if he remains."

Neither one has any consideration, thought Victoria, or cares one whit that I am in agony with this swollen knee. They are both bound and determined to have a row. She dismissed Brown with a wave of her hand. "We shan't be needing your excellent help for just a few hours. I would like you to run an errand, however. There is on the skirted table a small package and note for Lady Florence Dixie, who you know was attacked by Fenians and rescued by her St. Bernard."

"Aye, I'll take it. Then I'm going to make myself useful. Not like certain people. I'm going to search the grounds. There are assassins lurking everywhere; what happened to that poor lass should tell you that." He turned with hauteur to the Prince of Wales. "Take care she does not become overwarm," he cautioned. "The Queen does not like to be overwarm."

"You are talking about my mother," said Bertie, who caught the thinly veiled reference to his enforced inactivity but who decided that it would not do not to get into a scrape with a menial, "with whose wants I am entirely familiar."

"It's raining," said Victoria to the kilted Scot. "Search for Fenians when it stops."

"Fenians," replied Brown, "do not wait for fair weather to strike. Ye mun have noticed that."

The Prince of Wales was older than Beatrice, the sixteen years between them enough of a separation so that she really didn't know him except as a portly and affable older brother who seemed to have a penchant for getting into scrapes, even though he was a married man with grown children. He was discussing his recent trip to Berlin and saying that he did not like the way Vicky was being treated by Bismarck and her son Willy and that he would really like to give his nephew a punch in the jaw. What was unforgivable was that when Bertie slipped on the highly polished parquet eagle in the center of the ballroom floor, Willy laughed. "Why should he not?" asked Victoria. "That's very funny." Bertie said that Vicky was concerned for Prince Sandro of Battenberg, who had been made ruler of Bulgaria under the patronage of Tsar Alexander II, but that his cousin, the present Tsar, Alexander III, disliked him.

"I know why," said Victoria. "It is because of his looks. Sandro is tall and very handsome, while the Tsar is uncouth, surly, dull, and looks like a pugilist. I hear he worries about softening of the brain. He should. His brother's head melted."

Bertie laughed. "Sandro is a pawn in the political machinations of Germany and Russia. His task is an impossible one. The Tsar looks on Bulgaria as existing only for Russia's benefit, and Sandro is truly concerned for the Bulgarian people. Bismarck loathes him because of his status and objects to the morganatic marriage of his parents. While Sandro's father was of royal blood, his mother was not. Bismarck is telling everyone that Julia von Hauke's father was a pastry cook."

"What of Alice's children?" asked Victoria.

"Ella has fallen in love, it seems, with the Grand Duke Serge."

Beatrice kept her eyes in her lap and wondered if he was going to mention the rumor that she had heard from her sister Louise that Louis of Battenberg and her own niece, Alice's daughter Victoria, were in love.

Victoria shot him a warning look, but the damage had been done, and her curiosity was piqued. "How could she refuse Fritz of Baden for a Russian? Her health will never stand the climate. Besides, we all know the dreadful state Russia is in. What does Augusta say about all this?"

Bertie's image of the aging German Empress was of the chestnut wigs that slipped and slid over her palsied head. "She was very upset, enough to cut Ella dead at a ball. But Ella is determined. There is something brooding and mystical about her which should do very well in Russia."

"Nonsense, Bertie. I will write to her immediately. Benjamina, please make a note that I wish to write this afternoon to Ella." Beatrice rose and glided to the writing desk, which was smothered like a stall in a bazaar under trifles and a dense phalanx of ornately framed photographs. "How could you?" whispered Victoria. "You know very well that I do not want mention of such things in her presence."

"Forgive me, Mama. It is difficult for me to remember what I may and may not say before my little sister."

"It is not very difficult and certainly no mystery. No talk of love, engagement, or marriage. Really, Bertie, I had hoped to have your cooperation on this matter." The Prince of Wales, who fought with his mother on many issues, most of them concerning her prevention of his active participation in government, did not want to make this his cause. It was not important enough to press.

Before the tea things had been removed, Bertie had left, and there were no more visitors seeking audience. Sir Henry had seen to that by strongly suggesting to those remaining that it might be difficult returning by train to London because of the flooding and that the daylight hours, under the circumstances, would be more prudent.

By nightfall, Victoria's knee was badly swollen, and nothing Dr. Reid or Dr. Jenner did helped, not the purging of her peccant humors, which collected daily, not the mustard plasters to give counterirritant or the draft every three hours of digitalis, calomel, and opium. Fräulein Bauer suggested leeching, but Lady Ely ridiculed her suggestion, saying in her whispery voice that no one with any sense did that anymore.

Victoria wanted Brown and was annoyed when she was told by Lady Ely that he had gone to bed with a chill. Upon further questioning, Lady Ely informed her that he went hunting for Fenians in the open dogcart, which he preferred to the closed carriage, going over every inch of ground himself, which meant he most certainly got soaking wet. At first, Victoria thought he was so dear to have done that for her. The sentiment lasted only for minutes. Then she began to complain, vociferously, pettishly, to her ladies-in-waiting, her maids of honor, her dressers, Sir Henry, Dr. Reid, Dr. Jenner, and primarily to Beatrice, asking in a tired voice why she must suffer so.

Beatrice was privately glad, although she would never admit to such a selfish thought. It lodged between the layers, like sand in an onion. With Brown in bed, she could help Mama, do things for her that no one else could but Brown and she could do, show her how much she was loved. The next day they learned that Brown's face had swollen with erysipelas and that he was in bed with a fever. Only months before, an elevated temperature would have been determined with a hand on the patient's forehead or a clumsy glass bulb, which was no more accurate, but now there was the new thermometer to confirm what hand and lips could guess. It became apparent that he was very ill.

Victoria sent Dr. Reid and Dr. Jenner, both wearing neckties of white piqué over their glazed white linen collars, to his room in Clarence Tower. Dr. Jenner, fingering the cameo brooch that held his knot in place, reported back that Brown was suffering from an acute disease that manifested in inflammation of the subcutaneous tissues. The hours of exposure in the icy wind proved too much even for his strong physique. He did not tell her that Brown's alcoholism was a heavy factor in his illness. Instead, he said that the weather had done him in. Victoria visited her servant in his room, leaning on her stout two sticks, but could not believe that his illness was as serious as the faces of Drs. Jenner and Reid would suggest. She told Beatrice that somehow she would manage until he got better but that it would be an effort.

Leopold broke the news to his mother in her private suite. The task became his through default. Louise did not want to do it, Bertie abstained because he said it would be difficult not to laugh, Alfred was disinterested, and Beatrice said she would not know how to begin. Leopold said he would take the sad duty upon himself. He found her in her dressing room, searching for earrings in the drawered compartments of an opened velvet jewel case being presented by a dresser. "Dearest," he said.

She heaved a great sigh. "Is it about him? Have you come to tell me about Johnnie?"

Leopold nodded, kissed her cheek, sat beside her on an empire divan, and took her hand. "Yes, and I'm afraid it's very bad. He is gone," he said.

Victoria said nothing, but turned her back on the jewel case and slumped in her chair, with Leopold's arm around her for support. She wept silently.

Beatrice met Leopold in the hallway and clutched his arm. "How did she take it?" she asked.

"Very hard. As we knew she would." He looked at her with concern. "The burden, I'm afraid, will fall on you."

She lifted her chin when he had gone. He's dead, she thought; he's really dead.

Victoria threw herself into Brown's loss the way one dives into a lake, as if embracing the water. The court, which was already in mourning, was plunged deeper. Beatrice's white weeper cuffs came off. Unrelieved black, long veils, and crepe on everything was the order of the day. A funeral knell from the tower tolled his death. He was to have a life-sized statue fashioned by the sculptor Boehm erected on the grounds of Balmoral. The beautiful exiled Empress of France, Eugénie, a favorite of Victoria's, came to console Victoria, whispering to Beatrice that she would always have special feelings for her. Lady Florence Dixie sent a letter telling of the Scot's kindness when he delivered Her Majesty's gift and note, writing that he had asked for a picture of the dog, which she was enclosing. Perhaps the Queen would wish to have it, anyway.

Before his death, Victoria could not walk. Now she could not stand. White and exhausted, she clutched her youngest daughter and sobbed into her neck. "You're all I have, Baby. There is no one else."

Beatrice had heard those words spoken before in the same desperate, impassioned tones. The memory jarred her. Somehow it was connected to the nightshirt. She fought the image off as one would a fly. Mama always used to say, "You're safe with Brown." She had been hearing it for years, but it was not true. She was safer without Brown, for now she could have Mama all to herself.

Victoria became disconsolate, alternately maudlin and macabre, telling Beatrice that she wanted a guard posted at his body until the embalming was complete, if it was to be done, because she had once heard that when Napoleon was embalmed, his heart had been tugged by a rat to its rathole.

She demanded that Beatrice remain at her side from morning till night. Beatrice did not object. It was enough that Mama needed her. She cared nothing about the fatigue that flung her exhausted into bed each night, too tired to assist her dresser or Fräulein Bauer in removing her clothing. She no longer had bad dreams; in fact, she had no dreams of any kind that she could remember. She was even too busy to be concerned that it was becoming impossible to play the piano, that the compensatory movements she taught herself no longer worked, since now it was not only her right hand that was affected by rheumatism but her whole arm.

She listened for hours upon end to a threnody of Victoria saying, "He was my dearest and best friend whom I have known for thirty-four years and who for eighteen years never left me for a day." Then she would not speak again for hours, sitting in weepy silence, only to break the quiet with heavy, dull-toned tragedy. "His loss is irreparable." Beatrice was waiting for her mother to stop mentioning him. Then all would be fine. It would not take much longer. Another month or two, perhaps by the time they were in residence at Osborne. The sea air always had a salutary effect on Mama.

Tennyson came to console them. The poet laureate had grown very old and came for his audience on shaky legs, his eyesight dim. He was allowed to sit and gratefully did so, talking of the many friends he had lost and what it would be like if he did not know that there was another world where there would be no partings, and then he spoke with horror of the unbelievers and philosophers who would make one believe that there was no other world, no immortality. Victoria agreed that if such a thing were possible, God, who was love, would be far more cruel than any human being.

Beatrice was thinking of her sister Louise, her brother Affie, his wife, Marie, the Tsar's sister, and Bertie, who were all delighted that Brown was dead and said so. They even made jokes. Affie's was the one that made everyone laugh the most. It had something to do with Dr. Jenner. Victoria was saying what a comfort *In Memoriam* had been and that his words "Tis better to have loved and lost than never to have loved at all" sustained her through her own grievous losses. He replied that he had received shameful letters of abuse about the poem. "Dreadful," said Victoria. He told her she was so alone on that terrible height and quoted Shakespeare's *King Henry V.* "O hard condition! Twin born with greatness, what infinite hearts-ease must kings neglect which private men enjoy." She agreed, adding that few have had more trials and none have been in such a solitary position.

The poet remarked on what a comfort Princess Beatrice must be and said he remembered Princess Alice bringing her in to him at the drawing room in Osborne, a fair-haired child. This caused Victoria to weep afresh. He waited in respectful silence; when she seemed to have sobbed her last, he began to speak the bitterness and black desolation of sorrow being short-lived, that sorrow has a purifying effect, and then he spoke of duty, calling it this world's curse, and said that love could not find fulfillment if duty was not honored.

Beatrice remembered the joke. It was about a Scotsman sick in bed whose doctor prescribed a bottle of pills and a bottle of whiskey. On his next visit the doctor asked the Scotsman if he were taking his medicine regularly. "I may be a wee bit behint wi the peels, Doctor," he replied, "but I'm six week ahead with the whiskey." When Affie told it, the Scotsman sounded just like Brown.

Tennyson had assembled four quotations, from Shakespeare, Pope, Byron, and one that was anonymous, one of which was to be inscribed on Brown's statue. He recited the anonymous one last. "Friend more than servant, loyal, truthful, brave, self less than duty, even to the grave." Then he modestly recommended Pope, as being the best for the purpose, since even though it missed some of the qualities of Her Majesty's exceptional servant, no record could go beyond "the noblest work of God." Victoria guessed that the anonymous one had been his.

"The last," she said, "is best. Yours?"

"Mine, ma'am."

By the time the court went to Osborne, as it did every summer, everyone but Victoria was out of mourning. The gray Solent, the channel between the Isle of Wight and the mainland, was shining like oil, covered with steamers bearing harried ministers and gaily buntinged yachts.

Beatrice, in a seaside costume of cream serge trimmed with rows of green mohair braid, was coiffed in the newest fashion, the influence of Eugénie, her long blonde hair, which took hours to arrange, coiled and twisted, with plaits that wound round and round her head, on top of which was a straw hat covered with wheatears and fir cones.

Riding beside her mother and the exiled Empress of France in a claret landau, the spokes of which were painted in yellow and black, she was forced to listen to Victoria lament, while waving crowds cheered their carriage, that she could not live without Brown's faithful service. By now, Beatrice was convinced that somehow the fault was her own.

She agonized over her deficiency as they continued past tangles of thickets and clumps, masses of ivy, honeysuckle, blackberry, and holly, rolling hay fields, the sea circling everything like a celluloid collar. Eugénie was trying to amuse Victoria with a story of her yellow diamond, a jewel the size of a walnut, which she declared she would never wear again.

"It was during the ransacking of the Tuileries," she began. "This German person, a horrid man, broke into our apartments and found my jewels. Most of them had already been taken, but there were still a few lying about the floor. And my dears, can you imagine, just as he was apprehended, he swallowed it. They took him into custody and waited until nature took its course." Her eyebrows shot up. They both knew what that meant. "It was recovered and washed, but naturally I would never wear it again."

"Naturally," said Victoria, continuing to look despondent.

Eugénie launched into a better tale of the false funeral of Tsar Alexander I, in which she assured them, the corpse in the coffin was of a soldier look-alike, while the real Tsar had became a hermit, who wandered about begging alms because of guilt over his plan to assassinate his own father.

"I do not think," said Victoria, "that there is anyone who looked like Johnnie Brown."

"I was not suggesting," said Eugénie.

Getting down from the swaying carriage took the assistance of a footman in a long scarlet overcoat, equerries of both Victoria and Eugénie, who had been riding alongside, and Brown's successor.

"That man," said Victoria to Eugénie of her new attendant, "cannot lift me out without showing all of my petticoats."

Beatrice walked behind her mother, wondering how Tsar Alexander I got away with his deception. Wasn't he recognized everywhere he went? How does a member of royalty simply fade into anonymity.

"You must entertain your mama," whispered Eugénie as they neared the steps. "She needs to be amused and diverted with stories. Lots of stories. It is not enough to walk behind her as a shadow. You must be a force." Beatrice thought she did not know enough stories to tell, certainly none that her mother did not already know. And as for being a force, perhaps Eugénie was not making the proper translation from French to English. She nodded, anyway. Then Eugénie began to tell her that she must plan a trip to Paris to visit Worth for gowns and Doucet for lingerie.

"Mama and I find the English modistes more than adequate," replied the Princess.

"Pooh," said Eugénie. "That is because neither of you have been gowned by Worth. Your mother is set in her ways. But you are young."

"What are you talking about?" asked Victoria. They each looked to one another.

"I was telling Benjamina," said Eugénie, "that she must visit Worth."

"Nonsense," said Victoria. "English seamstresses are as good as any in the world. Benjamina must set an example, as must I."

When they reached the top of the steps, Victoria began to weep, withdrawing a black-bordered handkerchief from her reticule. "It is too much to bear," she said, sobbing, to Eugénie, leaning upon her arm.

"I know," replied the exiled Empress. "I know."

For a moment, Beatrice stood alone on the terrace. In the distance, fountains sprang from the slender throat of a bronze swan, and from the half-opened buds of pewter, water lilies. Anchored in the Solent beyond was a ship fitted with canvas walls, the royal swimming boat, where once Willy, only two years younger than she and desperately jealous, had called her Aunt Baby and had tried to stuff jellyfish down her bathing costume.

Suddenly, with the memory of the frightful jellyfish, she began to hate Brown, with teeth-clenching relish. The feeling was wrong, immoral, sinful; one did not think or speak ill of the dead, but she could not help it. The thought that she was not in command of such shameful, unacceptable feelings made her sad. That night, with the scent of salt air and the soft splashings of the Solent, she dreamed she was falling through space on her back; then somehow she became the donkey at the bottom of the two-hundred-and-fifty-foot well at Carisbrooke Castle, turning with cracked and plodding hooves, its fifteen-foot wheel to which she was tethered. She woke with a start and a cry and the sheets wrapped tight around her body. She could smell the cloves. How could that be? Her bed was sprinkled nightly with musk and rose.

CHAPTER FIVE

The bedchamber was less royal than homely, furnished with over-stuffed sofas and chairs covered in the same green-and-red patterned chintz, with mahogany wardrobes wedged against the walls. Victoria sat in bed beneath a heavy fringed canopy, facing the open bay windows through which she could smell the fragrant wild thyme and watch ivory gulls fan across the brilliant blue and silver Solent.

Dr. Jenner, who had twenty years before distinguished the germs of typhus and typhoid, stood patiently with Lady Churchill, while Dr. Reid, sitting beside the bed, placed a wooden stethoscope upon Victoria's chest, its India rubber tubing connected to two small ebony cylinders placed against his ears.

Victoria's eye was on a white gannet with black-tipped, widespread wings circling round and round. "I don't know what you learn," she said, "from your tappings and rappings."

"He can't hear you clearly, ma'am," said Dr. Jenner. "But I can tell you that the sound elicited from a healthy chest resembles the stifled sound of a drum covered with a thick woolen cloth."

"What is that thing? I have never seen you use it before."

Dr. Reid took the cylinders from his ears and wound the rubber tubing around the wooden instrument that he had only recently purchased. "It is the new stethoscope, ma'am. With it I can hear your heart sounds with more accuracy than I can by placing my ear against your chest."

Dr. Jenner moved forward, averting his eyes from the framed photograph of the deceased Prince Consort attached to the headboard and the memorial wreath that hung above it. His expression was serious. "Your Majesty, Dr. Reid and I are concerned with the health of Princess Beatrice. Over the past few years the condition of Her Royal Highness has worsened. At first, the bouts of pain in her hands seemed a form of neuritis, flaring up in the colder months, improving in the warmer months. But now she is quite disabled, and it is summer. What concerns us most is that while there is moderate inflammation and reddening, the nodule which is characteristic in these disorders is absent. So is certain thickening of the connective tissue that we normally see. Her reflexes are normal, yet we observe flexion contractures."

Dr. Jenner was forecasting doom again. It was an irritating trait. He had been predicting her own nervous breakdown for years. Victoria pursed her lips and turned her head toward the window. The gannet suddenly folded its wings like a parasol and dove headfirst into the water, sending up a frothy jet to mark its entry. "Spare me these disgusting details. What you tell me sounds positive, Dr. Jenner, not negative."

"Yes and no, ma'am. What causes us confusion is that we find nothing to support the severity of Her Royal Highness's disability."

Lady Churchill helped to fasten Victoria's tucked and pleated white lawn nightdress, while Dr. Reid reached for her wrist to take her pulse.

"What do you suggest?" asked Victoria. "Surely you have a suggestion."

"I have read of a new course of treatment in the *Lancet*, using salicin," replied Dr. Reid.

"What is that?"

"An active principle of the willow bark, ma'am. Some practitioners are using it with success, fifty-grain doses every two hours, with a quarter grain of morphine hypodermically."

The dark-moustachioed Dr. Jenner sought to reaffirm his seniority. "It is here, Your Majesty," he said, "that my young colleague and I are in disagreement. I must warn you that this is a new treatment, ma'am, and not without unpleasant side effects—headache, giddiness, ringing in the ears, loss of appetite, excessive perspiration, and melancholy. There may even be deaths attributed to its use, although no one is certain. Without further trials of the drug, I am reluctant to submit the Princess to its effects."

"Well, then, Dr. Jenner, we shall not consider it. Why can't you increase the dose of what you were giving her before?"

Dr. Jenner stroked the cameo on the knot of his tie. "Iodide of potassium and opium are certainly tried and true, a respected and effective treatment for neuritis. There is no question that opium subdues the inflammation. However, the effect on the Princess is soporific. If we were to increase the dosage, it would produce a lethargic state, which would be unacceptable. In addition, there is increasing evidence that quinine might have a deleterious effect on the heart."

"We are somewhat at a loss," said Dr. Reid. "We cannot simply take Her Royal Highness off sugar the way we would a diabetic; that is why we grasp at straws. There are two remaining possibilities." He looked to Dr. Jenner, who almost imperceptibly shook his head as if to say, You're on your own. "There is a physician in Nancy, a Dr. Bernheim, who has reported some success with young women such as the Princess without the use of drugs."

Victoria sniffed. "What kind of a doctor is he?"

"Dr. Bernheim is a neurologist," replied Dr. Reid.

"Why have you not suggested him to me before?"

"I was reluctant, ma'am, because of his mode of treatment."

"And what is that?" Lady Churchill helped Victoria swing her legs over the side of the bed, then signaled to a dresser, who had been standing at the door with a pair of black kid slippers.

"Dr. Bernheim explores the mind in the way Darwin has the flora and fauna of the earth."

"In what way is this done?"

"He hypnotizes his patients."

"You mean like Mesmer?"

"The technique, I believe, is similar."

"Have you, Doctor Reid, taken leave of your senses? Mesmer was a fraud, the joke of the continent. He and his barbaric hokus-pokus were completely discredited. You would throw us back into the Dark Ages."

Lady Churchill enveloped the Queen in a combing sacque and fastened its multitude of lacy closings while Victoria eased herself down, leaning on Dr. Jenner. One of the dressers removed her night-cap, while the other began to brush her graying hair.

"Believe me, ma'am." Dr. Reid was perspiring, thinking, as he often did, that he would forego the honor of being resident royal physician in exchange for a modest practice where patients paid one in potatoes and on rare occasion gratefully kissed one's hands. "I have considered very seriously what I just advised. I took the liberty of writing to Dr. Bernheim, who assures me that the visit would be handled with the greatest discretion. Bernheim is no Mesmer. He has studied under Charcot, who, you may recall, is the chief of medical services at Salpêtrière and was one of his most promising students. Dr. Bernheim has treated thousands of patients."

"And how many princesses of royal blood?"

"That I cannot answer. I believe that if Dr. Charcot and Dr. Bernheim are correct in their theory, it is possible that the rheumatism Her Royal Highness suffers is a form of hysteria, the result of some early trauma."

Victoria's eyebrows drew together like signal flags. "I don't like the way that sounds."

"The word hysteria," interrupted Dr. Jenner, "derives from the Latin *hysterus*, or womb. That is because the disease is seen primarily in women. Dr. Reid is suggesting that the key to the illness of Her Royal Highness may be in her mind."

The suggestion was onerous, reminiscent of whispered stories of her grandfather, George III, who raged into lunacy, then fizzled like a Chinese cracker into the phantom existence of the utterly insane. "Then," she said, her voice like ice, "you must believe her to be either mad or a fraud."

Dr. Reid mopped his forehead with his handkerchief, while Dr. Jenner, who had, through his years with the Queen, achieved a certain diplomacy, stepped in. "Your Majesty, I assure you that Dr. Reid had no such thought. We are both certain that she feels pain in her hands, and severely enough so that she experiences limitations."

Victoria was not mollified and sniffed her disapproval. "You are mad to suppose that I would consent to send the Princess to some humbug hypnotist. And you dare not say that I am not for progress. Without my example, there would be no chloroform in childbirth."

The dresser retrieved the hairbrush and smoothed Victoria's hair behind her ears, pinning it in place with large black hairpins that she held between her lips.

"Dr. Reid would be remiss, ma'am," said Dr. Jenner, "if he did not inform Your Majesty of all the options, even if I did not agree. Under the circumstances of your very strong feelings, which I assure you I understand, and until we learn more about the properties of salicin, there is just one course open to us. We recommend taking the waters. Perhaps Aix-les-Bains, which has certain mineral springs containing sulphur and alkalies. This may help alleviate her pain and hopefully improve her disability. The principle is a sound one. Alkaline waters promote oxidation."

Victoria smiled. "I thought you didn't believe that Her Highness's disease was subject to whatever it was you said those waters did."

"We cannot discount the possibility, ma'am," said Dr. Jenner, "that the disease is organic."

"When do you suggest she go?" The dresser rubbed pomade between her palms. It smelled of rose geranium, and she wiped it on Victoria's hair, slicking it into place until it shone.

"Immediately."

"And for how long?"

"Three weeks, ma'am," replied Dr. Jenner.

"The Princess has never been abroad without me before. Now you suggest a separation of three weeks. That would be very hard on her, indeed."

"At the present," said Dr. Reid, "it is the only remedy we can offer Her Royal Highness."

"We will think on the matter," replied Victoria.

The decision to send Beatrice to France was both benevolent and prudent, settled a few days later on the contents of a courier pack that contained a letter from her granddaughter, Victoria of Hesse, who wrote that she would like to come to England to discuss her engagement. Also to visit, with her grandmother's permission, was her fiancé, Louis of Battenberg, a naturalized Englishman with a commission in the Royal Navy, and her father, the widowed Grand Duke of Hesse. To complicate matters further, Victoria received word from Bertie, a good friend of both men, who said he was planning to sail across the Solent in his yacht in order to spend some time at Osborne with them.

Victoria directed the packing in Beatrice's sitting room before a skirted table on which was piled medicines, remedies, ointments, pomades, syrups, headache powders, soaps, papillotes, brushes, combs, hairpins, camphor cakes to prevent chapping and chilblains of the hands, a bottle of jasmine and orange hair oil, and tooth powder compounded of pumice stone and cinnamon. Fräulein Bauer and a maid were gathering armloads of garments, which they carried from the wardrobes, while Lady Churchill bustled about ticking off items on her fingers and saying, "I want oil of lavender to drive away the fleas. Her Royal Highness will require her own sheets, pillows, blankets, and a small flask of brandy in case of faintness."

Beatrice stood beside her mother, rubbing her right hand with her left. "But why, Mama," she asked. "Why must I go to Aix-les-Bains? I don't want to go. I want to stay here at Osborne with you."

"Dr. Jenner recommends taking the baths," said Victoria. "So does Dr. Reid. They point out that you are becoming more disabled despite the course of treatment which they have prescribed. Apparently it is no longer adequate."

Beatrice extended her fingers, curled them, and winced. "Look, Mama. See, I can move my fingers much better than I could last week. They are improving every day. Isn't that so, Lady Jane? I have been neglectful. I should have been in the sea more often. I will correct that."

"The matter is settled," said Victoria. Fräulein Bauer carried past an armload of summery frocks of sprigged lawn and gauzy grenadine to the trunk, which stood open on the oriental carpet. Victoria waved her tiny dimpled hand. "Those will not do, Fräulein. The princess is not on holiday. She goes to Aix for her health. Serviceable clothing. Comfortable clothing. That is your keynote."

"Mama"—Beatrice's voice was tear edged—"you know what a disaster it is when I am about by myself. I don't know what to say. My tongue ties; I suffer so."

"You speak to me of suffering? I find that a frivolous complaint. You forget I still mourn the loss of Johnnie Brown."

"I'm sorry, Mama. I had forgotten."

"Dear ones have fallen on all sides, one by one, and now I have lost one, who, humble though he was, was the truest, most devoted of all, who had no thought but for me, courageous, unselfish man. Without him I am desolate. The comfort of my life is gone. That is suffering."

"Am I not your comfort, Mama?" Beatrice knelt on the carpet to lay her head on her mother's lap.

"When you do not oppose me. When you are sweet tempered, good, and obedient. Then you are a comfort."

"I don't know what to say to people. I stand about like some awkward lump, and everyone else becomes uncomfortable. I can feel it; I can see them blinking me away as if their eyelids were blotters."

"Nonsense. You have made the matter entirely too fanciful. You are not going for conversation. You will be there for the cure. See to the packing, Lady Jane. I am very tired."

Leaning on two canes, Victoria stood and hobbled to the door. Beatrice called after her. "I will bathe here, at Osborne. Every day. I will not miss a morning. You always said the salt was beneficial. It hardens one. Your very words."

"The seawater at Osborne will not do. It is far too cold, and it lacks the minerals. Everything is arranged; I wish to speak of it no more. I have more serious matters on my mind. The Sudanese are about to revolt. Men of a totally different stamp. They could not stand against regular troops at all."

When the doors had closed behind her, Lady Churchill came to put a hand on Beatrice's arm. "On the road from Dieppe to Rouen, Your Royal Highness, the resemblance to our countryside is remarkable. You might suppose one side of the Channel had been transported to the other." She signaled to Fräulein Bauer, who returned with the summer frocks and carried them to the maid, who folded them in tissue paper and tucked them out of sight between sprinklings of lavender and rosemary.

Beatrice was detached, uninterested in which slippers were being packed or whether or not the brown linen petticoats one wore in the baths should be made up quickly by one of the seamstresses at Osborne or purchased at the spa. The thought of traveling abroad without her mother made her heart beat faster and her breath come in sharp, painful gasps, as though a steel stay had come loose from her corset. She sat down, feeling faint, and was startled to feel a hand on her shoulder. She turned to see her brother leaning on a cane.

"What's this I hear?"

"I am to go to France," she said. "For the cure. For my hands."

"Is Mama going with you?"

"No, that is why I am so desolate."

"Sly puss. You didn't tell me you had good news. Perhaps you will meet someone exciting in Aix-les-Bains."

Beatrice dropped her head. "I don't want to meet anyone exciting. I want to stay home."

Leopold looked at her. "Such a strange little bird, that never wants to leave the nest. While her wicked brother fluttered out at every turn. How can you stand it?"

"I don't know what you mean."

Leopold limped to the lace-draped mantel where he rested his arm upon the fringe. "Aix-les-Bains is more than a spa where people steam open their pores in stinking sulphur. It is nightly illuminations at the Grand Cercle, some of them fairylike, it is balls and regattas and concerts and theater, and in the evenings, after the baths, one who is so disposed may stroll, tilt one's head so, and have a flirtation."

"You know I am not like that. We have gone through this over and over again, and it is no use. Why don't you accept the fact?"

"I accept nothing. You should know that."

"It is so easy for you, Leo. You know exactly what to say, all the time."

Leopold pulled her toward him and whispered, "Listen to me; I have suffered most of my life from not being able to enjoy what others took for granted. I watched all of you, even my baby sister, who came after me, tumbling, falling down, crying, and getting up to laugh and fall again. For me, jubilance, enthusiasm, always ended in disaster, with the doctors and Mama and Papa watching over me to see if I had bled my last. I have decided that while my time may be short, I am determined to enjoy it to the hilt."

"Don't speak that way, dearest Leo."

Leopold turned toward the mirror. "One faces only oneself and the truth. Do you remember what you called mother's white cap when you were very small?"

"I called it her sad cap."

"Her sad cap, yes. It was what she wore immediately after Father died. It was her mourning cap. She has placed a sad cap on you. It is an invisible one, but when I put my hands thus, I can feel it. You cannot get freedom by asking for it. You have to take it."

"Why can't you see that I am perfectly content with things as they are."

Leopold took her chin in his hand. "You have to fight to live life. There is no footman to offer it to you on a platter. Listen to me. You see this knee? No, look at it. That's the point. I regard all this lumpy swelling as a minor inconvenience, as payment for a wonderful game of golf. It pains me, yes, but I have learned to live with it as Vicky lives with the existence of Bismarck. More importantly, I have learned to live, Benjamina, as you must. Browning says the denial of passion is a cardinal sin."

"I told you before I do not like Browning. He is licentious."

"Those are Mama's words, not yours. You even purse your lips like hers when you say them. Take her cap off, Benjamina. Take it off and feel the breeze through your hair."

Wearing a frock coat, stiff wing collar, striped gray cashmere trousers, and watch fob over his waistcoat, Dr. Bertier observed the somber young woman who sat before him. She looked like any young lady of discrimination, demure, fastidious, carrying a closed lace and satin parasol, her long chamois gloves, which she had just removed, folded across her lap.

She was traveling under the name of the Countess of Kent, but he knew, as did most people in the village of Aix-les-Bains, that she was the youngest daughter of the Queen of England. If he was successful in her treatment, his practice was assured.

Dr. Bertier was prescribing baths and massage. He was comparing the various movements of the body of a person of health to the wheels of a watch, which resolved themselves into a harmony of periodic action. Each organ of a living body in perfect health, he said, did the same. To cure sickness, he said, one must make the body keep perfect time, in the pulse, in the breathing, in the functions of the various organs, eating, sleeping, waking, through the mainspring of the movements, the brain.

He searched her face for understanding, for the nod of the patient who is in accord with what is being said. She appeared to be comfortable, placid, even calm, and it was this that was disturbing him. At first, he could not think why. He judged her manner to be the natural restraint of royalty and breeding. Then he noticed, as he examined her ungloved hand, that she did not seem to mind the pain or the disability. She was casual, indifferent. He recalled something Charcot, whose crowded lectures he had attended as a medical student in the gallery, had said as his assistants carried out a tranquil young woman on a cot, supposedly paralyzed from the head down, yet able to breathe. La Belle Indifference, a classic symptom of hysteria. That was it. The indifference to the malady, in contrast to the scores of other invalids and chronically ill, in his experience, who did nothing but complain.

Dr. Bertier wished he could recall more of Charcot's lecture. He asked her if she had any anxieties. She said no. He remembered that in such cases it was found that the patient's mothers clung unnaturally to their children, but how does one ask that of the Queen of England, and truly, do not all mothers cling to their children? He would have to read the literature. There had been a few articles published, a few addresses made. He would have to familiarize himself with what was being said.

He moved to ordinary questioning. Yes, she experienced early afternoon fatigue, a sign of rheumatism. No, she did not experience melancholy. Well, not all did. Yes, she had morning stiffness; perhaps he had been hasty, as one must not be in medicine. He felt her hands, with the practiced feel of the experienced clinician, comparing one to the other. The affected hand had red swollen joints; he could feel the heat, yet no synovial thickening, but then again, that was not always seen. Perhaps he was wrong. He would have to find out. He resorted to what he did know.

She must take the baths, and massage. That would help to neutralize and eliminate the rheumatic poison. She must at the same time warm her blood—sherry wine, carriage rides, if she could manage it, horseback riding. If she were a man, he would recommend pursuits of a carnal nature, but in this case it was unthinkable. If these remedies were not successful, he would try blistering the inflammation, and if that did not provide relief, he would prescribe coca, which gave energy and exhilaration and no harmful effects. Many doctors were prescribing it with success. In addition, Peruvian Indians had been using it all their lives.

The whitewashed village of fountains and clock towers was the site of the ancient Roman baths of Sextius, built over hot bubbling springs that surged through the faults and fissures of the entrapping shale beneath. Aix-les-Bains thronged with the sickly and the fashionable, those with bandaged gouty feet wheeled in wooden bath chairs, the more desperately ill carried on litters and draped with blankets despite the heat. Others, on their way to the casinos or to the Savoy to sample the reblochon cheese, were dressed in holiday clothes with lace and silk parasols, top hats, and gloves, some of the younger modish men wearing bowler hats and open morning coats over tattersall jockey vests.

Beatrice saw little association between herself and the ailing rabble and had refused to ride in the sedan chair. She chose instead to walk to the baths, wearing a hat with a veil, decorated in the current mode with dried insects, in this case, beetles. Lady Churchill was at her side, commenting on the offices of quacks that lined the way, in whose windows were neatly printed signs peddling earthworms, elf's hoof, and sun-dried goose dung mixed with saffron and sugar candy.

Inside the dank and foul-smelling stone-and-brick bath building they were led by a bowing administrator and his scraping assistants past a central loggia where a dozen people, their skin covered with an oily film, sat drinking or bathing various body parts in hot water from brass cock spigots, some of them, they were told, swallowing fourteen half-pint glasses in a morning. The adjoining chamber was a great smoking kettle where patients bathed together, standing up to their necks in steaming water, the brown linen petticoats of the women floating like water lilies. A man was being hoisted in a sling attached to a pulley, his atrophied legs flopping like sticks. The administrator also informed them that the waters contained sulphur, lime, and carbonic acid, that there were rooms for inhaling sulphurous vapors for those with chronic catarrh, there was a special spray for rheumatism and gout, and luncheon or tea could be brought in from any of the nearby inns.

Beatrice was led to a marble bath with an adjoining bedchamber. With the help of Lady Churchill, who soon left to supervise unpacking, and two attendants in white caps and long white aprons, she was undressed, stripped of everything but a chemise. The attendants were oblivious to her, speaking above her head as if she could not hear, guiding her, as if they were leading a horse, into the shallow square pool while they turned jets of sulphurous water against her body, plastering her chemise to her skin. The odor was terrible, the water strong, and the wall against which she leaned to keep herself from falling was cold, eternally sweating. She was led back into the bedchamber, where she was massaged and dried, then led back to the pool where a shouting attendant with a hose told her that later, when she was better, she could remain dressed and merely extend her unclothed arm into a sleeve attached to one of the pumps.

For the third time, Beatrice was brought back into the bedchamber and again pushed and pummeled, kneaded and draped with wet packs. She began to tremble. It certainly was not for lack of warmth, for the room was steaming. She hoped they would not notice. They were talking between themselves of a delicate fish that came from the nearby Lac du Bourget, which could only be fished at dawn in very cold water. One with chestnut brown hair plaited over her shiny scalp stopped her kneading. "You are chilled?" she asked.

They both dropped perfunctory curtsies at Lady Churchill's reappearance and resumed their massage as she fluttered a perfumed handkerchief in the air. "The odor of the sulphur is unbearable," she said. "And I have complained about our rooms again. They are totally unsuitable. We're going to be moved this afternoon, or I shall know the reason why."

Beatrice picked her head up. "Was there a letter from my mother?"

"No, my lady. I looked only an hour ago."

"Will you look again? Please."

The attendants wrapped wet packs upon the hands of the Princess, bobbed curtsies, and said they would return.

"Very well, but as I have told you before"—she lowered her voice, resorting additionally to English—"the Queen is preoccupied with the terrible situation in Sudan." Beatrice lay her head down again on the massage table. "It is difficult to be a sovereign and a mother, Your Highness. One cannot always do what is most natural." Beatrice closed her eyes. Lady Churchill could not tell if she was sleeping.

Dr. Bertier had located a few published articles, which he found somewhat confusing, although enlightening. Theoretically, of course, they were beyond the pale of accepted medical practice. A Viennese doctor who had authored one of them had suggested that hysteria was the failure to achieve full adult sexuality. The Princess was unmarried. Even if she had been, it was well known that females did not share the same drives as the male. The same author suggested that what was key to hysteria was the suitability of the organ to express symbolism. The patient, he wrote, having felt anger, an unacceptable unconscious thought, turns the guilty feelings toward the parent into the development of similar symptoms. Symptoms result when the conscious mind can no longer repress material from the unconscious. Dr. Bertier frowned on such nebulous concepts, and yet they deserved a test. If hysteria was the result of a conflict expressed in symbolic form, he would ask about her mother.

Beatrice spent the next afternoon in Dr. Bertier's office, being asked strange questions about her feelings toward her mother. He seemed apologetic to be asking them. Her responses were global, general, like the verses on a paper valentine. She was devoted to her mother. Her mother was a paragon of maternal virtue. She was wonderful. She was good. He asked about her mother's rheumatism. She described it, wondering what difference it made and when he was going to talk about her pains. She wanted to be able to tell him that she was better.

Dr. Bertier was at a loss. This was ridiculous. The whole theory was unproven. He distrusted the Austrians in any case, considering them to be the most arrogant of any in the profession. He would go back to what was solid and sound in medicine. He knew that alkaline waters promoted oxidation and protected the tissues from rheumatic poisons by eliminating them; therefore, she must drink as much as she could. And he knew that sulphur, when applied to affected joints and muscles, had long been known to be palliative. He would double his efforts in that direction.

Victoria sat on a sloping terrace, listening to the shrill of crickets and the drone of bees, posed motionless with her favorite granddaughter, pretty blonde Victoria of Hesse, and Victoria's father, Louis, the Grand Duke of Hesse. Arranged in a tableau of domesticity, they faced the gardens and a china palm with a black hairy trunk while a photographer, shrouded under a tent that covered his shoulders, was fixing the picture.

The Queen hissed out of the corner of her mouth as the photographer bobbed up and down beneath his tent. "Nine years your senior is as it should be. A young bride needs to be able to learn from her husband, and I think you have done well to choose a husband who is quite to your way of thinking, in many respects, as English as you are."

"Your Majesty," came the muffled voice from under the tent. "If you please. The picture will blur."

They sat for another minute. Then the photographer withdrew his head, holding a piece of glass covered with a white scum. His assistant poured a liquid over it, and the cloudiness cleared.

"There is only one drawback," continued Victoria, "and that is the fortune, or lack of it. I understand your Louis has a modest allowance from his father. His wages as a lieutenant can only be adequate. Not that I think riches make happiness, but I do think a certain amount is a necessity if only to be independent. That is where you come in," she said to her portly, bearded son-in-law.

"I will do what I can, Mama."

The photographer held the glass plate against his black coat sleeve; his assistant inspected the image and nodded, then dried the glass and coated it with black. The photographer mopped his brow, replaced his hat, and bowed.

"The main thing, dear," continued the Queen as the photographer and his assistant packed up the tripod and glass plates, "is to be a good, steady wife and not run after amusements but find your happiness chiefly in your own home."

"I know that's how it will be, Grandmama."

"Good, very good." She turned to the Grand Duke Louis of Hesse. "I am sorry to hear that Ella's marriage is to be. Ella herself says there is no hurry, that she doesn't want to go to Russia, that, if possible, arrangements should be made for her and Serge to live out of Russia. I think you should make this an absolute condition and not hurry it. Ella ought to be twenty before she marries, like Victoria."

"I am looking into it, Mama." The Grand Duke, who had come to Osborne to spend time with the Prince of Wales, always such a jolly good companion, dreaded these visits with the Queen. They were suffered while his wife was alive, but without Alice as a buffer, he was finding his mother-in-law's interference intolerable.

"You will see; you will look into it. For heaven's sake, man, where is your spunk? You are her father, and a Grand Duke to boot. You can't be wishy-washy. Like Gladstone. March into the Sudan, I say, now. Put down the revolt of the Mahdi, and they will soon see what kind of a holy man he is. He also replies, 'We will see.' People say, 'We will see,' when they don't see at all. Vicky says that there is some feeling, which of course she does not share, against the marriage."

"The principal drawback from the Prussian court, Mama," said the Grand Duke, "is their objection to the fact that Louis of Battenberg's mother was a commoner."

"Nevertheless, she was a countess, and lady-in-waiting to the Tsarina. Not an unimportant position by any standard. Further, there are few royal houses that do not have something a little out of the ordinary. For example, Milan of Serbia was an Obrenovitch; his grandfather was a swineherd. Worse than that, he makes a great noise when he eats." She turned to young Victoria. "The primary advantage is that your Louis is dark and handsome. And you are fair. I like the infusion of the dark. It strengthens the blood. All that blue eyes and blonde hair makes the blood lymphatic."

A tall naval officer in summer whites strode up the path from the Solent, accompanied by a heavier bearded figure that could only be that of the Prince of Wales. Victoria of Hesse gave a little cry, blushed, picked up her ruffled skirts, and ran to meet them, her bustle jouncing behind her like some fallen carapace, despite her grandmother's admonition that such spontaneity did not do.

"I don't know why Bertie has to muck things up," said Victoria. "The entire purpose of this visit was for me to advise them on their marriage plans. Now there will be so much noise no one will hear anything." She turned to the Grand Duke and dropped her voice. "You will be interested to learn that the bill permitting marriage between a man and his deceased wife's sister has been approved by the House of Lords. The way is entirely clear."

The Grand Duke appeared distressed, as if his collar were too tight. Since he could not, with good manners, slip a finger into his stiffened shirt, he craned his neck, easing it from the starched, confining linen. "I am surprised, Mama. I did not expect that it would."

Soon he would be able to discuss with Bertie the German Army maneuvers that were being planned for the Rossbach battlefield, where Frederick the Great defeated the French. There, dressed in regimental uniform, all of them would participate in military exercises —thirteen regiments of infantry, six of cavalry, and three of field artillery, he, the King of Spain, the Grand Duke of Saxe-Weimar, Milan of Serbia, Bertie, Affie, Arthur, Fritz, Willy, Louis of Battenberg's father, Alexander, and brother Henry, the Crown Prince of Portugal, the Grand Duke of Saxony, Prince Waldeck, the father of Leo's wife, even Vicky, dressed in the uniform of the Hussars regiment. He would bring his darling, of course, and she would watch from the sidelines as he led a frontal cavalry charge. Women always thrilled to men in uniform, especially astride a horse. It made the man deucedly attractive, it enflamed their passions, which they were not supposed to have, and stirred them out of the coma that they affected in the bedroom.

The tall, handsome naval officer who had arrived with Bertie held his head high. His face seemed molded, his mouth firm; even his dark moustache was elegantly shaped. "I hope, sir," he said, "that Her Majesty is not going to be difficult."

The corpulent Prince of Wales puffed beside him, wearing a belted Norfolk jacket, knickerbockers, and a yachting cap. "Asking Mama not to be difficult is like asking Ruskin not to rail. Be satisfied that she is content to let you out of exile. Now that you are marrying, she has probably concluded that it is safe to have you returned. It's not everyone for whom Mama makes a special request of the First Lord of the Admiralty to keep them in foreign ports. You should be complimented."

"The amusing part, sir, is that I was never interested in your sister. Beg pardon, but Her Royal Highness is, she is, well—"

"Dull," said Bertie. "You can say it, man. Dull and mousy. It's not news to any of us. Just look at that delightful creature running to meet you. You are lucky, Louis, just plain lucky. Who else picks red, to have it come up nine times running, scoops up his pile of gold just before the black comes up? And you do have an enviable way with the ladies. I for one am grateful for your castoffs."

"All that is behind me now."

"What has one thing got to do with another?"

The visit went well. Victoria sent the Grand Duke and Bertie to represent her at the regatta so that she could have luncheon alone with the engaged couple. This gave the Prince of Wales an opportunity to present his brother-in-law, who had complained that such things were difficult to obtain in Darmstadt, with two volumes of the newest pornography, one with colored plates, the other's illustrations artfully contrived with strings behind the page to animate the figures.

Victoria and Louis of Battenberg talked of the Royal Navy. Louis, who had joined the Navy as a midshipman when he was fourteen, said that steam was more than auxiliary power, that polo playing ashore and showing the flag in leisurely cruises around the world would not long substitute for competent seamanship. Victoria arched her eyebrows and challenged him for improvement. He replied that if the Royal Navy wished to continue to rule the sea, as it had done since Trafalgar almost one hundred years before, it must learn to handle ships under steam.

He would be difficult, thought Victoria. No matter, she would manage him through her granddaughter. More important than what he thought of the Navy was how he regarded young Victoria. She watched them carefully. That the girl was in love became obvious; she could see it in the way her eyes sought him out, in the way her fingertips brushed and connected with his.

Victoria asked Louis about his family. He replied that his younger brother, Henry, was a cavalry officer of the Hussars at Bonne and that his father, Alexander, and his brother, Sandro, had just returned from Moscow and the Tsar's coronation. Louis said that it was clear that Tsar Alexander III had no love for his brother and was making things more difficult for him.

Victoria asked if he knew that Moretta, Vicky and Fritz's daughter, was in love with Sandro. Louis replied that he had heard something about it. "But Bismarck," he added, "says the marriage is out of the question. He thinks it will give offense to Russia."

"All the more reason to go through with it," said Victoria. "I for one would like to see this match brought about, not only for the sake of Moretta and Sandro but to show up the Tsar and that meddlesome Bismarck. Vicky writes that Moretta has vowed she will never marry anyone else; she has refused to even look at other princes. It is difficult for Moretta to write. Her letters, Vicky is almost certain, are intercepted by Bismarck. It is up to you, Louis, to see that Sandro knows of Moretta's feelings."

"I believe my brother already does, ma'am," replied Louis.

"Then tell him, impress upon him that for the moment he must not come forward. Not yet. He is to wait. What is needed is time."

"I'll do my best, ma'am."

"This must be done confidentially and secretly," she said. "There can be no mention that you have heard this from me. Now I want to hear where you plan to settle. Close by, I hope. And is it true you have an enormous blue-and-red dragon tattooed on your arm?"

Young Victoria was surprised that her grandmama would ask such an intimate question that even she would not dare ask, and yet to criticize her or express disapproval in any way was just as unthinkable. Instead, she linked her arm through that of her handsome fiancé. "How is Auntie?" she asked. "Poor dear sweet Auntie, such a duck. Do you think, Grandmama, that the waters will help?"

CHAPTER SIX

While evenings were spent attending concerts and an occasional fete, which Lady Jane said would take Beatrice's mind off the daily routine of doctor and bath, nothing Beatrice did, no powder, perfume, pumice, soap, no long soaks in glycerine and orange water, dispelled the odor of sulphur that clung to her nostrils or completely removed the oily residue on her skin.

It was the night when they were to attend a gala at the villa of Count Waldersee that Beatrice received a black-bordered letter from her mother scored with bold underlinings. The Queen expressed the hope that the baths were beneficial, told her how much she was missed, and added, almost as a postscript, that Victoria of Hesse had come to visit with her father, the Grand Duke Louis, who sent his very best regards (very best was underlined), and their cousin, Prince Louis of Battenberg, who was now, did she mention, Victoria's fiancé?

The memory flared and fizzled, like the illuminations in the sky, set off the night before at the Grand Cercle. It had been a long time, almost ten years ago at Osborne, when Beatrice was seventeen. She remembered that she had thought him attractive. The thought had been secret. She had told no one; not Bertie, who had been telling stories in his loud, expansive, irritating manner, or Alexandra, who was hard of hearing and not one to whisper a confidence to, and certainly not Mama. Somehow Mama found out and had forbidden her to speak to him or to have anything to do with him. Beatrice remembered feeling his eyes on her face at dinner and once glancing covertly at him when Bertie made everyone laugh with a story of how Willy pushed everyone out of the way when he danced, which was really a joke on Bertie, since that was the way he danced. She would obey her mother, of course, but she had kept the memory of the young ensign fresh, the way one polishes an apple, even when she could scarcely recall what he looked like. It was different with the Prince Imperial, whom she had known since they were children. The thin, sad-faced youth, who was passionately dedicated to retrieving his father's lost throne, was her dearest friend, but he did not make her tremble.

The implications in her mother's letter were suffocating. She did not disclose her mounting anger to Lady Jane, who kept asking what was wrong, but said nothing. Louis and Victoria, her niece. Happy. Not telling her. Secret. Sent away to be smothered by the stifling miasma with horrid cripples. The rage was unfocused, as steaming as the baths. Beatrice brought it down, into herself, deep into the secret place, before it could form acid droplets to eat away at her soul, and the pains began, the stiffening, the aching. Lady Jane, who noticed her rubbing her fingers, said they would go to the baths first thing the next morning, immediately after breakfast.

Beatrice stood still as the maid fastened red satin roses in her up-swept hair, the same satin roses that lay in scattered clusters over her ruched and furbelowed gown of tulle and satin, and declared that she would not dance, that no one was to be presented to her for that purpose, that she wished to leave before supper, and that her maid was not to accompany them and wait with other ladies' maids in the dressing room, but instead to have tea ready upon their return.

By the time they entered the villa at half past eleven, a fashionable time to arrive at a ball that began at eleven, she was tranquil. They stood beneath a high, frescoed, intricately molded ceiling while their wraps were removed by liveried servants. Beatrice noticed that the chandeliers in the entrance hall, the prisms of which sparkled like diamonds, had been electrified. The new incandescent light made her feel naked, exposed. She hoped the ballroom had not been fitted with electricity. Then there would be no secluded shadows in which to hide, no dusky sanctum where one could sit unnoticed and sip a claret cup.

Followed by their equerry, a uniformed officer of the Queen's guards, they made their way slowly up the wooden staircase, each step flanked by velvet-tunicked footmen standing like statues. The ballroom was blazing with light and furnished in sky blue silk with banks of potted hyacinths and tulips. They stopped at the entrance while the equerry spoke briefly to the majordomo, who interrupted his droning proclamations to announce Beatrice and Lady Jane to the assembled guests. The two women glided over the parquet floor, Lady Jane a discreet few steps behind, with the equerry at her side, Beatrice, as she was taught, catching the eye of no one until she had been greeted by her host.

Many of the men were in brilliant uniforms of red and blue, some all white, embellished with stiff gold embroidery and splashed with medals and ribbons. The women wore clouds of tulle over their shoulders, stars and coronets in their hair, and carried fans of ostrich or spangled gauze, behind which they could whisper, as they now did at Beatrice's entry. As she neared, the fans were folded shut with a practiced snap, and everyone bowed before her, most of the women, even some of the dowagers, well advanced in age, sweeping elegantly to the floor, their dresses rustling like leaves on a poplar tree. The men bowed stiffly, some from the waist, some only with a drop of the head to the chest; most considering with experienced discretion her bosom, neck, and shoulders, the only features a man could judge of the figure of a woman. Such things as hips, thighs, belly, buttocks, and legs were hidden beneath tea gowns and bedclothes, subject to speculation and touch and only seen with ladies of the night, or if a man were lucky, lasciviously displayed by his mistress.

Count Waldersee kissed Beatrice's hand, like other farsighted noblemen, with his nose. His American wife, whom Vicky disliked—she had said once to Beatrice that she was parvenu, an adventuress—rose from her seat and quickly advanced, dressed in a white velvet gown with bands of blue fox fur and three buds of yellow roses at her throat. How ethereal and pure she looked in blue and white, thought Beatrice. An ice maiden. Vicky said she had killed her first husband, elderly Prince Frederick of Schleswig-Holstein, through excesses on her honeymoon. That horrid act, thought Beatrice, that women endured. Why in the world, how in the world, could such a lovely woman bring herself to do that more than was her duty, and with enough excess as to kill a man.

Beatrice was provided with a gilt chair near a bench of bony dowagers dressed in black, one with a goiter girthed in jewels. They were members of the family of Liechtenstein, and having already risen in creaking curtsies, now lifted their aristocratic noses in the air.

The dancers before them, tutored by dancing masters with inexhaustible patience, were performing the courtly figures of a quadrille. While the women on the bench criticized the dancers, searching for flaws and reporting them to one another, the equerry, who had been well instructed by Victoria on the protection of the Princess, returned with a list of suitable dancing partners, all older men with fluffy white side whiskers—rheumy-eyed ambassadors or heated and breathless elderly dukes, hopelessly out of practice, whom one had to prompt and push through the figures.

Lady Jane motioned to the equerry with a gloved hand to put the list away. The Princess had no wish to dance, and even if she had, the Queen's lady of the bedchamber would not encourage such a doddering assembly. It was a pity, she thought. The girl was lovely and should be like the other young ladies, who gave away their dances weeks before and flirted behind the safety of a potted fern. Even princesses were allowed a harmless dalliance.

Beatrice accepted a claret cup while she watched the dancers break into a rattling galop, noting the shocking bad style of an officer in the yellow-collared blue tunic of a Prussian dragoon, his gloved hand spread out over his partner's back. Her fingers tapped her cup to the music of an orchestra suspended on a jutting balcony above. The movement was imperceptible, a prosodic tremor that beat the orderly, rippling, vigorous tempo of the pianoforte. She followed the couple. The woman made no move to shrug away the offending hand, as other women would have done. Instead, she was smiling, just barely, the corners of her lips turned up, her mouth parted, her eyes downcast.

The next hour passed uneventfully. Small groups, moving as if they were skewered on ramrods, approached, bowed, and were presented, most presuming to do so because they were already acquainted with the Princess or had some connection to the royal family or to the English court. Laughter was smothered behind fans, and conversation, for the most part, was forced, exploring into tedium the weather,

the effect on a lazy liver of Enos Fruit Salts, or the cholera that raged
rampant in Egypt.

Beatrice continued to watch the officer and his partner who had
stopped dancing and had moved behind the screen of a potted palm,
leaning toward one another like flowers toward the sun. The officer
stood over the woman beside him, listening to her speak and caressing
the ends of his blond moustache. Suddenly, so fast that no one else
could have seen unless they, too, were watching, his fingertips trailed
to brush her naked shoulder. What was particularly shocking was that
he had removed his gloves. The woman blushed.

It was soon after that, that the ball became unbearable, Beatrice's
face a frozen mask from maintaining the placid expression that was
demanded of her. She and her entourage left before the supper of
quails stuffed with foie gras, salmon cutlets, a variety of mousses, petit
fours, and creams. Her departure upset the Countess, who concluded
that it was the presence of certain guests that caused the Princess to
leave, probably the Blanc girl, and that now her husband would not
be able to lead the way to supper with an English princess. The
Count, on the other hand, was glad. Victoria's youngest daughter was
far too somber, an arrogant, disdainful young woman with few graces.
She scarcely smiled, she didn't converse, she didn't dance, she didn't
even know how to use a fan properly, but held it closed, like a cudgel.

That night, Beatrice dreamed she was wrapped in a nightshirt that
smelled of cloves and tied to a bath chair at the dock while a yacht
sailed away from Osborne with everyone on it. On board was Victoria
of Hesse, dressed in white velvet banded in pale blue fox. She woke in
a sweat.

The sun streamed in through the skylight of the steaming baths,
illuminating the bathers below in chiaroscuroed shards. Beatrice sat
beside a metal tank, the hair on her head pinned up, her arm thrust
through a funnel, as her attendant toweled the sweat that beaded on
her forehead. She was thinking of that morning's visit to Dr. Bertier,
who had said, as he wiped his monocle on a handkerchief, that while
improvement had been at best modest, at least matters had not gotten worse.

For some reason, that had made her think of Papa, not the portraits
of the unsmiling, haughty man in boots with hunting dogs and dead

fowl at his feet but of sensation, of being lifted in the air and held close by the strong arms of a big warm man, whose laughter resonated from his chest, who tickled her neck with his moustache, and whose familiar smell she somehow connected to ham and jet beads. A curious combination. It was so long ago. The memory teased. Just when she grabbed its edge, it was gone. She was straining recollection when two attendants carried a woman on a litter into the adjoining bath. She watched as the attendants cradled the woman's head on a folded towel, preparing to settle her into the giant sling that would lower her into the water.

"That one chooses her whole body," said her attendant.

"I don't understand," said Beatrice. She was fluent in French, as she was in German, but the provinces introduced nuances of dialect that were sometimes confusing, not to mention idioms that made no sense. Besides, she had been thinking of something else. She must have missed a word. "What do you mean, she chooses her whole body?" she asked.

"One chooses whether they will embrace illness like a lover or whether they will shake their fist at it and send it packing. Most of those you see have chosen illness. It nourishes them, gives them something of their own. They clutch it to themselves as tightly as the blankets that cover them. Some of them choose more illness than others. Some less. A shoulder, fingers, a neck, a back, legs; that poor soul had chosen her entire person."

"You keep saying choose," said Beatrice. "Perhaps it is the language difference between us. In English, to choose means a deliberate selection. I see three ribbons, for example. I say, I pick the green one. That is to choose."

The attendant nodded. *"Oui,"* she replied, then folded a towel and placed it beneath Beatrice's elbow.

"I don't think you realize what you are saying. You think I have chosen this?"

"It is not for me to say, your ladyship. That would be presumptuous and not my place."

"But you have said it."

The attendant shrugged, a typically Gallic shift of her shoulders, a delicate movement. "I speak only in generalities. If I have offended you, I am sorry."

"You have not offended me. But you have surprised me. For one who spends so much time in the company of the ill, you have very little compassion." Beatrice withdrew her arm from the funnel, dripping foul-smelling sulphurous water over her dressing gown. "Enough. The odor is worse than Dieppe."

The attendant realized that she had upset this young English noblewoman who everyone said was really the Queen of England's youngest daughter. She did not really believe that this unhappy person was the daughter of the greatest queen in all the world. People let slip such things all the time in order to get special attention. "But you are not finished," she protested.

Beatrice brushed her aside and ran to the adjoining bedroom to pour geranium water from an enamel pitcher over her arm. The distressed attendant followed after her and tried to assist her into her garments, managing to close the fastenings beneath her skirt before the Princess dismissed her with a curt "You are no longer needed." Wearing the suffering expression of one who has been wounded unfairly, the attendant curtsied and left.

Beatrice tried to fasten her dress alone, but her hands would not cooperate. She used palms and then fingers held together like a wedge and managed to slip the frilly white fichu about her neck, but she could not marshal the fine pincer movements necessary to button her corsage, not to mention the smaller buttons from elbow to wrist on her sleeves. She began to sweat as she worked, twisting and pulling her buttons, becoming increasingly frustrated as buttons and buttonholes slipped out of her grasp. She dropped her hands to her sides and shrieked for Lady Jane. Then she became frenzied, pulling at her dress, her hair, in a fury of self-loathing.

When Lady Jane arrived to accompany her to the hotel, she found Beatrice weeping, her hair in disarray, her corsage open, the fichu halfway around her neck, two pearl buttons pulled off and lying like dewdrops on the moist marble floor.

The lady-in-waiting was unprepared when Beatrice later told her she wished to go to Paris to visit Monsieur Worth's establishment. She had been ready to make return arrangements to England, to order a sedative from Dr. Bertier, but Paris? It would be difficult to manage, as travel arrangements for royalty were not something one did on the spur of the moment. An appointment with Monsieur

Worth would have to be secured, the Hotel Bristol notified; they would need outriders in front and behind the coach and, not the least of all, the permission of the Queen. All of this meant nothing to Beatrice. The Princess seemed like someone possessed. She was single purposed, clear in one overriding idea. She wanted no more ball gowns with sleeves that came to the elbows. They were out of fashion; not even old women wore them. Lady Jane decided to make the arrangements, sending word on the day they left of their plans; hopefully, the overnight excursion would not offend Her Majesty too much. She would deal with the Queen later, saying in truth that Her Highness was so determined that under the circumstances of her bout of weeping the night before, it seemed the best thing to do.

The ride in the closed brougham over the winding, hilly, often rocky road to Paris took twelve hours. The equerry, who had registered his protest with his sovereign's lady of the bedchamber, rode beside them. They arrived after dark, to see the city glowing with lamplight as whirlpools of people surged down the boulevards, some spilling into the sidewalk cafés to sit at marble-topped tables under red awnings. The air that drifted into the carriage was soft and warm, filled with the odor of absinthe, Havana cigars, and the fragrance of flower stalls.

They were ushered into the Hotel Bristol quickly, before any of the other guests noticed their arrival. Beatrice fell asleep still wearing her wrapper, enjoying the freedom from her stays and listening to the clop of horse's hooves and the shouts of an angry woman below.

They left their rooms early, as baker's boys in white linen caps ran with baskets on their arms, and went directly to the shop of Monsieur Worth. Quiet and hushed, the salon looked like a conservatory, with potted palms and ferns everywhere. Modistes and their assistants carrying frocks ran over the Aubusson carpet from one part to another; green taffetas with flounces of curled feathers, mauve moiré covered with lace, white brocade trimmed with gold and silver flowers, and a red velvet, embroidered with beads, that looked to Beatrice like something that Marie, the Russian wife of her brother Affie, would wear.

Beatrice was escorted to a private mirrored room and helped to undress, her measurements taken by a team of modistes. It was noted that her waist was twenty-one inches. Privately, they thought this overmuch; unmarried young ladies of fashion scarcely measured over nineteen inches, except for the German royalty, whose figures were hopeless. Milkmaids, all of them, which explained things, since everyone knew the English Crown was practically German. Otherwise, her body was good, the hips supple, the back straight, the neck a slender column.

When Beatrice was again dressed, she and Lady Jane sat in consultation with Monsieur Worth. With grave courtesy, the former Englishman studied the pink and white young woman with red blonde hair and blue eyes and said that the Princess reminded him of Botticelli's *Venus* rising from the sea. He would make her a sea gown. Would she leave it to him? She would, provided the gown would be ready before she returned to England and that the sleeves did not come to her elbows. He assured her on both counts. They returned to Aix-les-Bains that afternoon.

"The Empress Eugénie," declared Beatrice solemnly on the return drive, "never wore the same gown twice, you know. Now she must, of course, her circumstances have been so sadly reduced, but when she was Empress of France, never. She says the magic is lost when one is seen wearing a gown a second time."

Beatrice received a letter from her mother two days later by special courier in which the Queen said how lonely she was without her dearest baby by her side and that if she had any thought for her at all, she would return to England as quickly as possible. She added that the absence of her youngest daughter was grievous and unpleasant, increased her depression, emptiness, and bereavement, which nothing could remove. Beatrice flexed her fingers and forgave her. Mama needed her. She would be able to write letters for her again. She would be able to help her in her work. Mama did not tell her about the visit of Vicky and Louis, because she wished to spare her. As always, she had her best interests at heart. Nothing had changed. She loved her best. Did she ask any of the others to stay at her side? If her sister Louise resided with them from time to time, it was because Mama worried about her. Certainly Mama considered Louise impractical. She said as much. How could one trust with state matters a daughter who did not always wear stays, smoked cigarettes, and had been a close friend of the novelist George Eliot, who, it was said, had shared a habitation with a married man. Did Mama ask any of the others, other than the occasional ribbon cutting and medal pinning and troop reviewing, to help her in her work? Not even Bertie was given as much responsibility as she. She was ungrateful. She was the most fortunate person in all the world. Victoria was not only her Queen; she was her mother and her dearest friend. She would make it up to her.

Dr. Bertier was informed. He told the equerry he would have preferred his patient to remain under his care a little longer. She was somewhat better but still in need of treatment. Another two weeks, at least. Privately he thought, royalty were the most difficult patients to treat. Anyone with any experience knew that.

The next week, within hours before they were to return to England, the gown, in its nest of tissue paper, was delivered by a messenger on horseback. The skirt was of pale green satin, hand painted with shells and starfish, the bodice of soft green crepe, powdered with silver foam, covered with white lace encrusted with real seashells, epaulets of oyster shells half open with real pearls, on her left shoulder a silver net glittering with gold and silver fish.

"It's exquisite," said Lady Churchill. "Do please try it on."

"Not now," replied Beatrice. "It's far too delicate. Later, perhaps, if an occasion warrants." The maid closed the box and carried it from the room while Beatrice thought of Osborne and the Solent, and of Mama, waiting patiently for her return. Then she thought of black-necked grebes giving snakelike twists to their necks as they glided together, slipping noiselessly into the water. Her skin felt strange— she stroked her hand, her wrist, her neck—the sensitive feeling one got when one became feverish. She thought of the dancing couple. Did the man touch the woman's neck as he had her shoulder? Or was it accidental. Did it feel like this?

CHAPTER SEVEN

The frost had been sharp, the ground was hard, and the short dark days were set against a pale blue brittle sky. Golden leaves, iridescent with morning dew, still clung to the beech trees, waiting for the first gale to bring them down to form a carpet of burnished copper. Partridges with exquisitely penciled feathers, veined like the gauzy wings of a fly, heard the sticks and the thudding boots of the beaters and whirred in little eddies through the purple-misted bracken.

In the castle's library where leather-bound volumes of men and women authors were carefully separated, Princess Louise stood before the mirror over the fireplace, tipping her black silk top hat more rakishly than fashion decreed over her pretty face. Seated on a sofa behind her were Beatrice, wearing fingerless woolen mittens and a fringed pelisse with shawl-like sleeves for warmth, and Leopold. A footman set a pile of newly cut magazines on a table, then took his place silently against the wall.

"It seems cruel and unfair," said Beatrice. "Grouse are driven before you, and there you crouch hidden behind the turf and blaze away."

Louise turned from the mirror. "You have become such a blue stocking, Benjamina. No fun at all. It's not as simple as you make it sound. You have to give instructions to your loaders, and you have to wait for precisely the right moment, for the birds come thick and fast and you have to get them on the rise, and sometimes they fly in packs, and the gamekeepers are not always successful in breaking them up."

"Benjamina is not a blue stocking at all," said Leopold. "That suggests someone prim and forbidding. As a matter of fact, she had a very enthusiastic reception at Aberdeen."

"It's a small way in which I relieve Mama of her burden," replied Beatrice softly.

"You're such a goose. When are you going to marry, for heaven's sakes? You're fast becoming everyone's old auntie. They all giggle about you, did you know that?"

"You're married," said Beatrice, thinking of the handsome eldest son of the Duke of Argyll, Louise's husband, who had been appointed governor general of Canada, "yet you're not living with your husband. Why is marriage in my interest and not in your own?"

"She has a point," said Leopold.

Louise inspected her buttons, embossed with the hunt master's horn. "That is another matter."

"I'm sorry, Louise," said Leopold. "Has it been difficult?"

"It is more difficult to live with him and pretend. But I won't speak against him, nor will I permit anyone else to do so. Lorne has been my best friend. Our differences stem from something out of his control. He has no interest in the physical side of marriage."

Beatrice looked into her lap, rearranging the fringes of her pelisse, astonished that Louise would openly mention such an intimate particular, however fortunate it might appear, and in the presence of their brother. Leopold was unmoved by Louise's disclosure. Such revelations were not uncommon with negotiated alliances. He withdrew a cigarette from a silver case. "It can't be because you are lacking in beauty," he said.

"The truth is," replied Louise matter-of-factly, "no woman attracts him."

They were speaking of a gray area of Beatrice's understanding, a matter she knew very little about, yet nothing she could question or discuss or find explained in any book. Was Louise saying that her husband was not interested in physical matters or that he was not interested in women? In men? Somehow it meant more than just being close friends. Bertie had made some such remark about Oscar Wilde before Alexandra quieted him with a look. What did men do with one another? The thought of two men kissing was disgusting. Surely handsome Lorne was not interested in that. It must be simply that his interests were aesthetic, spiritual, placing him one step higher on Dr. Darwin's evolutionary ladder than other men, more bestial in their tastes.

Louise took a puff of her brother's cigarette, then turned to her youngest sister, who had pulled her pelisse more tightly about her. "I hear you went to the black country, to Dudley, to open something or other."

"A school," said Beatrice.

"Weren't you embarrassed?"

"No," replied Beatrice, pleased that lately she was less and less afraid to be afraid, no longer upsetting cream jugs, although hostesses with pitying eyes still brought her the usual refuge of the awkward, photographs to look at. "Actually, I'm getting better at that sort of thing." She turned to smile at her brother. "Leo has suggested that I imagine them in their nightcaps."

"I don't mean that sort of embarrassment. I mean to be so privileged in the face of such wretched poverty?"

"I don't understand," said Beatrice.

"She means," said Leopold, "that her sympathies are with Salisbury's elegant nephew, Balfour, and Bernard Shaw."

"Do be quiet, Leo. There are many kinds of cruelty. I am suggesting that it is cruel to appear in silks in a landau with a half-dozen servants in attendance and snip ribbons in the sight of those who have to live in a forest of smokestacks."

"But you're wrong, Louise. They were happy to see me. They threw so many posies they filled the landau. And I did not travel with a half dozen. There were only two. The third was Lady Ely. Besides, all that you speak of is being changed. Mama is changing it."

"How is it being changed?"

"Education. Available to the very poorest. There are already improvements. Drunkenness and brutality are on the decrease."

"What about the women who crawl harnessed and half clothed through the mines," asked Louise, "for two shillings a day? How is their lot improved?"

"I was assured," said Beatrice, blushing, "that there are much fewer women employed in the mines, proof of the moral and social improvement that has taken place."

"When we were children," said Louise, "we were made to repeat the words Papa, potatoes, poultry, prunes, and prisms to give proper regal form to our lips. That is exactly as yours look now. As if you were about to spit out an egg. Why can't you see that laborers live in appalling squalor."

Beatrice gathered her defense, hoping that her voice would not desert her as it did in contention. "Herbert Spencer writes," she said in a treacherous quaver, "that when distress comes upon the imprudent, and starvation upon the idle, it is the decree of a large, far-seeing benevolence."

"Horse manure," said Louise, striding from the library. "Vicky was right. You are not only in Mama's shadow. You are Mama's shadow. That is exactly the sort of thing she would say." The footman sprang forward to open the doors.

"Louise was never known for her tact," said Leopold, pulling his tweed vest down over his kilt. "I suppose that is the Bohemian in her."

"She unsettles things," said Beatrice. "Like a poorly trained dog at a hunt that barks at horses." She stood, gathering the folds of her skirts, as was correct, to one side before she switched them behind her. "Mama is expecting me."

By the time she entered the chilly, homely parlor of the solitary little shiel that stood in the shadow of Lochnagar, Victoria was regarding her Prime Minister out of the corner of a baleful eye. Beatrice acknowledged his bow and that of Sir Henry as she hurriedly took her place at the writing desk.

Gladstone sighed, shifted his feet, and blew on his hands. "I concede that we have a moral duty to help the Egyptian government, but I am firmly resolved, ma'am, to undertake no fresh adventures in the Sudan. Prolonged Egyptian occupation will freeze all cordiality between ourselves and the French. In the case of war, the task of holding Egypt would weaken us. I am still of the mind that the means of negotiations, while remote, are still available. It is wholly possible that the Mahdi, who has no quarrel with us, might be disposed to accept us as mediator."

"Mediation is unthinkable." Victoria turned to Sir Henry, who stood stroking his beard. "What is next on the agenda?"

Sir Henry consulted his list. "There remains one final issue, ma'am. Africa."

Victoria folded her hands in her lap. "Everyone is taking pieces of it. I hope you are thinking of doing the same before it is too late. Three tiny protectorates and one colony at the bottom seem rather insignificant when one considers the size of the place."

"Africa is not a pie, ma'am," said Gladstone. "We do, however, have a sphere of influence."

"I don't know what that means, a sphere of influence," said Victoria. "It doesn't sound like land to me."

The droning conversation was shattered with a barrage of gunshot. Beatrice flinched as she hastened to compose her cramped notes, the pains in her hand now only an occasional ache. Louise said everyone laughed at her. Who, she wondered, and why?

The Prime Minister was speaking. "Bismarck has inquired on what title our claim to Africa is based. We have replied to him that we are claiming the southern point of the Portuguese jurisdiction to the frontier of Cape Colony and that any claim to sovereignty by a foreign power we would consider an infringement of our legitimate rights."

Victoria turned to Beatrice. "I asked you what it was that Vicky wrote on the subject in her last letter?"

"Africa. Yes. I beg your pardon, Mama. That the sole aim of Bismarck's colonial policy is to drive a wedge between Willy, who wants expansion, and his parents, who do not."

"Thank you, dear. Try to concentrate on the business at hand."

"That is also our understanding, ma'am," said Gladstone. "Bismarck's sudden moves toward southwest Africa and New Guinea were not a matter of flag following trade. They are sugar plums for Prince William."

"I was not aware that Bismarck had designs on New Guinea. You did not tell me this. We cannot give you our opinion unless we are informed of all the facts." Victoria set her lips in a downward pout. Her Prime Minister was making it odiously clear that he considered her only a figurehead and that it was not her opinion that was needed but her signature.

"Will you stay to lunch, Mr. Gladstone?" she asked. "We are having trout and oatmeal."

"No, thank you, ma'am." The audience was over. Gladstone, whose legs had begun to hurt, bowed and backed out of the small room.

"The people's William, indeed," said Victoria. "He is a dangerous old fanatic. Why does he not retire? He will soon be seventy-four. A man must know when it is time to relinquish the reins to another."

Beatrice's fingertips had gone numb, and she rubbed them as Victoria began dictating alternately to both Sir Henry and her, notes to the kitchen to cancel Louise's request for plover's eggs, to Miss Phipps, whose ridiculously tight skirts did not allow her to curtsy properly and which had caused her to fall flat, an accident unbecoming to those in waiting, and to the Indian viceroy about widows being burned alive.

If she persevered, she thought, and forced her unwilling fingers to comply, she might be able to see Leo once more before he left for London.

One day followed another like a ribbon, continuous, flowing, fraying. By March, the court had gone into full mourning for the Infanta of Portugal. Victoria Station had been dynamited, presumably by Fenians, leaving a gaping hole in its glass roof, a Parisian lying-in hospital reported the use of a wooden box with a shelf for a pan of hot water as a successful incubator, and Leopold, feeling the pinch of marriage, went to Cannes.

Victoria, with Beatrice at her side despite a nagging toothache, was preoccupied with other matters. A valiant eccentric named General Gordon had been sent to Khartoum to rescue the stranded garrison. On arriving at the junction of the Blue and White Niles, littered with the masts and felucca sails of rivercraft, Gordon, carrying a cane, which he called his wand of victory, and a Bible, telegraphed that the people kissed his feet and called him Savior. A fatalist, who believed that the devil was lodged beneath Pitcairn Island, Gordon had a mystical flash that a slave trader named Zebehr be set up in opposition to the Mahdi. His demand was followed by the Mahdi and his followers cutting the telegraph lines to Cairo, leaving the only communication, in or out, little scraps of paper carried by runners. Khartoum was under siege.

Gladstone and his Cabinet shuddered, for Gordon, a famous warrior, was unlikely to conduct an inglorious defeat. Victoria said she trembled for Gordon's safety and held Gladstone personally responsible. "We can do nothing now," she said, "but pray."

In the midst of alarming hourly communiqués from Egypt, Victoria received word that Leopold had fallen down a flight of stairs at the naval club in Cannes. That it occurred on the anniversary of Brown's death did not escape her. On the one hand, the news created great anxiety, for one never knew how long it would take to bring this mysterious disease, which Victoria declared could not possibly have come from the House of Hanover, under control. On the other hand, she had been informed that Cannes was populated in season by the most promiscuous society in Europe, including the Russian Imperial family, German royalty, and an international assortment of nobility, not to mention Bertie, whose doings were reported on by Lord Wolverton, who in turn was kept informed by Baron de Stoekl, equerry to the Grand Duke Michael. It was at Cannes that the widowed Grand Duchess of Mecklenburg-Schwerin became pregnant by a member of her staff, a tall, good-looking aide-de-camp, and went abroad in flowing gowns, although she did maintain the fiction that she had chicken pox and had to go into quarantine. Only at Cannes could Grand Duke Michael sit on a chocolate soufflé and squirt his dinner guests. The Tsar, however crude he might be himself, would never allow such a thing in Russia.

If, however, a fall down a flight of stairs was the way to bring Leo home, then perhaps it was as they said, an ill wind that blew no good. They waited anxiously for word, particularly how long it would take before he could return to England.

It came the next day. Victoria was receiving a massage to her knee in her sitting room while Beatrice was reading aloud the itinerary for young Victoria's wedding, which included traveling by rail to Darmstadt. Victoria was saying that the Grand Duke should be informed that she wished to be met privately, no fanfare, just family. "Poor lonely man," she said, "sometimes I think it is more difficult to be a widower than a widow."

Beatrice felt light-headed as one did before a swoon when Sir Henry entered. Perhaps it was the look on his face. Without preliminaries, he informed them that Leopold had died during the night of a cerebral hemorrhage.

Victoria was stricken. She began to sob, calling Leopold the dearest of her dear sons, her darling child, so gifted, so loved, so like his father, cut off too soon, and that happiness for her was at an end, although she was ready to fight on. She wished her subjects to know that. Sir Henry must prepare a message for the dailies. She reminded them that Leopold had come to her this exact time, on this exact date, to tell her in his gentle way of the death of John Brown.

Beatrice, staring at the delicate tracery of yellow garlands on the crimson carpet, was numbed, wounded, unable to articulate her grief as was her mother. She excused herself and somehow found the way to her apartments where she found her maid cleaning her kid boots, rubbing them with a mixture of egg white and ink. She was noticing one in particular which she had scuffed on a cobblestone when she slumped to the floor.

They went into the deep mourning of bombazine, crepe, and veils and still Beatrice could not speak of it to anyone, not even to Helen. Neither did she feel the scratches of the black veil rubbing on her nose and forehead or on her swollen weeping eyes. The dreary, edge-less, funereal days that followed were dreamlike—meeting the coffin at Windsor railway station with Bertie dressed in a field marshal's uniform, hearing the muffled drum rolls and the melancholy peals of the church bells, visiting the glass-lidded coffin at night in the chapel, lit by silver candelabra, viewing the recumbent stranger in the violet satin frock coat, the baton-carrying Queen's marshalmen wearing their Waterloo shakos, and the pallbearers with shoulder knots of white satin.

Lord Tennyson composed a poem, the first few lines beginning, "Early and wise and pure and true, prince, whose father lived in you." Leo makes jokes about Tennyson, she thought. He will laugh at this.

That night her tooth still ached; there had not been time to see the dentist. Mademoiselle Noreille gave her a sleeping draft and placed, with a needle, cotton wool soaked with oil of cloves into the cavity. Don't go, Leo, don't go. The others won't play with me, Leo. They say I'm too small. Stay with me. Stay. Papa, who lived in Leo. Cloves in mouth. Cloves in shirt. Mama, no, no, no, no, don't do it, I can't breathe. She crawled into a closed, sheltered position, her face becoming softened and vulnerable, like that of a small bewildered child, and cried herself to sleep. The maid, folding and putting away the mourning garments, noticed how they seemed to have picked up every bit of dust in Windsor Castle.

CHAPTER EIGHT

The woman's body was opulent and full, her flesh as plush as the velvet hangings that draped the canopy of the regency bed and the wall behind it, which minutes before her fingers had pulled and twisted, smudging the nap with telltale tracings. She was heavy lidded with full pouting lips, her rich dark hair spread over the pillow and covering her eyes like a veil. A servant had removed the satin brocade fire screen, and the flickering fire cast the woman's skin with the glisten of a pearl.

Now, in a corset with loosened ribbons, her belly made tumescent by its pointed stays, she lay in the shirted arms of the Grand Duke Louis of Hesse. The carved and painted bed smelled of musk and rose, and they accommodated to one another in its narrow confines, intertwining arms and legs, sloughing off the bedclothes, flinging a lace pillow to the floor.

His fingers traced over one moist breast, circling the aureola of one brown nipple that had escaped from its corset confines. She murmured and moved toward him, her head back, her lips open, feverish; he dug his fingers harder into her breast, seeking the other.

Suddenly, she turned her head. "She has come for you, Louis," she said, "to marry the daughter. She has come for you, that sour old widow, and she won't rest until she takes you back to London, trussed up like the boar you hunt in the forest."

"Darling," he said, breathless, "you worry so. I tell you not to worry. Would I leave you? Would I let you go? Out of my life?

Impossible; you are my life." His fingers reached again, his lips sought her breasts, and he burrowed between them, crooning, gasping.

"She has come for you. I feel her presence," she said, "in this very room."

"No, no," he murmured, "no one has come for me. She is here for the wedding. Only the wedding. You are my *Geliebte*. My own darling." He pressed one knee between her legs and bent his head toward her, seeking her lips. She groaned, her legs parted, their rounded kneecaps mounding beneath the bedclothes.

Later, she lay staring at the frescoed ceiling high above them, its fleecy clouds and gilded, smiling cupids lit by shafts of twilight from the lancet windows.

"Princess Beatrice is pretty," she said. He sighed, reaching to the dais beneath for a wine goblet that rested on its ledge. "Isn't she?"

He rolled the wine around his tongue. "She's passable," he replied. "Her eyes are not bad, nor her mouth, but she seldom smiles. She should be a nun, that one, except she is not a Catholic. I like a woman who smiles, with dimples, here, and here." His hands moved again, squeezing, pinching, kneading the flesh as if it were dough. "She's not you." He sighed. "No one is you. I am young again with you, Alexandrine, as desperate as any student. I am young and strong, and feverish, always feverish . . ."

"That is because you are in your prime. A man is nothing until he is in his prime."

"And when is that?"

"When he has lived, and suffered, as you, when he is wise, as distingué, as august, as you. When his chest is like a barrel." Her fingers reached beneath his opened collar.

"Even if he is not as handsome as his cousins?"

"The Battenberg brothers are too young. They are unseasoned."

"Not so unseasoned as to diminish the relish with which you danced with Henry."

"Only because he waltzes like an angel. Don't be foolish, darling. There is no one but you."

A beech log began to spit. He pulled at the bedclothes. "Off, off," he said.

"Louis." She turned her face to the velvet wall. "It is not yet dark."

"I don't care. I want to see everything. And then I want to impale you. Like a boar."

The crumbling red-gabled roofs of the court city clustered with an air of feudal allegiance. Their half-timbered houses, rich with carvings of mermaids and dwarfs, stood on little crooked streets below where a uniformed street sweeper, wielding his broom like a scepter, swept the night's gleanings into the gutters.

The Prince of Wales, in tweeds, gaiters, and a soft felt hat wound with a piece of crepe, strolled in a cluster of relatives with his hands behind his back. The bridal party, still in mourning, was subdued, all except eleven-year-old Alicky, who was chattering beside her older sister Ella, telling her that if she went to Russia to marry Serge, she would come to visit. Behind them, paced discreetly apart, walked an equal number of equerries and attendants of various ranks.

Bertie turned to Louis of Hesse. "It's way past time she were told, old fellow. Everyone in Europe knows about Madame de Kalomine, the duels her husband fought, the time he caught you both in the woods and then was mysteriously recalled to Russia and sent on a special mission to Japan. With Mama at Darmstadt, it is only a question of time. And then there will be the devil to pay, I assure you."

They passed a signboard painted with the head of a red ox. The Grand Duke, in frock coat and bowler, nodded in response to a woman who had been scrubbing the stone steps behind it and now stood to curtsy. "But how? How can I tell her?"

"Simple," said Bertie. "Say that in deference to her terrible loss you felt it was best to wait until you might tell her in person."

"Would you do it?" asked Louis of Hesse. "Speak for me?"

Bertie laughed. "You're joking. Me? If anything is guaranteed to put Mama into a rage, it would be if I were to tell her that you are not going to marry my youngest sister but instead—now please take this in the very best way, Louis; I have very high regard for the lady—but instead, a divorced Catholic, and to make matters worse, a Russian. Don't you agree, Sandro?" He turned to a tall man with full dark beard who had been walking solemnly behind him, telling the bridal couple that the Empress Augusta and Bismarck were dead set against him.

Prince Alexander of Bulgaria nodded and continued to relate to his brother Louis that now it seemed Bismarck had brought Willy into his camp. "Bismarck calls us the Polish Specter. He sees all of the Battenbergs as possible occupants of the Polish throne."

"He has my abdication in advance," said Louis.

"It is very well for you to laugh," said Sandro. "I can't live without her; that much I know."

They neared the citadel of the old schloss, a pile of windows, roofs, and chimneys, irregular courts, archways boring into darkness, and a yellow bell tower where storks nested in a wheel. Soldiers hung over the parapets of the little bridges, some standing idly in front of striped red and white sentry boxes, their spiked helmets bristling and twinkling in the sunlight.

Before them, a green moat yawned out of the marketplace where old women under colored umbrellas sold cabbages and plums, rabbits peeped out of boxes, and men, sipping coffee at tables of old moss-grown millstones, argued whether or not people with eyebrows that met became werewolves.

Bertie withdrew a cigarette from his pocket and held it beneath his nose. "Mama must be told," he said, "and quickly."

"I can't do it," said Louis of Hesse. "Whenever the Queen sees me, she starts to talk of Alice. It is so dreary and depressing, and I have to sit there while she pats my hand and tells me she understands. How can I tell her when she starts to talk of Alice and when I know she promotes the deceased wife's sister bill in the English Parliament?"

Young Victoria disengaged her arm from that of her fiancé and put her gloved hand on her father's arm. "I will tell her, Papa," she said. "I will explain everything. Do let me. You know how close Grandmama and I are. She could never be angry with me, certainly not for explaining things."

Bertie laughed. "My niece is both beautiful and clever. Actually, she is the only person who can tell Mama. The only other possibility is Vicky, and she won't be here until tomorrow. Frankly, we can't wait that long. This cigarette is stale." He signaled to a servant in Highland dress, who came forward with a silver case.

Prince Louis of Battenberg took the moment to walk to the embankment of the moat and call below to the young officer standing at an umbrella where a woman was polishing plums on her apron. The officer's black boots reached to his thighs. His impeccably tailored white tunic, trimmed in gold braid, was wound about the waist with a silver sash. Beneath it hung a sword belt with a gleaming sword. "Henry, for heaven's sake, how long does it take to choose a plum? We can't wait all day. The Empress's train is scheduled to arrive in half an hour."

The woman behind the umbrella smiled with toothless gums and indicated with a wave of her hand that payment was not expected for the plum. Nodding his thanks, the officer strode up the embankment to join the others, carrying beneath his arm a helmet surmounted by a silver eagle.

He was handsome, with dark moustache and deep, lustrous, chocolate-brown eyes, his dashing uniform molded to his vigorous young soldier's body. As he reached the top of the grade, a clatter of horse's hooves and wagon wheels announced the approach of a carriage. Riding in an open landau sat Queen Victoria in a crush of black lusterless skirts, with Alexandra and Beatrice, attentive and somber, beside her. Henry was surprised to see how small the Queen was. He had expected to find her more imposing. The carriage stopped, and the footman on the box sprang down.

Young Victoria turned to her sister Ella. "Don't say anything about Serge in front of Grandmama," she whispered, then, without waiting to be helped, jumped up unaided into the carriage. "Do let me ride along with Grandmama, Aunties. I have so much to say to her, and I'm afraid that with all the wedding plans I will not have the opportunity. Besides, you will find it so much more lovely to walk. The lilies of the valley and the fuschias are in bloom, and the swans have had cygnets, and they are adorable."

Alexandra murmured something to the Queen, patted her hand, and stepped down, neither hurriedly nor stiffly, accepting the hand of the footman with grace and dignity and lifting her dress in front as she descended so as to show the point of her shoes. Beatrice continued to sit beside her mother until the Queen persuaded her to follow Alexandra down. She descended reluctantly, also on the hand of the footman, glancing backward once or twice, then standing to straighten the bouffant drape of her overskirt with her black kid gloves.

When she lifted her eyes, she saw him at once. It was the high shiny black boots that caught her attention. He was not as tall as Sandro or as ebullient as Louis, but there was something familiar about his shining vigor, and yet something foreign, mysterious. A vague memory rustled in the corner of her mind. She blushed and looked about her. Louis stepped forward. "You know of course," he said, "my brother Henry."

Henry, who had watched Beatrice alight from the carriage with downcast eyes, came forward and bowed before her. She did not offer her hand to kiss. She said nothing. Her eyes were what compelled him. They were infinitely sad. He knew she was grieving for her brother, but that did not explain the depth of sorrow that he saw, like looking into a tunnel of dark mirrors.

As the carriage drove off with young Victoria and her grandmother, there was some confusion in the small cluster having to do with who would go to meet Augusta. It seemed no one wanted to, and yet they felt that the German Empress should be met with a delegation of family. While those that remained were deciding who would go to the station, Henry took an unhurried step closer.

"I would offer you the plum," he said, "but I'm afraid it will run all over your gown, and I should not want you to be angry with me."

She did not do what other young ladies would have done, royal or no. Although Louis had told him that she was incredibly shy, Henry was somewhat surprised to see from one so pretty and ripened—after all, she was not eighteen—no coquetry, no practiced flick of eyelash, no delicious smile that curved pink cheeks into scimitars, no badinage such as English and Frenchwomen were so clever at making. Instead, she looked directly into his eyes and extended her hand. He noticed that her blue eyes were as clear as water. "I'll take the plum," she said in a soft, gentle voice, "and have it later."

"I did not expect to see a Valkyrie so soon," he replied, smiling and handing her the plum.

Her hand went to smooth the scarf beneath her linen collar. "I don't understand."

"I thought perhaps you came to take me to Valhalla, and I am not yet ready to make the journey."

It was decided that either all or none would go to meet the Empress, and the cluster moved with dutiful resignation toward the railway station, with Henry and Beatrice following along. Ella and Irene turned to watch the couple, who walked silently side by side and began to giggle until Alexandra took the arm of each and told them that when she returned to the palace, they must show her the Holbein *Madonna.*

By the time the party passed the pond, on which were gliding black and white swans with downy cygnets streaming behind them, Sandro had rehearsed his speech to Augusta, Beatrice had flung back the heavy crepe veil over her hat to let the spring breeze cool her forehead, and the Grand Duke, feeling relieved, began to amuse everyone with the story of Ludwig of Bavaria, who dressed in the Swan Knight's costume and rode around on his lake in a boat drawn by mechanical swans.

That evening, Victoria, Beatrice, and young Victoria, who was hemming a linen napkin, sat in Alice's sky-blue boudoir, a musty room in which everything—ceiling, walls, couches, chairs, and hangings—was of pale blue satin yellowing in the folds.

Victoria's chair creaked as she shifted her weight to watch the attendants bring in the bridal gown for her to admire and note that the bodice has been altered to her specifications—high in the back and square in front, in respect to the mourning of the court.

"I have told you this afternoon," said Victoria as she inspected the gown, "that I shall never turn away from your dear papa, but he must see how ill considered this whole thing is. In England, his remarrying such a person would lower him so much that I could not have him near as before. It is unladylike, dear, to sew with such a long thread. Only seamstresses do that. Believe me, breaking off the engagement will be infinitely less painful than hurting all those he loves."

"Grandmama," said young Victoria, making the proper knot, "Papa is marrying Madame Kalomine for the sake of his children and his country."

"Ridiculous," snorted Victoria. "He is doing it for his own personal happiness. She could never be a mother to you. And if that were his concern, your papa has only to look about him for a partner more suitable." Victoria stopped, aware that she was tipping her hand, as Lady Ely, always annoying, did at whist. Beatrice did not appear to be listening. Victoria turned to one of the attendants. "When Her Highness is dressed, her veil must be arranged so as not to conceal her face. Don't you agree, Benjamina?"

"I beg your pardon, Mama," replied Beatrice. "I was not listening."

"I know how you are thinking of Leo, dear," said Victoria, "but you must not let your sorrow affect our duty to the bride. She and I both need your help and attention." She let fall a satin fold and turned to young Victoria.

"I could never defend such a choice. And Prussia would not put up with it for one moment; you can be sure of that. Believe me, you do not want Augusta to hear one whisper of this. If Papa should feel lonely when you three elder are married, I should say nothing, though it would pain me, if he chose to make morganatic marriage with some nice, quiet, sensible person, but to choose a lady of another religion who has just been divorced would be a terrible mistake. He would repent, I know, but then it would be too late."

"Papa is determined."

"Nonsense," replied Victoria, signaling to the attendants to remove the bridal gown. "That is what he now says, but when he thinks over what I have said, he will change his mind. Your papa is a sensible man."

The attendants backed out of the boudoir, their arms draped with white honiton point lace and satin. Beatrice only partially took note. She was thinking suddenly of Henry's lips beneath his moustache.

That night she tossed on her bed, trembling, thinking of his eyes, his high black boots, the muscles of his shoulders and arms, hinted through the cloth of his tunic, his deep, vibrant voice that somehow resonated in her own body. The thoughts were keeping her from sleep, and she shook her head from side to side to thrust them out.

"I will not grant him an audience, and that is final. I do not care how long he waits." The woman who spoke sat holding a hand mirror while a lady-in-waiting adjusted her skewed russet wig. She was Augusta, Empress of Prussia, her face chalky white, coated with a maquillage of some pasty substance, her white silk jet-trimmed gown cut in a low décolletage, more fitting for a young woman, its ruffles coyly displaying her wrinkled, pearl powdered breasts. She smelled of verbena.

The Crown Princess stood before her. "I beg you to reconsider."

"The matter is closed, Vicky," said Augusta. "His father may be a

Hessian prince, but when he married a Polish nobody, he laid all that aside. His mother's title means nothing. Julia von Hauke's father was a pastry cook, her brother a Hebrew socialist killed in some sort of military riot. There's your royalty. It is the joke of all Europe. He is a commoner. Prince of Bulgaria? Another joke. He is a puppet on a Russian throne, and even they do not want him. Victoria will get no dowry money from the Hessian Parliament because they do not consider his brother Louis a real prince. There's your answer. Sandro a suitor for Moretta? Impossible."

"This is very difficult on all of us," said Vicky. "The girl is miserable. She is losing weight. I implore you only to meet with him. Allow him to plead their case."

"I'll tell you this, Vicky. You and your daughter risk disinheritance if you pursue this any further." She turned to Ella, who sat obediently waiting, gazing at a deeply pigmented portrait of St. Elizabeth of Hungary, an ancestress of the Hessian royal family, shown leading her children through a snowstorm. "I will speak now to this silly selfish girl. It is not enough, Ella, that you rejected Willy, who will someday be Kaiser, but you refuse the Grand Duke of Baden, all because you fancy yourself in love with a Romanoff? What is it about Serge that is so special? It cannot be that miserable country in which he lives."

Ella remained silent, the words she had been composing now lost.

"Answer me," commanded Augusta. "Let us see if your tongue is as strong as your will."

"It is his eyes, Your Majesty."

Augusta put down the gilt hand mirror. "I cannot believe what I am hearing."

"They are gray-green," said Ella. "He also waits in the alcove, Your Majesty."

"You will do well to reconsider, Ella. The Romanoffs are a brutish lot. And the country is all bears and ice. No culture at all. I have had a difficult journey. That is all I have to say on the subject. What is this I hear of your father? Someone told me he is also interested in a Russian."

"Your information," said Victoria, walking in on the arm of Beatrice, her other hand leaning on a walking stick, "is as incorrect as your gown." Victoria and Augusta bowed to one another with inclinations of their heads. "Fritz doesn't look well, dear," said Victoria to

Vicky. "He should have remained behind instead of trotting off hunting boar."

"What is wrong with my gown?" snapped Augusta.

"We are in mourning. Did you forget? Ella, go and tell Serge that he may join us later in the yellow salon."

"What shall I tell poor Sandro, Grandmama? He has been waiting for hours."

It was clear to everyone in the room, including the ladies-in-waiting, who stood holding shawls, fans, and wire-framed reading glasses, that there had been a subtle shift in supremacy from Augusta to Victoria. Vicky took courage from her mother's reclamation. "Tell him that it would be inconvenient at this time." She followed Ella to the door, her skirts rustling as she walked. "Better yet, I will see him myself."

Victoria settled into a sofa. "I, too, Augusta, am opposed to the marriage," she confided when Vicky and Ella had left.

"Which one?" asked Augusta. "There are two under discussion as I see it."

"Three, dear," replied Victoria archly, "but you and I both know that talking of marriage and actually marrying are as far apart as Moscow and Berlin."

Augusta's palsied head shook beneath curls fixed with ale into perfect scrolls. "I see," she said, "that Beatrice is a devoted daughter. It is good to find attention paid to the old values. Too often they are forgotten in these times."

Beatrice was thinking of that afternoon when Mama had been engaged in a private audience with the Grand Duke Louis from which even she had been excluded. She had been taking a horse to ride, an Andalusian with flowing mane, when suddenly he was there, pushing the groom aside. "May I?" he had asked. And before she could recover her wits, she had gathered up her skirts in her left hand, while he stooped and held his hand so that she could place in it her left foot, then gently lifted the heel of her boot as she sprang up into the saddle, and as a groom would have done, put her foot in the stirrup and smoothed the skirt of her habit.

He said she mounted the horse well, that with such a military seat she should be in the cavalry, as he was. She had wished that she could have thought to say something witty. Instead, she said something about the actual difference between the military and the hunting seat. How stupid he must have thought her.

While the groom waited patiently behind with his own mount, Henry asked if she were planning to canter or to trot. She said she would try both. He said that the canter was safer for horse and rider when both were unknown to one another, as was here the case. He advised the canter. The horse, he said, would have his haunches more under him in the canter, thereby making the animal more able to recover himself in case of making a mistake. There was silence. He smiled, and she placed her right hand on the pommel, thanked him for his advice, and led off, but he checked the reins, saying that the horse seemed awkward. He suggested that if the horse struck off falsely again, as it had just done, she should tighten the near rein, which would incline the beast's head to the left, naturally advancing his right shoulder. Some horses, he said, were safe in all their paces; others were stumblers in one and safe in another.

Her horse became restless, and he held the reins more tightly. They spoke briefly of horses that stumbled. He said that it depended on whether the stumbling arose from a defective formation of the limbs or whether occasioned by carelessness on the part of the handler. Can this defect be removed? she had asked.

He replied that if the former, the hand of a good rider, by throwing the horse on his haunches, converted the stumble into a harmless trip. Did she know, he asked, that the Romans tied clogs to the pasterns of their mounts to train young horses to elevate their feet and look where they walked?

The courtyard suddenly swarmed with hounds with curling, pointed tails, hunting grooms carrying guns, pad boys rolling up horse cloths and buckling them with straps, stable grooms leading in the horses, and huntsmen wearing scarlet frock coats, taking glasses of sherry from trays held by liveried footmen. He bowed and left to join the hunt, and she went off to ride, with the groom behind her, through honeysuckle and little daisies, the wind loosening her hair from beneath her hat and, with each pound of the horse's hooves, thinking of him—how he had held her fast and how she had permitted him to do so.

"You have been daydreaming, Beatrice," said Augusta. "I am waiting for your response."

"To what, Your Majesty? I am so sorry."

"You must forgive Benjamina, Augusta," said Victoria. "The loss of our dear Leopold has upset her terribly."

"Understandably," said Augusta.

They left for the yellow chamber, a handsome reception room lit by gilt chandeliers and sconces engraved with roses, to listen to a concert of Mozart given by a banner-carrying choral society. Everyone was there, sitting stiffly upright in their jewels and decorations on gilt chairs, the bridal couple side by side, Moretta sitting between Sandro, who was telling her of the château he was building like an eagle's nest high on the cliffs above the Black Sea, Vicky, Fritz, the Grand Duke Louis, surrounded by his children, behind him Serge and the gray-haired Prince of Hesse, aloof and imperious, with his son Henry at his side, Alexandra with a special trumpet to help her hear the music better, and Bertie, whose forehead was scratched, the result of a nasty brush with a thorn bush, arguing with the Grand Duke behind him that the best place to fatally wound a boar was in the middle of the forehead. Henry's eyes were on Beatrice. Vicky saw it, even though she was occupied with Moretta, pining beside her.

It was during selections from *The Magic Flute* that Vicky tapped Beatrice on the shoulder. "You dropped your program," she said.

"No, I didn't," replied Beatrice. "My program is here in my lap."

"Take it," said Vicky. "You will see that you are mistaken."

Beatrice opened her program. Someone had scribbled in the corner . . . "I have been more fortunate than Tamino. He had only a portrait."

She blanched at this reference to the operatic Prince who fell in love with a portrait. Lady Ely produced a vial of smelling salts from her reticule, but Beatrice brushed her hand away. She knew he was looking at her, but she was afraid to turn. If only Leopold was there. Leo would tell her what to do.

"I think," said Vicky after the concert to Beatrice, "that tomorrow we should pay our respects to Alice's memory."

A late supper was served in a hall of stiff silk furnishings, dark ancestral portraits, and mirrors reaching to the floor. Ella took her father aside, clutching his arm and importuning him with earnest pleadings as the company made its way to the gold and silver epergnes laden with aniseed cakes and goose pâté, the women carrying their trains over their arms like bales.

"I love him, Papa. I have always loved Serge. You know how much we care for one another. Can they tell you what to do?" she asked.

"No," he replied at length. "Your grandmother and the Empress forget that they are in Hesse where I am still the Grand Duke."

Henry and Louis regarded them from a table where Moselle cup was being ladled from a crystal bowl. "Your future father-in-law seems distressed," said Henry.

"Probably because he has been doing something he shouldn't. He and his inamorata have been making some rather serious plans."

"What sort of plans?"

"Nobody is certain. You know how rumors are; first a faint buzzing, then a steady drone, until one whines near your ear, like the one I heard from my valet, who heard from the woman's dressmaker that the Grand Duke has arranged for a private wedding ceremony following my own."

Guests turned toward the gilded doors as Beatrice entered the hall at the side of her mother. Henry put down his Moselle cup. "Why in the world would he want to marry the Kalomine woman?"

"Why, indeed. Who knows? When they get on in years, they get a little crazy." Beatrice glided slowly at her mother's side, escorting her over the smooth parquet floor through the aisle of bowing men and women rustling in deep curtsies, to the chair that had been placed on the dais. "She is good-looking but stiff, like a skiff that has been in drydock. You spoke to her. Is she still so afraid of her own shadow?"

"Her Royal Highness is very shy, more like a young girl of twelve," replied Henry. "One must go slowly with her. She still will not look at me, even though this morning we had a conversation."

"Can it be," said Louis, smiling, "that you are losing your touch? You told me yourself that women can't resist a man in uniform, especially the uniform of the Gardes du Corps. It sends shivers down their spine, your very words."

"You and I both know, Ludwig, that there are women and there are women."

Louis of Hesse called for attention. Ella stood at his side, her eyes shining, as he raised his goblet, lifted his chin, and faced the assembly. Everyone expected a toast to the bridal couple. Instead, he announced Ella's engagement to the Grand Duke Serge. The hush was palpable. Serge made his way through the crowd to reach Ella's side. Augusta's rage showed in the flush rising through her maquillage, while Victoria concealed her disappointment behind narrowed eyes, her major concern the information of Lady Ely that the Kalomine woman had not yet been sent packing.

The next day, Vicky arranged the picnic at Rosenhohe, the wooded bower of densely woven arcades where Alice lay entombed. Beatrice was not surprised when Henry appeared on horseback with Sandro. She had been half expecting him, wishing he would not come, yet hoping that he would. They arrived just as a half-dozen servants were laying the tables with fine damask so crisply starched as to appear glazed and carrying hampers of lobster salad, jellied tongue, and salmon dressed in green sauce. Vicky was angry that the napkins were damp and was reprimanding the steward, saying that it was unhealthy to serve damp napkins to someone like her sister, Princess Beatrice, who suffered from rheumatism.

Moretta jumped up and ran to meet Sandro as the groom took the reins of his horse, her sheer black stockings showing over the tops of her shoes. Beatrice remained where she was even though she yearned to see his face, trying to listen attentively as Fritz detailed the changes he would make when he became Emperor, although he was not wishing any ill to his father, saying he would never place such blind trust in Bismarck as did the aging Wilhelm, who signed everything Bismarck placed before him.

"It is very hopeful," said Vicky, watching the young men pick their way through the brambles, disengaging branches from epaulets and braid, "a large part of the Reichstag is ready to support Fritz when he comes to the throne."

Vicky placed Henry at her side, Moretta and Sandro opposite. Moretta wore a blue enamel watch with a diamond rose on its face, a gift of Sandro. "Look, Auntie," she said. "It is tinier than a six-kreuzer piece."

The situation proved awkward. Sandro and Moretta, so attentive, so wildly, so obviously in love, were an embarrassment, making her uneasy. It was the sort of thing one did not witness. Beatrice found herself endlessly stirring her coffee cup and looking down as she did so.

"Did you know I would be here?" he asked, eating grapes behind his half-closed hand.

"I wasn't sure."

"But you thought it was possible."

Such things were never said. She felt her ear tips burn. "Yes."

"And still you came. Why?"

"To visit my sister's tomb."

He wiped his lips and moustache on his napkin, then dropped it to the Turkish rug beneath them as he was handed a fresh replacement. "You don't like picnics?" he asked. He began to peel a pear with his silver knife.

"I don't mind them."

"To tolerate a thing and to enjoy it are not the same. One should only picnic when one wants to eat outdoors." He lay the quartered pear on her plate. "Permit me. Why did you come—ah yes," he said. "Forgive me, to visit Alice's tomb."

Placing the pear on her plate was a forward gesture. If Vicky and Fritz noticed, they did not seem to think anything of it. The footmen served strawberries in wine with tiny lace doilies between saucer and plate. "Do, dear, at least have dessert," said Vicky. "You've been picking all afternoon."

A violinist lifted his instrument, its gleaming finish made mellow with beeswax, and plucked its strings. Henry said that Vicky had told him Beatrice liked to read. She said she was going to the castle library that afternoon to get something of Schiller.

"Schiller was a deserter," he said, his handsome face set in earnest protest. "He left his post of duty."

"But surely he can't be faulted for his early life," she said. "He has given great poetry to the world."

"Schiller is hopelessly sentimental."

"Perhaps you prefer Fichte," she said, "or Schopenhauer. One can never call Schopenhauer sentimental. He wrote that a happy life is impossible, that the highest summit one can attain is a heroic life."

The violinist began to play a waltz, and Sandro led Moretta to dance on a carpet of fir needles.

"I prefer Nietzsche," said Henry. "You may not yet have heard of him. He pleads like your Carlyle for giants and says that the truly free man is a warrior. He scorns the comfort favored by grocers, cows, women, and forgive me, Englishmen."

"And the free woman?" asked Vicky, standing to take Fritz's arm and join the dancers. "What of her?"

"Her job is to bear warriors," he replied, then turned to Beatrice. "Shall I have the pleasure?"

The fecund smell of forest was too intimate, the dancing on fragrant fir needles too abandoned. "I am in mourning for my brother," she replied, suddenly wondering what she was doing there, like dreaming of parading in one's shift on the long walk at Windsor. She excused herself and said she had to return at once. Vicky picked up her skirts and followed after her, looking like a partridge skimming over the ground, asking what was wrong.

"How can you dance, Vicky?" she asked, with tears in her eyes. "It has not yet been a month."

The windows of the castle library were tightly closed, the air as dry as iron filings. The high room smelled of old bindings and the insides of old books, of dust and snuff. Here and there someone was burying his nose in a folio. She felt safe. Alone, she could think. A polite librarian with a green eyeshade came to offer his assistance. She replied that she preferred to find the book herself.

The gray light seemed to add a coating of dust to the tiers of long brown shelves through which she browsed. She couldn't concentrate. Her eyes scanned the titles, but there was no registration, just a flashing assortment of letters in German script. She finally found Schiller and stood on tiptoes to reach a particular volume.

A hand took the book from her outstretched fingers. She turned to see him standing in the shadows. "You did not go to the Rosenhohe to visit Alice's tomb. I think you have had enough of death."

"Yes," she replied.

He took her hand and brought it gently to his lips. "I would rather," he said, "this were your brow. I would then be able to make you safe and tell you that it is time for life."

She swayed, and he stepped closer to kiss her brow, slowly, gently, a brushing pressure, the briefest touch on her closed eyelids; then ardently he sought her mouth. She had never been kissed on the lips before. It took away her breath, sharply, sweetly, and they embraced, knocking Schiller to the floor.

CHAPTER NINE

The wedding took place in the palace chapel, where oaken pews and pulpit were carved in linenfold. The bride, demure beneath an orange-blossom-and-myrtle wreath from which fell the rich lace folds of her veil, knelt before the Lutheran minister with her head lowered, promising to obey her groom, whose hand she held. She was flanked by standing family and members of the Hessian court.

Henry and Beatrice were only yards apart, separated by silks and braid, glancing at one another in cautious flickers. They had not been alone since the library when his kisses had left her in a strange turmoil, longing, yet fearful to see him. Once or twice he looked at her quizzically, and she thought with dismay that it must be her white gauze gown trimmed in satin ribbon, identical to the one worn by Ella and Irene and much too childish. She should have worn white jet beaded silk like Alexandra.

It had been two days of aborted plans and disappointment. He had suggested that at a certain time she walk beside the gardens near the miniature lake. She had agreed but forgot to reckon with the business of government. Victoria had letters to write: to Lord Wolseley, applauding his efforts to launch an immediate British expedition to Khartoum; to Gladstone, asking if he realized that the fierce summer heat to come would seriously affect the dash of one thousand cavalry across two hundred miles of desert; and notes to make, such as the one concerning Tennyson, who now sat in the House of Lords. A private meeting was to be arranged when they returned, in which Victoria would ask the poet laureate not to support Gladstone's move to increase the electorate. There was no way to send word to Henry. One could not simply walk to a man's apartments, call to him in passing, or risk a message. And there were always family and staff underfoot preventing any exchange other than the most perfunctory.

At the time they were to meet, she had gotten up and down so many times to peer through the bubbled window into the gardens below that Victoria asked in a pettish voice what was wrong with her and demanded that she read back the letter to Gladstone. Later, driving in the open carriage with Victoria, she had seen him, but he merely bowed, formally, correctly, with no sign in his eyes that anything had ever passed between them. By then she was convinced that she had acted foolishly, and as any woman who allowed a man liberties, deserved his disregard. Soon, soon, she would be home in England with Mama.

The ceremony over, she hurried to the wedding banquet, enveloped in a din of pealing bells. Vicky caught up with her, tugging kid gloves to her plump elbows. "He's been asking for you," she whispered.

"Who?" replied Beatrice.

"Who. Darling, don't be coy. Henry, of course."

Beatrice's heart began to race. "What does he ask?"

"He wonders if he has offended you."

The unfamiliar feeling lifted her feet as she walked. She was wrong. He had been merely cautious. Before Beatrice could reply, Victoria, stiff and aching on the arm of Lady Ely, announced that she would not attend the banquet and that Beatrice was to accompany her to their apartments.

Beatrice's uncommon buoyancy fizzled like Apollinaris water left to stand.

"Surely Benjamina will remain," said Vicky.

"Baby is still grieving and is every bit as tired as I." Beatrice dutifully stepped to her mother's side and offered her arm, but Vicky stood before them.

"Nobody could possibly fault you for wishing to retire early, Mama. You were brave and courageous to come to the wedding in the first place, and everyone will understand if you don't come to the banquet, but Beatrice doesn't have the same excuse. It would be considered a grave slight if neither of you were present. Besides, we are all together so seldom. I long to reminisce about the old happy times when Papa used to skate with Benjamina in his arms. Do you remember, Benjamina?"

Beatrice was torn between her mother and her sister. "I don't know, Vicky, I—"

"Do you wish to stay, Beatrice, or do you wish to retire?" demanded Victoria. "I cannot stand here all evening while you discuss skating."

Vicky signaled to a lady of the Prussian court. "Of course not, Mama. How inconsiderate we have been. I am certain Fräulein Kohausen will be happy to see you and Lady Ely safely to your apartments." Vicky firmly took her sister's arm and held her fast, while Victoria hitched painfully away. "He has been miserable. You will tell him yourself what he can do to put things right."

They sat at a long table on satinwood Hepplewhite chairs. Beatrice and Henry were far enough apart that any attempt at conversation between them would be awkward and improper. He looked anything but miserable. Instead, he was affable and charming, and extremely attentive to Irene, who rested her chin on a rounded shoulder and fluttered her lashes, flirting with him in an easy, careless manner. Beatrice felt as if she had been suddenly dropped down to some hollow place from which there was no way to climb. Vicky surely must be wrong. How could he be concerned with what she thought and still be so absorbed in her silly niece?

Ella was talking. "Auntie, I asked if your hands allowed you to play."

"Play what?"

"The new game of tennis that we hear has taken over all of England, for which everyone is clearing their trees."

"A rather pointless game if you ask me," said Augusta. "Chasing a ball over one side of a net to the other. We Germans are too purposeful to engage in a pastime so silly."

There was a pause. Everyone looked to Bertie, who dabbed his lips with a napkin. Fritz broke the silence. "We risk making our family feel unwanted in Germany, Mama, if they are led to believe that we dislike things English."

"What rot," said Augusta. "We all admire Carlyle, and he is English."

"Then you agree with Carlyle, ma'am," asked Bertie, "that man's earthly interests are hooked and buttoned together so that society is founded on cloth, for if that is so, my earthly interests must be very broad indeed."

The tension dissipated in laughter. "And thus," said Serge, "the beginning of wisdom is to look upon clothes until they become invisible."

Irene giggled at his indiscretion. Ella silenced her with a censuring look. Their father spoke. "Serge's German is not yet perfect. I believe what he means is that the philosopher, unhampered by the material, is finally able to see the true man."

"Beatrice's German," said Vicky, "is excellent."

Unwanted attention was to Beatrice like hailstones, something to avoid. They were all waiting for her response. She cleared her throat. "Perhaps Serge meant," she said tentatively, then quickly, like dipping herself into the Solent in May, "that philosophers are tailors who clothe men with their beliefs."

"Well said," declared Bertie. "Very well said, indeed." Vicky smiled. Henry, engaged in conversation with Irene, did not seem to notice.

The Grand Duke left the hall as the wedding guests scraped back their chairs to stroll beneath dark-canvased Vermeers. No one noticed his departure. The supper had taken several hours, and everyone was anxious to move legs grown numb and backs grown stiff.

Vicky came to take Beatrice's arm. "Leave it to me."

"Please, Vicky, this is very awkward," said Beatrice.

"Don't be such a goose."

Vicky led her toward Fritz, Henry, and Bertie, all in full-dress uniform, in earnest argument beside a medieval coffer carved in wreaths and helmeted warriors. Bertie was pontificating. "My dear fellow, the new firepower will cut you to pieces. You are left behind, I am afraid, in the march of military progress. Your own medical field reports illustrate how utterly ineffective is the saber. We have seriously reconsidered the use of cavalry."

"That is because your horses were in deplorable condition by the time they got to Egypt," said Fritz.

"Besides," said Henry, "we no longer employ tactics of only saber and lance. The combination is steel and pistol, or steel and carbine, in which the Americans have shown such skill, although we still employ the principles of Frederick the Great, for which we are world famous. While others ride stirrup to stirrup, we ride knee to knee in the closest formation possible. This makes us, double armed, a rather invincible war machine. And always with a second line. That army which brings the last reserve is always the most successful." He heard the rustle of skirts and turned. "Cavalry is never weaker than after a success, when men and horses are blown, lines disordered, orders are not heard . . ."

"A fresh force falling upon such confusion," said Vicky, putting her arm through that of Fritz, "will always put it to rout. The infantry may be steadfast, but there is something dashing and chivalrous about the cavalry."

"You see," said Fritz, "my wife has grasped the elemental difference."

"My sister forgets," said Bertie, "that Frederick the Great did not know his right from his left. He painted two terrible pictures when he had the gout, one, which hangs in Potsdam, of an unclothed female with two left feet."

"Potsdam is full of strange things," said Henry. "Some of the men swear that the white horse of Odin wanders nightly on the long bridge, looking for a rider."

An aide came to whisper in Bertie's ear. He excused himself and followed after him. Vicky led Fritz away, saying she wanted to say a few words to the bride.

Henry and Beatrice were left standing. Her impulse was to run. Her hands began to perspire inside her gloves. He spoke first. "Do you believe that Odin's horse appears? I think not. That is a soldier's yearnings. For what does an English princess yearn?"

Beatrice seemed discomfited. "I can't engage in the sort of conversation you are accustomed to," she said.

He stepped closer. A lock of his black hair escaped the slick of scented Macassar oil and fell over his forehead. "You are quite formidable, you know," he said, "for one so reticent."

"You make fun of me."

"But I don't." He turned toward a window slit high into the thick wall. "You are forbidding, distant, like any star out there I cover with my finger. Just when I have you fixed in my sights, one blink, and you are gone."

"I'm not distant, just unable to say entertaining things, and I'm not capricious." She dropped her voice and looked about her. "I couldn't get away."

He gazed intently into her eyes. "I do not find you a Valkyrie at all. They are too strident. You are more like the Lorelei, gentle, utterly feminine, no ability to make idle conversation, only the power to drown men in your eyes."

Lady Ely was suddenly at her elbow, whispering in her ear. The Queen was waiting for her.

"Excuse me," she said, blushing, wondering how much her mother's lady-in-waiting had heard and turning to scurry past the milling wedding guests, with Lady Ely behind her.

The bridegroom came to put his arm around his brother. They watched as Beatrice left the hall. "Well?"

"She is not backward as you say," replied Henry. "She is merely inward. Like a flower at night."

"And you are the sun to shine upon her and cause her to open her petals?"

"I am surprised that one who has been through the ordeal of a wedding ceremony would have wits left for metaphor."

"Passion has honed my mind," said Louis.

"Then remind me not to ask you anything important next month. I will expect to find you very dull."

"I hope so," said Louis.

"He did what?" asked Victoria, eating a boiled egg in a gold egg cup. "He married the Kalomine woman? This I cannot believe. When?"

"The night of Victoria and Louis's wedding, Mama," replied Bertie.

"That stupid foolish man. How dare he?" She placed her gold spoon down. A Highland servant cleared away the egg cup. "He has placed me in the most awkward position. If I leave Darmstadt, it creates scandal. If I remain, it looks as if I approve the marriage. It must be annulled. That is clear. You must see to this at once, Bertie. You must arrange for an annulment immediately."

"Annulments, Mama, are only possible under certain circumstances."

"That is what I want you to find out. Untying a morganatic knot is simple. Your grandfather's marriage to Julie de St. Laurent was annulled. The lawyers find a suitable form as soon as they agree on the aims. You will interview the woman. You will first find out if the marriage has been consummated."

"Forgive me, Mama, but don't we have every reason to believe that it has?"

"Nonsense. The man drinks sherry whenever I see him and is certainly exhausted from his daughter's wedding, not to mention his own. After seeing that woman freely for two years, and no longer twenty years old, I doubt he was ruled by passion stronger than his dyspepsia."

Bertie stroked his beard. "Mama, we really can't—"

"Don't tell me what we can't do, Bertie. Tell me rather what we can do. Call the Grand Duke at once, Sir Henry. I wish to see him immediately. Now go, Bertie. There can be no delays."

Within minutes Secretary Ponsonby ushered in the Grand Duke Louis.

"How could you, Louis?" she asked. "How could you place us in such an awkward position?"

He bowed from the doorway, then came forward quickly to kiss her hand. "Mama, I did not realize that you would react in this way." Sweat beaded on his forehead.

"Why? Can you answer that? I appealed to you, and you disregarded my appeal. I told you that if you married the Russian woman, you would lower yourself so much that you would have no place near me, nor any of your brothers and sisters-in-law, ever again. I told you that you could not marry before Irene, and she is much too young. Selfishness has no place in royalty, Louis, none at all. I would like to understand you but find that I cannot."

"We are deeply in love, Mama."

"Love? You have a sacred duty to Hesse, to Germany, to England. What does love have to do with royal position and responsibility?"

"It is everything to me, Mama."

"You are simple, Louis, and you are foolish, incapable of managing your own affairs. I shall have to manage them for you. This marriage is to be annulled at once."

"Mama, that is impossible."

"Indeed, it is very possible. It is not only possible, it is essential that it be done immediately. The Prince of Wales is interviewing the woman at this very moment. You are not to see her again."

The Grand Duke strode to the window and back again. What was happening to him was beyond belief. "But she is my wife," he explained softly, as if perhaps the idea had not occurred to her.

"A technicality. She is a crafty schemer who has duped you and made you the joke of all Europe. Did you really think you could defy all convention, all that is moral, and not bear any repercussion?"

He lowered himself slowly into a chair with twisted pilaster carvings, shaking his head. "I did not dream that you would take this harsh position."

"Did you think at all of the matter? It is inconceivable to me that you thought of it. If you did, you would have concluded another course of action. Marriage! You are not yet in your dotage to be so gullible. You have caused us great pain."

He put his head in his hands. "Mama, I am so sorry."

"Leave me. You have done enough. You are not to see the woman, Louis. We must drive her away, this very night, and you must sign this decree of expulsion which I have already had drawn up by your own ministers. Good God, if I could drive the creature out with my own hands." She signaled to Sir Henry, who lay the paper on the desk and offered the pen. The Grand Duke's shoulders sagged. He took the pen and signed, then turned toward Victoria.

"She will be devastated. I am afraid she will do something tragic."

"Don't delude yourself with such romantic notions," replied Victoria. "The tragic thing has already been done, and I aim to remedy it with the swiftest speed. The Prince of Wales will communicate with her. You are to remain apart. Guards are being posted at her doors to ensure that she does not leave the palace until escorted under guard."

The news that the Grand Duke's bride had been escorted to the frontier with forty mounted policemen and now languished in some convent spread quickly through the village. That the English were to blame was also known. Flags and bunting were taken down. The narrow streets on which Beatrice rode with Vicky were empty; the only movement was an occasional pair of eyes peering from round oriel windows flanking the gables of the roofs. Inside a rough-stone lower story, a cobbler, hearing the carriage, looked up from his bench, put a handful of tacks in his mouth, and ducked his head.

"Are you certain, Vicky," asked Beatrice. "I so dislike leaving her alone."

"The bow should rest just beneath your ear," said Vicky, retying the velvet ribbons of Beatrice's straw bonnet, "to show up your chin. You have a nice chin, not like some of us, and you should show it to advantage. As for Mama, she is hardly alone. Ministers rush in and out of her apartments like flakes in a storm, at least those that have not taken to their beds. Lady Ely and Sir Henry are at her side, as well as Bertie, who tells me he still has a headache from the Kalomine woman's shrieks. Mama will be quite preoccupied this afternoon, I assure you."

They reached a wide clearing in the forest where a wall of thick canvas had been erected under the trees. In the center of the clearing was a pavilion covered with branches cut from fir trees and decorated with wreaths of flowers and laurel. Vicky led them to wicker chairs upon which they sat with other ladies of the wedding party, while the men, Henry among them, stood at the pavilion's opening, holding their guns firmly to their shoulders, lining up breech to muzzle. At a signal, the canvas fence was drawn back to form a gateway. There was dead silence, then the hunting cry of the chasseurs, the thunder of hooves, the crash of branches, and the sight of frightened stags and hinds driven into the clearing. The guns fired all at once, and a band, hidden in the trees, began to play martial music.

The whole affair took less than ten minutes. Beatrice was shaken, visibly pale.

"Try to collect yourself," said Vicky as huntsmen crouched on the red grass to slit the throats of animals that had not been killed outright. "He's coming this way, and he's desperate for a chance to talk to you again."

Henry disengaged himself from the knot of men, one complaining that his gun was breech heavy, another arguing that his method of keeping both eyes open accounted for his greater success. He bent to kiss Vicky's hand, then clicked his heels with a smart snap before Beatrice, who greeted him with a proper inclination of her head.

His presence was overwhelming. He seemed to fill the pavilion. Vicky initiated conversation, gay chatter as effortless as the trilling piccolo of the hidden band. Beatrice tried to contribute but was distracted by the sight of deer and rabbit dragged across the grass and slung from poles, with black drops of clotted blood oozing from their hides. She turned her face.

"I think you do not like this place," he said.

"No," she replied, grateful for his understanding.

"I should be honored to escort you back."

They left while the Grand Duke berated a huntsman for beating the bushes with a cocked gun, Vicky asking under her breath why Beatrice always had to make things so difficult and the German women laughing in whispers behind their coffee cups about the frightened *Engländerin*.

At first they rode in silence, Vicky annoyed, Beatrice ashamed that she had been so silly, Henry sitting opposite, looking over both their heads. Soon they were on the cobblestone streets of Darmstadt, the woods and clearing out of sight, hidden by the rooftops.

"May is your month," he said to Beatrice.

"Actually it isn't," she replied. "I was born in April."

His saber, glinting in the sunlight, flashed across his thigh. "I wasn't speaking of your birthday, only of the quality of the light, pale, golden, soft. It matches you."

Beatrice masked her delight with a bland expression, eyebrows only slightly raised, lips shaped in the proper aristocratic pout, as if some iron had pressed flat her smile.

They decided to walk. Beatrice, wishing desperately for something to say, lifted her skirts to clear a curbstone and noticed with dismay that her maid had neglected to fasten one of her boot buttons.

"In that direction," he was saying, "although you cannot see it, is the Rhine where the Lorelei waits." He looked at her and smiled, and she wondered if he had noticed the open scalloped buttonhole. "And over there, the palace theater. Are you familiar with Gilbert and Sullivan? I am very fond of them."

"Every Englishman knows of Gilbert and Sullivan," she replied.

"They have become a staple," said Vicky, "like kidney pie. I heard they're collaborating on a new operetta, something about Japan. So little is known about that quaint little country. Whatever will they find to write about?"

"Their music is so engaging, ma'am," replied Henry, "I do not believe it matters very much how the libretto reads."

"I disagree," said Beatrice. "Gilbert and Sullivan promote their satire first. The music's purpose is to make it palatable. It is because your native tongue is not English, Prince, that you did not see the satire."

"Perhaps so. But then, please tell me, what is satiric about"—he began to sing—" 'let us gaily tread the measure, making most of fleeting leisure, hail it as a true ally, though it perish by and by.' "

Beatrice, to Vicky's surprise, joined him, in a light, sweet voice. " 'Every moment brings a treasure, of its own especial pleasure, though the moments quickly die, greet them gaily as they fly.' "

By the time they reached the high wall of the palace and the gardens inside where willows drooped over drowsing lily pads, Vicky had fallen back, and Beatrice had put the incidents of the shoot out of her mind. Bystanders strolling between careless beds of roses and rhododendrons nodded and bowed to the royal party, then turned to whisper behind twirling parasols.

"The Crown Princess walks farther behind us by the minute," said Henry. "I expect to learn soon that she is back in Berlin."

"My sister is considerate."

"Does that mean it is with your approval?"

"What else could it mean?" Her blue eyes were open, trusting.

Any other woman, he thought, would have parried the question. "You are quite disarming. Now I am at a loss for words, except to say what a luxury it is to be uninterrupted." He walked more closely beside her over snapping twigs, the tops of his boots brushing against the silk of her crackling gown. For a while they were silent. He stared ahead. "I long to touch you," he said. She did not reply. "Did I offend you?"

"You could not offend me."

"I did when we first met. I spoke to you as if you were another silly woman with whom one only fences."

"You frightened me. You didn't offend me."

"And do I frighten you now?"

She lifted her eyes and smiled. "Not since I've learned that you sing off-key."

He laughed. She saw that his teeth were even, white. "There is a pulse that beats at your temple. There," he said, pointing with a gloved finger. "Just above the bow of your bonnet. If we were alone, I would untie your streamers and place my lips on it."

"If we were alone, I would turn my head."

"To foil me?"

"To assist you."

A blue-jacketed officer of the dragoons came quickly across the grounds toward Vicky, his golden epaulets quivering as he ran. He began to speak in urgent hushed tones. Vicky seemed distressed. Her hand flew to the jet and gauze capelet that covered her shoulders. She hobbled toward Beatrice and Henry with the subaltern beside her.

"Who told her?" she was heard to ask. "Everything was kept secret."

"It is believed that Herr Stumm sent the telegram."

"That busybody. And where is he now?"

"Herr Stumm has been sent on a special mission to Carlsruhe."

"Coward. He has run to Carlsruhe, you mean. Very well, please inform the rest of our entourage." Then she turned to Beatrice. "The Empress has commanded that we all return immediately to Berlin. It is the Kalomine situation, of course, as we had feared. She is furious and insists that we all leave at once from what she calls a contaminated court. Beatrice, please, see to Moretta. I am told she is in our apartments, terribly upset. Perhaps you can think of something comforting."

With a tentative backward glance, Beatrice hurried in mincing steps toward the castle. When she was safely out of earshot, Vicky put her hand on Henry's arm. "A few words of advice, Henry. Don't return to Potsdam, not yet. Use any excuse that you can. This is very difficult for me to say. If you love my sister, as I think you do, you must make her return that love with ardor, for when she goes back to England, the campaign against you will be dreadful. Do you understand my meaning?"

"Clearly. It is essentially a matter of endeavoring to deploy more quickly than the adversary, of surprising him if possible, and of seizing the advantages of the terrain."

Vicky smiled. "Is it possible for you to think in other than military terms? Of course not. You are a soldier."

Victoria and Vicky sat side by side on a fern and floral satin brocade settee. Victoria wore her wire-rimmed spectacles, and she rubbed the space where they rested on her nose. A black-bordered pencil sketch of a back view of Alicky in flounces and sash lay beside her. "I must say I cannot blame her, although I disagree with the haste. Surely Augusta realizes that I do all I can to remedy the situation. At this moment, decisive action toward annulment is under way. A messenger has ridden to the convent to offer her a title and a sizable estate if she surrenders all rights as Louis's wife."

"I don't understand," said Vicky, "why the Tsar cannot recall her. Surely Serge could be trusted with the request. That would settle matters quickly enough."

"That is exactly what he will not do for England," said Victoria. "Louis is quite disconsolate, but he will get over it. I have invited him to Balmoral. Under the circumstances, I would not push the matter of Sandro with Moretta when you return. I would wait. This is not the time. And Vicky, do not think that because I have been occupied I have not noticed certain occurrences."

"What occurrences are you referring to, Mama?"

Victoria resettled the spectacles over her ears and picked up her pencil and sketch. She began to feather in the sash. "The meetings between Henry and Beatrice. They have been seen, combing the grounds like pigs searching for truffles, with you bringing up the rear."

"Henry and Beatrice are only part of harmless excursions, Mama. An afternoon's diversion in which all of us participate."

Victoria was having none of it. "Baby is not used to men. All of this can be quite confusing for one who is unaccustomed to such attentions." She wet the tip of her pencil and blurred a flounce.

Vicky decided to change tactics. "Beatrice is twenty-seven years old, Mama. If she is not accustomed, it is time she were. She should be thinking of marriage."

Victoria lifted her eyes from her sketch. "She is to remain with me. I have told you the last time we had this discussion that it is her duty as the last-born child and her wish. Someday you will see, Vicky, that your baby is the last link to your husband. You must not interfere in matters that do not concern you. In any case, the matter is closed. Beatrice and I leave for England as planned. Two days is hardly time to gather one's staff, much less undertake the complications of a dalliance."

Hurried preparations to return to England had been speckled with restless, meager moments, furtive brushings, veiled glances at tedious coffees, and one clandestine meeting beside a gargoyle, to grope their way down a crooked passage into a wine cellar with romanesque vaulting, kissing until breathless beneath a fresco.

As the time grew nearer, desperation made them bold. They conspired to meet a last time in the castle in a little-known music room dating from the time of round-barreled Mecklenburg coaches.

Beatrice selected her dress with care, standing imperiously in a six-pound petticoat that had been inserted with steel loops, while she exchanged a black mohair for a costume of pleated gray woolen skirt and black velveteen tunic with frilled white cuffs. She insisted that her maid also change her black kid boots for bronze kid with patent leather toe caps. She wanted Spanish wool to rouge her cheeks and pearl powder to dust her nose; there was none. The crisping irons were missing. She complained because a freckle that her maid had treated was still there. Her maid bobbed a curtsy and explained that it would have worked had they had one part of Jamaican rum to add to two parts lemon juice. As it was, the remedy was only half effective.

Beatrice did not examine the implications of such a meeting. She had only two concerns. The first, that he would not find her comely; the second, that she needed to see his face, hear his voice, feel his lips and arms about her once more before she left. That her thoughts were indelicate and shocking did not matter. She put such things aside, as she had learned to do with other feelings that were cumbersome.

Henry would be there first. She was to follow a very old half-blind retainer with an old-fashioned three-cornered hat and a staff, who would lead her to the chamber. It was clear that the porter did not know who she was. He kept calling her lady, telling her, in a long, rambling story, of the death of Frittie, the little son of the English Grand Duchess who fell out of a window and bled to death and whom he sometimes caught glimpses of in lonely corridors. Leo. Tears flooded her eyes. What would Leo say? Leo would be glad for her.

She entered the dimly lit room, and the hall porter closed the door behind her. Candles flickered from cobwebbed crystal chandeliers. The walls were covered with elaborately carved gilded panels of bow knots and musical instruments, harps, horns, pipes, violins, mandolins, and tambours, and large, rounded chairs with fluted, tapered legs lacquered in flamelike iridescence still bore indentations.

He was leaning against the back of a sofa, his gloves off.

She walked toward him, her heels clicking across the parquet floor. As she drew nearer, she noticed that the back of his hand had black curling hairs.

"I am weary," he murmured, "of bits and pieces of you, of moments like unfinished thoughts, a glance which I must mask, a sigh which I must turn into a cough, a touch on your sleeve that I pretend is a courtesy, and the servants, everywhere as always, like the dust they chase."

He kissed her hand, lingering, rubbing, pulled back her gloves, to kiss the inside of her wrist, grazing her palm with his moustache. She gasped, remembering how exquisite were his kisses. Suddenly, he grasped her wrists and pulled her close, kissing her lips first softly, then crushing his mouth against her teeth. She found herself yielding open her mouth, yearning for his tongue, ashamed of such wanton kisses, yet resolute. She thought for only a moment, somewhat with surprise, that only Frenchmen kissed in that way, according to what her sister Louise had said; then she dissolved in his arms like sugar in tea. He unbuckled his sword, which he set on a console, then led her to the sofa.

"I must have word from you," he said, "the moment you return. You must write immediately and tell me when I may visit."

"Yes, yes," she said.

"I do not want you to forget me."

She wondered how he could have thought such a thing was possible. He told her he loved her. He said it in German, and it sounded like whispers. Then he took her hand and kissed it, brushing his lips across her knuckles as he engaged her eyes, and turned her hand over to kiss her palm, gently nipping the fleshy part in his teeth until she thought she would surely swoon. Nothing she had ever known, least of all the concept of pure love, which promoted devotion as a chaste abstraction, prepared her for the swimming heat, the mindlessness, the urgency.

She unbuttoned slowly the top button of her high-necked bodice. Her fingers awkwardly, stiffly, at her throat, slowly and deliberately.

"My dearest love," he said, closing her fingers in his hand, "you cannot know what you are doing." That she was under seal brought him up short. He was astounded that her passion matched his, that, inexperienced, she wanted him in the way of courtesans and older married women and a recent mistress whose expenses caused his father in fury to terminate the affair. He had gone too far. The responsibility was his. It was his duty to put things right.

He held her on the narrow sofa, stroking her hair, which had come undone, and kissing her eyelids, thinking they had come narrowly close to ruining his chances. In addition, the strategy was sounder. She would want him all the more.

She buried her flushed face in his tunic, her skin itching from his moustache. Did anyone else feel this, she wondered.

He was silent.

"Is something wrong, Henry?" she asked.

"I am worried."

"There was no one in the corridor except Franz. We're quite safe, as you promised."

"It is not our privacy that concerns me. It is the Queen, my darling. She will oppose us, of that I am quite sure, and she can be a formidable foe. We see of what she is capable when she is opposed. I fear that when you return to England, you will not have the strength to hold your own against her. You are so gentle, so sweet. You are simply no match for her."

She lifted herself on one elbow, her hair streaming over her eyes. "What happened with Louis of Hesse has nothing to do with us. Mama was in love herself. When I explain how we feel, she will be all for us."

"And how do you feel? You have not yet told me."

"I feel like a thistle spinning in the sun."

Leave-taking at the train station was, as with most royal journeys, chaotic. A dispirited band played while a guard of honor stood at attention, and a bustling retinue, under the direction of Ladies Ely and Churchill, dealt with the Queen's bed and desk, couch and mirror, and gallery of family pictures, which went with her everywhere. Sir Henry, who was trying to decide whether to reveal his information that there was something between Fräulein Kohausen and the Prince of Bulgaria, sprinted forward to the engineer to give him instructions for strict speed limits and frequent stops, to allow the Queen time to change clothing, take her meals, and the numerous notables waiting along the way to make their addresses. Victoria and Beatrice stood waiting on the platform, while a few meters distant, an abashed and sorrowful Louis of Hesse kissed his children good-bye.

Henry was waiting in the shadows of a clock. He came to bow before Victoria and Beatrice.

"Prince Henry," said Victoria, "I am surprised to find you still in Darmstadt. Your party was ordered back to Berlin two days ago."

"Other matters detained me, ma'am," he replied.

"I cannot imagine what could have taken precedence over royal command," she said.

Lady Churchill, who had been watching, stepped closer. "Which of your small cases, ma'am, do you wish close at hand?" she asked.

"It does not seem possible, Lady Jane, that after the pains I took to point them out, you have forgotten."

"Forgive me, ma'am," said Lady Churchill. "I have been feeling unwell. My memory needs jarring."

Victoria was clearly annoyed. "If you knew you were feeling ill, you should have left such details to Lady Ely." She took Lady Churchill's arm and pointed with her stick to the mound of parcels that lay before the door of her personal saloon carriage.

Beatrice glanced nervously in the direction of her mother, clearly uncomfortable. "You should not have come, Henry. It was dear of you, but it will only lead to questions."

"It is my intention that it should lead to questions. And to answers."

"This is not the time for answers. Not when the matter of the annulment of Louis's marriage is so fresh in her mind. Not when she knows she will go back into mourning as soon as we return. She has been unhappy all morning."

He looked worried. "When do you propose to tell her?"

"Soon."

"Make it very soon. Do you wish me at your side when you do?"

"No, dearest. It's better I tell her myself. I'll pick my moment."

Victoria turned, saw them in conversation, gave Beatrice a cold, commanding stare, then, with assistance from Lady Churchill and a servant in Highland dress, boarded the train.

"You will be strong?" he asked.

She turned and hurried after her mother, with Sir Henry at her side to assist her into the dark blue satin and velvet saloon with white quilted ceiling. The train pulled away. Henry stood watching it a long time, even after the band and honor guard dispersed, thinking that in all the rush he had forgotten to ask for a lock of her hair.

CHAPTER TEN

Beatrice sat through subdued and dismal meals served by flitting scarlet footmen in the dark oak-paneled dining room of Windsor, unable to find the right moment to tell her mother her secret.

For one thing, she was afraid. For another, Victoria, returned with relish to dispatches and knightings and audiences with her ministers, was preoccupied. Especially since the Queen had learned that the military was waiting for the Nile to rise so that Gordon could retreat by way of Berber and that Madame Kalomine's attorney published a copy of the marriage document in all the German papers in the same week that Victoria's uncle, Prince Leopold of Saxe-Coburg-Gotha, died.

Just before an audience with Gladstone, Beatrice got so far as to clear her throat, a sound that startled even her, when a footman with violet powder sprinkled into his hair ushered in the Prime Minister. The speech she had so carefully rehearsed, beginning with reference to the bridal couple, proceeding in general to the Battenbergs, and leading finally, specifically, to Henry, scattered like seed puffs as Gladstone explained that Gordon's plan to join forces with the slaver Zebehr was ill founded, since the African general was responsible for the capture and sale of two hundred thousand slaves and the manufacture of forty thousand eunuchs. Beatrice wrote a note in flowing Spenserian script to remind herself to include in her appeal that Victoria always considered German men a cut above.

"Are these eunuchs manufactured," asked Victoria, "in the usual way?" Gladstone, who had put his hands behind his back, folding them together as if they had custody of one another, took on a look of sober resignation. "No, ma'am, my information indicates that the alteration is more . . . complete. The men are buried in the hot sand for their wounds to be cauterized; the half that do not perish in agony are given glass tubes and sent to eunuch farms."

There was silence, the ticking clock issuing a metric rebuke. Beatrice blushed and folded her note, Sir Henry adjusted his stock, and Victoria changed the subject to the franchise bill on which the Commons would soon vote. "You have warned the peers," she said, "that a collision between the two houses would end in the defeat of the House of Lords. Your language, Mr. Gladstone, is inflammatory and far too strong. You must couch your opinions in more conciliatory tones."

Victoria's silvery voice had an edge to it. Beatrice felt the shift as keenly as a blade, and hastily, with perspiring hands, she crumpled the note.

"Your Majesty's concerns," replied Gladstone, "will be given serious consideration, but one must also consider the mood of the nation. It cannot be ignored."

If the days were bad for Beatrice, filled with the anxiety of false starts and aborted attempts, the nights were worse. She yearned for his face, his eyes, his moustache, his shiny high black boots, his impeccably tailored uniform, the way he strode and turned, the tones of his warm, modulated voice resonating through her body, his kisses, the way his tongue licked shamefully between her fingers, memories that made her toss with fever.

It was during the viewing of a new improved magic lantern that Beatrice finally found the courage. The darkness gave her the strength. They sat in the ornate white drawing room, Victoria wearing the blue ribbon of the Garter across her black satin bodice, Beatrice, Louise, short, rude Affie and his lavishly costumed, sullen wife Marie, telling Ella beside her that she need not fear the nihilists, as the Okhrana had them all deported to Siberia. Behind them were Lord Rosebery in the uniform of the Royal Scottish Archers, and his wife Hannah, the daughter of the financier Rothschild, wearing a belt of large single precious stones, the tall, white-moustached and Piccadilly-whiskered Duke of Cambridge, who had just returned from Vienna where he had retrieved his renegade brother-in-law Frank from an elopement with a governess, and in the rear, members of the household, except for Lady Ely, who had poked herself in the eye with the point of her parasol and now lay in bed with cold compresses and a stiff whiskey toddy.

The footmen were extinguishing the candles in the chandeliers with long, tapering silver snuffers. Aleck Yorke, the corpulent groom-in-waiting, was assuring the assembly that what they were about to see would be different from the old flickering stereopticon, from which they all got nauseating headaches.

Two footmen and the diffident inventor wheeled in a wooden apparatus. An assistant set up a screen. Within moments, the drawing room was dim except for a gas lamp glowing behind a pane of glass in the magic lantern.

"I find it unforgivable that Louis did not take supper with us," said Victoria, "although I do not know why I should care. He is so woebegone; he quite takes away my appetite."

Beatrice thought of her portly Hessian brother-in-law wandering dispirited through the halls of Windsor. "He is deeply in love, Mama," she said. "It will take time."

Victoria adjusted her ribbon with a shrug of her shoulder. "Nonsense. He might as well realize that his great love is planning to blackmail him. She refuses to return his letters."

The inventor bowed in the darkened room. His oiled hair flapped forward like a pennant.

"Perhaps it is because they are so dear to her," said Beatrice.

"You know nothing of the world, Benjamina. Remind me to write to Ambassador Ampthill that he must request the German government to speed the annulment."

"If Your Majesty pleases," said Mr. Yorke, "Mr. Donisthorpe will explain just what it is that makes his gadget an improvement."

The inventor brushed back his hair and spoke into the darkened drawing room. "Your Majesty, Your Royal Highnesses, I have eliminated the passage of the shutter which was responsible for the formerly violent contrast of light and dark." With a crank, he began to rotate the whirring, clacking drum, and on the screen before them the figure of a man in a white gym suit enacted a jerking run. There was some applause. This was followed by a man in a gym suit executing a jerking leap into the air.

"The illusion of movement, ma'am, is based," said the inventor, "on the theory of persistence of vision."

He fiddled with the apparatus as his audience rustled and whispered in the dark. Someone laughed. Beatrice leaned close to her mother. She could smell the scent of roses from her mother's center-parted hair. "I wish to marry, Mama."

A duck flew across the screen in spasmodic flutters. "A baffling phenomenon," said the inventor, "this deficiency of the human eye, which persists in seeing the object when it is no longer there."

"What did you say?" whispered Victoria.

"I said, Mama, I wish to marry."

A horse raced on a track, all four hooves lifting off the ground at once. "This is done, ma'am," said Mr. Yorke, "with several cameras, a whole battery of them, I am told."

"It still jerks," complained Victoria. "I don't see the value. If I wanted to see a horse running, I should prefer the real thing without headaches."

"Persons are working, ma'am," said the inventor, "on a continuous strip of thin paper covered with a gelatin emulsion which will do away with any remaining flicker."

Victoria turned to Beatrice. "Is it the married state in general that interests you, or is there a particular person you have in mind?"

"A person, Mama. Prince Henry."

"Louis of Battenberg's brother? You know nothing about him. How can you possibly think you want to marry him?"

The inventor continued his explanation about gelatinous paper heretofore not being thin enough or playing sorry tricks when drying like buckling and shrinking. No one was paying attention. The candles on the chandeliers were lit, bathing the drawing room in soft yellow light. Everyone waited for Victoria's polite applause, while Mr. Yorke, with jeweled fingers flashing, hustled out the bowing inventor and his equipment.

The moment was awkward. Beatrice reproached herself for not having waited. Now she had to stand through an hour of tedious conversation, as tamped and as useless as had been the smothered candles.

Conversation was hushed and tepid. Marie continued to instruct Ella in things Russian, saying that she was disappointed in her brother the Tsar for doing away with the gorgeous uniformed guards of her childhood, especially the Circassians in their chain armor. Lady Rosebery had seen *Lohengrin* at Covent Garden. Victoria inquired as to what she thought of the performance. Lady Rosebery replied that Madame Albani as Elsa showed refined grace and poetic charm, and in the duet with Lohengrin in the bridal chamber, displayed tragic power.

Affie led Lord Rosebery to the Chippendale carved doors, telling him of an old laborer on his estate at Eastwell named Plant who could neither read nor write but who was, according to tradition, a Plantagenet, an illegitimate son of Richard III. When they were safely through the doors, he reminded Rosebery that he had promised to obtain for him a golden key, which Bertie, as well as all the male members of the Rothschilds, held to the foyer of the Danse at the Grand Opera, where one could converse at one's leisure with the posturing ladies of the corps de ballet.

Lord Rosebery smiled and slipped an object into the Duke of Edinburgh's gloved hand as Victoria rose to bid good night to the assembly.

Beatrice quickly stepped to her mother's side and followed her out of the drawing room, as did the lady-in-waiting, the maids of honor, and the equerries. Louise, her pretty face dusted with luminous pearl powder, sought to join the sober entourage, but Victoria pleaded fatigue, adding that she found Louise's stayless gown unsuitable for court.

Beatrice and Victoria rode the crimson and gold lift in silence. Once in Victoria's sitting room, the Dowager Duchess of Atholl removed Victoria's diamond coronet and veil as Victoria spoke in derision of Princess Mary, the sister of the Duke of Cambridge, married to the penniless Prince of Teck, who lived far beyond her means. "Fat Mary," Victoria said, "is served right for marrying a man so many years her junior. Keeping Frank straight takes up as much of the Duke's time as his duties as commander in chief of the Army."

"Yes, Mama," replied Beatrice. She came to sit at her mother's side, carefully settling the drooping puff of deep blue satin of her skirts and the butterfly bows of Chantilly lace that covered it. She drew a breath, then spoke in a rush, her words like a freshet suddenly released from ice, spilling over pebbles and rocks and splashing over mossy frozen banks.

"You asked before how I know that I love Henry. It is a feeling that has accumulated. I don't wish you to believe that it was some sudden silly thing such as are in novels. My sentiment is too tender, too profound, to be so trivialized. I know I want to marry him as clearly as I know my name. I know I am miserable without him, empty, incomplete."

"You're still on the subject." Victoria shook her head, now free of the weight she had borne all evening. Her diamond and emerald ear bobs glittered as they swung. "I would have hoped you had forgotten by now. You speak as if you were a vase, dear. You met the man once, twice. That is hardly enough time to decide upon what breed of dog one wants to add to one's kennels, much less a husband."

"I know all I need to know."

The Duchess left to instruct the maids, who waited in the green-and-gold dressing room beyond. She was heard to say that the Queen would need three hot water bags in her bed, as her knee was especially paining her.

"Would you really leave me all alone, Benjamina?" asked Victoria, her voice now soft. "With everyone off and married and Leopold gone along with Alice and Johnnie Brown and your dear papa. I will soon be sixty-five. You are all I have left, and yet you would desert me in my last years?"

Beatrice began to pull at a bow, fingering its edge with her kid glove. "Perhaps leave is too final a word, Mama. We might think of it in another way. If I married, I would simply take up residence elsewhere, but I would visit often, as do the others, more than the others, for I would come every day to help you."

"You would live in Germany. Your income would be drastically reduced. So would your station. Your rank would be the lowest of any, except for the woman whom Cambridge calls his wife."

"That is unimportant to me."

Victoria pursed her lips. "Never," she said.

"Please don't say never, Mama."

"I will say what I please. I will never allow you to marry Henry of Battenberg. You are my baby. I need you with me. Do I not favor you over the others? Did you not hear me tell Louise not to join us? Surely that should tell you something. If nothing else, it should show you in what special regard I hold you."

For a moment, Beatrice faltered. The skirmish was over, and the battle had not yet been joined, all because Mama looked so helpless, so vulnerable. She paused, then remembered her resolve. This time she would begin more slowly, mention all the positive aspects, and remember to speak more gently. Mama must not think this urgent. She must see the reason, the logic, the clarity of it all. Then surely she would understand. It had not been presented properly. Sir Henry said presentation was everything. "I am not unappreciative, Mama, you know that, but I'm twenty-seven. Ella is getting married next month, and she's not yet twenty. I want . . . I want a life of my own. Before it is too late."

"That sounds like Vicky or Louise. Did they tell you to say that? You speak in romantic notions. You do have a life of your own, and you are living it as far as I can see." The Duchess returned from Victoria's bedroom, her feet aching from her long stand. Victoria turned to her. "Please tell Lord Rosebery to wait outside, Duchess. I shall want to see him."

"I love Henry," Beatrice said as the elderly Duchess teetered to the door, mastering the discomfort of her swollen feet with an elegant lift of her brow.

"How are you so sure that that is what you are feeling?" asked Victoria. "That you don't simply require a tonic?"

"Love is easy to recognize."

"What do you know of love? I loved your father, truly, deeply. You cheapen the word. One must love, but one must not fall in love. The two are completely different. The first is sublime. The second is a sorry spectacle. Henry is very handsome and used to women making fools of themselves over him, as I begin to suspect you have. He knows exactly what to say and what to do in such matters. You do not. Further, he is penniless. Bismarck has seen to that, and he is the product of a morganatic marriage. He is only partially royal."

"So is Louis." Beatrice's voice rose in pitch. It began to tremble. Tears flooded her eyes and shimmered in the candlelight. "You didn't deny him to Victoria. So is Sandro. You don't discourage Moretta." The threads that held the bow in place began to rip.

"You speak of my granddaughters. They are not the daughters of the Queen of England."

"Surely, Mama, that can't be the reason. With six brothers and sisters before me, I'm too far down the line of succession for that to make a difference."

"Events have a way of happening. One never knows what the future will bring. For the moment, there are certain things about Henry that if you were to know, I am confident you would see how silly is this whole business. What are you doing to your gown? For heaven's sake, leave it alone. If you are nervous, Beatrice, ask Dr. Reid for a sedative."

"I don't care what has happened before we met. I only know of what I feel today."

"You are too innocent to be so certain. Since your judgment appears to be impaired, you must trust mine."

"It doesn't matter."

Victoria's words became sharp and crisp, and she spit them out as if they were melon seeds. "It has to matter. You are no ordinary person. If you have learned nothing else, surely you have learned that. Everything royalty says, everything royalty does, matters. Consider the Duke of Cambridge here tonight. He was so foolish as to believe that he could do as he pleased. The Dublin actress he calls his wife may not appear with him at any public function. I cannot receive her, nor can any member of the family. Because I never sanctioned the marriage, the union is illegitimate, as are his five children. They are no different from that Plant fellow, the gardener on Affie's estate."

"I did not know, ma'am," said the Duchess of Atholl, "that Mrs. Fitz George had been an actress."

"You forget yourself, Duchess," said Victoria sharply.

The Dowager Duchess of Atholl begged pardon and shifted her feet, thinking how lucky Lady Ely had been to poke herself in the eye.

"What has that to do with me?" asked Beatrice.

Victoria regarded her youngest daughter as if she had never seen her before. "You are being very stubborn. Very well. I did not want to tell you, but I see that I shall have to make you understand. Henry has been on the books of a Madame La Croix, a notorious French match-maker whose husband translates Greek plays, which certainly does not recommend her. Do you know what it means for a man to be on the books of a matchmaker? It means he is merchandise, like a pair of gloves in a shop window. He was listed with other minor princelings of no money and dubious title. Now the truly absurd part. No one wanted him. She almost matched him to the niece of General Gallifet, a silly heiress who eloped with some Turk. The marriage was annulled, and the girl was dragged back. Then the La Croix woman offered the family Henry. The family turned him down. And that after the girl had been disgraced. Madame La Croix had to let him go. He was unplaceable."

"Perhaps there are things about me that might be unattractive to him. In any case, it is gossip. Petty and malicious, and I don't believe it."

"Why not? Because he is above registering with a marriage broker?"

Beatrice looked up. "Because he is too wonderful. No woman in her right mind would not have him if she could."

"This is giving me a headache," said Victoria.

The Duchess of Atholl reached into her reticule for the bottle of crystal salts from Karlsbad prescribed by Dr. Jenner and stirred a spoonful into a glass of Apollinaris water and Auld Kirk whiskey.

Victoria took the nightcap and drank the contents, then handed back the glass. "Tell Lord Rosebery, if you please, Duchess, that I will see him now."

"I'm sorry, Mama," said Beatrice, as the lady-in-waiting, her hands clasped above her waist, walked slowly toward the door. "It can wait until the morning."

"We shall never speak of it again."

Beatrice stood and found that her knees were trembling. "You can't mean that."

"Let me make myself clear, Beatrice. I mean it strongly and irrevocably. There will be no more talk of marriage to Prince Henry or to any man. As long as you persist, I have nothing further to say to you."

With a sickening feeling, Beatrice realized that she had gone too far. It had been so easy to do, like slipping down a mossy bank. Why did she think of that? So long ago. Who was it standing before her laughing, whose boots she had slid into with green-stained pinafore, tall, very tall, smelling of cloves. She tried to bring the memory into focus when Lord Rosebery entered the sitting room, his clean-shaven face boyish, ruddy. "Your Majesty," he said, bowing. "Your Royal Highness."

Victoria seemed pleased to see him. "Gladstone has suggested, Lord Rosebery, that you plan to ask for a select committee in the House of Lords to consider means to expedite the passage of the franchise bill. I had hoped that you would work to shut the door on the thing."

"Forgive me, ma'am, but one cannot shut the door on two million working men." He stood before the fireplace. Behind him, on the marble mantelpiece, flanked by china vases preserved in glass domes, chimed an Empire clock.

"I can see," she said, "that you are going to be obdurate. It is a peculiar trait of Gladstone's which you seem disposed to mimic. It does not become you. Very well. There is another matter in which you can be of assistance. I have heard some unpleasant gossip," she said, "that I expect you will be able to put to rest."

"I will do all I can to be of help, ma'am." His blue eyes were as clear as water. Beatrice looked away. Perhaps if she withheld hospitality, he would leave more quickly. Then she could resolve Victoria's ultimatum. Surely Mama did not mean what she had said. Surely the threat was made in anger. When Lord Rosebery was gone, which should be soon, they would settle things.

"You are acquainted with that Lumley person," asked Victoria, "from whom my dearest departed son obtained the villa in Cannes?"

"I am, ma'am. Augustus Lumley is a friend."

"Then you are privy to information to which others are not."

"That depends, ma'am."

"I will come to the point." Victoria's lips trembled. She quickly mastered the tremor. "I have heard of a certain party at a Villa de la Bocca. I have heard that the Duke of Albany was at this party. Does this bring anything to mind?"

"It does, ma'am."

Victoria lifted her head. "I heard that the party was given by Americans."

"The Hoffmans, ma'am, are German Americans."

"It's the same thing. And that the Duke was persuaded to dance by these persons of little sense, who knew that he had hemophilia, that any pressure, any scratch, would cause the bleeding. I have heard"—

her voice caught like a sleeve on a fence post—"that he danced all night, that the dancing killed him, and not the fall down a flight of steps, as we had been told."

"I was not there, ma'am."

"Don't fence with me. Is this what you heard to be true?"

"It is, ma'am."

Victoria seemed to slump into herself. Her ribbon buckled over her breast. "Who else knows?"

"I don't have the answer to that, ma'am, but I'm certain that it can only be a trusted few."

"It is my understanding that other members of my family knew," said Victoria. "I am referring to the Prince of Wales." Lord Rosebery paused, his light blue eyes steady and direct. "Your silence confirms our suspicions," said Victoria. "It is late, Lord Rosebery. Good evening."

There would be no rejoinder, no explanation, no salvage. The audience was terminated. Adjusting the tartan at his shoulder, the Scots nobleman bowed and backed out of the sitting room.

Beatrice hung her head in her lap. "Say you did not mean what you said before, Mama, about not speaking to me. I do not think I could bear it if you meant it."

"How heartless you are, Beatrice. After what you have just heard. Helen, of course, is not to know of the party at Cannes and the dancing. It would break her heart."

"Leo loved to dance," said Beatrice.

"Do you understand the implications of what Lord Rosebery has told us? I cannot think that you truly understand when all you have to say is nonsense."

"I understand that Leo is gone," replied Beatrice. "Nothing anyone says, good or evil, will bring him back. And I'd rather think that he died from dancing. A fall down a flight of steps is much too ignominious."

"You shock me. I think it is the influence of Louise. Whenever she visits, everything is unsettled. Do I understand, then, that you will continue to press for Henry?"

"I cannot help myself."

"Then I will help you to help yourself. Do not address me again until you have given up this preposterous idea." Victoria signaled to the Duchess that she wished to be assisted from the sofa. Beatrice moved to help, but Victoria turned from her and leaned instead on the arm of her lady-in-waiting. "The varnish on the sofa arm," she said with irritation, "comes off like jam. Please speak to Sir John."

For a few moments, Beatrice stood alone in the sitting room, waiting for her knees to stop buckling. An impulse to sweep the chiming clock from the mantelpiece was transformed into clenched fists. Yeomen of the guard in embroidered tunics closed the doors behind her. Mama would change her mind, she thought, when she was rested and not out of sorts. It was the news of Leo's dancing. Why could not Rosebery have altered the truth? What difference did it make? Leo was gone, and nothing could bring him back.

Louise was standing in the corridor, idly examining curios in a cabinet when Beatrice left Victoria's sitting room. "I remember these jade elephants. One has a chip on its trunk. When I was little, I thought that the other one had bit him. Rosebery looked upset. Did Mama give him a wigging?"

Beatrice picked up her skirts. "You know that I can't reveal privy information," she replied.

"Don't be such a prig, Benjamina. For heaven's sake, tell me what it was about. I promise to be satisfied with a clue."

They descended a white-and-gold staircase, touching lightly with their fingertips the crimson velvet rail. "Bertie has kept certain information from Mama. She's furious with him."

Louise sniffed. "I shouldn't worry about Bertie. He's more of a despot than she is."

"How can you say that?"

"Because it's true. Bertie wields a sovereignty of his own design. He is far more powerful and autocratic than Mama ever could be."

"You exaggerate."

Two footmen carrying kettles of boiling water stepped aside to permit them to pass into an octagonal hall with a ribbed Gothic roof.

"But I don't," said Louise. "Bertie is able to decree life or death. A few hints, and one is ostracized; a word of recommendation, and life becomes paradise on earth for the lucky one. He made the social position of the Rothschilds. In his own way, Bertie has strengths Mama never had."

"What kind? They can't be very important. Bertie knows very little of what is going on."

"You don't know? The people, silly. They adore him."

"They adore Mama." The pain had returned. It had been so long. Like something hidden, lying in wait. She clutched her hands together.

"They revere Mama, but she is distant, unapproachable. Bertie, on the other hand, is jolly and accessible. He likes the ladies; he doesn't dress in regimental uniform and spurs but prefers a pot hat and a rumpled hunting jacket. Underneath it all, though, he is a tyrant. Believe me. If you give me the tiniest hint of what Bertie kept from Mama, I will tell you what Vicky wrote to me about Darmstadt." Louise laughed at her sister's blush. "You are as transparent, darling, as a piece of crystal. You must learn how to conceal your feelings. They are there for anyone to read, even for someone who doesn't understand German."

"Mama is right," snapped Beatrice. "Stayless gowns have no place in court, or anywhere else that I can see."

"We both know that stayless gowns are not the issue. For my part, dear, I am delighted. I despaired of ever seeing you enamored. Vicky says he is frightfully handsome. How has Mama taken the news?"

There were tears in Beatrice's eyes. She would not turn to look at her sister as she walked away. "Going about like a dustman's wife has loosened your manners as well. You speak of matters that do not concern you. Your own life must be put to right from what I hear."

"I doubt that Bertie will approve, if it is marriage you are thinking of. He didn't approve my marriage to Lorne, you know. As a matter of fact, he made life very unpleasant for us. That's why Lorne jumped at the chance to go to Canada, among other reasons. Of course, Lorne's nobility was never in question. There is a bow loose on your dress. Have your maid see to it. It needs a few stitches."

CHAPTER ELEVEN

Beyond the parade grounds of Osborne, Victoria could see the opal sheen of the Solent and the pennanted yachts gliding over its surface. Seated in the open barouche with Beatrice beside her and Vicky and Fritz opposite, she turned her attention to the chin-strapped battalion of Seaforth Highlanders in their pith helmets and white gaiters standing before her, to address them in her high treble as fresh breezes slapped the unfurling gold-fringed new colors and whipped about their gold and crimson tassels.

"I see before me men who have upheld the honor of the country in Afghanistan and in Egypt, and it is with confidence that I entrust these colors to your charge. I cannot forget that were it not for the great loss which we have all sustained, my dear son would have performed this duty."

She handed the officer nearest the carriage two pikes spearheaded with the royal crest to which the silken standards were fastened. A kettledrum rolled a final grand tattoo, the men broke into rousing cheers, bagpipes began to play, and the carriage, drawn by four matching grays and flanked on either side by cantering equerries, drove off with postilions in sober black-jacketed livery leading the way.

Victoria dabbed at her eyes with a handkerchief edged in black. Reference to Leopold still saddened her. "The ceremony had more substance," she said, "on horseback."

She regarded Beatrice, who held a parasol, amazed that after three months her youngest daughter preferred silence between them rather than drop her foolish cause. The girl would come to her senses, she thought, just as the War Office, which at that moment was making plans for an expedition to relieve Gordon at Khartoum, had finally come to its.

"God bless you, Mother," shouted a voice over the cheering soldiers. Victoria nodded in its direction. The din increased. She found the roaring pleasant. It reaffirmed things. The Crown, for example, an amalgam of three crosses, St. George, St. Andrew, and St. Patrick, stretching over centuries and over water to every continent on earth.

Victoria thought that Beatrice looked pretty in her brown felt hat with the blue jay wings stuck in the band. It was a matter of time before she would once more be the loving, dependable daughter on whom she had come to rely. Balmoral and the solitude would do it if the others would not interfere. She blamed Louis of Hesse. Were it not for his silly escapade, Benjamina would never had had the idea in the first place. Now it appeared that Vicky, sitting so primly in her black dress and white bonnet beside Fritz, resplendent with stars on his chest and an embroidered sash—in the manner of all the male Hohenzollerns who loved decoration—was determined to plead Henry's suit. She would remind Vicky of the insult to Louis of Battenberg, who was separated from his wife Victoria, at Ella and Serge's wedding reception where he was seated with officers of the royal yacht, while Victoria had been placed at a table for royal princes.

Of course there was no contest. Baby was timid, afraid of her own shadow. Even now Benjamina showed signs of capitulation, as would that troublemaker Chamberlain when he realized that the House of Lords, which had vetoed the franchise reform bill, spoke for the people. Victoria saw it in the solicitous manner in which her youngest daughter tilted the parasol to make certain that her mother was shaded.

Even so, it had been a difficult three months. Their only communication, notes passed between them. A trying time, with weighty matters, the Commons and the press branding the peers as ancient monuments and expeditions to Khartoum and South Africa more dangerous than the cholera that raged in France.

Vicky was saying that the Shah of Persia was an absolute savage and that one must wear an old dress when at dinner with him, as he had a habit of throwing any food under the table that he did not care for, especially bones.

Fritz laughed, his smiling face, seen through an aureole of yellow and white beard and whiskers, turning somber when Beatrice asked for details of Serge and Ella's wedding. Willy, their own son, had been sent in their place to St. Petersburg to attend the ceremony, a slap in both their faces. Victoria secretly thought this served Fritz right for waiting meekly behind the throne but did not say so. Instead, she said she hoped that Ella would not be spoiled by the admiration and the adulation of the Russian people. Glitter and grandeur, she pointed out, were enough to turn the most sober head.

There was silence, only the clatter of the horses' hooves and the sounds of the carriage wheels jouncing between the double line of cedars, over the Royal Avenue to Osborne. Fritz said he hoped Victoria was pleased with the Grand Duke Louis's annulment, granted because the German presiding judge suddenly determined that the Grand Duke held a command in the German Army and that officers were not allowed to marry without the Emperor's permission.

"I knew the judge would see reason," said Victoria, "when the promise of a title was held out to him. Who in the world does not wish to be noble? And what would not certain people do to achieve this end?"

Beatrice stared straight ahead. The sun had gone behind a cloud. She folded the parasol and lay it across her lap.

"I understand," said Vicky, "that an expedition to South Africa is underway."

"It was necessary to check the Boers' territorial greediness," replied Victoria, vexed for having to answer to her oldest daughter, now decidedly German in her allegiance.

The carriage stopped. One postilion held steady the lead horse; the other, with the aid of an equerry, and Fritz who had already alighted, stood ready to hand the ladies down.

Vicky gave her shawl and ivory fan to the waiting equerry. "Could the expedition," she asked, gathering her skirts, "have anything to do with the fact that the military has not forgiven their defeat at Majuba Hill and hope to pick a quarrel with the Transvaalers?"

Beatrice stepped down last, handed her mother a folded note, then walked ahead, holding her skirts with tan kid gloves. Vicky waited until her youngest sister was safely inside the stuccoed villa.

"You have not spoken to each other in three months, Mama. That is entirely too long a breach for a mother and daughter."

Victoria leaned heavily on her son-in-law's arm. "Your wife, Fritz, is a busybody. First she meddles in English colonial policy, then with very personal matters. Vicky already knows that I will agree to speak to Beatrice when she renounces all ideas of this ridiculous marriage."

"You're being unfair, Mama, and cruel," said Vicky.

"Sometimes a mother must be cruel to be kind."

"There is no kindness in this," replied Vicky. "You put Benjamina to the same torture Bismarck and Willy and the Emperor apply to our poor suffering Moretta. I can at least understand Bismarck's objection to Sandro. He thinks he is the tool of England. That it is all your instigation. Bismarck says he expects you to appear in Berlin with a pastor in your satchel and Sandro in your trunk. But what has Henry done? He is not political at all."

"You are the one who is being unfair, Vicky," said Fritz. "Mama is tired."

"Nonsense," said Victoria. "I am going to have tea and dunk my cakes in my cup. One cannot be tired to do that. The cakes float about, and the tea becomes crumbly if one is not alert."

A maid was washing Beatrice's black silk waists in water in which potatoes had been boiled in order to stiffen them and make them glossy. Beside her, another maid was cleaning silk ribbons, rubbing them with a piece of flannel. They both bobbed curtsies at the arrival of the Princess. The first maid wiped her hands on her apron.

"Please take care," said Beatrice to the servant who continued to rub the ribbons, "not to take the color out."

"This is a special mixture, Your Royal Highness, to keep the color fast. Gin and molasses have been added to the soap," replied the woman.

The first maid unpinned Beatrice's hat and placed it on the waiting wooden form, then unbuttoned the jacket of the Princess's brown corded silk tailored suit, careful not to let her still-damp fingers touch the velvet collar. Beatrice heard the rustle of her sister's skirts before she saw her. Vicky rushed in, untying her bonnet strings.

"I didn't want to say this in front of Mama, but you must know

that Henry wants to come to England. He has asked me to beg you to
allow him to help."

Beatrice stood in a white ruched muslin wrapper. "I know," she
said as the maid reached discreetly beneath the garment to loosen her
laces. "He's said so in his letters to Victoria and Louis, but it would
not do."

"He is half crazy with worry," said Vicky.

"It's odd," said Beatrice, sighing with relief now that the stays of
her sateen corset no longer dug into her ribs and waist. "I've not
forgotten his touch, nor his face; it's the sound of his voice I can't
remember. Does he speak of me often? What does he say?" She sat
before her dressing table. A maid took down her golden hair, which
she began to brush.

"Only to remind you of his deep abiding love. You do not falter? I
hope you do not falter. That worries me. Let Henry speak to Mama.
You know how charming he can be. Let him charm her and make
everything right."

"Henry can't say anything for me that I can't say for myself." The
maid moistened her hair with water into which oil of thyme had been
added, then rolled it into coils.

"But darling, if you allowed Henry to meet with Mama, I am
confident he would convince her how fine and true he is, how right
you are for each other, how good he will be to you, and what a fine
husband and father he will make."

"That's the point. If Mama gives in to Henry and not to me, then I
have lost."

"What does it matter why she changes her mind so long as she
changes it?"

"I have gone this far, and I must succeed. Otherwise, this will all
have been wasted. Besides, Henry should not have to account for
himself to Mama or anyone."

"You are as stubborn as she."

Beatrice addressed one of the maids. "I will wear my lace tunic at
dinner, the point d'Alençon, the very very old one. Take care when
you handle it." She turned to Vicky. "It belonged to Katharine of
Aragon. It is very fragile, very delicate. When I wear it, I feel as if I
have put on spiders' webs."

The dining table, standing beneath the Winterhalter painting of luscious frolicking nymphs, was crowded. At one end sat Prince Peter of Oldenburg, with a large wen on his forehead, whose hobby was peace. The aging Prince had given a pamphlet to Alix, seated beside him, and was discussing, his false teeth creaking on their hinges, universal disarmament.

"War is of course hellish," agreed the elegant Princess of Wales, whose deafness prevented her from hearing what he said but who was familiar with his cause.

"Nonsense," interrupted Victoria. "It gives a needed tonic, without which man would become effete and lose all virility and courage. What was the name of the major, Sir Henry, who reports that the Nile has risen four feet, that seven steamers have successfully passed the second cataract, and that camels are being trained this very moment? A most optimistic man."

"Kitchener, ma'am," replied Sir Henry.

Georgie, the Duke of York, Bertie and Alix's second son, in conversation with his father, turned to Victoria. "Sixty-six especially designed boats, Grandmama, have sailed for Alexandria."

Victoria smiled. She preferred this grandson to his older brother Eddy, sitting across the table with a long brooding face. She considered the Duke of Clarence not only constitutionally unsound but unsteady as well, which she put down to his father's flagrant conduct. Somehow it had affected his conception.

Eddy was growing a beard and pulled at his chin. "They will never get up the Nile," he said. "They will have to be towed over the cataracts. Then it will be too late."

Victoria pursed her lips. "I don't see why you insist on a beard, Eddy, just because Georgie has one. There are those who are suited to beards and those who are not. You fall into the latter category."

Alix noticed her eldest son's glower. "What is the matter?" she asked. "What has been said?"

"The Queen does not like his beard," shouted Prince Peter.

"And what is wrong with his beard?" asked Alix. "I think he looks splendid."

Bertie switched the talk to Kilimanjaro. He said it was eminently suited for European colonization and that within a few years it must be French, English, or German. Bertie was priming the well. He did not say that he had information that Lord Granville had already instructed the British consul at Zanzibar to use his discretion as to the action to take if, in the meantime, there should appear to be an attempt of another power to interfere with British interests. He watched his mother and Sir Henry for any flicker in their expression that would confirm his information.

Victoria turned to Louis of Hesse. "If your face were any more sunken, it would be in the soup. Please, please, make an effort."

"I beg your pardon, Mama," he replied. "I was lost somewhere in my thoughts."

"It is not healthy to think when one eats. If nothing else, imagine what it will be like to be a grandfather."

"The implication of that estate has crossed my mind," said Louis.

"Well, then, surely the thought of Victoria's baby should keep you buoyant. Between you and Beatrice, who sulks at my other side, mealtimes have come to be quite unpleasant. When you write to Victoria, tell her to walk regularly every day, regardless of the weather; it is the one thing she must attend to." She scribbled on a piece of paper, "Find out from Helen's nurse if she can recommend a reliable woman," and shoved the note at Beatrice.

Beatrice scribbled a response that read, "I wrote to Helen last week."

Victoria scribbled another note. "Where did you get that ancient thing you are wearing? It has a most distasteful odor and looks as if it has been eaten by moths."

Vicky called across the table, an infraction of her mother's dictum against speaking from a distance. "Are we to be kept in the dark? Whatever are you two writing about?"

Annoyed at the turns the conversation had taken and at her eldest daughter's breach of manners, Victoria signaled that dinner was at an end. A footman sprang forward to pull back her chair. She left the table, on the arm of her private secretary.

Bertie came to take the arm of his youngest sister. "If it is information you want about Kilimanjaro," she said, "I have nothing to tell you."

Bertie smiled. "I only want to talk." They strolled beneath the candlelit open gallery of the loggia where one could hear the waves slapping the beach and see the winking lights of the sailing vessels. Always awkward with this youngest sister, whose personality was so different from his own, Bertie wished that she would not cast her eyes down when he spoke. "This plan of yours to marry Henry of Battenberg, don't you think it's time you reconsidered?"

"Did Mama ask you to say that?" The air was soft with the taste of iodine. She relished it. The aroma was Osborne.

He laughed. "Heavens, no. I assure you, Benjamina, it is my own idea. I ask you to reconsider because of the implications of such a marriage. Henry is, after all, of somewhat blemished background. To marry someone beneath you, well, there are repercussions of such rashness, dear, unpleasant ones, that I don't care to enumerate. You must take my word for it, as someone older, perhaps a little wiser."

"I don't understand," she said. "I thought that you and Louis of Battenberg are the greatest friends. Wasn't Louis responsible for saving the life of your own sons?"

"Friendship and gratitude must not be confused with responsibility. I hope you don't object," he said, withdrawing his cigarette case. A white-gloved footman emerged from the shadows with a match.

Beatrice waited until her brother's cigarette was glowing. "I love him, Bertie," she said.

The Prince of Wales, the cigarette clamped between his teeth, folded his hands behind his back. "Ah, yes, love. It mucks up things a bit, doesn't it? One never knows when or where it will strike. Royalty, however, must arm against it. Those in our position must have a clear head at all times."

"Do you, Bertie? Do you always have a clear head?" Beatrice referred to her brother's much-publicized peccadilloes.

"See here," he replied, suddenly angry, "I am steadfastly devoted to my wife. Nothing alters that. And I am just as steadfast in my duty to the Crown. Which is what you have not considered, it appears to me."

Alix appeared on the arm of Georgie. "What's the matter? Everyone seems to be out of sorts this evening. Beatrice, where did you get that marvelous tunic? I have never seen such lace."

The smell of lemon oil filled the bleak interior of Crathie Kirk. The aroma came from the gray-shadowed, gloomy wooden pews in which earnest, sober parishioners sat in starched and stuffy piety while the sexton moved silently, extending the wooden offertory on its long pole to the Queen and her party, each of whom dropped in a coin, then to the pew behind them in which sat an old man with an ear trumpet and a mother holding a baby in a lace christening gown, made soporific by laudanum.

The clean-shaven dominie in black alpaca gown, enlivened only by the double streamers of his white stock, appealed to the Almighty to send down his wisdom to the unruly demonstrators in Hyde Park and to the House of Lords, who sorely needed it. The baby woke up and began to cry as Reverend Campbell switched to damnation, intoning, "Dearly beloved brethren, the Scripture moveth us, in sundry places, to acknowledge and confess our manifold sins and wickedness . . ."

Beatrice knelt with the congregation and bowed her head, her hands clasped before her. "We have erred," she prayed in response, "and strayed from thy ways like lost sheep." Victoria knelt beside her with the assistance of Lady Southhampton and Horatia Stopford. It seemed to be more difficult for her than ever before. Beatrice heard her mother utter a groan as she sank painfully to her knees.

"We have followed too much the devices and desires of our own hearts . . . we have done those things which we ought not to have done . . . not to have done . . ."

Groups of travelers bound for Ballater alighted from their coaches in the fog of the gray still morning to troop over fallen bronze and yellow leaves to Crathie Churchyard. Some had had their ten-minute stop at John Brown's grave and were on their way back with souvenir labels and strings that they had torn from the wreaths when they saw the Queen leaving the church.

"Barbarians," said Victoria amid the cheers. "Why can't they leave the man in peace?"

It was cold; the west wind, bearing the smell of woodsmoke, had picked up, sending the leaves whirling in the road before them. Beatrice settled her mother's skirts with a lap robe, tucking it in place around her legs and beneath her black elastic-sided boots to ward off the chill. They passed a stone cottage on which a man lay thatching the roof with barley sheaves while below his redheaded children and an aged grandfather, sucking his gums and doffing his cap, plaited straw into collars for oxen.

The lap robe had slid to the floor of the carriage where it lay in a crumpled heap. Horatia Stopford bent forward to retrieve it. Beatrice, her eyes moist, stared ahead at the purple mist that shrouded the woods and the turf hut beyond where shearers, wearing sheepskin vests, crouched on their haunches.

She was weary and close to tears. The strain was becoming unbearable. At first, it had been simple. After a few mealtimes when Victoria would not speak, when Beatrice thought she would die, and did not, it became easier. All that had happened was that she had lost weight. Her clothes, despite their myriad tapes and fastenings, hung loose; especially wrinkled were the bodices of her gowns, which had to be discarded. But she had gotten used to the silence. Then, with each successful encounter, she had felt stronger, more resolute, as flinty and as stonelike as the rocks on Lochnagar. Lately, however, in the chill of autumn, the memory of her passion withering like the leaves, she wondered what she was doing, and why. She had placed herself in a remote and lonely cranny where it was cold and hard and inaccessible to the sun. Henry, after five months, was a sheaf of letters tied with ribbon. Mama was a silvery voice and fluttery hands, all that was comfortable and certain. Mama was love.

Days later, Beatrice galloped with Louis of Hesse over the sedge-covered braes of Deeside on her little Highland pony. While the pain in her hands made holding the reins difficult, the cold wind that whipped over her face and stung her eyes helped her to think.

They dismounted, the grooms behind them running forward to take their reins. To their left was a roaring cascade that splashed over ledges and crags and plunged to a marshy basin into a narrow glen where juniper, birch, and tall, skinny firs rustled in the breeze. Above them was a browsing herd of red deer.

"Have you been able to forget a little, Louis?" she asked.

"I have no problem forgetting," he replied. "The trouble is, I forget the wrong things. I forget people's names; I forget where I put my spectacles. Other things are not forgotten."

The waterfall sent its spray to dampen them as white gannets with pale yellow heads flew to their colony on the cliff. "To fall in love at my age," he said, "is a matter of luck. With Alexandrine, I had new life. I was young again. She was so vital, so alive. For the first time since your dear sister died, I looked forward, not backward. You see, it isn't only that I have lost a love; I have lost the rest of my life."

A thrush sung sweetly in a beech tree. At their approach, it flew to hide among the hazel catkins.

"She will win, you know. It is no use, all this pointless suffering."

"That remains to be seen."

"You don't know her as I do."

Beatrice's cheeks became pink. "I think that is presumptuous. I know my mother better than does anyone."

"You have been at her side longer than anyone. To know the Queen, you have to be the target of her rage. How long since she has spoken to you? Five months? You must find it unbearable."

Beatrice put her hand to her cheek. "It has been difficult."

"Don't fight her, Beatrice. She is not only your mother; she is the Queen of England, the most powerful monarch in all the world. It will make your life easier. Perhaps it is just as well. You know how your sister Vicky is treated. Do you think it will be any less so for you? And as the wife of a Hussar? What protection could you expect from Bismarck? Or Willy?"

"Easier is not better," she said. "Why are you going on so much about this? You muddy the issue. You make it unclear." She poked back stray wisps of hair beneath her veil.

"When I see you with your hair in disarray," he said, "I cannot help thinking of the picture Alice once described. A pathetic picture of her little sister, four years old, with blonde hair streaming over her eyes, being carried from her bed by her sobbing, bereaved mother, who wrapped the child in her dead father's nightshirt, then took the baby to her bed to cry over her through the night. Of course you cannot remember."

The cloves. Papa's scent, in his neck when he snuggled her close, in his chair, among his pillows, in his nightshirt, wrapped around her, tight, tight. Let me go, Mama. I can't see. I can't breathe. You're getting my hair all wet.

It was like inhaling frigid air, which burned into her lungs, making her gasp sharply to take in even more. Events rushed to her mind, presenting their credentials like ambassadors, demanding to be seen, noticed, sorted out, and filed away.

"I remember," she said. "I have been wrapped in that shirt for over twenty years. The clouds are coming down, Louis. Shall we return?"

A signal toward the grooms caused them to rush forward with the mounts. Beatrice gathered her long black skirts in her left hand as she placed her right hand on the pommel. Her groom stooped beside the horse and made a step of his hands. When she had sprung up and was seated sidesaddle, he adjusted her skirts and placed one boot in the stirrup. Beatrice ran her hands over her pony's mane. "After you have used the curry comb," she said, "he should be wisped, and take care to keep him covered so that you do not set his coat."

They rode back, their mounts setting their hooves carefully over the pebbly edges of the dee. Clouds were settling fast. Beside them, swirling waters flashed blue and silver, eddying away in little circles from the giant boulders set in their path, while salmon, their back fins pattering its surface like rain, darted in the fading light. A woman stood beside a boulder scrubbing potatoes, her head covered with a close cap, her dress up to her knees. When she saw the royal party, she dropped her skirts and curtsied. Some of the potatoes fell into the stream.

By the time they dismounted, it had begun to rain. Beatrice walked over the cobblestones, shielded by the umbrella held over her head by the waiting footman. She would stand firm, she knew, if it took a year, if it took ten years. Time was her ally. Mama was the one who could not go on alone. Not she. Mama.

CHAPTER TWELVE

The court returned to Windsor, those in waiting grateful to exchange the piercing drafts and isolation of Balmoral for the chilly damp and proximity to London of Windsor Castle. The Nile campaign to rescue Gordon had begun, as troops under the direction of General Wolseley whipped untrained camels toward Khartoum. Beatrice continued to assist her mother from morning till night, relaying instructions to plume-helmeted equerries, writing memoranda, reading aloud dispatches with grim-lipped, stoic dedication. Everyone was acutely aware of the silence between the Queen and her youngest daughter, a feature that made mealtimes an ominous obligation. Some made private wagers as to when Beatrice would capitulate. Lady Ely whispered that it would certainly be before the anniversary of Prince Albert's death, since Her Royal Highness could not possibly be so cruel to her dear mother the Queen.

If their silence discomfited others, it did not seem to affect Victoria, who had submerged herself in delicate negotiations between the House of Commons and the House of Lords, a venture that she undertook with relish. Reminding Sir Henry, who acted as go-between, that Disraeli had taught her that all matters were publicly introduced and privately settled, she first met with Gladstone. He thought she wanted to discuss the Sudan and told her that Gordon was hemmed in but not surrounded. She forgave his duplicity and insisted on a private meeting between him and Lord Salisbury. To her surprise, he agreed. Then she met with Salisbury, who faced her with knitted brows and domed forehead and said such a thing was impossible if for no other reason than that Gladstone tended to muddle issues with long discourses. She promised that Gladstone promised that were he to meet with Salisbury, he would keep his parentheses and suppositions to a minimum. Victoria then dictated a note to Gladstone. "Tell him," she said to Sir Henry, "that I expect him to expound only when asked." Sir Henry tactfully suggested she change the words *expect* to *earnestly trust.*

Gladstone and Salisbury met for tea in an unprecedented tête-à-tête and discovered that there was no insuperable discrepancy of view between them. The meeting ended with Gladstone promising to introduce a redistribution of seats bill, provided he was assured that doing so would not endanger the franchise of two million new voters.

Victoria was lauded by both sides for her wise and gracious influence in averting a dangerous parliamentary crisis. To Sir Henry she confided that she expected Lord Salisbury to rise to the occasion. Of Gladstone she said that she did not think he had it in him. "Now," she said, "they will want me to give him the Garter. As if it were a piece of millinery."

The Queen was in high spirits. She put aside Dean Stanley's four-volume biography and had Horatia Stopford read to her nightly from a new novel. She even saw a new side of the Prince of Wales. He congratulated her one evening after dinner as the court retired to the white drawing room for two or three rubbers of whist.

"It appears, Mama," he said, "that since we cannot seem to create a third party of moderates, an informal coalition of party leaders under your supervision may, after all, be best."

"Exactly, Bertie," said Victoria, crinkling her cheeks beneath her puffy Hanoverian eyes and leaning on the arm of young Victoria of Battenberg, whose flowing gown and artfully arranged, crocheted magenta wool shawl announced her condition. "You are beginning to have a grasp."

Victoria leaned closer to her granddaughter. "You told me that you felt sick when you returned from Russia at the end of June," she said. "This led me to calculate that the event should take place between the twentieth and twenty-seventh or so of February. Now Louis writes you only felt the first movement at the end of October. Are you sure of that?"

Young Victoria began to blush. "Grandmama," she protested, "please."

"The rest can't hear us, and your uncle Bertie isn't interested," said Victoria. "What one feels is often so slight at first that one hardly knows. You can't really rely on that for time. I am anxious to make your *accouchement* as safe as possible. Think, Victoria, think. Was it like a butterfly or a bubble? The difference is very important."

Beatrice walked behind them on the arm of Bertie's friend, the piccadilly-whiskered Matthew Arnold. She carried a small gift for her niece, with whom she was anxious to speak, but aware of her duty, cleared her throat. "My brother tells me that you lecture in English and not in Latin, Mr. Arnold. What has been the response?"

"Oxford, Your Royal Highness," he replied, "the hope of lost causes, steeped in sentiment as she lies, spreading her gardens to the moonlight and whispering from her towers that last enchantment of the Middle Ages."

Lost causes. How does one know when a cause is lost? And is that why they are lost? Because the moment never comes when one admits the folly. Is that what was happening to her? Beatrice wondered why he didn't simply answer her question, thinking that even Lord Tennyson could come to the point, and then realized that she didn't care. What really mattered was how she was going to speak to her niece, Victoria, with any privacy. She had something to ask her, something she had read in a letter from Willy's wife, about which she needed assurance.

Mr. Arnold was smiling at her with eyebrows lifted. He seemed to be patiently waiting. "I beg your pardon, Mr. Arnold," she murmured in chagrin. "I didn't hear the question."

When they reached the white drawing room, they found the room ringed with scaffolding left by gilders who had been restoring the moulding and pots of gypsum and glue, a reminder of the scagliolers. There was a minor commotion. Bertie herded everyone out. "Mama's landlord, the Office of Woods and Works," he said, "is making improvements." They strolled instead to the crimson drawing room where an octagonal table and a scarlet morocco card case were brought in. There was an additional stir when it was discovered that the pack was one card short, but another was quickly fetched, and the game, with Victoria, Sir Henry, Mr. Arnold, and Lady Churchill, began, with two shillings on each hand and a half a crown on the rubber.

Sir Henry dealt the cards around. They were smaller than ordinary, made to fit the Queen's grasp. Victoria arranged her hand, looking all the while toward the gilded beech-wood settee upon which her grand-daughter and youngest daughter were seated. Lady Churchill led with the ten of hearts, the others followed suit, and her partner, Mr. Arnold, collected the trick. Victoria watched the young women settle themselves on the crimson and gilt brocade, guessing by Beatrice's rising blush what the discussion was about. She called Lady Ely to her side. "Tell Princess Louis," she said, "that it is time for her port wine."

"Two by honors," announced Lady Churchill.

"Observation and reasoning," chided Victoria. "One must recall, Sir Henry, and try to remember very carefully the cards that are played."

"I will try, Your Majesty," he said, "to draw more accurate inferences."

Beatrice watched Victoria of Battenberg unwrap her gift. "Be careful," she said, spreading her white ostrich feather fan across her lap. "Don't prick your hand." Her new steel-wire bustle, designed to collapse when its wearer sat, creaked as it folded beneath her.

With a little cry, Victoria held aloft a small white satin pincushion on which tiny pink and blue pins had been arranged to say, "Welcome, sweet innocent." She leaned forward to kiss Beatrice on the cheek and began to describe the layette that was being made with each tiny button wound from linen thread. Then she laid her gloved hand on Beatrice's arm and whispered in her ear, "We have invited him. Louis and I. We have invited Henry to Kent House. What do you think? Are you pleased?"

Beatrice quickly looked about the drawing room to see if anyone had heard. The closest was Prince Christian, the husband of her sister Helena, standing behind them in the center of a small group. Prince Christian had sent for his collection of glass eyes. Everyone was examining the contents of the case. The only person who looked their way was the Queen, peering over her wire-rimmed glasses. Beatrice glanced down in her lap, smoothing the feathers of her fan. "Henry? Here? In England? What did he say? Is he coming?"

"What do you think?"

"Don't tease me, Victoria, tell me."

"He's coming, and he's determined. He said this will be the major campaign of his life."

Lady Ely approached, holding a crystal goblet mounted in rubies. "The Queen is anxious that you drink this, Your Highness. It will make your blood strong."

"Thank you, Lady Ely," replied Victoria. Lady Ely remained standing beside the settee. "I will finish it, Lady Ely, I promise. But I want to sip it slowly. It has a nice bouquet."

The lady-in-waiting pivoted on one heel, kicking the other behind her to reverse her short train, and rustled away.

"But nothing has changed," said Beatrice. "He knows that nothing has changed."

"That is why he is coming. He says he can no longer wait. That he has already waited a lifetime. He is crazy to see you. He says he can't go on without you. He says . . ."

"What?"

"It's very extravagant. He says you are his life!"

"But I thought—I had been so worried." Beatrice closed her fan and clutched tightly the mother-of-pearl sticks. "I had heard that he has been seen with another. That he has been more than attentive to the pretty wife of old Prince Carolath. Is that true? Have you heard that to be true?"

"Darling, that's so silly, so insignificant. Henry is very handsome. Sometimes I tease Ludwig that Henry is the most handsome of all the Battenbergs. If women are so foolish as to make themselves cheap over him, well, what can you expect a man to do, for heaven's sake, dear auntie. That's the way of the world. Who told you such a malicious tale?"

"Willy's wife. In a letter."

"Well, that should tell you something. You know Willy is against Henry, as he is against my own Louis, and Sandro, as well. The Germans and the Russians are being so silly about the Countess and her birth and so forth. Besides, I thought that Princess Carolath had eloped to Italy with Bismarck's son? Aunt Vicky told me that. Months ago. Believe me, Henry is frantic to be near you, to hear that you still care, that nothing has changed. I can assure you that his devotion is constant."

"Tell him," Beatrice searched for words, looking for them in the ornate embossed and painted ceiling above. "Tell him for me that I have been strong."

Victoria seemed disappointed. "Auntie, can't you think of something more romantic?"

"Tell him that my devotion is also constant and that I will succeed. There, that is the best that I can do. Does my mother know that you have invited him? Did you tell her?"

"Not yet. Louis will tell her. It is entirely his idea. He says he will mention it matter-of-factly, as if Henry's visit were an ordinary thing, as it would be if there was nothing between you. After all, he is his brother. It is natural that he should want to visit."

"Drink the wine," said Beatrice. "Mama has not taken her eyes off us, and Lady Ely looks like an arrow in a bow."

Lady Churchill and Mr. Arnold won the rubber. Lady Churchill returned the cards to their morocco case. Everyone bowed and curtsied, while Victoria, nodding to one side and the other, accepted dutiful kisses on her cheek from the family, and left on the arm of Sir Henry.

"They have invited him to Kent House," said the Queen. "They plan to tell me in the next few days. Louis, I believe, has been chosen as the bearer of the glad tidings. Why is my daughter so obstinate? Surely she would have forgotten by now this ridiculous notion."

A maid of honor, following close behind with a Highland servant, hurried ahead to ready the Queen's dressers.

"Her Royal Highness is, as you said, ma'am, your daughter."

"And what does that mean?"

The corridor in which they slowly walked glowed with scarlet window stools, Venetian paintings, gilded candelabra, and oriental cabinets. A yeoman of the guard with rosettes on his black shoes stood at attention, as motionless as the statues and objets d'art beside him.

"Simply, ma'am, that the Princess has most likely inherited a certain tenacity, or steadfastness, if you will, that same quality that will not allow Your Majesty to knuckle under to anyone, the same quality that now causes the empire to cheer its sovereign for averting a parliamentary crisis."

They stopped at the Queen's private lift. The Highland servant noiselessly stepped forward and offered his arm. Sir Henry deftly withdrew his own.

"You would compare her silly stubbornness to my commitment to principle?"

"The aims may be different," he replied, "but a similar strength of will propels them both. A feather or a ton of rocks. They both rush to meet the ground. You press to win, Your Majesty," said Sir Henry, "yet you above anyone know that everything in life is negotiated, even love."

Victoria was anxious to get on with her novel. Horatia would read to her while Annie MacDonald took down her hair. He was right, of course.

The next morning's dispatches were more tedious than usual. Beatrice could think only of Henry and if he would find her changed. When a woman reached the age of twenty-seven and was not in her first youth, it was well known that she changed for the worse at an alarming rate. The scarlet-coated guards with their high black bearskin busbies could be seen through the frosted window mounting in the quadrangle, their boots stamping smartly in unison on the cobblestones. Beatrice had just handed a reprimanding note to Harriet Phipps to take to Count Hatzfeldt, who was reported by the maid to have been seen lying on his bedroom floor and blowing smoke from his cigar up the chimney. She began to read aloud to Victoria a letter from Cecil Rhodes, who suggested that if the colonies and protectorates of South Africa were ever to be united, it could only be through a force majeure, either British or Boer.

Victoria turned to Sir Henry. "They say he is a woman hater," she said, "but I cannot agree. Mr. Rhodes has always been very civil to me." She nodded to Beatrice, indicating that she was to continue reading.

Beatrice complied. Rhodes advised that since African potentates sometimes ceded their territories to several European nations at once, it would be in England's interest, and actually best for all civilized powers, to report to one another any new acquisitions.

Beatrice scribbled a note reminding Victoria of the Berlin conference from which emerged the tacit agreement among civilized nations of the right to seize and govern any part of Africa not already imperialized and placed it before her.

Victoria squinted, then crumpled the paper. "I am tired of reading your notes, especially in that cramped hand of yours," she said. "Tell me, Benjamina, what you wish to say."

Beatrice felt time stand still. Sir Henry and his undersecretaries, sorting communiqués and handing leather packets to waiting pages and equerries, seemed captured on some frieze. The yellow roses in the Chinese porcelain vase, forced in the greenhouses of Windsor, held drops of moisture on their velvet petals. Even her own heart seemed to cease its beat. The only sounds were the military band and the corps of drummers in the quadrangle below. She looked at her mother, mastering with great effort her voice. "Mama," she said, "what does this mean?"

"I don't know what it means. It means I'm tired, and I need new glasses. It means I have exchanged my dearest baby for a wan, thin stranger who scribbles notes. It means I have been hasty."

Sir Henry signaled to his undersecretaries. They discreetly withdrew, leaving only the Highland servant standing silently against the wall. Beatrice knelt beside Victoria and threw her arms around her knees, laying her head in her mother's lap. "It's been so long, and I've been so lonely." She began to weep.

"It has occurred to me," said Victoria with a great sigh, "that the loss of Leopold had been as great to you as it has been to me. It is natural that you seek a replacement for the loss."

"Henry is not a replacement for Leo," said Beatrice, lifting her head. "No one will replace my beloved brother. I love Henry for Henry."

"You are too close to see it. No matter. Let us not argue so close to the anniversary of the death of your dear papa and your sister Alice. It is harder and harder to face December." Victoria fingered her diamond bracelet, in the center of which was a miniature of Albert and a lock of his hair. "When your father was alive, the rooms rang with his voice and the voices of your sisters and brothers, everyone romping, trooping, scolding, sounds of life from every cranny. There are no sounds around me anymore except for what you hear in the quadrangle, and those are the sounds of sovereignty and its lonely isolation.

Tzo," she said, in the German fashion, "I need cozy sounds again. I will see your Henry."

Victoria of Battenberg reclined on the regency-style sofa, which was upholstered, as were all the other pieces in the room, in the same flowered damask as the walls. The drawing room of Kent House had been garlanded and festooned for Christmas. A yule log decorated with sprigs of fragrant rosemary lay on the grate waiting to be lighted on Christmas eve with the log from the previous Christmas. Windows, mantelpiece, and smoking oil lamps were adorned with evergreens.

In the center of the room stood dark-bearded Louis of Battenberg, wearing the gold-fringed epaulets of commander, the rank to which he had been recently promoted. Before him was a footman on a ladder, preparing to hang from the center of the ceiling entwined hoops garlanded with sprigs of ivy and holly, colored ribbons, paper roses, apples, oranges, tiny presents, and a piece of mistletoe tied to the bottom.

"That is not high enough, Ludwig, darling," called young Victoria from the sofa. She leaned on her elbow. "Try to walk beneath it. See, you cannot. It is too low." The footman raised the garlanded hoops.

In the corner of the room, Beatrice stood beside a fir tree, the bark of which had been peeled from its lower trunk. Beside her waited two maids and her attendant, Mademoiselle Noreille, holding trays of decorations, while two footmen stood on stools. Beatrice carefully selected ribbon streamers, candles, wafers, gold foil, sweets, little dolls, and eggs painted yellow and red, handing some to the footmen and fastening others to the tree herself.

"Isn't it wonderful," said Victoria, arranging her shawl over her abdomen, "that Grandmama has agreed to see Henry? You are halfway there; I know it."

"I'm afraid that if I think about it too much," replied Beatrice, "it will somehow slip away, like a butterfly one chases through the garden." She draped a shimmering festoon of silver on a branch. "Mama has only agreed to see him. She has said nothing about anything else."

"You know," said Louis, stepping back to admire the garlanded hoops, "stranger things have happened. At my boyhood home in

Heiligenberg, there are those who swear that the cattle kneel and speak at midnight on Christmas eve."

"Begging your pardon, Your Highness," said the footman, stepping down from the ladder, "but I have seen it myself."

"Have you then, Crawford. You see? An eyewitness."

They heard the muted sounds of a fiddler accompanied by laughter and shouts and tinkling bells. An underbutler, the balls of his thumbs swollen from polishing silver, stood before Victoria and whispered to her.

"The mummers, Ludwig, they want to come in," she said.

"I don't know," he said. "In your condition, won't they tire you?" He was smiling.

"Nonsense," she replied. "They bring luck to the house."

"What do you think, Beatrice?" he asked. "Shall we let them in?"

Beatrice returned a yellow egg with a cracked shell to a tray. It was strange, she thought, how she could be in his presence now and not feel a thing, even feel, all things considered, quite comfortable. Did Henry make the difference, or did she? "Do," she replied. "They are always such fun."

The doors to the drawing room opened rudely, and in trooped a fiddler with a blackened face leading seven masked men wreathed in holly and dressed in brightly colored paper strips that hissed as they moved. On their ankles were jingling bells. One, called Bessy by the others, was dressed in women's clothes. Another was wearing the frock coat of a doctor, a third was garbed as a fool in the skin and tail of a fox, and a fourth, holding a wassail bowl, was dressed as Father Christmas. A fifth, in tinsel armor, astride a hobby horse, represented St. George. The two remaining identified themselves as Blue Breeches and Ginger Breeches. Except for Father Christmas and the fiddler, they all carried wooden swords, with which, with dexterity, they began to dance, laying their sham weapons upon the ground and nimbly stepping around them, then making a hexagon of their swords while chanting verses, lopping off in pantomime each other's hands and feet, and causing the servants to clutch at various objects that threatened to crash to the floor, including a pair of petit point fire screens, a Sèvres figurine, and a tray of ornaments in the hands of the shrieking Mademoiselle Noreille.

Suddenly, St. George slew Bessy. The prancing doctor, grinning through his papier-mâché mask, revived the victim, and the mummers continued the dance, first a round, then, laying hold of each other's hilts and points and wheeling around faster, changing their order and forming another hexagon, to finish by dancing rapidly backward and vehemently rattling the sides of their swords together.

They made an elegant bow, in the manner of old-fashioned courtiers of another time, a stylized pose made grotesque by their masks and their jingling bells. Louis gave them money, and they left as they entered, raucously, merrily, waving their rustling paper-strip costumes, knocking each other about, all except Father Christmas.

"See," said Louis to Beatrice, "Father Christmas has taken a liking to you, Beatrice. He wants you to drink from his bowl."

Father Christmas shuffled across the carpet to stand before Beatrice. She hung back, repulsed by his garments and the heavy smell of varnish from his mask.

"Go on, Auntie," said Victoria. "You must take a drink. He will be terribly offended if you don't."

Beatrice reached forward hesitantly and sipped from the wassail bowl while Father Christmas slipped off his mask. She lifted her eyes. The bulbous nose and long white beard were gone. So was the costume. In its place stood Henry in the white uniform of the elite Gardes du Corps.

He looked different from her remembrance of him, different from his picture. His face was older, leaner; if anything, more handsome than she recalled. He bowed, then took her hand and gently brushed his lips against it.

"Henry," she said.

They stood together wordlessly, soundlessly. She hoped she would not cry. "My darling," he whispered in German. The servants busied themselves with the decorations, taking care not to be seen observing any intimate exchange.

"Father Christmas," said Louis after an embarrassing silence, "have you no good wishes for the rest of us?"

Henry reached over to clasp his brother's shoulders and kiss the hand of his wife. "I would have been here sooner, but the roads are jammed with post chaises filled with schoolboys on holiday. You can't imagine what a time my driver had."

"I was fooled as well as Auntie Beatrice," said Victoria. "I thought, surely, Liko, you would choose to be St. George."

Henry laid down his razor next to the basin of hot water on his washstand and stood in his dressing gown as his valet trimmed the points of his moustache.

It had not been difficult to convince her, due less to his skill at persuasion than to her innocence, a virtue that was strongly in her favor. He had explained everything as they walked a snowy footpath, Beatrice in a gray velvet redingote trimmed in chinchilla, her hands in a chinchilla muff, with Mademoiselle Noreille trailing discreetly behind, while sea fog, like rolling fleece, passed through the leafless trees like wool through a carding comb. Beatrice quickly understood that Willy, really the tool of Bismarck, had a strong interest in thwarting the marriage. Under those circumstances, it was natural that Willy's wife would have written such a letter.

He let drop his dressing gown to the floor. His valet held out a white linen shirt, starched, with the help of a piece of wax candle and a bit of gum arabic, to a glossy sheen. A wife, he thought, could never be too virtuous. In addition, she was shy, adoring, qualities that he found delightful, and she was courageous as well. He had never expected that she would have been able to carry this thing so far.

That afternoon, everyone had picked raisins out of a dish of burning brandy and dined on a great wensleydale cheese upon which a cross had been scraped and roast, boiled beef, hams, hares, geese, cinnamon cakes, cider cakes, elderberry and dandelion wines, plum cakes, puddings, and mince pies. There was mutton suet in the mince pieces, the Queen had told him, in honor of the shepherds in Bethlehem.

They took turns stirring the Christmas pudding, each person making a wish as he stirred; the Prince and Princess of Wales; the Princess Louise, a pretty, flighty woman who Henry noted looked at him under her lashes; her husband, Lord Lorne, from whom, he understood, she lived apart. It was clear that the Prince of Wales was against him. The heir to the throne never once glanced his way. His son Eddy, an arrogant fellow, followed his father's lead and would not look in Henry's direction. His only allies were Vicky, who was not there, the Grand Duke of Hesse whose recently developed heart condition prohibited any contention, and Louis and Victoria, whose impact, while one of affection, was minimal. The yule log crackled on the fireplace. He told them that it was the custom in Westphalia to preserve the yule log and rekindle it during a storm to protect against lightning. Bertie changed the subject as if a servant had become overly familiar.

Through the windows had come the sound of carolers accompanied by oboes and clarinets. They had all gone to peer outside at the snowflakes sparkling in the soft yellow light of the carolers' lanterns. Several youngsters, wearing holly berry wreaths, could be seen riding on stout exmoor ponies. Beatrice came to stand beside him, despite the lack of propriety of such an untoward move. She seemed to be defying all of them. "They are holly riders," she explained. "They will want cider and pennies."

She was adorable. They were the same age, she was even a few months older, yet she was naive and inexperienced, more like a girl of seventeen, closer to Louis's Victoria than to unmarried women of twenty-seven. She would be easy to handle. What troubled him was not Beatrice, it was what he knew to be powerful opposition of the German and Russian courts. If they brought their influence to bear on the Queen, he could be sent packing.

The valet held out his coat. A slight odor of spirits of hartshorn emanated from the collar. "You should have cleaned this in time for the smell to disappear," said Henry. "How can I possibly visit Her Majesty?"

"I beg your pardon, Your Highness," said the valet. "It was difficult to find the things I needed, especially after the confusion of our valises. Perhaps some cologne?"

"Don't overdo," cautioned Henry as his valet sprinkled his collar with musk.

Secretary Ponsonby led Henry to the dead Prince Consort's study in which he found a kneehole desk, a stand for walking sticks, plaster studies of the hands and feet of all the royal children, and the Queen, seated with her hands folded in her lap. Henry bowed low before her, knelt, and kissed her hand.

"I trust your crossing was uneventful."

"Without incident, Your Majesty."

The wind beat upon the windowpanes as the shutters creaked on their hinges.

"Your good looks have been heightened by the cold, Prince Henry. I mention that to show you I am aware of your considerable physical attributes. Do not try to use them."

"I earnestly hope, ma'am," said Henry, "to persuade you to my cause with only the force of my argument. And what you see is not the cold but my excitement at being granted an audience. I have dreamed of this day. I have prayed for this moment. I am encouraged by your kind reception."

"Yes. My daughter, the Princess Beatrice, tells me that you love one another. She is very sheltered. I doubt if she knows what love is. Do you?"

"I do, ma'am."

"Yes, I should imagine so. Does your definition of love include the concept of sacrifice?"

"I'm afraid I don't follow, ma'am."

"Your career, Prince Henry, is the military. How are you regarded?"

"I am considered a competent horseman by other officers and an excellent groom by my stallion."

"You are modest, Henry. I have been told you are an excellent soldier and officer and that you have a promising career in the Prussian cavalry. How do you feel about your chosen occupation?"

"It is one to which I have devoted my life."

"Then you could not leave it?"

"I beg your pardon, ma'am?"

"I asked if you could leave the military."

"The thought has never occurred to me."

"It occurs to me that if you and Princess Beatrice were to marry, she would be forced to follow you from one part of Germany to another or wait for your return in some lonely schloss, in considerably reduced circumstances. Both situations are unthinkable. In addition to which, I would be left entirely alone, also unthinkable. There is only one condition under which I would permit you to marry."

"And that is?"

"Give up your military career and come to live in England. With us."

"I was prepared to do that, ma'am. I was hoping perhaps to receive a commission in the British forces, as my brother Louis serves Your Majesty's Navy."

"You don't understand, Henry. I mean give up your career. Totally. When I said live with us, I didn't mean Beatrice. I meant us. Both of us. I mean live under my roof, with me. Follow me when I go to Balmoral and Osborne and back to Windsor, or perhaps if I should travel abroad, I would expect you both at my side, at all times. A career in my own forces would serve no good, for then you would be off, and Beatrice, of course, who would worry, as do all military wives, would be clamoring to follow and be no use to me at all."

"What you ask, Your Majesty, is very difficult. It never occurred to me that you would require such a thing."

"I do not require your union in the first place, Henry. Nevertheless, be assured, it is the only way I will allow the marriage. And by the way, if you are interested, the plaster studies, second from the left"— she pointed with a cane—"are those of Princess Beatrice."

The audience was at an end. Henry bowed and backed out of the room. Sir Henry returned soon after. "He will accept it," said Victoria. "The terms are, after all, not so bad."

They sat huddled together against the bitter cold in the small palatinate pier house, Beatrice, Henry, Louis, and young Victoria, looking out onto the gray water, which was indistinguishable from the sky. A few terns picked over the desiccated and frozen contents of clam shells.

"And so," Henry explained, "she will allow the marriage only if Beatrice and I will live with her."

"What do you think of that, Auntie?" asked Victoria. "It's quite an about-face, wouldn't you say? I told you you were halfway there."

"I would have preferred a home of my own," replied Beatrice. "I must speak to Mama again, assure her that I will continue to be of help in any way I can. She is afraid to be alone, you know."

Henry shook his head. "The Queen is adamant, my darling," he said. "Take my word for it."

"The price is high," said Louis, who stood to toss breadcrumbs onto the beach. The terns left their pickings and skittered over the sand.

"At least she trades," said Henry.

"Could you not do it, Henry?" asked Victoria, whose cheeks were rouged with cold, making them almost as red as her cherry-velvet bonnet. "Would it be so bad?"

"It is something I never considered," he replied. "One plans one's life along certain lines. It just never occurred to me. I imagine it is because I have worried so much that the Queen would never permit me to discuss the matter that somehow the question of terms never entered my mind. I don't see that I have a choice. I cannot live without Beatrice. I love her. I want her to be my wife."

Beatrice felt rage. Her hands hurt. She thrust them deeper into her muff. Why did Mama have to make things so difficult?

"I thought it would please you to hear that," said Henry.

"I was thinking of your regiment, your responsibilities," replied Beatrice. "You mention them in every letter. How could you abandon all that you have trained so hard and so long to achieve?"

An equerry crunched over the sand, touching his helmet with his gloved hand. The terns retreated to the water's edge. "I beg your pardon, Your Royal Highness," he said to Beatrice. "Her Majesty wishes you to return."

"How did he find us?" asked young Victoria. "I thought we had been so careful."

Beatrice sighed. "Do you mind, dearest?" she asked.

"Not at all." He kissed her hand. She left, with the equerry following behind.

"There is another price, you know," said Louis, "for living under Her Majesty's roof."

"I am aware of it," said Henry, watching Beatrice hurry, with skirts raised in one hand, to the villa.

"Well, if you are reconciled to that point," said Louis, "I don't see that there is a problem. The solution is quite simple. Switch to the British cavalry or join the British Navy."

"But that's really the issue," said Henry. "The Queen wants me to give it up. All of it. I would be something like a Prince Consort, only not quite as dignified or as purposeful. I would be the German husband of an English princess, like Christian examining his glass eyes."

CHAPTER THIRTEEN

Sober and resigned, Henry waxed his moustache into points with lemon-scented resin and acceded to Victoria's demand. He told himself he was a soldier and a German, and what one lost through renunciation, one gained in valor. It was the nature of men of honor to sacrifice. His own father, for example, forced to choose between the panoply of the Russian court in which he enjoyed a favored position as brother to the Tsarina, and the love of a Polish maid of honor; his brother Sandro, who relinquished his homeland to take the uneasy crown of Bulgaria, which rested its cabochon-studded crown on the capricious mood of the Tsar; or the Grand Duke Louis, who gave up the Kalomine woman for the honor of Hesse. The theme of the noble warrior was threaded through him in Wagnerian tone poems of concentrated power and splendor, in the dicta of Nietzsche and Fichte, in legends of Knights of the Holy Grail who sailed in swan-drawn vessels.

The contemptuous Prussian court waved their pedigrees like banners and sneered. Stiff necked with starch and braided military collars, they said that Henry's action was exactly what they expected. Of course he would give up his commission. What else would an ambitious upstart do when given a chance, however remote, at the Crown of England? Vehemently opposed to ingress of inferior stock into their tightly guarded bloodlines, they said so, even Vicky's Fritz, in snide dispatches or in messages couched by envoys who clicked their heels and coughed behind their hands.

Victoria's response was to remind the Empress Augusta, whose white-enameled face made her look to Victoria like a corpse, that if one were to look carefully enough, there were even worse black spots in the background of most of the royal families of Europe.

The Russian court was no less disdainful, especially so because of Sandro's unpopularity in St. Petersburg. They laughed in overheated palaces filled with wooden reliquaries, clocks with diamond streamers set in motion to resemble waterfalls, and red-and-yellow-fissured icons; the women in fur-trimmed velvets, the men in spurs and epaulets, declaring that the Battenbergs, as all lower orders, must be put firmly in their place.

In Paris, the minor royalties who played along the boulevards whispered slander behind marabou fans and potted palms, and over petit point screens in darkened boudoirs, that the joke was on the matchmaker, Madame La Croix.

Beatrice was oblivious. If the British press expressed mild disapproval that another royal princess chose for her husband a minor German princeling, she was uninterested. Since the announcement of their engagement and the kaleidoscopic events that followed, one nagging worry emerged. Beatrice could not be reassured that he would not change his mind. Nothing anyone could tell her, including the solemn imprecations of Henry, would relieve the dread anxiety that caused her to roam over the curry-colored pebbled paths of Osborne or trod in sodden boots down to the pools that formed at low tide at the water's edge to search for the answer in starfish.

Victoria said very little about the coming marriage until after the lavish ball given at Sandringham by the Prince and Princess of Wales for the twenty-first birthday of their oldest son. The ballroom had been brilliant with guests displaying the dazzling certainty of aristocratic nonchalance. The dissolute Eddy, his eyes limned with blue-black smudges, a telltale sign of excesses, had warned Beatrice, while staring at her powdered bosom, that she take care never to sit on Henry's helmet. Beatrice reminded herself that Eddy had been caught drinking sherry cobblers in a West End oyster saloon with a girl in satin and rouge and that his insolence deserved no reply. That he would someday inherit the throne was unthinkable.

When Beatrice returned to Windsor, Victoria dismissed her ladies of the bedchamber and her maids of honor, then spoke to Beatrice of man's animal nature, not as delicate as the sensibilities of women, and experienced beneath his kisses and his restless, breathy murmurings against her throat, her ears, her eyes, now aroused by the lacy hem of a nightdress brushing her knees, a mindless focus, to the center of her being, a stretching up and forward to something. Her breath was coming faster. Was she afraid, as Mama had said she might be? Perhaps that was what also caused the trembling in her legs. Beatrice let drop her gown and shrugged it to her ankles.

Henry returned to his barracks at Potsdam just before Victoria received a coded telegram announcing that despite Gordon's elaborate fortification of wire entanglements and mines and paddle steamers patrolling the Nile, Khartoum had fallen and the Mahdi's followers had slaughtered everyone in sight, including Gordon, whose head they severed after they speared him to death. Gladstone was blamed for the fate of Gordon and his men, who had been mutilated in ways the dailies would not even hint at. Victoria was not alone in her utter condemnation of her Prime Minister and in her anguish over the news of Gordon's death. The nation was outraged and stricken. Black-draped portraits of Gordon appeared in shop windows, while Victoria suffered a renewed bout of neuralgia, which Sir William Jenner said was due to her upset over Gordon. In addition, Vicky wrote that Bismarck was laughing up his sleeve, since he had knowledge that the Russians were planning an advance toward Afghanistan.

While England and Victoria went into outraged mourning over the death of their hero, Beatrice stood on a wooden platform, revolving slowly as a modiste on her knees slowly turned the crank. A team of others, with pins in their mouths, fluttered about to drape the fabrics of her trousseau, a cardinal silk from Dublin, so rich and lustrous it resembled velvet, a pale blue crepe de chine trimmed in old gold passementerie and a cream bengaline embroidered with loops of pearls. As they tightened the corsage of her white satin wedding gown, she pictured Henry's hand guiding someone's silken waist before the solid silver musicians' gallery of the old schloss. When they overlaid the tulle undersleeves with lace, she frowned, thinking that the German court would offer Henry something more appealing. Vicky had written that it was entirely possible that Bismarck, to spite Victoria, would be behind such a move. "I beg your pardon, Your Royal Highness," said a modiste. "Was I careless with a pin?"

of a husband's prerogatives. Of course, she was speaking of c
union. Beatrice began to blush. Victoria assured her that the
thing took less time than it took one's maids to undo one's
Besides, it was done in the dark, beneath the quilts and linens
need not even loosen one's nightdress, so that modesty was prese
at all times. One thought beautiful thoughts at such times, of
sanctity of marriage, for example, of England, or of the flowers
wished to press, and if one began to breathe hard, as did one's h
band, one need not be ashamed, since it was fear that caused a
female breathlessness and not, as in the man's case, brute desire. Th
was their nature. In no way did it indicate that the wife was less loved
it was just, the dears, for them a peccant humor that collected, caus
ing them great pain if it was not spent. They could not help themselves. She advised Beatrice to lie on her back, remain quite still, try
not to turn over afterward, since immobility ensured the desired result, which there was no need to go into.

When Beatrice went to bed that night, she lay in her high-necked
lawn nightdress, with its tucks and ruchings, and trailings of lace at
the wrist and front panels. Henry would find her thus, she thought;
her maids would have tucked the silken coverlet about her and
tamped the candles. Her hair would be loosened as it was now, spread
about the pillow beneath her lace and ribbon nightcap. Since it would
be dark, he would not see its gold and copper glints. That was a pity,
since her hair was one of her best features. Perhaps a candle could be
left burning. Beatrice dismissed this idea as indecorous.

She slipped her hand to the hem of her nightdress. Would she lift
it, she wondered, or would he? What was correct? She listened to the
footsteps of the guards on the ramparts and heard them giving the
watchword, then thought of their last meeting. His attentions, while
on the one hand more tender, more solicitous, were more restrained,
as if he were holding himself from her. She had only a few proper
embraces, flavored by the lemon scent of his moustache, the minty
taste of his lips, once the heady feel of his muscular thigh right
through the chambray and horsehair of her undergarments and the
taffeta of her gown.

Beatrice raised her nightdress to see how it felt and imagined
Henry doing it. The lace brushed past her knee. She felt a vague
yearning that became exquisite, almost painful. The same urgency she

In the spring, when the Russians had moved on Afghanistan and the security of India appeared to be in jeopardy, Victoria and Beatrice visited Aix-les-Bains. This time there were no crippling pains in Beatrice's hands, although she did not seem to notice. Perhaps it was the crowds that ran cheering alongside their carriage, the pealing church bells, the band of the 4th Dragoons, stationed at Chambéry, playing in the gardens of the villa, or the brilliant illuminations of the night skies, flaring rockets, showers of roman candles, exploding star shells, and a lance-work portrait in white fire of Victoria.

Darmstadt was more subdued, having just witnessed the funeral of the Grand Duke's mother, the Princess Charles. Storks from Africa, clapping their bills to attract mates, settled on roofs broken by little gable windows, where below old women in black knit beside the rough-stone lower stories of its red-timbered houses.

The drawing room of Henry's parents' home was darkened; the only objects clearly visible were an Easter egg jeweled with emeralds and rubies resting on an ivory stand and a six-foot malachite vase with gilded lip and handles. Victoria offered condolences to Henry's father. Henry's mother offered them Madeira in goblets made from ostrich eggs and told them that the Hessian people, who still believed in vampires, were very superstitious and that the servants rushed to shut the door after her sister-in-law's coffin had been carried out so that her spirit could not return and do mischief. "Those in her service," she confided, "swore they saw wailing women with eyes of fire."

Beatrice shuddered. Henry's mother offered her burned feathers to smell, but Beatrice said she was not faint. Henry turned up the lamps and diverted everyone to the stereoscope. They placed their foreheads in turn against the eyepiece and peered at the illusion of three dimensions, ghost pictures, moral tableaux, snow-capped mountains, and men in fezzes before the Pyramids. Victoria had seen most of them and asked if there were more. There were, in the locked drawer beneath, bare-breasted Zulu women, tattooed Japanese men in loincloths, child nudes, and women being whipped.

Prince Alexander said he was afraid that was all, then spoke abruptly of Afghanistan, which, in his opinion, was the most vulnerable part of the British Empire. Despite Victoria's lack of encouragement, he continued, saying that the Afghans were savagely independent, composed of many clans, each with their own characteristics and their own loyalties. Impossible to govern. Add to that the fact that Russia was immediately north, well, there it was. Henry's mother, seeing Victoria's face, changed the subject to Moretta, Vicky's daughter, who threatened to throw herself into a Venice canal if she and Sandro could not be married. "A terrible situation." Victoria agreed, and asked if Prince Alexander knew that South Bulgaria might move to unite with North Bulgaria, expecting Sandro to lead them against opposition, which meant, of course, the Turks and the Tsar.

"I had heard such rumors," replied Henry's father, reluctant to discuss before his wife matters she would not understand. "The Tsar would order all Russian officers to leave the Bulgarian Army."

It was suggested that Henry take Beatrice for a walk. Henry's parents sat facing Victoria.

"She is highly strung," said Henry's mother.

Victoria was piqued. "Princess Beatrice is a sensible and level-headed girl."

"I did not mean that as an affront, Your Majesty, only that it is natural for a bride to be nervous."

Lady Churchill, who had followed to chaperone, busied herself picking lavender as the couple picked their way down the hillside, Beatrice holding out her hand to Henry, toward the crumbling ruins hidden among the shrubbery.

He led her past an old font in which a swallow bathed. Beyond it was an escutcheoned tomb of a knight banked with tall waving grasses and yellow cowslip. "Ludwig and I used to play here as boys," said Henry, yanking away the grasses. "We had a Polish cousin, much older than us, with dreamy eyes. We would play at freeing Poland. He would always make one of us shoot him dead; then he would fall to the ground with outstretched arms."

"My brother Leo used to play like that," she said. "Whenever he fell too hard, he would get horribly pale and have to go to bed for days. He bled, you know. I think you would have liked one another. What happened to your cousin?" she asked. "I never hear you speak of him."

"A Polish revolution broke out. He disappeared from Heidelberg.

One day Mama told us he had been killed. Fallen in his country's cause."

A breeze rustled through the mossy ruins. The swallow flapped its wings and flew over a wall. "Has it been too much," she asked, "what Mama has demanded? Do you regret your decision?"

Henry's back straightened, and he gazed toward the sunlit meadow where the swallow had flown. "Sacrifice has been demanded of both of us. You have your duty. I have mine." It was she who kissed him first, closing her eyes as she had learned to do. At first it was a chaste kiss between an engaged couple; then, with abandon, she allowed herself to go limp in his arms so that he was forced to half carry her to the marble slab. He pressed her tighter, a groan escaped his lips, then leaned over her until she was leaning back and cupped her breasts over the fabric of her gown. She felt his heat, but it was he who desisted, sitting bolt upright, straightening his tunic, taking her hands and helping her to her feet, even before they heard the footsteps of Lady Churchill and her discreet cough. "My dearest," he said, "I have been importunate. Forgive me."

Bertie was outraged when he discovered that Victoria had decided to confer upon Henry the Order of the Garter but found there was nothing he could do to prevent it. The Queen was determined to elevate Henry's status and assure Henry, if he had any misgivings, that his decision had been a sound one.

The ceremony was private. Victoria, assisted by Arthur, the Duke of Connaught, buckled the dark blue velvet garter around Henry's left leg as the prelate intoned, "To the honor of God omnipotent and in memorial of the Blessed martyr of St. George, tie about thy leg, for thy reknown, this most noble garter. Wear it, that thou prayest be admonished to be courageous, and having undertaken a just war, thou mayest stand firm, valiantly fight, courageously and successfully conquer." While the Gentleman Usher of the Black Rod placed the broad blue ribbon over Henry's left shoulder and Arthur pinned the star to his left breast, Henry considered the absurdity. He had been called to fight and conquer for a just cause, while his means to do so had been denied. He told himself that the ceremony was symbolic, deriving from ancient days when a monarch sought to ensure an elite military group upon whom he could depend, and that his duty was to

Beatrice, who stood beside him, her eyes downcast, clasping the ribbon ends with a jeweled badge, to his Queen, before whom he now knelt, and who placed a mantle and the golden collar of enameled Tudor roses on his shoulders, and to his adopted country, whose ways he did not fully understand. Sadness, regret, a yearning for what was not possible was for old women, like his mother, who constantly spoke of returning to the Russian court.

The wedding was in July. Mr. Gladstone, whose government had fallen in June, was not invited. The island was covered with flowers, everywhere the letters H and B entwined with blossoms. Sailing craft, decorated with wreaths and flags, speckled the bay, piping greetings to the floating bridge that ferried carriages to the pier. Scarlet-coated Sutherland Highlanders and seamen from the royal yachts lined the way to the church, along with the overflow from the viewing stands who stood in the open fields, gazing and waving over the hedges.

At Osborne there were two irritations: the length of the bridesmaid dress, to which Alicky, who was twelve, objected, and Lord Tennyson's poem, written in honor of the marriage.

Beatrice, in tears, paced in her Watteau wrapper with a paper in her hands. Her attendants stood by helplessly, holding out her wedding gown on outstretched arms as if it were an offering. Victoria was sent for. The Queen entered, her eyes swollen from crying, followed by her dressers. Beatrice waved the paper. " 'The mother weeps at that white funeral of single life.' Why did he have to write that? Why does he make my wedding funerary? I dislike the poem intensely. It has ruined everything."

"Poets cannot be made accountable for what they write. If one does not like a work, one has simply not to read it. You are making too much of this." Victoria signaled for the women to come forward with the gown. "I am terribly depressed. I cannot think of how I will walk down the aisle. My baby is getting married, and my eldest daughter has been forbidden by her father-in-law to attend. Do not add to my sorrow. Let them dress you."

"But he goes on. 'Her tears are half of pleasure, half of pain, the child is happy, even in leaving her.' It makes me sound cruel, uncaring."

"Put your arms up, Benjamina. How can they drop it over you if you do not put your arms up."

"It is the ending that is the worst. 'Thou true daughter, whose filial eyes will neither quit the widow?' It is not Lord Tennyson's affair where I am in residence."

Everything inside the church was scarlet and gold, the specially built wooden floor carpeted in crimson Persian rugs, the slanting beams of sunlight on the large gold cross at the altar, the golden tassels of the crimson velvet hassocks placed before it, and the jewels of the guests. The only sounds were the rustle of silk, the clink of swords and spurs, and from a distance, booming guns. By the time Beatrice entered, mollified by a few drops of laudanum mixed in sherry, she was composed and radiant, in time to see four chamberlains walk slowly backward up the aisle. Someone gently pushed her forward. Flanked by Victoria, wearing a figured black grenadine woven at Lyons on a special loom, and Bertie, in the uniform of a field marshal, she trod in measured step to Henry, who stood waiting with Sandro at his side, wearing the blue ribbon of the Garter over his white dress uniform. As the couple knelt at the altar, Beatrice could not bring herself to look at him, afraid that if she did, she would betray feelings too intimate for propriety.

That evening, in a villa six miles from Osborne, her maid sprinkled perfume on the sheets, then turned down the silken coverlet and helped Beatrice into the canopied bed, letting fall one of the musty, fringed, velvet draperies so that only one side was open. The maid dipped a curtsy and left. Beatrice leaned against the pillows and folded her hands on the sheet, wondering suddenly if Secretary Ponsonby knew where to find the new ink.

There was a discreet knock. Henry, wearing a silk dressing gown, entered and sat on the edge of the bed, as if he did not wish to presume. "How beautiful you look."

"You don't have to say that," she replied.

He smiled, loosening his sash. "You must learn how to accept a compliment. It is my pleasure to give it. You should make it easy for me and learn to regard it as your due. After all, a man wants to be able to tell his wife she is beautiful." He kissed her hand. "And courageous. All has come to pass because of your strength. You are very German, you know."

"I am English, Henry," she replied. A pearl button had been left open on her lacy cuff. She moved to close it.

"Of course you are English, but your father was German; your mother, the Queen, is half German. It is a fact; you cannot deny it. What is the matter? You have nothing to fear, my darling."

"I'm worried about the new ink."

"Ink?"

"Mama's eyesight is worsening, and we have ordered special ink as black as boot polish so that she can read our writing. Sir Henry may not know where it is."

"Surely he will look for it? If you like, we will send a messenger in the morning."

"Then it will be too late."

"Very well, we will send one tonight. Later."

His fingers toyed idly with the pale blue satin ribbons that fastened the front of her dressing gown. There seemed to be no purpose in their movements, just a vague and random examination of the fabric. Then Henry checked himself in the manner of all upright and correct men of breeding. The things one allowed oneself in bed with women of sport did not apply, could not apply, to one's wife. It was unfair, uncivilized, to make them, against their delicate natures, too desirous. It took them from their primary task, which was to bear children. You had to make them ready, of course, so that it was not painful, while taking great care not to overexcite them. One was tender, gentle, and spent oneself as quickly as possible. He had been imprudent with her in the past; that was because he had had so little time, and he wanted her to want him enough to fight the Queen.

Her hair was beautiful, he thought, spread upon the pillow; so was her body, the outlines, which he could see vaguely beneath the coverlet, lush, full, molded like an hourglass, even without stays. He doused the candle, then lay beside her in the bed and kissed her gently, his hands caressing her neck, straying down to the lacy ruchings that covered her breasts. He listened to the quickening of her breathing, her sighs, gently slipped his hand inside her nightdress and withdrew it. Then he raised the hem of her nightdress, as she had imagined he would. She felt the yearning, the painful wanting, turned her head so that she would not have to look at him as he entered her, quickly, expertly, his hand parting her legs. It was not necessary to think of anything else, as Mama had suggested. She could only think of him, above her, entering her, reaching for her secret places, making her his own, his wife. It was over.

He lay beside her. "Did I hurt you?" She could only murmur no, while silently admonishing herself. How stupid he must think me. I should have known to do that myself. Embarrassed to be so awkward, she hoped he would not find her clumsy.

It happened a second time. This time she was quick to part her own legs, turning her head again, closing her eyes, and hoping he would notice that she knew what to do. It happened a third time. No one had told her that it could be repeated. Perhaps, she thought, he is anxious to start a child. She lay still, as Victoria said she should. Then he kissed her on the forehead, said they were both very tired, and turned on his side.

She listened to his breathing. How quickly he fell asleep. She put out a tentative hand to touch his ruffled nightshirt. He stirred softly and flung an arm across her shoulder. She lay still while pins and needles crept into her arm. The messenger would have to wait till morning. Now they were each other's. It was like affixing a seal.

Two days later they returned to Osborne and to Victoria to find that their quarters had been arranged down to the last detail, including a washstand for Henry fitted with a razor strop to his specifications, a razor, and lemon-scented wax. Beatrice resumed her responsibilities at once, leaving after breakfast to join Victoria and her secretaries for the docketed papers of the morning. When Henry stood to accompany her, those at the table, Louis of Hesse, Louise, Helena, sallow-faced and dyspeptic Prince Christian, looked away in embarrassment.

"But my dearest," she said, "you can't be privy to the morning's agenda. I thought you understood."

Henry clicked his heels and kissed her hand, his handsome face expressionless. "Of course," he replied.

There was silence when she left, the only sounds the clink of flatware against the plates and the deviled kidneys that lay frizzling on a hot water dish. The Grand Duke Louis wiped his mouth and suggested they go for a sail on one of the royal yachts. "It is one of your prerogatives," he said to Henry. "You should get used to it."

Writing a letter to the Tasmanian museum to protest on Victoria's behalf the exhibition of the skeleton of the last female Tasmanian, which had been strung on wires and made to dance to a fiddler's tune, Beatrice heard them in the marble corridor, laughing, hurrying to the carriage, which would take them to the quay.

Victoria was speaking. An invitation was to be issued to Randolph Churchill. "It is amazing," she said, "the resemblance between Lord Randolph and our Leo."

A tear rolled down Beatrice's cheek. She wiped it away with her finger, thinking it was foolish to be jealous. Henry was her husband. Devotion was assured. "I forget," said Victoria, "you still mourn him as I do." In September, when Gladstone was conducting a new campaign and there was talk that ladies such as Randolph Churchill's wife were electioneering, many of them unchaperoned, the court went to Balmoral where Henry began to realize what it meant to be on perpetual leave. Leisure had, however, its compensation. He discovered rough terrain over which a skilled horseman could ride, picnics in the hills with goblets sparkling in the open air, over peat mosses tufted with cotton grass, where one could gather handfuls of wild raspberries, and find orchids rambling through the pine needles. And there was deer stalking. Henry, wearing a kilt ordered for him by Victoria, got up at five with gillies, who were given a bottle of whiskey each, ascended Lochnagar beneath rain clouds that drifted like heavy smoke, waded up to his knees in bogs, and returned after dark with roe deer and a brace of grouse, complaining that the gillies were too drunk to be of help.

By now, Beatrice adored him beyond all reason. She wished away the day, for night in the darkened bedroom was the one time they were alone without interruption, although never enough, like having one's plate pulled away by a footman before one was finished, which could happen if you did not keep up at table with Mama.

One night he lay on his back, unable to fall asleep. He had gone stalking and was particularly exhilarated. "Why can't you go salmon fishing like Louis?" she asked. "Then you can take lunch with us."

"My cousin goes fishing because his heart is weakened. Climbing and crawling are too grueling for him. Besides, the gillies prod the fish from the stones and even hold one's net. All one has to do is not fall in the water. But today you cannot imagine. Excitement mounting as my labor became more strenuous, in the final climb and crawl, my heart pounding like it would burst; then a stag rose and stood superb, his great head high, and turned a little towards me, his foreleg crooked at the knee for action. I put up my rifle and fired. There the stag lay. He was dead, and yet I loved him dearly. I suppose I loved him because he contributed to me."

"Contributed? I don't understand."

"I did not expect you would," he replied. "It was a profound and exalted feeling, because I had driven my body to exertion, because the kill was clean and instant, and we stood two thousand feet above the sea, with the bare enormous forest all about us."

"Do you love me dearly?" she asked.

"How can you ask such a question," he replied. "Do I not show it in a hundred ways?"

When they returned to Windsor, the unspoken question on everyone's mind was whether or not Beatrice was in a family way. Victoria told Lady Buccleuch, her lady of the robes, that if she were not, it was due to all the riding after Henry she did at Balmoral. A suite of rooms in the south turret between the Victoria and York towers had been prepared for them, close by the Queen's sitting room and private audience chamber, overlooking the long walk. In the Victoria tower, space had been prudently allocated for expansion.

After a few weeks, it was clear to Henry that Windsor was the center of the Queen's life, ruled by strict etiquette and tradition, her every word law, including the agenda of their daily lives, and her every whim, such as requiring them to stand in nightly attendance in the drafty corridor as she sat in a stiff-back chair, to be met. Henry had stepped into a routine where each coming and going was preordained, where meals were parades, dress for all occasions dictated. His wife was in service to her mother most of the day, often into the evening. Their rooms made them accessible, so that there was no privacy, no place to get away, and the final authority on any problem was Prince Albert, who had died a quarter of a century before.

Being master of one's own house, carving out a career, managing one's estates, these were not to be his, nor would they ever be. It began to rankle. First Henry sought to change their rooms. He told Beatrice he wanted to set aside an area that could be closed off in which his male visitors might smoke. Beatrice twisted her hands. They could not both be pleased. "Mama will be hurt," she said. "She has gone to so much trouble. Besides, she is opposed to smoking in the castle."

Henry was adamant. "If you are determined," she said, "speak to Sir John."

The master of the household informed Henry that the arrangements were under the explicit directions of Her Majesty and were not subject to change without her approval. When the young Prince smartly snapped away, Sir John wondered how long this former officer of the crack Prussian Gardes du Corps would remain tied to the apron strings of his mother-in-law.

Victoria wrote to Vicky. Time was what Henry needed. Papa, as a young bridegroom, had settled in more quickly, but that was because he enjoyed helping her with the blotting paper when she signed and had no need for derring-do. Vicky responded by first asking permission to burn Victoria's letters because of Bismarck's surveillance. Then she wrote that her father-in-law, the aged Emperor, was failing, complaining, as he had begun to do, that Moretta's tears and all the fuss about Sandro were killing him fast, that when he walked, he shuffled his feet so that the least crease in the carpet sent him tumbling. Last she advised that the young couple be given things to do together.

Victoria sent Beatrice and Henry to Chatham Hospital to visit wounded soldiers from the Sudan. Henry wore a vicuña morning coat and a narrow black stock tie and stood in a crowded ward beside Beatrice, who had prepared a brief speech. "Her Majesty wishes you to know," she said, her voice tremulous and quaking, "that the nation is forever in your debt."

"Speak up, if you please, Your Royal Highness," said a man whose head was swathed in bandages. "We can't hear you."

Another, in a bath chair, held in his pocket a bullet that had been lodged in his nose. He asked Beatrice if she wanted to feel its weight. She declined. Then, with a peculiar snort, one who had been lying quietly, died. The hospital staff, clearly chagrined, quickly pulled a white screen about the bed. In the awkward silence that followed, Henry stepped to the bedside of the man in bandages, asking him what kind of action he had seen.

"It is difficult to describe, Your Royal Highness," he replied, "to someone who has never had a tour of duty."

"But you're wrong," said Henry. "I am a cavalry officer."

"Ah, sir"—the man sighed—"but where have you seen duty? You're too young, begging your pardon, for the Franco-Prussian business."

That night Henry disappeared after dinner. A yeoman of the guard came to report he had been seen walking in the home park. Victoria asked if they had words. Beatrice related what had happened at the hospital. "He's sorry, Mama. He wishes he were back in Germany. If he's unhappy, I will die. I cannot live without him."

"You need a baby. Does Henry exercise his rights with regularity?"

Beatrice looked into her lap. "Yes, Mama," she whispered.

"Then it must be something else. Perhaps you bathe in water that is too hot. Your bath water should be tepid, and it should contain no salts."

Victoria conferred with Drs. Jenner and Reid. Dr. Jenner advised that moderate gratification was the answer, that excess, which incidentally led to heart failure, paralysis, softening of the brain, and loss of memory, also devitalized the impregnating fluid. Dr. Reid was dispatched to counsel Henry.

Henry was offended. Of course he knew that his wife did not require the excitement one employed with a courtesan. He folded his arms behind his back. "Good," said Dr. Reid, "then Your Royal Highness understands that the majority of women are not troubled by sexual feelings of any kind. Her Royal Highness does not have the strong passions as yourself. Love of home, children, nation, these were the passions she felt. As a general rule, the modest woman submits only to please her husband; but for the desire of maternity, she would rather be relieved from his attention. These things work themselves out," explained Dr. Reid. "Assuming the married female conceives every second year, during the nine months following conception, in addition to early months of lactation, she experiences no sexual excitement, which works to diminish the husband's desire. A healthy thing. Sensual feelings in the husband become gradually sobered down, preserving the potency of the vital fluid, which leads me, sir," he said, "to Her Majesty's present concern."

CHAPTER FOURTEEN

Wearing a crimson robe with an eighteen-foot train held by four pages in scarlet and yellow livery, Victoria entered the House of Lords to a fanfare of trumpets to open Parliament. On her head sat a crown covered with thousands of jewels, including the Black Prince's ruby, worn by Henry V, a sapphire from Edward the Confessor, and pearls belonging to Elizabeth I. "There are few ordeals worse," she said to Eddy, on whose hand she leaned, "than trying to deliver a speech while balancing a crown." Minutes before, a detachment of yeomen of the guard with lanterns engaged in a ritual search of the cellars.

While the pageantry and pomp belonged to Victoria, Henry, who sat with Prince Christian in a section reserved for the corps diplomatique, noticed the stir when Parnell arrived with members of the House of Commons. Strikingly handsome, urbane, moving with languid elegance, the Irish champion appeared as if he despised the Parliament in which he came to sit.

After the ceremony, Victoria remarked to her ladies that Gladstone, who intended to introduce a bill for Irish home rule, was in the hands of Parnell. "He will ruin the country if he can," she said. The Duchess of Buccleuch lifted the crown from Victoria's head and whispered that Parnell was involved in a sordid alliance with the wife of one of his own followers. "He calls her wifie," she said. "She has even borne him children."

The issue of home rule for Ireland split the nation. It also was a point of contention between Beatrice and Henry, more symptom than malady. It was not a good time for Henry. He had suggested to

Victoria that the British red coat might be impractical in modern battle. Why not adopt, he asked, a uniform that blends with the natural surroundings? There was a new color being used for wear in the field; khaki, he thought it was called. Victoria thanked him and said such matters were in the hands of the Army. There were more serious concerns than merely feeling useless. Louis's baby daughter, Alice, had been found to be stone deaf, and a cipher from Berlin said that danger was impending for Sandro. Since these were matters over which he was powerless, Henry focused on the larger, less immediate issue of Ireland.

Victoria, of course, was against home rule. The idea of separating the home islands stood against the trend of the times, the coming blaze of empire. Beatrice's sympathies were with her mother. The couple argued at night.

"Ireland is stagnant," he said, his hands folded beneath his head.

Beatrice quoted Lord Randolph. Home rule was Rome rule. The priests were so primitive they sprinkled holy water on their congregations from mops dipped in zinc buckets. "You have much to learn about England," she said.

"I see a land desperate to be free." His accent became thick. "How can that be ignored? They want only a stronger say in their own affairs."

"They are a lawless breed," she replied.

"They fester," said Henry, "for a separate legislature."

"You are confusing Ireland with Hesse."

Henry was outraged. "That is an intolerable statement for you to make. Open your eyes, Beatrice. Think with your own mind."

"Whose mind do I think with, Henry?" she asked.

"You sound like your mother. Try to think not with arrogance but with reason. We never travel to Ireland. We go to Scotland but never to Ireland. The Queen has only been there twice."

Beatrice turned from him angrily, pulling the silken coverlet to her chin.

"Do not turn your back on me," he said.

"You have been very rude," she replied.

"Do not turn your back." His voice was cold, like steel.

He flung back the coverlet, gripped her shoulder, and turned her, his eyes blazing, then fell on her, roughly, angrily, ignoring the flickering candle, holding her wrists with his hand and pulling up her gown with a violent tear of silk. "Open your eyes," he demanded. "Open your eyes!"

Beatrice lay awake all night, weeping silently into her pillow. What he did was not a marital embrace but an assault. The next morning she would not speak to him. He was immediately contrite, angry with himself for his loss of control. She looked through him and around him as if he did not exist. The only time she spoke was to issue requests on Victoria's behalf. When the new council met at Osborne after the outgoing ministers had given up their seals, Beatrice told Henry in icy tones he was wanted by the Queen. He left, certain that Victoria, who knew everything that went on, wanted to discuss what he had come daily to regret more profoundly as a reprehensible impropriety.

He found her seated in an audience chamber, the new foreign secretary, Lord Rosebery, standing before her, advising her that the real danger to Bulgaria was the Tsar's rooted hostility toward Sandro.

"You are in a position, Henry, to be of great help," she said.

Lord Rosebery explained. If Prince Alexander sided with Turkey, there was the risk of simultaneous occupation of Bulgaria by both Austria and Russia. England's task was to prohibit a naval attack on Turkey by Greece, thus ensuring Turkey's obligation to come to terms with Sandro. In addition, the German ambassador, Hatzfeldt, said that Bismarck was wholly with England in this matter and had sent an ironclad to the Mediterranean on their behalf.

"Hourly there are matters vital to convey. Your Royal Highness is in correspondence," said Lord Rosebery, "with Prince Alexander. We should like to provide you, sir, with a cipher, a code, so that we can relay important messages through you."

"It would be my greatest privilege," replied Henry, "to be allowed to be of service both to my Queen and to my brother." He bowed. Something in the way he did so reminded Victoria of Albert. The dapper moustache, the physique, the handsome, aristocratic, young face, perhaps in the Teutonic roll he gave to the word privilege. It had not been easy at first for Albert, who had the status of consort. Even Francis of Teck grumbled because he had only the post office volunteers to command. How much more difficult must it be for Henry, whose responsibilities were so ambiguous. Victoria asked him to remain after Lord Rosebery left. "I have no objection," she said, "if you wish to permit smoking in your apartments, providing your servants keep the rooms well aired."

Soon afterward, the little white-haired abbé, Franz Liszt, garbed in a black soutane, brought his grand piano to Windsor. Beatrice and Henry sat stiffly side by side in the crowded green drawing room with the elaborate courtesy of a couple that is estranged. The recital began.

Henry had just supplied Victoria with ciphered messages from Sandro that the Army was solidly behind him and that the traitors who had smuggled a chemist into the court dispensary to mix headache powders with arsenic had been caught and executed. Henry was feeling expansive. It seemed a good moment to try to heal the breach. He would be charming, as if they were not married. Henry had already decided not to mention that Liszt's youngest daughter had borne Wagner an illegitimate child. Instead, he whispered behind his program, "Maestro sounds like Wagner, an achievement for a Hungarian."

Beatrice lifted her eyebrows in disdain. "Wagner derives his leitmotifs from Liszt. It has to do with transformation of themes, which I expect you know nothing about."

When the concert was over, the Empress Eugénie took Henry aside, first speaking of the musicales at the Tuileries where her husband, the Emperor Napoleon, beat time with his head to stay awake. Then, when Beatrice was at the other side of the room, she said, "Buy her a hat. Not jewels, not gloves. A hat. Make it one that is wildly extravagant in style. Make it the sort of hat one does not buy for one's wife."

He took Eugénie's advice, particularly because he knew Frenchwomen to be thoroughly knowledgeable in such matters, and presented Beatrice with a towering box filled with tissue in which nestled a black velvet bonnet with black plumes and white hyacinths under the brim.

She did not try it on as he had expected. Instead, she asked where he got it.

Louise helped him make the purchase, he replied.

"How did she come to shop with you?"

"She did not shop with me. I mentioned that I wanted to buy you a hat but did not know where one went for millinery. She volunteered to help."

"Do you discuss Ireland with my sister?"

"Why would I do that? She brought two boxes. I chose one."

"Then give it to her," she said, turning on her heel.

Later, Ludwig's wife, Victoria, said that he had made the wrong selection, that Beatrice might have liked the other one better, the one he described adorned like a meadow, yellow straw with ribbons and grasses, that Louise had said was too frivolous.

In April, Gladstone spoke for Irish home rule before the House of Commons. His supporters said the speech, which took more than three hours to deliver, was one of transcending eloquence and power. His opponents denounced it as the dream of an old man in a hurry.

Victoria was outraged. With spectacles perched on her nose, she read an excerpt to Henry, Bertie, and Alix, who were dressed for a diplomatic reception. "Ireland stands at your bar, expectant, hopeful, almost suppliant. Her words are the words of truth and soberness. She asks a blessed oblivion of the past, and in that oblivion, our interest is deeper even than hers." Victoria peered over her glasses. "What perfidy. Gladstone wrote to me—Beatrice has gone to find the letter— that nothing could be more improbable than that he would ever advise home rule for Ireland."

"He has managed to split his party," said Bertie. "Chamberlain has resigned. The Scots are against him. There are angry crowds milling about Downing Street. I cannot see how the bill will not be defeated."

Henry adjusted the Star of the Garter on his white tunic. "It does have some merit," he said. "I do not believe the Irish would be so dangerous in an Irish Parliament as they are in a British."

"The Star is worn to the left," said Bertie. "Actually the issue is complex. They are a mystical, unpredictable lot. They greeted me with coffins in Dublin. One needs to be more than a naturalized subject to have a sense of Ireland."

"What nonsense, Bertie dear," said Alexandra. "I had a perfect grasp of England the moment I came ashore, and I, too, wear the Star to my right, especially when it interferes with my arrangement of jewels."

Beatrice returned with a letter. "The Irish are a disorderly people. They will never be satisfied no matter what Parliament does. They cannot be allowed to disrupt the empire." She turned to her oldest brother. "When you went to our apartments to smoke, Bertie, you didn't close the door to Henry's room. Now the smell is everywhere, and it has made me quite ill."

The two couples drove in silence to the Rosebery mansion. When they entered, lackeys wearing silver epaulets sprang from the walls to take the Princesses' sable-trimmed velvet cloaks, while Henry and Bertie doffed their helmets. Bertie remained apologetic. "I'm frightfully sorry," he said to Henry. "She still seems quite upset."

"It is not you," whispered Henry, checking the shine on his eagle. "It is me."

Lady Rosebery was the first to greet the royal party, saying to Beatrice that her pale complexion was as delicate as porcelain. Those in the drawing room bowed before them like rushes in the wind, then came forward with smiles as glittering as their decorations—the Turkish ambassador, Rustik Pasha, the Chinese ambassador in mandarin costume, and the American ambassador, who presented the American novelist, Henry James.

Everyone in the room knew that Sandro's situation had become more critical. Many also knew that ciphers had gone back and forth throughout the day. Only a few were aware that Sandro's only choice was to flee the revolution, which would surely be organized by Russia, or declare himself independent and so bring war with Russia. Yet there could be no open mention of any of it to members of the royal family. Only in the most indirect and circuitous way could it be addressed, if at all.

The Russian ambassador, Staal, presented his wife to Beatrice and Henry. The greeting was formal, polished, and cold. The woman's curtsy was awkward, and her husband had to help her up. "Your Royal Highness was wise," he said to Henry, "as was your brother, Prince Louis, to make your life in England."

There was silence. In Germany, his remark would be addressed in the way gentlemen resolved insinuations, by the saber. Henry had no such recourse. As Victoria's son-in-law, he was officially bound to silence. As Sandro's brother, his restraint was less mandatory than it was political. He could not afford to tip the precarious scales in any way.

Beatrice watched Henry's jaw clench and the color rise from his neck. He seemed so solitary. She took his arm, her voice tremulous but firm. "We in England, Your Excellency, are fortunate to have both my husband, Prince Henry, and my brother-in-law, Prince Louis, at our side."

Later that night, as Beatrice opened her arms to his embrace, Henry said that now he felt that they were truly married. "I am for you," he said, "always, and you are for me."

When Vicky came to visit in May, Beatrice had recognized in herself the early signs of pregnancy but had said nothing to anyone, not to Victoria, not to Vicky, who asked immediately upon her arrival how she felt, certainly not to Henry. The subject was too indelicate, especially for one's husband. It was at the dedication of the Colonial and Indian Exhibition that Vicky also recognized the signs, along with something else less pleasant.

The family had stood upon a carpeted dais in Albert Hall, as Bertie and Victoria each addressed the enthusiastic crowd of commissioners, officers of state, kaffirs draped in blankets, representatives of the colonies in top hats and cutaways, their wives in hopelessly outdated fashions, parsis in white with black-glazed headgear, scarlet-coated field officers who had provided the escort, and turbaned rajahs in bright rich silks. Just after Madame Albani sang "Home Sweet Home," Louise turned to smile at Henry, but his attention was on Beatrice, whose arm he steadied. When Madame Albani went on to sing "Rule Brittania," Louise leaned closer to whisper in his ear.

Vicky and Louise rode back to Paddington Station in an open landau, through a narrow cordon of black-lacquered hansom cabs, omnibuses with stairways curling to their tops, gigs, ponderous and solemn broughams, and brewer's drays with drivers in red stocking caps, which had pulled to the side to let them pass.

Vicky was faced with a decision. There was little question in her mind about what she had seen in Albert Hall. Was it better left alone? Would saying something to Louise in some way spur her on? Would saying something to Beatrice, who was certain to say something, in turn, to Henry, help or worsen the situation? If a wife accuses a husband who is innocent, would it not give him the idea where there was none before? Vicky acted on impulse. Her reasoning was that Beatrice's condition was delicate and Beatrice too naive to manage the situation. "What did you say to Henry on the dais?" she asked. "How could you think of speaking when all eyes were upon us?"

Louise tugged at her gloves. "I don't know what you mean." A crossing sweeper with a broom, a boy of about nine, took off his cap.

"I think you do," said Vicky.

"Your ways are so German, Vicky. One would hardly know you were born an Englishwoman. Your prudery makes you see things that don't exist. Actually, I remember now. It was a harmless comment. I think I told him he was stepping on my skirts."

"If you are unsettled in your own life, Louise, that is your affair," replied Vicky, "but Benjamina may be in a family way. To encourage your own sister's husband is at best cruel. To do so at such a time is vile and unconscionable." She nodded to a crowd of shopkeepers in long white aprons and an oyster vendor with a barrel on his head.

"You behave as if you were already Empress of Germany," said Louise. "How do you have the temerity to speak to me of Henry, with whom I enjoy the most circumspect and sisterly relationship, when you take Count Seckendorff with you everywhere you go. Everyone talks of it. They say he is your lover."

"I expect such slander from Bismarck. Not from my own sister."

"This was learned from your son."

"Count Seckendorff," said Vicky, mastering her voice, "is my faithful chamberlain. He runs my household, he is devoted, honest, thrifty . . ."

"The last may be his most important asset. I know that the Emperor has threatened to disinherit you if you persist in marrying Sandro to your Moretta and that one of the reasons you are here now is to ask Mama for money."

"You must nod," said Vicky. "The people expect it." A muffin man had stopped ringing his bell to cheer. "The money you refer to was my inheritance when Papa died. I asked Mama at that time to exclude me from his legacy. Actually, I did that because all of you were young and unmarried. Matters have changed. If you had children of your own, you would understand how I must consider Moretta."

Vicky was silent, thinking of Fritz; so many colds, his throat swollen again. Willy was dead set against the marriage. If anything happened to Fritz, she would have no protection, and neither would Moretta when Willy became Emperor. She waved the back of her hand to an old soldier on the curb doing rifle exercises.

By late summer, the Irish home rule bill had been defeated, Gladstone presented Victoria with his seals, and Beatrice was in purdah, a semi-invalid in dishabille and knitted shawl, confined for the most part to her apartments. She reclined on a sofa in her sitting room, drinking port wine twice daily and eating, when she could force them down, raw beef sandwiches on the advice of Dr. Reid, who reminded her that she was now eating for two. When Dr. Williams gently palpated her abdomen over her skirts, he said all was proceeding normally. At least the dreadful sickness was over, with the vomiting and fainting spells, which disappeared when she loosened her stays.

She felt the baby kick and could sometimes trace its feeble course. Ludwig's wife, Victoria, said it must be a boy, since girls did not kick that early. Eugénie told her that a woman in a delicate condition must remove herself from the world and confine herself to a place of safety and serenity, preferably indoors. When Beatrice went out for walks, which Victoria made her take daily, she was to be careful not to look at animals. Eugénie had heard of a woman frightened by a heifer who later had a baby with cow's eyes. To be startled at such a time was a calamity. The unspoken question was what had frightened Victoria of Hesse to make her baby deaf. Eugénie privately thought it had been a clap of thunder.

Beatrice's sister, Helena, said the desire for a certain food told one if the expected newcomer was going to be a boy or girl. Salty foods indicated a boy; sweet foods, a girl. The Princess of Wales said that was nonsense. That in all her confinements she craved walnuts and had both boys and girls, that what mattered was whether one carried high or low.

It was difficult for Beatrice to imagine a baby at all. Pregnancy was a condition, an embarrassing illness of several months' duration from which one ultimately recovered. She didn't know how she would feel toward the result or if she would feel anything. That she could include anyone else into the tight circle of Mama and Henry seemed unlikely.

At first, the early news of Sandro's disappearance was hidden from her. Then the dispatches came too swiftly to be contained. First came the terrible cipher that Sandro had been kidnapped; no one knew by whom or where he was. Victoria told a distraught Henry that the sickening treacherous act could only be Russian fiends, a stepping-stone to getting Constantinople, a slap in England's face. Russia must be unmasked. Then came the news that Sandro had been carried off to a vessel, taken to Russian territory on the Black Sea, and sent to the Russian frontier by rail, the destination not yet designated.

Vicky had been right all along, said Victoria. Lord Salisbury always claimed the Crown Princess's fears were exaggerated, but now Russia was intriguing right and left. We must make a formal protest at the very least, she said.

Victoria broke the news to Beatrice. "Of course Henry's wild to dash off to the Ukraine with Louis. Naturally, it is out of the question. He can do more good for Sandro here."

Beatrice found Henry with his head in his hands, his fingers raking through his hair as if to punish himself. She sat awkwardly at his side, her arms resting on the shelf of her abdomen. "Tell me what you know," she said.

"He was working late at night, there was a noise in the corridor, his aide rushed in shouting that they wanted to kill him. 'Run,' he said, 'before it's too late.'

"My brother sprang out of bed and seized his revolver; then he heard a military command and thought he was rescued, but his aide cried out, 'No, no, run. It is the soldiers who want to kill you,' the very army he led to victory."

Henry began to pace. "Then shots from all sides, the palace was surrounded, bullets rattling and a hundred voices crying, 'Down with the Prince.' He put out the lights and in the darkness got into his uniform, not stopping for socks or underwear, only his uniform, so that he might be shot in it. The noise and clash of weapons and shouts grew louder. He went into the corridor; he could have escaped —there is a passage—but he did not. A crowd surrounded him, and by the light of the candle, he saw the glint of bayonets of a hundred men. They pushed him in the entrance hall. An impudent cadet, a traitor, tore a leaf out of the signature book, and the whole insolent drunken crew shouted for him to sign his abdication. A captain pointed a revolver at him. Sandro cried, 'Write yourself and give me a reason for my abdication. I know of none.' One of the bystanders took the pen but was too drunk to write with it. Then Sandro tore the paper out of his hand, and wrote, 'God Protect Bulgaria.' They told him he was going to Russia, forced him into a carriage. Ninety officers quietly looked on, said nothing."

It was daybreak when Henry finished. Footmen were already in the halls trimming the lamps. Beatrice eased her neck, then rang for his valet. "His Royal Highness will want to bathe and change his clothes," she said. "And throw up the sash. Fresh air is needed in this room."

"Louis is going to the frontier to bring him back," he said. "I am desperate to go with him."

"I know," she said.

The baby was born at Windsor. It was on an evening in November when Beatrice and Henry were dressing for dinner. The new Chancellor of the Exchequer, Lord Randolph Churchill, and his attractive American wife were among the guests, and Beatrice was requesting Henry not to speak too fondly of Parnell. Just as her maid was clasping the ruby-and-diamond choker about her throat, her water broke, drenching her kid slippers and staining the carpet in rivulets. Mrs. Brotherstone, the monthly nurse, was sent for, as were Drs. Reid and Williams.

Beatrice was put to bed. The pains were severe and continual, pulling her lower back inside out, in a tug both sweet and excruciating, involving her against her will, grunting, sweating, causing her legs to tremble. When the pains were bad, Dr. Reid gave her chloroform, which he dripped onto a piece of gauze. She heard Victoria in the room, whispering encouragement. Then, with a final tearing expulsion, the baby slipped into Dr. Williams's hands. Someone wiped Beatrice's forehead with rose water. The experience was to her untidy, animal, shameful, humiliating. The nurse dipped her fingers in brandy, laid the baby on its side, and quickly and sharply rubbed its spine until it began a lusty cry. Then she wrapped it in flannel and a Shetland shawl and showed it to Victoria. "Your Majesty shall be the first to see him," she said.

Victoria said he was not very big, that he had a large nose like

Bertie's but very pretty, small ears. "As a rule," she said, "I like girls best."

They laid the baby at Beatrice's side. Still groggy from the sweetish chloroform, she watched him wrinkle his face to cry as someone bound her waist and stomach tightly beneath her fresh lawn nightdress. "Is he ill?" she asked. "Why is he crying?"

"Crying is a benefit," said the nurse. "It is necessary to the wee one's full development."

Beatrice did not think his nose looked anything like Bertie's. The baby was beautiful, like Henry. He put his creased small fists to his ears. Tiny lashes fringed his eyes. It had already been decided to call him Alexander. Beatrice thought the name unlucky but wanted to please Henry. "Alexander," she whispered, "do you know that you are mine?"

The baby was removed when the doctors explained that it was not healthy to keep him in an atmosphere loaded with the breath of adults, which contained an excessive proportion of carbonic acid thrown off by adult lungs and mephitic acid given off by the adult skin. "Do not," admonished Victoria to the nurse, "sleep with the baby at your side."

"Of course not, Your Majesty." The nurse was offended.

Beatrice suckled him in the first few weeks. Her full recovery would take a month, and it was the appropriate thing to do. They accommodated to one another, she learning the feel of his fuzzy head and the expression of his mouth when he had had enough, he associating sweet-smelling softness with satisfaction. She discovered how his hand curled and tightened about her finger when he was intent and how his deep blue eyes seemed to engage hers, although he clearly could not see and would not for a few weeks. At the end of the month, when his wrinkles turned to folds, Victoria said she was finding it increasingly difficult to go on without Beatrice's services. Weak at first and lightheaded when she rose too quickly, Beatrice resumed her schedule, including evenings, from ten to eleven, when she wrote down Victoria's recollections of the day.

It was decided that the baby be put on supplementary feeding as soon as possible to make him independent. The decision was made between Victoria and the nursery staff. Beatrice was not consulted.

Beatrice went to speak to Mrs. Brotherstone. A nursery maid was rinsing glass bottles mounted with India rubber nipples tied with twine. Mrs. Brotherstone held the baby on her lap before the fire, a heated napkin over his naked belly, and explained. "It is good to accustom a child as early as possible to an artificial diet, not only that it may require more vigor to help it over the ills of childhood but that in the absence of Your Royal Highness, it will not miss maternal sustenance." She gave the baby castor oil from a tiny spoon, placing it back on his tongue, and lay him in his crib.

Another nursery maid was stirring arrowroot and water, cooking it into a paste, which she removed to mix with milk in a pap saucepan. Mrs. Brotherstone adjusted the watch that she wore pinned to the bodice of her apron. "Baby actually likes this better; it sticks to his ribs," she said. "You will see, ma'am, that your rest will not be disturbed."

The nursery maid added milk until the mixture was like cream, then poured it into the bottles as the baby drew up its legs and began to cry.

"After the third month," said Mrs. Brotherstone, "we will add an egg for baby Alexander."

Beatrice lifted her skirts to hurry to the crib. "Is he in pain?" she asked. "He sounds as if he were in pain."

"No," said Mrs. Brotherstone with a patient smile. "Nurse knows his cries. I can tell you with confidence, ma'am, he is telling us that he has been handled too much."

Beatrice moved to pick him up. The baby's eyes met hers.

"I shouldn't do that, Your Royal Highness," said the nurse. "We don't want to spoil baby, now, do we? And the physick will take effect much sooner if he is left alone."

When Beatrice went to discuss the matter with Victoria, her mother told her that she was falling into the trap of many new mothers who made too much of tiny infants. Victoria had had nine, and countless grandchildren. She considered babies rather ugly creatures and liked them better when they got older, when one could reason with them. She assured Beatrice that in due time she would feel the same. The nursery was directly above Victoria's sitting room. Beatrice turned anxious eyes to the faint wails heard from above. "The nurses handle tiny babies better than anyone else," said Victoria. "There is nothing you can do for him now except get in the way."

Sandro arrived in England in time for the christening. When the ceremony was over, they sat in the drawing room and listened to Sandro recount the perilous moments when the soldiers took him to a point on the road bordered on both sides by fir, looking for a place to shoot him, but changed their minds, then dragged him to his yacht, forced him into one room, tortured him in ways he would not disclose, closed all the windows, and sailed down the Danube with ship's engines overheated to hasten the journey. It was unbearably hot.

Alexandra began to weep. "How horrible," she said.

Victoria hoped his story would soon be over. While she was sympathetic, its outcome was patent. She was tired from preparations already underway for her golden jubilee. Jubilee medals and jubilee coins had to be examined; remissions of sentences releasing prisoners in her honor, signed. One of a man who had been convicted of cruelty to animals she had refused to sign. "One of the worst traits in human nature," she had told Sir Henry.

In addition, her rheumatism was painful, and she looked forward to the massage she would get when she retired. There was an Irish singer yet to follow, arranged by Mr. Yorke. Victoria's idea had been that it would be prudent to show her regard for all her peoples. Besides, an entertainment would cheer them. Dignified and charming Sandro was nevertheless broken, in body and in spirit. She had already written to Vicky that the engagement must be reconsidered, since it would be unfair to both to contemplate marriage with everything so unsettled. She had not mentioned this to Sandro. It seemed not the time.

"How were they successful?" asked Prince Christian. "We understood the Army to be behind you."

"Three quarters of all the officers were involved in the conspiracy," replied Sandro. "The ministry knew of the plot, but they did not seek to prevent it. The whole clergy is also implicated. It is over. Russia will occupy Bulgaria, and everyone will be powerless to prevent it."

"The indignities you have been put through," said Louise to Sandro, "treated like a common felon, sent without even a servant."

"Despite everything that's happened," said Sandro, "it is my dearest wish that I be buried in Bulgaria."

"What will you do now?" asked Bertie.

"I have asked the Emperor for either a place at court or a commission in the Army. It is only a matter of time before I will have an answer. If I do not have the crown of Bulgaria, so be it. At least I can be happy serving Germany."

"You would be better off with a commission," said Henry.

Victoria wondered if Henry was happy serving her. His remark about a commission suggested that he still yearned for a military career. Always at her side with Beatrice, he had become important to her. She was as fond of him as if he were her own son, so much so that Bertie was becoming as jealous as a six-year-old. The other day, she had fallen asleep in her chair after tea and had opened her eyes with a start to see his reassuring smile. When her memory failed for dates or names, as it did from time to time, he and Beatrice were there to supply them. Henry was beginning to advise her as Albert had done, clearly, simply, sincerely. Arthur Balfour, Salisbury's nephew, who would likely be appointed Secretary for Ireland, had come to call, telling her that the cancer that was sapping the vitality of Ireland was not political injustice as much as the poverty and wretchedness of the people. Could it be, she wondered when he had left, that the evils were mainly economic? Would Balfour be able to calm the Irish? She had asked Henry his opinion. Balfour, Henry said, promised to succeed where Gladstone failed because his approach was one of reason.

Henry was trying hard not to look at Louise. Victoria knew what that was all about. It was not his fault; that was certain. Secretary Ponsonby had informed her that a footman had been present in the blue closet where Louise, wearing a smock over her dress, had set up a small table for her sculpture. She had asked Henry to help her bend the wires of her armature. Their fingers brushed and lingered, overly long, according to the report of the footman. Henry, to his credit, had moved away even though Louise told him that he was too serious, that everything was not life or death, honor or dishonor. That there was something in between, such as the piece she would sculpt, that would have intrinsic value only in existence.

Louise could never speak her mind straight out even as a child. Victoria wondered what she had done differently to this daughter to make her so factious. Something to do with the artistic temperament. And yet Victoria had artistic gifts herself, painting, drawing, and singing. Had not Mendelssohn complimented her when she was a girl? And she was never flighty.

The singer was ushered in. She was beautiful, young, and poised, her black-fringed green eyes unwavering and grave, her dark hair, unlike the elaborately upswept coiffeurs of the women present, brushed down her back like a child's. She curtsied before Victoria. Her silence was respectful. Mr. Yorke, who had heard her sing that morning, had assured Victoria that the girl's voice was excellent and very well trained.

Victoria nodded; then the girl sang, songs of wild, rebellious Erin, as two candles flickered on the piano like pins of light. The harmony wandered on, then moaned, and returned bruised and weary. A solemn stillness had fallen upon the listeners as the voice threw out its imperious flood of protestation and defiance, thrusting its music into the silence like flashes of a spear.

All at once the headlong cadence fell and died away. A few words were murmured, some polite clapping, a contrast between the singer's excitement, her extraordinary force and talent, and the apparent coldness with which it was received.

Alexandra rose and gave her words of congratulation. "How well you sing," she said, "and how very near your heart this music must be."

Victoria saw them all watching her, waiting to take their cue. Was she as obdurate as the papers had said? Perhaps the paucity of Albert memorials in Ireland was due to their poverty and not their arrogance. Yet hadn't she sent them a statue of Albert, carefully packaged, crated, and dispatched to Dublin, and hadn't the mayor returned it? "I want to hear 'The Wearing of the Green,' " she said.

An uncomfortable murmur floated through the audience, a few whispered words. Beatrice leaned over. "Mama," she said, "it's an angry song. You would not like it." Victoria repeated her request. "Sing that song, please. I wish to hear it very much indeed."

"Yes, madame," answered the girl. Her face was set. Her eyes shone with a strange glow; the song she sang was a popular anthem, a shriek for mercy and pity, a defiant challenge from the weak to the strong, the stanzas quickened, each measure full to the brim of vehement desire for justice and victory.

It ended. There was silence, this time no applause, only shuffling and whispering and the crackling of programs. Henry knelt at Victoria's side and took one of her hands. "What a great Queen you are, Mama, and how sure of the affection of your subjects, to permit such a song to be sung in your presence."

"But the song is splendid," she said, "and I wanted to hear it. Besides, I am very fond of the Irish; you may be sure of that."

The evening was at an end. Beatrice brought Victoria's thick ebony walking cane. As she stood with Beatrice on one side and Henry on the other, Bertie handed her a present. "For the new year, Mama," he said. "A bit early, for your golden jubilee." It was an inkwell, a crown forming the lid, and inside, Victoria's face gazing into a pool of ink.

"Very pretty and useful, Bertie," she said.

To Henry and Beatrice, who escorted her to her apartments, she confided that she didn't like the idea of closing her own face upon all that repulsive black ink.

CHAPTER FIFTEEN

Beatrice conceived again during the time when the doctor had told Henry she would be uninterested in the conjugal embrace. It was she who initiated it, feeling distant and jealous after a ball, where, as a matron who had just emerged from a confinement, she had been expected to sit and flutter her fan while Henry danced.

Alexandra had confided that she and Bertie still occupied the same bedroom, despite what people whispered. "He cannot help it," she said, "if women gush after him, flagrantly set their caps at him, hunt him down like a quarry. Henry, too, cannot help it if he is handsome and silly women make fools of themselves. It means nothing. It is you he loves. It is you who bears his children. It is you he sleeps beside." So far Beatrice had managed to keep the facts of her condition from everyone except her maid who laced her stays.

With her hair coiled in an elaborate mass on top of her head, the latest according to Alexandra, she sat with Victoria and Bertie, taking breakfast on Chantilly plates in a hut mounted on a turntable so that it could be turned away from the wind. Swallows had alighted on nearby magnolias and deep red maples. Some picked at the ground between clusters of grape hyacinth and crocus, looking for worms, as Bertie told his mother and sister about his visit to Berlin and about the Emperor's birthday celebration. He was describing the elderly Emperor wearing a lock of hair swept around his head and tied to his ear with a string, while tartan-clad gillies labored to swing the hut around.

Victoria asked about the deposed Prince of Bulgaria.

"The situation is not good with Sandro, I'm afraid," replied Bertie. "Bismarck had misled the Emperor into believing that Sandro intends to become the leader of the opposition in Germany. The old man has denied him both a place at court or a commission in the Army."

They were suddenly confronted with a row of lemon-scented verbenas. "The gillies have faced us into the bushes," said Victoria. She turned back to Bertie, who leaned closer.

"I'm afraid I have even more unpleasant news, Mama. You know that Fritz has reconsidered his position on the subject of Moretta's marriage to Sandro and has given his blessing. The reason is clear. They are saying, to be blunt, that Fritz's throat infection is cancer."

"Surely your information is wrong," said Victoria. "Vicky said it was simply hoarseness from a cold."

"It is more serious than that, Mama. A specialist, a Professor Gerhardt, discovered a growth on his vocal cord. He tried to remove it, first with a snare, then with a ring knife, and finally through galvanic cautery, the heat of an electric wire. He told Vicky that it's gone, but Fritz has trouble swallowing. Worse, he can't speak. He begins but cannot finish a sentence."

"Perhaps it needs time to heal," said Victoria.

"Perhaps." Bertie reached for his cigarette case, then remembered Victoria's injunction.

"How sad," said Beatrice. "If Fritz passes on before his father, he will never have been Emperor."

There was silence as the Indian servants removed their plates. She could have been speaking of Bertie.

"When Willy succeeds," said Bertie, "he will support Russia against England and plunge Europe into war."

"Where is Henry?" asked Victoria. "Why is he not taking breakfast with us? I like having him near."

"May I point out that I am here, Mama, entirely at your disposal?"

"Of course, Bertie, and it is indeed appreciated."

Beatrice excused herself, wondering where Henry was. He had risen early, just as the first light slipped over the sash, saying he needed exercise. That was hours ago.

The nursery smelled of poppy syrup and linseed oil. She found Alexander lying in his cradle, dressed in a tucked white nansook gown, lavishly adorned with lace and ribbons. The baby did not appear to recognize her but seemed to prefer his dimpled hands, which he brought before his face, then the nurse, to whom he lifted his arms. Beatrice stood by feeling inadequate as the nurse reached beneath his voluminous skirts to change his napkin.

It was not the baby's fault. She was to blame. Before she had left for Cannes, she had seen him daily, if only for a few minutes at a time, to bring his chuckling face close to hers, to kiss his fingertips. He had smiled at her then, cooing when she approached his cradle, trying to kick his feet beneath his ruffled gown. She had begun to feel for him in a way that she had not thought possible, different from the devotion she felt for Victoria or the passion for Henry. This was an exclusion of all others, as if she and Alexander shared some secret of self.

Her hand was swollen. Perhaps from all the writing. One's hands tended to cramp from holding a pen. She rubbed it before she picked up Alexander, kissing his temple where a tiny blue vein throbbed beneath his translucent skin, as he struggled from her grasp.

Henry returned just before the morning dispatches, dressed for riding in tight-fitting trousers and dusty boots. One can only go so far at Windsor, he said, where everywhere are gates and guards and people staring over hedges. "If I am to be so confined," he said, "I should prefer to ride in Rotten Row as Bertie does. At least in Hyde Park one meets this one and that one and has a bit of a good time doing so. Of course, one has to live in London. It scarcely pays to do so otherwise." What he was saying was out of the question. They both knew it. It was like Alexander trying to kick beneath his skirts.

"The baby prefers his nurse," she confided.

"Isn't that what they all do?" he asked, allowing his valet to pull off his boots.

"Perhaps. It was different before we left for the Riviera."

"Nonsense. He was unformed then. A tabula rasa. You cannot rely on anything he did before we left as a sign of anything."

The next day a cipher telegram came from Vicky. At first, no one could locate the code. Then Sir Henry found it hidden beneath the crown of the inkwell Bertie had brought for the New Year. A transposition of letters for numbers was made, and Sir Henry was able to read that the German doctors wanted to perform a tracheotomy on the

Crown Prince but agreed to a consultation with the famous English surgeon, Dr. Morell Mackenzie. The Crown Princess implored her majesty to send him as soon as possible to save her husband from the terrible operation. "It must be arranged at once," said Victoria. Henry was sent to tell Dr. Reid to get Dr. Mackenzie started as soon as possible.

Concern for Fritz was not forgotten but put aside in the preparations for Victoria's golden jubilee, which included climbing over the timbers and scaffolding of Westminster with the dean to make sure there was room for everyone and everything. On the way back to Windsor, Beatrice suggested they visit Col. Bill Cody's Wild West Show. They sat with members of the court in the crimson velvet royal box in the center of a covered grandstand, Henry in top hat and morning coat, Victoria wearing her white widow's cap with its streamers fluttering down her back. Beatrice was dressed in pearl gray wool edged with chinchilla, on her head a red felt hat trimmed with red velvet, a red feather, and a gray ribbon.

Leading the parade was Buffalo Bill in a moustache and goatee, waving from a white horse. Behind him on a pony was the Sioux chief, Red Shirt, in war bonnet and paint, followed by a half-dozen buffaloes and a calf, a group of Indian squaws tailing a wagon of hickory poles, forty Sioux and Pawnee braves mounted and in war paint, cowboys, cowgirls, two strings of elk prancing about and dashing across the ground, a pair of burros with packs, a dog team, a goat team driven by Indian boys, a stagecoach, covered wagons, Annie Oakley and Lillian Smith, with their guns and skirts to the knees, a bewildered herd of Texas longhorns, and Mexican *vaqueros*. Last was a little half-breed boy that rode his brown pony up a stairway concealed in a backdrop of Western scenery, looking as if he were riding over a mountain. On its summit he stopped and unfurled the American flag.

Nothing the royal party had ever seen could compare to this unruly rampaging lot. Cowboys hazed a buffalo into the open, while another cowboy went after the beast, tossing a circling lasso in the air. As soon as the loop sailed over the buffalo's head, the rope snapped like twine, and the rampaging buffalo charged toward the stands. The crowd began to scream. Then the cowboy overtook the buffalo, grabbed its mane, and slid off his horse onto the bucking, grunting animal's back.

This was followed by a relay of pony express riders, *vaqueros* breaking in wild horses, sharpshooting with glass balls and pigeons, steers lassoed and wrestled to the ground, and a mule-driven stagecoach attacked by Indians in paint and feathers who burst forth from behind the shrubbery, shrilling their war whoops and firing blank cartridges at the rig, sweeping around the enclosure like a whirlwind. The mules bolted; then, with dust flying, Buffalo Bill and his rescue party dashed out, shot and scalped the Indians, and set an Indian village on fire.

When the blaze was over and most of the smoke had cleared, the little half-breed boy rode to the royal box and made his pony curtsy. Behind him was Annie Oakley with her rifle, the Sioux chief, Red Shirt, two squaws and their papooses slung behind them, and Buffalo Bill in white-fringed buckskins.

Annie Oakley and Buffalo Bill shook hands with the royal party, to their astonishment, while the Indians stood in silence. Buffalo Bill, a handsome man over six feet tall, did not wait to be addressed as was customary but spoke first. "Too bad," he said, "you had to miss Mustang Jack. He can cover thirteen feet with a standing leap, then jump over a horse sixteen hands high. Sometimes he varies his act, picks up a handkerchief from the ground while riding full speed."

"Colonel Cody was in the cavalry," prompted Beatrice.

Henry politely inquired about his military career, and Buffalo Bill replied that he had been in the 7th Kansas Volunteers.

"Tell us what it is like to live in the American West," said Victoria.

"Well, ma'am." His narrowed eyes were on Beatrice, who he thought was a little pale but otherwise just as a woman should be, especially with that red-gold hair peeping under that red hat. Princesses or one of Daisy's girls, they all got silly if you looked at them with your eyes squinted. "I wish you could come with me, ride alone all day, in a sea of prairie grass, the summer sun beating down on you, catch a drink from a buffalo wallow, then watch the blazing sun become a big red ball. You take off the saddle and bridle and turn your horse loose to roll and graze. You settle your saddle for a pillow, spread your blanket, open your grub sack, take out your hardtack and sow belly, and light your fire of dried grass, backed by dried buffalo chips, begging your pardon, fry the bacon in its own grease, then the legs of a jackrabbit browned to a turn in the bacon grease. Supper's over, you fill your pipe and settle down for a good smoke while you gaze up into a dark-spangled distance."

"It reminds me of Balmoral," said Victoria.

The Indian babies were quiet. Beatrice noticed that they had flat heads. Were they born like that? she asked. Buffalo Bill explained that the babies' heads were bound on boards to form them that way. How cruel, she replied. Do they never put the babies down? she asked. Only when they're chopping wood or skinning buffalo. Which one of the squaws was the wife of Chief Red Shirt? Both, said Buffalo Bill. Beatrice tried to imagine the implications of two women and one man living in a tepee. Buffalo Bill was staring at her. She blushed at his insolence, then wondered if he found her pretty and dismissed the thought as vulgar and immodest.

The Indian chief said something to Buffalo Bill. "Ma'am," said the scout, "the Sioux people believe that if they cross the great ocean, they will die unless they get some talisman to carry them back."

"A talisman? Oh, I see," she said. "He wants my feather."

"No, ma'am, your hat."

Later that night, as she lay beside Henry in the dark, he accused her of encouraging Colonel Cody. American men were rough, un-mannered, he said, worse than your Australians. It is because they are so removed from the courtesies of nobility. It has nothing to do with station. Even European draymen know how to behave in the presence of royalty. Then he said Buffalo Bill was merely a circus performer. "I am just as good a marksman; ask the gillies at Balmoral."

"Yes, Henry."

"And his riding is ordinary, showy. Of course he makes himself ridiculous with that saddle. Come with me tomorrow. I will show you feats of horsemanship you have never seen before."

"I can't ride with you tomorrow, Henry."

"Of course not. I forgot that matters of state take precedence."

"Not that."

"What, then?" She was silent, reticent to reveal the indelicacy of pregnancy. "When?"

"October."

"Wonderful," he said, then bent to kiss her forehead, brushing her face with his silken moustache. She offered her lips, putting her long-sleeved arms around his neck. "Are you sure?" he asked. "It might be harmful." She pulled his head down upon hers hungrily while he slipped his hands beneath her nightdress, then carefully, his elbows keeping him from coming too close, entered her in a guarded, cautious act more pledge than concupiscence. When it was over, her cambric nightcap lost among the pillows, she suddenly thought of Fritz.

"If anything happened to you, my life would be over."

"I am not yet in my prime," he said. "You do away with me too quickly."

She kissed the hollow of his throat, which had been laid bare by his open button, then set her cambric nightcap on her head. "There is nothing for me but you, Henry. You are my life." He turned on his side as the acrid smoke of the blown-out candle curled about the bed. After a while she said, "Do you mind so very much our life with Mother?" But he had fallen asleep, his breathing deep and regular. What were the nights like without him? She couldn't remember. How did she sleep in those faraway days without his warm shoulder to nestle into.

The evening before the jubilee, Willy managed to offend everyone in Buckingham Palace but his grandmother, including the Kings of Belgium and Denmark, the Prince of Wales, the Portuguese Infante, and the Japanese Prince, Komatzu. In Germany, he had been feted everywhere, his recent adulation a result of the whispers that a dumb sovereign could not rule, that Fritz would have to relinquish the crown to him. Consequently, he had become more insufferable than ever, even patronizing Bismarck, who proclaimed all over Berlin that there was no such law.

Balancing his left crippled arm on his sword hilt, he first told the King of Belgium that though Belgium might be ahead in colonization, Germany would soon catch up. Then he asked Crown Prince Rudolph of Austria, who had just thanked Victoria for giving him the Garter, if his inamorata, the delectable Baroness Vetsera, had really traveled to England with him for the jubilee, as everyone on the continent was saying. Rudolph declined to comment. Willy was not put off. "My dear fellow," he said, "to have a dalliance is one thing. To transport it is another."

Willy then praised Adolf von Stöcker, his court chaplain, for his anti-Semitic policies, asking Rudolph if he did not agree that keeping the German race pure was a noble goal. Rudolph, who had written editorials in Austrian newspapers on behalf of the Jews, took issue. "Your sentiments match my father's," said Willy. "Stöcker has dubbed him Cohen I. They are an insidious people, Rudolph. It is well known that the English doctor my mother has imported is not Morell Mackenzie but a Jew whose real name is Moritz Markovitz."

His greatest rudeness was to Beatrice and Henry when he and his haughty, shapeless wife, Dona, first brushed past them to greet Affie and his lavishly costumed wife, Marie. Then Willy insisted on filing into dinner before them, hissing first to Henry, "You are not fit to be at the side of my grandmother. I will make certain that your brother will never marry my sister." Mary and Frank of Teck, whose rank had also been reduced in the Almanach Gotha, and their quiet young daughter May came to commiserate on their cousin's arrogance and inquire about the baby Alexander.

When Beatrice went in on Henry's arm to a table covered with gold plate, she asked him who he thought was more unmannerly, Buffalo Bill or Willy. He threw back his head and laughed. She thought him divinely handsome.

The ball that followed was a spectacle of flashing jewels and sabers, lace and satin corsages crossed with ribands, and gold-embroidered tunics hung with orders. Since Alicky was too young for more than a few token dances with her father and uncles, Victoria had her brought to the dais by Harriet Phipps. At fifteen, Alicky promised to be a great beauty. The Queen said she did not want her snapped up by false and arrogant Russians, that she had someone in mind for Alicky, who was very dear to her.

"Who is that?" asked Alicky, her hair down her back, silk bows on her shoulders, the corsage of her gown higher and more modestly cut than that of the older women present, and skirts not yet long enough to suit her.

"He is in this very room," replied Victoria. Alicky looked around at the assemblage of royalty and hoped it was not the Persian Prince, who spoke no English. Victoria glanced in the direction of the Duke of Clarence in gold-braided uniform emblazoned across the tunic with stars. "Eddy, dear. He will someday be King of England, and it is my dearest wish that you will be his Queen."

Alicky made a face at the mention of her cousin's name and switched her hair away from her neck. "I'm already in love, Grandmama, with Nicky."

"The Tsarevitch? But you don't know him."

"I met him last year in St. Petersburg when we went to visit Ella. We fell in love, I with him and he with me. He gave me his picture."

Victoria did not take this admission seriously, especially as she was aching and anxious to retire. She signaled to her maid of honor, who began to gather her fan and shawl and ebony walking stick. "The marriage would be impossible, dear," she explained. "You are a devout Lutheran. You would not be happy in Russia in the Orthodox faith."

"Ella is."

"Ella is different from you. You are more sensitive. You need to be closer to people who truly love you. All your uncles and aunties would be here to guide you; your cousins would be here to give you friendship and loyalty."

"Is it true, Grandmama," she asked as Victoria leaned on her walking stick, "that you have allowed divorced ladies to attend the drawing rooms?"

Victoria refused a glass coach and robes of state, despite Lord Halifax's recommendation that the people wanted gilding for their money, and rode to her jubilee celebration with an escort of Indian cavalry in an open landau drawn by six cream-colored ponies, wearing a black dress, a white bonnet of Alençon lace with a Stuart brim, and a little plume of white feathers set off with a row of large diamonds.

The places of honor beside her in the carriage belonged to Vicky and Alix. Ahead on horseback was a cavalcade of her sons and grandsons, Henry for the first time in an English uniform. Fritz, resplendent in white with silver breastplate, golden bearded, taller than the others, was cheered as a Charlemagne by the enthusiastic crowd and applauded for his courage in the face of his serious illness. Somewhere behind, through the dictates of precedence, rode Beatrice.

Bands played, one giving way to another, as the procession wound up Constitution Hill, through the Arch, past a stand of old Chelsea pensioners, down Piccadilly, Regent Street, Waterloo Place, the Embankment, and Bridge Street, the way lined with an honor guard standing shoulder to shoulder. Emblazoned shields, legends, garlands of flowers, and banners crisscrossing streets hung where days before carpenters had erected balconies, platforms, triumphal arches, and pennanted Venetian masts. Every sidewalk, every window, was filled with cheering, waving people, a mighty roar that followed Victoria inside Westminster Abbey.

Met at the door by the Archbishop of Canterbury and the Dean of Windsor, both in purple velvet mantles sprinkled with embroidered gold crosses, the same robes that had been worn at her coronation, she walked slowly up the nave to Handel's "March," toward the great dais in the center. On either side were members of Parliament, the diplomatic corps, visiting royalty within the altar rails, their ranks enlivened by the Thakur of Limri wearing a gleaming aigrette of emeralds in the center of his white turban, the Queen of Hawaii in black satin brocaded with red roses, and the elegant Maharani of Kuch Behar in yellow silk. She noticed that Crown Prince Rudolph did not bring his wife, Princess Stephanie of Coburg.

Victoria was brought back almost fifty years, before the railroads, before the photograph—when one sent painted miniatures of oneself —before the empire, borne of imperial duty, which gave her title to the oceans, to when she was a girl of seventeen, dressed in crimson velvet trimmed in ermine, slimmer than Alicky. Her mother had been alive then, her beloved Albert only a cousin she had met, receiving the homage of the princes and peers. The Archbishop of Canterbury had crushed her ruby ring on the wrong finger, and she had risen from her coronation chair to help the aged Lord Rolle, who tumbled when his foot caught in his robes. She doubted that she could do that now. If anyone stumbled, it would be she. She was thankful that the rheumatism was not so bad. It made it easier to climb the steps.

The family advanced to kiss her hand, all her children, now grown, with lives of their own. Why was it that the troubles of one's children, no matter their age, become one's own. Bertie, Affie, Arthur, who had suggested that she wear something really smart, Helena, Louise, then Beatrice, in a bonnet of pink rosebuds, curtsying, bending low, kissing her hand, receiving, in turn, a ceremonious salute on the cheek. Baby, dear sweet Baby, in the early days, I would have died without you, loyal, steadfast, except when passion made you desperate. When it was Vicky's turn, Victoria gave her a long embrace, less because of Vicky's sorrow than because of all the children, she had been the most beloved of Albert.

The one-hundred-and-twenty-foot yacht, *Sheilah,* a gift from Victoria to Henry, with a crew of twenty, was under sail, running in the fresh breeze, its glossy black clipper bow cutting through whitecaps, which whirled back in great curls of foam. White sails and dazzling brass work glistened in the afternoon sun. Henry, wearing a yachting costume of pea jacket, jack-tar trousers, and a cap, stood beside the captain, who fondled the spokes of the wheel, telling him that he wanted the spinnaker set. On deck, beneath a brilliant canopy of flags, were Vicky, Fritz, Louis of Hesse, Helena, Christian, and Louise. They sat on wooden steamer chairs, banked by pillows and rugs, listening to creaking booms and flapping sails, while before them stewards in white duck and brass buttons offered cups of broth and peeled oranges stuck on forks.

Christian was commiserating with Louis of Hesse, whose heart condition imposed restrictions, complaining of his own torpid liver, while Vicky, in a jacketed woolen yachting costume, was telling her sisters that Dr. Mackenzie suggested she and Fritz visit Braemar where the air would do him good. Fritz had gone nearly every day to Dr. Mackenzie on Harley Street, she said, and Dr. Mackenzie snipped off the last of the growth on his vocal cord. The cure that he had promised was completed. Fritz would soon be able to speak in his natural voice. All he had needed was a peaceful convalescence. Fritz touched his neck. It was only slightly tender.

The schooner passed a beach reserved for ladies where bathing machines stood up to their wheels in water. Louis of Hesse took out his spyglass and scanned the shore. A dipping woman, stout, portly, wearing waterproofed clothing, bulging everywhere, bonnet secured tightly to her head, staggered through the water, intent on grabbing reluctant bathers firmly around the waist to duck them and earn sixpence for her trouble. It was agreed that she performed a useful service. "A wet body and a dry head," said Helena, "lead to an early death."

"There," said Louis to Christian. He handed him the spyglass. "Where?"

"To the right of the last machine. Frolicking with the others on the end of a rope."

"Do you mean the one in yellow and white?" he whispered.

"Your liver may be bad," said Louis, "but there is nothing wrong with your eyes. Well set up, don't you think?"

"It's difficult to tell. The waves get in the way."

"What are you looking at?" asked Helena.

Henry excused himself and went aft to check the shrouds. From where he stood, those on the nearest mast seemed slack. Louise followed after him. The deck officer turned to busy himself with his crew. "You really should not make yourself so distant," she said. "It is not polite."

"Are you not impolite to leave the others?" Music from a brass band blared across the water. He shielded his eyes and squinted up.

"All they talk of is sickness. I am alive and healthy. I don't want to talk of anything but the sea and the taste of salt spray and how you left me sleepless and tossing all night."

He was intent on the rigging, making no acknowledgment of the day before when he had suddenly pulled her into a doorway of the terrace garden, crushing her against his chest and kissing her with ardor, nudging, then thrusting his leg into the pleated flannel of her tennis skirt and its alpaca foundation until his knee was between her legs and she had groaned.

"Where?" she asked.

"Where? Where what?" He smiled.

"You taunt me, but you know that, don't you?"

"I thought it was the other way around." The strengthening wind began to whistle in the halyards, and swells from the open channel sprayed the decks with foam. Louise's straw hat slipped its long skewer and flew over the ship's railing as the crew set about to reef the sails, gathering them at the bottom to fasten to the booms.

"To look at you, one would never know that you are cruel," she said. "Yesterday at tennis, for example, I think you rolled your shirt-sleeves to your elbows on purpose, knowing that I would want to sculpt them . . . or be in them."

"You give me credit where none is due. Meet me in the pier house," he said, "tomorrow morning, early, before sunrise. Wear nothing beneath your skirts, no chemise, no drawers, no bustle."

"No stays?" Her eyes were bright.

"Yes, stays—I want your waist pulled tight, so tight you cannot breathe—and stockings, the black ones you wear for tennis, not the white ones. White is too maidenly. White is for nuns; you are no nun. I want to feel the naked flesh between your stocking and your corset. Wear your hair with only a few pins so that when I reach behind you, it will come down like a veil, and have your nipples out. I want them where I can reach them, and rouged as you did before. What was the taste?"

"Almond and rose."

The face of the island had changed. They sailed past towering breaker-battered cliffs that plunged in a precipitous drop to the sea, then miles of broken terraces created by landslides, strewn with a tumble of rocks, dense undergrowth, and fallen trees, clinging by twisted clawlike roots.

"Here you are," said Vicky, lurching toward them, one gloved hand on the railing. "We are all going below into the saloon, Henry, before you have to lash us to the wheel." She turned to Louise. "You should get out of the sun or carry a parasol. Your cheeks are flushed. Helena and Christian are keen to see *Spithead*, Henry. There are forty-three torpedo vessels and thirty-eight gunboats, not to mention a frigate, that Fritz wants to see. The back of the island is nothing but cliffs and rough seas. If you insist on following it, Henry, we shall have to stay below and listen to Christian recite Grey's elegy. He knows it by heart, you know, and it is not the thing for Fritz to hear."

"Henry is only interested in the back of the island because it is called the Bay of Death," said Louise.

"That is untrue," said Henry. "I cruise the back of the island to avoid other yachts. For privacy."

"What sort of privacy do you need?" asked Vicky. Her eyes went from one to the other. "Surely when you entered royal life you realized privacy was an impossibility? That everything one does is under scrutiny."

"It is not scrutiny one avoids, Vicky. It is its verdict."

It was very hot, the air still and heavy. A huge block of ice sat shimmering on a bed of straw in the center of the dining table. An

Indian servant with his hands clasped in front of his sash nodded to a footman wheeling in a trolley.

The footman removed trays of calves feet, shellfish, and cold grouse and placed them on the mahogany sideboard as Sir Henry cut into his mutton chop. "Bismarck wants the Crown Prince to return to Berlin," he said. "The British ambassador informed me that if the Crown Prince dies, it would be impossible for the Crown Princess to return to Germany. He said they are asking in Berlin how the heir to the throne can remain absent when he might be Emperor the next day? He also said they are saying that the Crown Princess prevents the operation in order to keep the Crown Prince alive long enough to be Emperor; then, untreated, he dies, and leaves her with the imperial dowry and Seckendorff."

"I do not understand," said Victoria. "What has Seckendorff to do with it?" The Indian servant filled her glass with Madeira wine and removed her plate.

Sir Henry explained, while his unfinished mutton chop was being removed, that Bismarck's informant, Radolinsky, had taken him aside to tell him that Seckendorff and the Crown Princess were lovers.

Beatrice had touched very little food. It was too hot to eat, and she was very uncomfortable. Her back ached, and her feet were beginning to swell. Was it true about Vicky and Count Seckendorff? Beatrice doubted it. Vicky was too concerned with her desperately ill husband, which she demonstrated by her irrational interest in tennis. Vicky had said that it was important as soon as the baby was born for Beatrice to have tennis outfits made with straw hats and long aprons to hold the balls. Why should a game be so important? Beatrice asked. When my hand doesn't ache, I have my piano and my paint box. It is not the same, replied Vicky. One plays the piano alone. One paints alone. One plays tennis with others; one's husband, for example.

Victoria was speaking. Something about Lord Rosebery. "I beg your pardon, Mama," said Beatrice.

"I asked, Benjamina, if you thanked him for the miniature of Queen Elizabeth?"

"Not yet. I'm sorry."

"When you do, you must tell him I am delighted to possess the locket but that I have no sympathy with my great predecessor, descended as I am from her rival queen, whom she so cruelly sacrificed."

Victoria went for a carriage ride with Lady Churchill and her new maid of honor, Miss Mallet. Beatrice had two free hours at best. She decided to visit the day nursery. Alexander was sitting firmly now, no longer wobbling from side to side, holding in his hands a crust of bread. He was peevish, his gums red and shiny, swollen at the place where overnight had appeared a fine white line. She felt the sharp edge of teeth with her finger. He began to cry, dropping the crust of bread and putting his hands to his drooling mouth.

The nurse bobbed a curtsy. "We need to increase his perspiration, ma'am," she said. "If that doesn't help, we shall have to think of lancing his gums."

"Is that necessary?" asked Beatrice. "Don't teeth simply come through?"

"Your Royal Highness must try not to concern herself with details of the nursery. Lancing is what the doctors order when baby has too much difficulty."

Beatrice's back ached. She arched to ease it. It seemed as if she would never have this new baby. "I should like to take him out," she said.

"Baby is best indoors, ma'am," said his nurse. "Where it is cooler."

"I thought you needed to increase his perspiration." Beatrice swept past the grim-lipped nurse, directing the reluctant nurserymaid to carry the baby and follow after her, out of the villa down the sweep of lawn sloping to the sea.

It was a silver summer's day, the sky and the luminous sea almost indistinguishable. They walked through flowering cotton grass and ox-eyed daisies bending in the sea breeze, picking their way to a cove with a shallow pool, a water meadow of anemones, urchins, gooseberries, sea squirts, and hermit crabs. Terns skittered to the shoreline at their approach.

"Remove his gown," said Beatrice, "his shoes, his stockings, and his corset." The unwilling nurserymaid, who knew she would have to answer to the nurse, disrobed the baby with the halting, meticulous movements of the grudging. "Surely he may keep his bonnet, madame."

Beatrice took her petticoated son to the water's edge, dropped to the sand, and placed him in her lap. Foaming ripples lapped the edge of her gown, soaking her shoes and train, and ran over his feet. He chuckled. She splashed his toes and moistened his forehead, then shielded her eyes toward the pennanted yachts. Henry was out there somewhere. She wished he were with her and Drino at the water's edge. She took the baby's dimpled hand and showed him how to splash. The water sprayed her coiffure. How lovely it would be if she and Henry could live alone with the children and only a minimum cortege. Perhaps if he had a commission he would be less restless.

Henry trod lightly toward the pier house, trying not to step on the gravel paths. Only hours before, Beatrice had raised the subject of their living independent lives apart from the Queen. What made her think of such a thing? Women who were expecting often had strange ideas. If life at court was tedious and restrictive, how much more so sequestered in some baronial estate with none of the glory and privilege of sovereignty and all of the protocol.

He stepped into the pier house and found her at once, catching her scent of roses and almond before he spied her shadow. He stood for a moment in the blackness, thinking that since she was the pursuer, he owed her nothing. There was no pretense, none of the protestations of affection one usually made, and therefore he was free to indulge himself, to do exactly as he pleased. That morning she had come without her knickers. He would take her on the bench. He would make her get on her hands and knees and face the villa; then he would blindfold her and tell her that she had to stay still and not turn. He would make her wait, while whispering randy things to make her squirm; then he would throw up her skirts and petticoats over her head, finger her like a servant girl, and take her not in the way she was accustomed but from behind. He would take her hard, make her gasp, then grab her hair and force her down in the sand as one would a whore. She had given him no peace. Now he would give her none. Her silken skirts rustled as she came toward him. A nightingale warbled its last notes before morning.

Beatrice gave birth to a baby girl at Balmoral, the first royal baby born in Scotland since 1600. The delivery was difficult. Beatrice had neither the strength nor the inclination to give the flannel-wrapped infant more than a fleeting glance, in contrast to the Highlanders,

who celebrated the birth with piping and whiskey and the discharging
of guns over a roaring bonfire.

Eugénie, who was staying nearby at Abergeldie Castle, came to
take tea on a day dreary with mist and drizzle. They say in the drawing room, lit by four branched candelabra held by marble statues of
Highlanders. Beatrice, in a loose flowing tea gown, wore a gift of
Eugénie's under her corset, the new Swanshill Belt, designed to restore and retain the maiden form after confinement. Eugénie, still in
her brown silk grosgrain redingote, asked for Henry. Beatrice replied
that her husband was off shooting. He is happiest at Balmoral, she
said; it reminds him of the Thuringerwald.

"Yes," agreed Eugénie. "Scotland had the same fresh bracing air."
Eugénie had heard from her lady-in-waiting palace gossip concerning
Henry. She observed Beatrice carefully, determining that she was wan
and pale because of her confinement. Victoria's youngest daughter
had none of the pinched-face look of the worried wife, most likely
because she was too innocent to recognize the signs of wanderlust.
Eugénie asked about Vicky.

"The news is very bad." Beatrice stirred milk into her tea. "Vicky
wrote from San Remo that new tumors had been detected below each
vocal cord. She puts ice bags on Fritz's throat day and night. The
doctors all agree it is cancerous, even Mackenzie, and are recom-
mending total removal of the larynx. All the Berlin doctors are accus-
ing Vicky, saying that they have been right all along, that an operation should have been carried out long ago, that Fritz shouldn't have
been traveling. There was a terrible scene with Willy. He arrived at
San Remo with a laryngolist from Frankfurt, burst into her room, and
told her to get Fritz dressed to return with him to Berlin for an
operation. She refused and barred the way into Fritz's bedroom with
her body."

"You know," said Eugénie, "there are ghosts at Abergeldie. Some
say they are the couple who fell to their death from the aerial cross-
way. I do not think so. The spirit I see is an old woman with long gray
hair crowned in white roses. When she speaks from beyond, it is to
foretell the future. She told me that Fritz is so bad he should not
accept succession but pass it on to his son."

"Will you tell that to Mother?"

"Of course."

The children were brought from the day nursery, each carried by a nursemaid. The baby girl was beautiful, but Beatrice's heart did not stop as it did for Alexander, nor did she feel the fierce connection. Something was wrong with her. Somehow she was unnatural. She did not discuss it with Eugénie but instead picked up Alexander and held him in her arms, wondering if he could one day behave toward her as Willy did to Vicky.

He struggled to get down. Beatrice set him on the tartan carpet. He made tentative steps, suspended from her hands, his little legs hidden in his gown. He was walking. When did that happen? A child lies idle, kicks a bit, crawls, then suddenly is on its feet. Beatrice felt a twinge of envy. The nursery staff had seen it first. Or perhaps no one saw it. Perhaps they had their backs turned and he had just walked. How lonely for him. How sad. She began to cry, tears spilling down her cheeks.

"What's wrong, dear?" asked Eugénie.

"He's walking," she replied.

"But that's nothing to cry over. Next he will begin to speak. When he calls you Mama, you will melt."

Miss Mallet was admitted by a footman into the drawing room. Wearing lavender, one of the few colors allowed a maid of honor, she curtsied. "Her Majesty wishes your presence, Your Royal Highness." Beatrice returned Alexander to his nurse and went to embrace Eugénie, who was gazing at the new baby. "This one is special," she said. "I am already planning her marriage."

"To whom?" asked Beatrice.

"The Infante of Spain, of course. There is no one else."

The waving flags of the beaters fluttered in the damp purple heather; then a roar like thunder arose as hundreds of grouse leaped simultaneously out of a fold in the moor, dark shapes sweeping toward the kilted men kneeling behind a bank of peat, each shouldering a rifle. Behind each one stood a loader holding an open bag of cartridges and a second gun. The wind was with the grouse, and they came in great numbers and speed, one covey after another, whirring, becoming dark specks, then copper and green and brown blurs over the hunters' upturned faces. The men fired in rapid succession, one gun after another, and the birds plummeted like meteors as the dogs ran to retrieve them.

When it was over, Henry put his arm around his brother's shoulder. "You did very well," he said, "for a naval commander. It was the very summit of marksmanship, the nonpareil of shooting." He turned to a hounds keeper. "That young bitch has her mother's nose and steadiness; in fact, she is the dead spit of her on the line, but she is inclined to pinch her birds when she picks them."

"I will see to it, Your Royal Highness," said the man.

They tramped through the heather, with beaters, loaders, keeper, and dogs following behind. "You are making a grave mistake," said Louis. "You know to what I refer. Your position, Liko, is an enviable one. There are those who would like nothing better than to see you disparaged. Why do you put yourself at a disadvantage and in a position to be slandered? There are plenty of women. Surely you are not limited to your own sister-in-law."

"What I do is my business."

"Yes, that is true. But I will give you my opinion nevertheless. Women are women, and they abound. Try to restrain yourself until you are safely out of sight, and then, in heaven's name, select someone unimportant. If what I heard gets to the Queen's ear, your position will be badly compromised. My God, man, what do you want? Beatrice is a loving, devoted wife. She has given you two beautiful children. The Queen has already said you are like a son. You and Beatrice go everywhere, do everything. You are privy to information that even Bertie does not have."

"It is easy for you to speak," said Henry. "You have responsibility, purpose, a new command. You can see your career moving forward."

"But you knew all this when you married."

"I did not realize what it would be like. Imagine if you can an evening shirt, stiff, starched, then imagine that it covers you from head to toe and that everyone around you is also covered in the same way. That is something of what it's like at court."

"And Beatrice? What of Beatrice?"

"She cannot be separated from her mother. It is like taking a woven piece and trying to tease the woof from the warp. When she speaks, it is the Queen I hear. Even in bed sometimes I imagine I am making love to Victoria."

CHAPTER SIXTEEN

A detachment of mounted carabinieri with strong-boned Tuscan faces escorted the carriages containing the English royal party from the Pitti Palace where they had just had luncheon with the King and Queen of Italy. They crossed the Ponte Vecchio, passing covered arcades of goldsmith shops where the morning before a shopkeeper told Lady Churchill that he was retiring to the coastal town of Piombino to live with his married daughter and was ready to sell his goods at sacrificial prices.

The Duke and Duchess of Edinburgh, Beatrice, and Henry, torpid with chianti, figs, melon, sausage, ragout, roti, and lemon ices shaped like famous composers, waved to the cheering pedestrians. They were discussing Fritz, now Emperor of Germany, his tracheotomy, and the wedding of Moretta and Sandro, which would not be too far off. Affie, lifting his stiff felt homburg to passersby, wondered aloud exactly how Fritz ate with the cannula in his throat. "Spare me such details, if you please," said Marie, tilting her parasol against the warm Florentine sun, careful not to poke the stuffed cats' heads on her towering Gainsborough hat.

They alighted at the Uffizi Palace, the women wearing the modish new tailor-made suits of long redingotes over unembellished skirts that barely skimmed the ankle while the carabinieri chased away a donkey cart. Before the gathering crowd pressed closer, the royal party and their attendants were ushered in by the bowing museum director and his assistants and led through long glassed-in corridors with vaulted ceilings encrusted with mother-of-pearl.

"Why must you go with Affie to Malta?" whispered Beatrice. She fingered a small silver watch slung from a chatelaine. "I still don't understand why you have to leave me and Mama?"

"This is my only opportunity to see my brother's ironclad. I would prefer that you accompany me, of course, but you cannot. I hoped you would understand."

"A ship is a ship. And Malta is no better than a rock. There is so much to do and see here. I find it hard to understand how a civilized man can leave the city of Galileo and Dante."

"Galileo and Dante are dead. Those that I meet are the King and Queen of Brazil, both ill and tedious, and their grandson Pedro, of interest only because he is the son of a Coburg, and I have frankly seen enough of the tombs of the Medicis."

The museum director was speaking. Affie was listening politely, while Marie seemed impatient. "Florence has always been the arena between pope and emperor. We Florentines, of course, were always for the popes, yet we are independent; we shut the city gates in the face of Frederick Barbarossa. We always stood for republican principles and for His Holiness. It was the guilds that ruled Florence, the merchants and craftsmen, not the nobles." Beatrice and Henry fell back as the director began to talk of the black death and how Boccaccio and his friends told bawdy tales while stinking cadavers piled up in the city squares.

"You insist on going even though you know I wish you not to," she said.

"You are making this unnecessarily difficult."

The director stood waiting before a canvas of a battle scene. Beatrice moved to catch up with the group. "The beauty of this Uccello," he said, "is in its depiction of the decisive moment when the leader of the Sienese, Bernadino, is hit and thrown from his horse, which rears before the compact ranks of the Florentines."

Beatrice held her parasol by its tip. "The obvious parallel of the Sienese flight is seen in the fleeing hares."

"Your Royal Highness has a well-trained eye. To be noted is the manner in which the artist has elaborated each form, horses, shields, lances, trumpets, crossbows, helmets . . ."

"From a tactical point of view," said Henry, "this is an excellent example of what cavalry ought not to do. Bernadino should have retreated behind the fighting line to retain strategic control of his troops. If a commander is bold, it is a calculated boldness. This man looks less bold than surprised that they have knocked him from his mount."

The museum director bowed. "If Your Royal Highness will permit, it is an allegory. Uccello has painted most of the men going into combat unseeing, with their visors down, blind, so to speak."

He walked ahead, opening his arms to the paintings. "This portrait of His Holiness, Leo X, is the masterpiece of Raphael's last years. Note the central figure in its three-quarter turn, the two bodies at the side like chapels built around a central apse."

Beatrice turned to Henry. "You will miss the archbishop's visit."

"I have nothing to confess."

"That isn't clever."

They moved on. "While Raphael was painting in Rome," said the museum director, "Titian was reinterpreting classicism in Venice, composing his splendid variations on the theme of feminine beauty. The most famous of these is this you see now, entitled *Flora.*"

Henry leaned closer. "She resembles you," he said. Beatrice's head was erect, her countenance fixed in immutable hauteur. "But look," he insisted, "the rounded shoulder, the red-gold hair, the mouth. I will ask your brother Affie. Let him decide."

Beatrice repressed a half smile and touched the loops of hair worn low on her neck. "You are incorrigible."

In deference to the English visitors, a Titian *Venus* had been draped with a diaphanous shawl suspended over the lower half of the canvas. "Usually they are stenciled over with vine leaves," said Marie. She and Beatrice gave the painting the expected cursory nod and moved on with the museum director.

"I like the look in the eye of that one," said Affie of the nude. An assistant director unhooked the drapery to let the prince view the balance of the canvas. "One could call it docile invitation. You will find that in the Maltese. You will also find that they are a dark hybrid; the Ottoman influence is very strong. And you have to be careful of the pox."

"I will be there only a week," said Henry.

"If I had one quarter the women who flutter their lashes at you, I should never see the light of day. Incidentally, my mother, the

Queen, is aware of your brother Sandro's present attachment to Mme. Loisinger. I can't say I blame the fellow. This marriage business has been on and off for three years, and everyone attaches to an actress or a ballerina at one time or another. Personally, I prefer dancers. They have stronger limbs. I hear the Loisinger woman is charming."

"All Sandro wants is to begin his life together with Moretta." Henry did not intend to confirm that Sandro's commitment to the Prussian princess was only that of honor since he had fallen deeply and hopelessly in love with the prima donna of the Darmstadt theater.

Their carriages clattered through narrow thoroughfares paved with massive blocks of white granite, past dun and ocher façades, piazzas with long arcades lofted in elegant apexes, to the thronged Piazza del Duomo with the bulky hump of the domed green, white, and pink marble cathedral, where beggars lay about the steps and men crying "Ciambelli" sold macaroons.

An equerry led them quickly to the ground floor of an orphanage with delicate Corinthian columns studded with blue and white Della Robbia medallions of swaddled babies where they took up positions behind a grated window.

"The ceremony you are about to see," said the equerry, "dates back to the Crusades."

"I am so glad Mama has taken her Indian servants back with her to the villa," said Marie, peering through the grating. "The Florentines bow before them as if they were princes, and they bow back in return. One in particular had the effrontery to tell me he was not of the servant class but the son of a surgeon general. Someone should speak to Mama."

"Which one of us?" asked Affie. "You know how Mama is when she forms an attachment. Incidentally, did any of you notice how she fell asleep after lunch? I've never seen her do that before."

"She is very tired," said Beatrice. "It is natural that she should need to take a nap from time to time."

Affie and Marie exchanged looks. "I'm sure your brother did not mean to disparage Mama," said Henry.

"He implies she is dotty. She is not in the least enfeebled. Certainly not in the way Affie suggests."

In the piazza, white oxen garlanded with flowers pulled a wheeled pagoda four stories high, gilded, paneled, tasseled, laden with fireworks, and halted in front of the Duomo. A cord to which a dove-shaped rocket was attached extended from the church to the pagoda. There was silence; then the strains of "Gloria in Excelsis" coming from the cathedral. "At this precise moment," said the equerry, "a priest inside is applying light from the holy candle to the rocket." Suddenly, the dove flew hissing from the church along the cord, igniting the fireworks. The spectators in the piazza cheered, and bells rang out from the mosaic campanile. "The peasants believe," said the orphanage matron, her hands tucked into her capacious sleeves, "that if the dove flies straight to the car, there will be a bountiful harvest."

Beatrice inclined her head toward Henry. "What will you do in Malta for a whole week?"

"Be bored," he whispered, "think of you, and wish I had not been so rash."

As they walked to the waiting carriage, Marie took Beatrice aside. "You are foolish to mind that he leaves," she said. "One would think you would welcome relief from conjugal obligations. I for one am grateful that the Mediterranean squadron is under Affie's command."

They sat in the saloon of their Aubusson-carpeted private railway car, listening to the clicking wheels and watching the foothills of the Po Valley leap into Alps. If Henry had been attentive to Beatrice and Victoria before he left for Malta, now he was more so. He brought them refreshments and notepaper, frequently taking them out of the hands of servants. When they talked about the riots in Ireland, Victoria saying that they were the result of parish priests who made inflammatory speeches inciting tenants to refuse payment of rent, Henry kept his sentiments to himself and adjusted the pillows behind Victoria's back. When Victoria talked of the unfairness of the discovery of the largest gold field in the world in the Transvaal, a territory in which she had only nominal suzerainty, while the Boers had jurisdiction, Henry reminded her of the diamond mines at Kimberley and the ruby mines in recently annexed Burma. They considered names for the part of New Guinea over which sovereignty would be declared, including British New Guinea, Papua, Papuana, and Reginia. Victoria squinted in a shaft of light from the window and said that Papua was a corruption of the Malay words pua pua, which meant woolly, while Henry removed the sashes from the fringed and tasseled velvet curtains and let them close.

At the platform in Innsbruck, they were greeted by the Emperor Franz Joseph of Austria, in scarlet dress uniform and frogged white cloak. Behind him, sparkling in the sun, was a coach of glass and gold with coachmen and outriders in black and gold-laced coats and three-cornered hats with ostrich feathers. As equerries rushed to place a red carpet before Victoria's saloon car, the Emperor swept his green-plumed hat from his head and bowed before her. She, in turn, with difficulty, curtsied to him.

Then the nearly bald Franz Joseph, with snow-white moustache and whiskers, led them into a station waiting room that had been transformed with carpets, jardinieres, priceless hangings covering train schedules and ticket windows, gold plate laid on a damask-draped table, footmen in scarlet tail coats and white knee breeches, and waltz music from a string ensemble hidden behind the ferns.

"How happy I am at the good relationship between our two countries," he said.

Victoria said she learned of the concentration of Russian forces on the frontier of Galicia.

"Your Majesty's intelligence is excellent," he replied. "Russia is an enigma, and Bismarck much too yielding to her. I was surprised to learn that your Randolph Churchill advocates Russian control of the Mediterranean."

"No more surprised than I," said Victoria. "Lord Randolph holds a dangerous doctrine. The Prince of Wales has been asked to restrain him if he can."

"It is useless to make agreements with Russia," said Henry, "for she always breaks them."

"That's very true, Henry," said Victoria. "What I have been saying about those half-Orientals all along."

They talked of Fritz's grave condition. The Emperor said that he had heard Bismarck threaten to resign if Victoria set foot in Berlin. Then Victoria asked why Stephanie, Rudolph's wife, did not come to her jubilee celebration. Franz Joseph seemed upset. "If it concerns the Vetsera woman," she said, "I know all about that."

"I can only offer my own apologies," said the Emperor.

Victoria was mollified. "One can't be held responsible for one's children."

"Did you see the look on his face?" Victoria asked when they boarded the train. "He wonders if I also know about Frau Katherina Schratt, who lives, mind you, on the palace grounds, an arrangement he has had with her for years."

Beatrice looked at Henry. His dark eyes were shining and clear. Does another woman look into them? she wondered. In Malta? Her stomach dropped, and she began to tremble. She would die if there was. Was inconstancy the true nature of men? Sandro, so devoted to Moretta one moment, involved the next with an actress—so she had heard from Marie—Crown Prince Rudolph, in love with the Vetsera woman, Bertie, Louise had said, with the Countess of Warwick, now the Emperor, Franz Joseph, as old as he was. There had even been whispers about Leo.

She had bought new lingerie with Marie in Florence, nightgowns and all-in-ones called combinations. Since the shopkeeper had said that no one wore white anymore, the nightgowns were made of soft pink silk with pleats and tucked yokes trimmed with lace, some with sailor collars and open sleeves gathered up with ribbons. She would have to wait to wear them in Charlottenburg. Mama, as always on a train, wanted her to sleep with her in her compartment. Henry would sleep alone.

She watched him stand to bring Victoria a news clipping, then resume his seat. The vibration of the train made her want him desperately.

"I should like to see you privately," she whispered.

"Is it about Malta?"

"Of course not."

They retired to the car and closed the door. She began to undress. "Help me," she said. "My hand is stiff."

"It is still daylight, dearest," he said. "Everyone is about."

"Then lock the door." She stood in a single garment, drawn down from the shoulders in a lace-inserted V, with knickers frilled at the knees.

He kissed her shoulders. "What happened to your chemise?"

"I'm wearing something new. It's called a combination."

"I can see that. What do we do with it?"

She wriggled out and stood in her corset. For the first time since they had been married, he saw her undressed. He removed his coat and trousers. "Are you in love with another woman?" she asked.

He studied her face. "What makes you ask such a thing?" He began to cover her with brushing frantic kisses.

The wheels continued to click. They found the bed too narrow. "How can we?" she whispered.

"There is a way," he said. "I will show you." He sat down and pulled her into his lap, and they engaged in a mindless, urgent embrace while mountains forested in blue-green spruce fir flashed before the open window. The moving train and the erotic sight of her bare white buttocks spilling over his thighs continued to arouse him. He held her firmly, his lips on her neck. "Not yet," he said.

Later, he helped her to dress, fastening with deft movements the closings at her throat.

"I really liked Reginia better, didn't you?" she asked.

"Actually, I preferred Papuana."

They started to laugh, a silly, raucous hysteria that had them both leaning against the walls of the compartment, weak and helpless, until a rap on the door and the discreet voice of Lady Churchill.

"I am terribly sorry, Your Royal Highnesses, but it is the Queen. She requests your presence. Particularly His Royal Highness. The Queen wishes to discuss with him what she will say to Bismarck and what he knows of Prince Alexander's recent involvement."

Victoria sent ahead a cipher telegram to Vicky telling her not to pursue the marriage without the full consent of Willy, since with Fritz so ill, she would soon have to reckon with him. They arrived at the flat gray outskirts of Berlin. Willy escorted them to a four-horse state barouche in which he, Vicky, Beatrice, and Victoria were to ride, assigning Henry to the carriage behind with Major Bigge, Sir Henry, and Lady Churchill. With Union Jacks waving in the cheering crowds, they drove to the royal palace, passing between members of the Gardes du Corps, Henry's old regiment, then beneath drawn swords of sentries at the palace gates, to the old rooms of Frederick the Great, which had been redecorated for their use.

After a visit to Fritz, ashen hued, propped up with pillows, Vicky tearfully told them that Fritz had been brought close to death by his doctors. It had to do with the insertion of the cannula. Mackenzie had a new lead cannula made, but in deference to Dr. Bergmann, asked him to insert it. Bergmann had brought along a cannula of his own without a rounded end, pulled out the old breathing tube, and thrust in his own, missing the incision in the windpipe and forcing the cannula inside the flesh of Fritz's neck. Time and time again he did the same thing, Fritz bleeding copiously; then, agitated, Dr. Bergmann pushed his finger into the wound to enlarge it. Bergmann's stabbing resulted in an abscess. Mackenzie said it was the fatal blow.

Then Vicky told how Bismarck had stopped Sandro from visiting Charlottenburg. When Fritz invited Sandro to Berlin, intending to reinstate him in the German Army as general, Bismarck raged. The Chancellor shouted that he had worked himself to the bone to conciliate Russia, who was only too ready to stick a knife into Germany's back; if the marriage took place, everything he had slaved for would be lost. Fritz was no match and acquiesced. Victoria listened to Vicky but didn't tell her that Sandro was in love with an opera singer. Instead, she said that Vicky should accept the fact that the marriage couldn't be and forget the whole business.

The Chancellor was escorted to Victoria's sitting room by Sir Henry. He bowed before her, deferential, nervous, snapping his heels, his full moustache covering his lips, the pouches heavy beneath his eyes. They shook hands, and Victoria asked him to sit. He referred to their meeting at Versailles thirty-three years before. Then he spoke of the German Army, which would put millions of men in the field against Russia or France. He hoped that the British fleet would help if Germany were attacked. While France did not want war, she was so weak and powerless she might be forced into anything. Victoria agreed that they had much to gain from mutual assistance, then said she was glad there would not be a regency under Crown Prince William. Bismarck assured her that even if he thought it necessary, which he did not, he would not have the heart to propose it. She asked him to stand by the Empress. He assured her he would, that hers was a hard fate. Victoria spoke of Willy's inexperience and his not having traveled at all. "Should he be thrown into the water," replied Bismarck, "he would be able to swim."

Then Victoria introduced the subject of the Battenberg marriage. Bismarck sat erect, prepared for battle. To his surprise, Victoria threw away her trump card and said she had persuaded her eldest daughter not to proceed with the marriage because of political complications. Bismarck came out smiling and wiping the sweat from his forehead. "What a woman," he said to Major Bigge. "One could do business with her."

When the train pulled out, Moretta was left lying prostrate in the castle, suffering from the vapors, and Vicky was left standing on the platform in tears.

Beatrice and Victoria wept in the saloon. Henry stood behind them, staring out the window. The visit had been unpleasant for him. For days he had swallowed the insults of Willy and Dona. Then he had met with his former comrades of the Gardes du Corps, the elite young officers of the cavalry who told him, in a gasthaus heavy with cigar smoke, of the spectacular field maneuvers they were preparing to display in Austria in the fall, a demonstration of Field Marshal Von Moltke's doctrine of encirclement. They had clapped his shoulder, praised him for having done well for himself, matched him drink for drink—aquariums, a pint of English ale mixed with a pint of German champagne—and told him how fortunate he was not to fall on his head weekly, as they did. Two of his comrades had fresh dueling scars, and one, recently returned from banishment to a garrison at the Polish frontier, told amusing tales of a village of one-story houses where everyone peeped into everyone's windows. Some were talking of the *Übermensch*, the rule of the best, saying that law and religion frustrated man's progress, that Christianity was sop for the weak, and that the superman had no need of God but was a law unto himself. There would be a new Germany as soon as Willy was Kaiser. They were all waiting.

The Prince of Wales took breakfast with his mother. Through the bay window of Balmoral Castle he could see bronze and scarlet birch branches dipping into the silvery dee, bracken of flaming orange, finches and long-legged whimbrels scouring the stubble, and distant towering conifers veiled in purple mist.

Victoria buttered a scone with her small dimpled hands. "Both Lord Salisbury and I deplore the way in which Lord Randolph, apparently with your approval, Bertie, proclaimed goodwill toward Russia, which neither of us feel. And the Tsar inviting him to Gatchina for a discussion of Anglo-Russian relations. I hold you responsible."

"Lord Randolph's visit has no political object of any kind," he replied. A covey of white-feathered ptarmigan flew from the bracken.

"I fail to understand your high opinion of a man who is clever, undoubtedly, but who is devoid of all principle, who is very impulsive and utterly unreliable. And it is disconcerting, Bertie, when you stare out of the window."

"Beg pardon, Mama." Bertie leaned closer. "Willy's ascent to the throne must drive Russia into the arms of France unless a definite English policy makes it more attractive for the Tsar to come to an understanding with us rather than with France. We should make new attempts to bring about an Anglo-Russian entente. The Tsar, according to Randolph, shows a lively interest in the project, providing there is a mutual definition of Asiatic interests."

Victoria dipped her scone into her tea. "Lord Salisbury assures me that the key is Austria. If Russia seizes the Bosphorus, without Austria, England will have to defend the Bosphorus by herself, for Russia, as always, can purchase the complicity of Italy and Germany by allowing them to do what they like with France. So long as Austria stands firm, Germany and Italy must go with her. The most important question is, What is the disposition of Austria? That is why it is so important for you to accept Franz Joseph's invitation to witness the autumn military maneuvers."

The Prince of Wales's personal footman removed his plate and napkin and laid a fresh napkin on his lap. "I am in wholehearted agreement, Mama. You have heard, of course, that Willy has informed Franz Joseph he will visit Vienna only after I am gone. It seems I have committed unpardonable crimes."

"In what way?"

"The offenses are as follows. I told the Grand Duke Serge, in passing, I might add, that if Fritz had lived, he would have given back Alsace-Lorraine. Second, when I went to Fritz's funeral, I treated Willy as a nephew rather than an emperor."

"That he expects to be treated in private as well as in public as His

Imperial Majesty is perfect madness. You are his uncle. If he has such notions, he had better never come here. He must understand that neither you nor I will submit to such insolence. Willy's behavior is like the Germans in Zanzibar, bullying everywhere they go."

They were interrupted by Miss Mallet, who came in saying the kitchen was in an uproar because the Indian servants insisted on killing fowl with their native rites and that the cooks were being sickened by the smell of blood, onions, and curry.

Partially shrouded behind velvet hangings of the royal box in the Trocadero Music Hall, Bertie, Henry, and Eddy were rolling brandy in huge snifters and smoking cigars.

"There are twenty-three turns listed in this program," said Bertie, "including the overture. Let's hope Albert Chevalier sings 'Mrs. 'enry 'awkins.' It's about a man who falls in love with the fat lady at a circus and travels with the show as an Egyptian mummy." He turned to Eddy sitting behind him. "Who is Vesta Tilley?"

"A male impersonator, Papa," replied Eddy. "She does 'Algy, the Piccadilly Johnnie with the Little Glass Eye.' "

Bertie leaned again toward Henry. "I hope this excursion brings you no repercussions."

"I expect none." Henry already had repercussions regarding his trip to London. Beatrice at Windsor, and expecting again, had made a scene. He had argued that he had not left her side since Malta and that he would be gone only a few days.

"Why must we go through this every time?" he asked.

"Why must you do it? That is more to the point," she had replied. It was only through Victoria's intervention that she had dropped the matter.

A female vocalist dressed as a charwoman sang a plaintive song.

"However did you manage to get away from my sister and Mama?" asked Bertie.

"I was given an assignment."

"Such as?"

"I am not at liberty."

"Come on, man, don't be an ass. I know just about everything that's going on, anyway. I'll bet anything it has to do with Scotland Yard."

Someone brought out a new card and set it on the easel. An actor wearing a black cape lined in red satin and a flowing tie bowed first to the royal box, then to the audience, and began to declaim, "Why did he forsake me, him I loved so well, hark the bell is tolling, bidding earth farewell."

"Great fun," said Bertie, who joined in, as did half the music hall. "Frantically, her hands high, in the air she throws, a sigh, a leap, a scream, 'tis done, and o'er the bridge she goes!"

The whistling, stamping crowd went wild. The sign was switched, and the actor was followed by a man who did imitations of musical instruments. He, in turn, was followed by Sarah Brown, jailed for three months on charges of indecency, dressed now in a fishnet over flesh-colored tights and wide studded belts around her ample waist and hips, singing "Daddy Wouldn't Buy Me a Bow-Wow."

"She has an insolent look," said Eddy. "She should be whipped with her own belts."

"That is precisely what she wishes to inspire in you, my boy," said Bertie. "Miss Brown understands the desire to chastise."

Soon after, Eddy left, saying he had an appointment. Bertie sighed when he had gone. "He is apathetic, lazy, and has no interest in the Army. When he was younger, he had none whatever in his studies. It was difficult to teach him anything. Alix and I hope to get him married as soon as possible. Mama is in accord. The ladies find him immensely attractive. Sarah Bernhardt claims he is the father of her son Maurice. More likely, I am."

The show was topical, cheeky, boisterous. They left after Marie Lloyd sang "Champagne Charlie" and "The Man Who Broke the Bank at Monte Carlo," while an actor improvised doggerel verse. Bertie sent an equerry to invite three of the women to a private supper.

"Do you fancy any of them?" asked Bertie.

"Not especially, except perhaps the girl in tights. The one jailed for indecency."

"That will be a disappointment, I'm afraid. You'll find her a pathetically tame little creature."

In the crimson drawing room of Windsor Castle, Victoria, Beatrice, Henry, Louise, Bertie and Alexandra, and members of the household had just witnessed a demonstration of the new Gramo-phone, an invention of Mr. Edison's, with stylus, horn, and wax cylin-der, that produced, when cranked, the sound of hissing and a man's voice. Victoria thought the man sounded as if he were gargling.

When the footman had borne away the wax cylinder and stylus, his white gloves smudged from the lampblack coating the wax cylinder, the conversation turned to the alarming situation of prostitutes in the poor district of Whitechapel who had been murdered, ripped by sharp surgical knives. Under suspicion were a Polish Jew, an insane Russian doctor in the habit of carrying surgical knives in his pocket, and an English doctor bordering on insanity.

Louise was all in pink, slippers, stockings, ostrich tips in her up-swept coiffeur, pale flesh pink gloves over her elbows, and pink faille gown draped with black dotted pink tulle. "Scotland Yard is derelict for their failure to arrest the murderer," she said. "Why can't they simply pick up suspicious persons and question them? And why hasn't someone come forward?"

"The police cannot arrest simply on suspicion or question anyone they suspect," replied Bertie, in white tie and tails. "And an isolated murderer with blood lust has no confidants."

"They bring it on themselves," said Louise. "The victims belong to the lowest dregs of female humanity; they avoid the police and exer-cise every ingenuity to remain in the darkest corners of the most deserted alleys."

"I do not agree that they bring it on themselves," said Alexandra, who had been reading lips. "Even the unfortunate class deserves pro-tection."

Henry stood to pour himself Madeira. "Whoever it is has become fiendishly savage," he said. "The murderer, according to doctors, spent some two hours at his last job before a bonfire of old newspapers and his victim's clothes. His fury and his appetite seem to be sharp-ened by indulgence."

Victoria looked at him fondly. It was clear to all of them that she favored this youngest son-in-law, perhaps even more than Arthur, the Duke of Connaught. "Bring me a glass, too, if you please," she said. Harriet Phipps stood to comply, but Victoria stopped her. "His Royal Highness will do it," she said. "The problem is that these wretched women are plying their trade under police protection. The police of the district should arrest every known street woman found on the prowl after midnight or warn them that the police will not protect them. Evil flourishes in darkness."

"Mama is responsible for the improvement of street lighting," said Beatrice. "She has—"

"I have also advised the home office," interrupted Victoria, "to recommend that the police examine all the cattle boats, as well as the lodgings of single men. Surely the murderer's clothes are saturated with blood. They must be kept somewhere. What are the numbers in plain clothes, Henry?"

"The city has put a third of its men in plain clothes. They have been instructed to hang about the public houses, sit on doorsteps, and pose as gossiping loafers."

"A good idea as long as surveillance at night remains high," said Bertie. "I understand a new police commissioner has been selected by the Cabinet."

"The problem is," said Victoria, "he is lame and rides with difficulty. There is the serious question of whether Mr. Munro during state occasions could accompany my carriage on horseback."

"Perhaps, Mama," said Beatrice, "his assistant could perform that function."

Two-year-old Drino, who had somehow found his way downstairs, toddled into the drawing room on chubby legs, making his way to Victoria, shouting, "Gan Gan," with a turbaned Indian orderly officer running after him. Beatrice stood to take his hand, but he pulled away and screamed. Henry signaled to the orderly officer, who caught him up in his arms and set him beside his mother. Beatrice solemnly took the little boy's hand. "You must go back upstairs, Drino," she said. "You have been very naughty."

When she left, Bertie and Alix escorted Victoria to her apartments, Victoria suggesting as they walked that they seriously consider either Alicky as a wife for Eddy, her choice, or Vicky's youngest daughter, Mossy.

"Mossy is too German for my tastes," said Alexandra. "She will not do at all. I prefer Alicky."

"Alicky has some childish idea about the Tsarevitch. I think it is only a young girl's fancy. Eddy would be more suitable."

Henry wandered into the grande corridor, strolling between mellow amber portraits, painted screens, and marble busts on ormolu pedestals. Louise followed after him.

"I know you were in London," she said. "I know you went to Scotland Yard for Mama. I also know you were out with Bertie. You were seen in the music halls and other tawdry places. You knew I was expecting you."

"It was not possible."

"Why wasn't it possible? You mean to say you had no time for me at all? Not one hour? When you knew I was desperate? You had time to ride in Rotten Row with Bertie; you were seen every morning for a week. Once you were seen riding with the Archbishop of Canterbury. There is no mistaking his black cloak and his curly silver hair. Since when do you prefer the company of prelates? I don't believe you."

He stopped before a gilt clock chiming the hour. "I will not abide this stupid, clinging behavior. Who I see and what I do is my affair. Not yours. I did not ask you to wait. I made no promises."

"You are unspeakably cruel," she said.

"I cannot abide hysterical women. Control yourself."

"You care for me. I know you do."

"Lower your voice. Others will hear you."

"Let them."

They turned to the rustle of skirts.

"Is something wrong?" Beatrice looked from one to the other, her face blanching as the import of their conversation took meaning. "Drino is getting more difficult all the time. I think perhaps we ought to engage another nurse. And there is a telegram for you, Henry, from your sister. It's about your father."

Why did she not die? How was it possible to feel this way and not die? She kicked her train aside and hurried away. Henry overtook her.

"How could you?" she whispered.

"It's not what you think."

"You think I'm stupid. I'm not stupid at all. I've just been blind. It was there all along for me to see. Vicky tried to tell me, Alix, and in her own way, Marie. I never saw it. What is so ironic is that I pleaded with Mama to have her with us."

Henry took her arm. "I'm sorry you heard what you did. You should never have been witness to such a display. I assure you there is nothing between us."

"I must see the children," she said.

"The children are sleeping. Mrs. Goode and her staff will attend to them. We should retire to our own apartments where we can talk in private."

"There is nothing to talk about."

She pulled from his arm and went into the darkened night nursery, wrapping herself with a shawl. The baby Ena was asleep in her bassinet. Drino was awake and tied into his bed. He had been crying, his pillow wet. With difficulty, she untied him as a nurserymaid jumped up from her cot. "Leave me," said Beatrice. "You are not needed." She lifted him in her arms and carried him to the rocking chair where she held him tight against her chest, withdrawing into herself as if wounded, sobbing through the night on top of his pale blond head, as he snuffled into her shoulder. Leo, Leo.

By February, after Henry's father's death, Sandro's marriage and retirement into private life, and Henry's appointment as the Governor of the Isle of Wight and of Carisbrooke Castle, at the time of the news of Crown Prince Rudolph's double suicide at his hunting lodge with his sweetheart, Maria Vetsera, the pain subsided. It was there, keen, a blade that had sunk into her flesh, but she did not feel it unless she moved. At first, she could not look at either Henry or Louise, but plunged herself into her work with her mother and the activities of the children, angering Victoria's favorite Indian servant with her sharp commands and driving the nurse and her staff to distraction with a dozen daily intrusions. Gradually, her sorrow eased, and she was able to pretend to Henry and to herself that there had never been anything at all, that she believed him. When the new baby was born, more beautiful than the others, with fine dark hair covering his head, she had buried deep her feelings and asked Louise to be godmother, then named the baby Leopold. Somehow, it would bring Leo back, the dear brother she had not missed till now.

CHAPTER SEVENTEEN

Beatrice had come to accept a swollen hand as a fact of life, much as she began to realize that Henry needed time away from court. He rewarded her for his solitary excursions to the Scillies, to the north of Scotland, to the Mediterranean, with loving attention on his return, even ardor. Their relationship took a new footing.

To demonstrate his devotion, Henry encouraged her to attempt activities they could enjoy together. She tried lawn tennis and found, despite painful stiffness in certain fingers and bustled skirts that brushed the grass, that she was able to return the ball. After Henry convinced her of the propriety of the divided skirt, she learned to ride the new safety bicycle, with two gillies and Major Bigge running alongside, while Henry led the way on the riskier penny farthing with its oversized front wheel. He even had a small tricycle made for Drino, who was allowed to accompany them as long as a nursemaid and an Indian orderly were in attendance. Finally, Henry urged Beatrice to perform in amateur theatricals, reasoning that it was also a way for her to overcome her shyness, especially since Victoria's calls upon them to represent her had accelerated.

To Louise, to all women at court, he was civil, even charming, but always correct. In January, after his father's death, he had made clear to Louise that anything between them was over, that they had behaved in a rash and foolhardy manner, and that he was principally at fault. Louise, who knew her welcome at court was on sufferance, displayed a faultless decorum. In addition, she appeared more frequently with Lorne, her handsome artistic husband, now a liberal member of the House of Commons committed to Gladstone, who would someday be the Duke of Argyll. Henry was grieving for his father. She would give him a year.

Henry was also devoted to Victoria, who had come to rely upon him even more, so much so that Bertie was now openly jealous. This came to light during the scandal of the raid on the homosexual bordello in Cleveland Street where Eddy was caught with Lord Arthur Somerset. Lord Arthur had fled the country, leaving his parents, the Duke and Duchess, in disgrace.

"It is a dreadful affair," said Victoria. "Really too shocking."

"Names will come out, I'm afraid," said Lord Salisbury. "One, a married man whose hospitality I have frequently enjoyed. That is to say, the hospitality of him and his wife."

Bertie turned to Beatrice and Henry. "I'm at a loss, Mama, to see why Benjamina and Henry must be present. The matter is of concern only to my family."

"Don't be silly, Bertie," said Victoria. "Benjamina and Henry are privy to all of it. Who do you think dictated and wrote the necessary letters? We are, Lord Salisbury, naturally concerned with the Duke of Clarence's name and reputation. What can you tell us in this regard?"

"That will be difficult, but it can be arranged. For certain considerations."

"I will not yield to blackmail," said Victoria.

"Not blackmail, ma'am," said the Prime Minister. "More of an exchange."

"What was he doing there, anyway, Bertie?" asked Victoria. "All of this would not have come about if he simply would go where he is supposed to go and do the things he is supposed to do."

"Eddy assures me, Mama," replied Bertie, "that it was as an innocent bystander. That he had no real idea what it was all about, that when he found out, he was surprised, naturally, but in consideration of Lord Somerset, whose guest he was, there was nothing he could do under the circumstances but remain."

"With all due respect," said Henry, "I find that hard to believe, as will everyone else should the matter ever come before public scrutiny."

"This is insufferable," said Bertie. "No one asked you your opinion,

Henry. Certainly I did not. If anything, it is you who are under public scrutiny. Do not think it has not been mentioned in my presence on numerous occasions that you live an indolent life at the expense of the British taxpayer. I refer to your yacht."

"I am not interested in the details of Eddy's predicament," said Victoria, "and since I gave Henry his yacht, what he does with it is his business and his business only. I am concerned with appearances, with maintaining a public decorum. After all, we should be setting examples for others to follow. Can we rely on this person's discretion?"

"I have every reason to believe so," said Lord Salisbury.

The meeting concluded with a discussion of Willy's visit to Osborne. Victoria demanded that before this grandson who had begun to take the shape of an enemy be allowed to come, he be required to apologize to his uncle Bertie. Lord Salisbury urged the Prince of Wales to pocket his dignity, saying that it would be in the Queen's interest to make the Kaiser's visit as easy as possible, that to mandate such an apology might be detrimental to the Zanzibar settlement. Further, English public opinion would not tolerate a diplomatic rupture with Germany because of personal quarrels within royal families.

That night the heat made the presence of bedclothes intolerable. Beatrice threw them off. "What is it that men do with one another?" she asked.

"It is not something you would wish to know," Henry replied.

"Do you know?"

"Of course I know."

"I don't think you do. If you did, you would tell me. You refuse to tell me because you do not know yourself."

"I cannot believe you would want to know such a thing."

"But I do."

"Very well. But you will find it offensive." He told her the two ways that he knew of. "I don't believe it," she said. "You have invented that to irritate me."

Henry continued to lie awake, his hands beneath his head, thinking of his brother-in-law's thinly disguised resentment. How strange, he thought. On the one hand, if I am in constant attendance on the Queen, I am a German intruder, far too close to her ear. And if I absent myself, I am an indolent drain on the taxpayer. A deadlocked engagement. Von Moltke would say to withdraw.

At the end of August, Willy came to the Solent with his warships, wearing the uniform of a British admiral. Even though Victoria let him know it was his Uncle Bertie's idea to confer upon him the title and the uniform, Willy insisted on entering the Royal Yacht Club first. After Willy's review of the fleet at Spithead, his penetrating questions about the Royal Navy, and his promise to his grandmother that he would never be rude to his uncle again, Victoria, Beatrice, Henry, and Alicky went to North Wales with bicycles and an entourage of ladies, dressers, valets, cooks, a half-dozen Indian servants, and Sir Henry.

Seen from the train, Wales was cottages and hamlets, sloping meadows of blazing gorse brakes, a golden flame of harvest glowing on the flats beside warm-tinted fallows, clear streams, sharp, craggy hills bordering ribbons of narrow valleys, and sheep pastures of emerald turf, where birch trees threw feathery shadows.

Victoria dictated a letter in the blue silk and yellow tasseled saloon car to Sir Henry regarding a Mrs. Maybrick, who administered arsenic to her husband. Since there was medical doubt as to whether it was the arsenic that was the cause of death, the Home Secretary, Mr. Matthews, requested Victoria to commute the capital sentence to penal servitude for life. "Thank Mr. Matthews," said Victoria, "and say that my only regret is that so wicked a woman should escape by a mere legal quibble."

"How could a woman wish to kill her husband?" asked Beatrice.

"Have you never had such thoughts?" teased Henry.

"Never." She looked out the window, tracing the course of a lane as it wound idly between waves of silver-tinted fern.

"I'm glad to hear that. I would have thought differently." Her features smoothed, made bland as if a hand had passed over them. He had gone too far, evoking remembrances under tacit agreement best forgotten. "Sorry." He kissed her fingertips. "Ena is making sentences."

"I know."

"She is very pretty, like her mother." He leaned closer to whisper in her ear. "Did you wish to see me in private?"

"I can't imagine why."

"There was a time you could."

Beatrice blushed and turned back to the window, resting her forehead against the cool glass. A woman in a tall black hat shaded her eyes to the passing train.

They entered a deep valley, wooded with arches of larch and copper beech. After an enthusiastic reception from dignitaries with speeches and bouquets, a robed choir, and an honor guard of Welsh Fusiliers, the royal party rode through narrow streets between gray houses with gray, moss-grown roofs.

"Wonderfully how well these choirs sing," said Victoria, "being that they are composed of shopkeepers and flannel weavers." She turned to Alicky to continue a conversation that had begun on the train. "You know that poor Eddy is devastated. When you come to reflect what a serious thing it is to throw away such a marriage, and in your mother's country where you would be received with open arms."

"Eddy is stupid," said Alicky, wisps of her hair flying out from beneath her bonnet of violets and magenta velvet Alsatian bow.

"He is not stupid, dear. He is good and affectionate, and handsome to boot. Allow him a faint, lingering hope that you might in time see what a useful position you will lose if you persist in not yielding to his wishes. 'I don't think she knows how I love her,' he writes, 'or she could not be so cruel.'"

"And I don't believe he composed those words," said Alicky. "Auntie Alix must have helped him. A gypsy has already forecast, Grandmama, that I will marry a Russian. It's my fate. I can't escape it."

"Say something to her, Henry."

"Perhaps when Eddy returns from India, you will find him developed more to your taste. Travel tends to broaden one."

"He would have to be gone a very long time," she replied.

In a round of receptions and a brief cycling expedition along a wooden banked canal, it was arranged that members of the royal party visit a coal mine. Ruabon was fiery furnaces and belching chimneys, where ladies-in-waiting draped Beatrice and Alicky in white sheets and veiling against the smoke, while a middle-aged fireman, whose job it was to check the safety of a site, was explaining seams.

He twisted his peaked woolen cap in his blackened hands, wheezing as he spoke. "Imagine, Your Royal Highnesses, getting under a chair and working with pick and shovel. Some places are hardly fit for a dog to go in, not being more than two and a half feet or so in height, and in such places many of our boys have to go for twelve hours or more a day on their hands and knees."

"It must be dangerous work," said Henry.

The fireman glanced at the officials, who stood waiting beside the open cage, holding glowing safety lamps. "One Sunday, sir, my grandfather went in at evening to examine the pit. Someone left a ventilator door open. He was blown to pieces by an explosion. They collected his remains with a rake and brought him home in a sack."

"That was years ago, George," said one official. "Conditions have improved since then."

"Begging your pardon, sir, but my son worked in the mines until his back was broken by a fall of roof. And my brother went nearly blind. Can't come out during the day at all."

"Must we go down there?" Beatrice whispered.

"Of course," replied Henry.

"I can't, Henry. I will feel like I'm suffocating."

"The men do it. Every day. Alicky is ready to go down. You must do it, too. To show them that you respect their efforts."

"What if the lift fails?"

"It won't fail. It has been checked and rechecked. And I will be with you. It means a lot to them." He put out his hand. "Come, you will see that it is easier than learning to ride a bicycle."

She lifted her chin with imperious grace, suggesting an assurance she only partly felt, and took his arm. With Alicky following, they entered the caged lift and descended into the shaft, lurching, then dropping quickly, jerking to a sickening stop, then plunging downward again into blackness, as Henry held her arm close to his side.

The lift stopped. Someone opened the rail. The pit was dark, dusty, hot, and stuffy. From somewhere came the sound of tapping. A man with a pail of water, wearing toeless black socks, appeared out of the blackness, dampening the ground around them to keep down the choking, swirling dust. Beatrice closed her nose to the foul smells. Despite the safety lamps, it was almost pitch black, a heavy dark that she could feel. Once Beatrice heard rats scurrying, but because she had been carefully trained as to what behavior one displayed, there was no sign on her face that she had noticed or that she was hot and close to fainting. She huddled beneath the beamed roof only inches above her head. "Will it fall in?" she asked, much as if she would inquire about the weather.

"It is well shored, ma'am," said the man, "with good stout timbers. Have no fear. Will Her Royal Highness care to fire a shot?"

A kneeling miner held a detonator. Beatrice depressed the lever. After a few seconds, there was a muffled blast.

"Well done, Your Royal Highness," said the smiling hewer.

Papa. Why did she think of him here, in this dark, smothering, grimy tomb. They returned to the shaft and were hoisted in the creaking, groaning cage. It seemed to take forever.

The sunlight was painful. Beatrice shielded her eyes and breathed deeply the fresh air. She felt as if she would never get the dust out of her nostrils.

"You did well," said Henry. "You should never again be afraid of anything."

"There is only one thing I am afraid of."

"What is that?"

"Losing you."

Alicky clapped her gloved hands together to rid them of their dust. "You're not going to try to persuade me to marry Eddy, are you?"

"I don't think so," said Beatrice. "I wouldn't dream of persuading you to marry anyone you didn't love."

That evening Victoria composed a letter to Bertie. Beatrice rubbed her hands to take the stiffness out before she dipped the pen.

"Your hand seems swollen," said Victoria. "When we get to Balmoral, let Dr. Reid blister the inflammation."

"My hand feels fine, Mama."

"Are you not taking the draft that he prescribed?"

"It makes me groggy."

"I have found potassium and opium very useful for rheumatism. I should think you would want some relief. I can understand refusing salicin; it's a bother taking powders every hour, besides the constant ringing in one's ears. Very well. Tell your brother of the excellent and enthusiastic reception we have had here and how much this sensitive and warmhearted people feel the neglect shown to them by the Prince of Wales and his family. Tell him it is only five hours from London, and as the Prince of Wales takes his title from this beautiful country, it does seem very wrong that neither he nor his children have come here often, and indeed the Princess and the children not at all."

Henry returned from relaying instructions to one of the ladies that someone somewhere was snoring in the household and must be identified.

"Bertie could not do what we did today," he said to Beatrice.

"Why not? Bertie is very courageous."

"I don't question his courage. It's the cage. It would never hold him."

Victoria turned to them. "I assure you, this is not funny at all. Bertie has a real responsibility to the Welsh. And it is time he saw it."

On the train from Wales to Balmoral, Henry outlined a vague itinerary of his forthcoming trip to the Mediterranean, a cruise that would take from the end of November to the early part of February, and which would include an expedition to Albania to hunt wolf.

"I'm not going to say a word," said Beatrice, looking into her lap. "You know my feelings very well that wolf hunting is very dangerous. I hope you know what you are doing."

He excused himself to smoke a cigar on the rear platform with Sir Henry. Beatrice found her mother in their sleeping car. A dresser was smoothing the Queen's hair with rose geranium-scented bandoline. "He's going away for two months."

"That seems excessively long. However, I shouldn't fret about it. At the beginning of the new year, you will be too busy to notice."

"I doubt it, Mama."

Victoria's center-parted hair shone. The dresser settled the white widow's cap securely on her head. "He is a man," said Victoria. "Men have to rush off to do things to feel like men. Thank heaven women have no such thoughts, or everyone would be flitting about like bees. If he were a soldier, dear, he would be in one campaign after another. You might not see him for many months at a time."

Beatrice's hand toyed with the ruffled fichu at her throat. "What does it matter why he goes. When he is gone, he takes my life with him. The first thing I think when I wake up in the morning is that he is not there."

Victoria looked into a hand mirror and tossed her head, loosening the cap. "This needs pinning," she said to the dresser, then, to Beatrice, "How can you say that to me, who has suffered all these countless years of that very thing. You talk of a few months, knowing he is alive and will return. Can you imagine decades? How cruel you are."

The children did not miss their father, primarily because, as all children of their rank, they saw very little of him. They did see more of their mother. When she could spare moments from her duties with Victoria, Beatrice towed them on the ice on a sled or sat with Drino on her lap with a linen book called *The Alphabet of Fruit and Flowers*, teaching him his letters. She would say things like "C is for the cowslip, for wine to make merry, the while after dinner we eat the plump . . ." "Cherry," would reply Drino, who was becoming headstrong and independent, scurrying about, knocking over priceless objets d'art, and finding his way into council chambers and drawing rooms. From this it was determined that it was necessary for Drino to feel the weight of authority. His nurse especially considered it her moral duty, as well as the conditions of her employment, to subjugate his will, as well as that of Ena, now that she was no longer an infant, subjecting them both to tight corsets, which were beneficial for future upright spines, and tighter discipline, such as castor oil at the slightest tantrum or going to bed for disobedience.

Leo, still a gurgling, contented, cooing baby in yards of ribboned cambric, promised to be not only the most beautiful of all the Battenberg children but the sweetest. Beatrice carried him about herself, often bringing him into Victoria's bedroom in the morning, laying him on the pink and blue quilted satin counterpane in his long trailing gown to kiss his soft plump neck, while Victoria, propped up with pillows covered in Valenciennes lace, took deviled kidneys in bed.

Despite a heavy schedule that often kept her working with Victoria late into evening, missing Henry was constant. Even when the white-haired African explorer Stanley came to Windsor, telling stories of frightful atrocities in Ashanti, of one tribe seizing the small children of another tribe and pounding them to death in great wooden mortars used for mashing yams, of lopping off the hands of the rest and sending them to carry the news to their people, her thoughts were on Henry, whose absence was as palpable as the blackness she had felt in the mines.

Ludwig, on thirty-six-hour leave from his torpedo cruiser, and Henry, both in woolen ulsters, leaned against the railing, huddling into their hoods against the salt spray. Asleep in his stateroom was Louis of Hesse, off to hunt wolf in Albania despite his doctors' warnings against exertion of any kind. It was dawn. Far away, they could see the still blinking beam of the lighthouse at Antibes, ahead, the dark strip of irregular peaks of Corsica, their snow-crowned mountain tops illuminated by the gold and purple rising sun. As the yacht grew closer to the savage coast, they could make out wild, desolate hillsides of brushwood, relieved only by an occasional vineyard and olive garden.

"I've spoken to Admiral Hoskins," said Ludwig. "He's anxious to meet you."

"It's a waste of time," said Henry.

"Perhaps if I went to see the Queen, or better still, if Victoria went to see her grandmother. We ought to put that to work for you."

"She won't hear of it," replied Henry. "Believe me."

"Beatrice?"

"My wife is not the obstacle. My mother-in-law, the Queen, rations all my activities, especially those that make her nervous. I expect to be fetched back at any moment."

"I don't like to see you like this. None of us do. Father, before he died, liked it least of all. Perhaps as you wait for something to change, you will find your life less difficult."

"It gets worse, not better," said Henry. "Our cousin Louis at least is middle-aged with a bad heart. I have no excuse. None."

"Don't regard it as a closed issue. Admiral Hoskins says that he would welcome your addition at any time, considering your previous commission and the fact that you are my brother. That counts for something."

They entered the harbor, maneuvering between rocks like murderous teeth that guarded the entrance to the Bay of Ajaccio. "The French have improved the harbor," said Ludwig, "although they have done nothing to mitigate the ferocity of the people. They are idle, fiery brigands most of them, but of a peculiar type."

"Thieves?" A black-petticoated priest stood on the quay talking to a fisherman who was hauling in a net of glittering sardines. Behind him was an equestrian statue of Napoleon.

"It has nothing to do with thieving. The Corsican brigand had murdered someone or other according to a strict code of honor that considers the act one of duty. There is scarcely a respectable family in Corsica who has not had one of its members *alla campagna.*"

The yacht was made fast, Louis was awakened and they leaped on shore, Louis with some assistance, striding through wide streets paved with broken rock, passing wine booths not yet opened and stalls of salt fish, stern and gloomy men on mules laden for the hills, and silent old women in blue-black mantles weaving in the doorways.

"Do either of you wish to see Napoleon's house?" the Grand Duke Louis asked. They laughed.

The rough granite, six-story inn, pierced with slitlike windows and narrow doorways, was mournful and desolate. Everything had been discreetly arranged. The hovering innkeeper seated them at a table with a fresh, white, starch-glazed cloth that gleamed in the light of the lamp and promised them girls. "Sirs, they are from good families, very clean, carefully reared, all virgins."

"He means he is raising the original price," said Louis. "Tell him, Henry, that virgins aren't essential but cleanliness is."

"I would rather you told him," said Louis of Hesse, "that his services are crude. In Paris, one can get virgins in bundles of six complete with doctor's certificates."

The girl brought to Henry's room was very young, not more than ten, with large dark eyes and shining coppery hair that had been piled and pinned on top of her head. The dress she wore belonged to a grown woman but had been shortened, so that the shoulders fell upon her thin arms and the bodice reached to her waist, revealing a narrow, undeveloped chest over which someone had modestly stretched a piece of silk.

The girl smiled, an artful, seductive smile she had been taught, at odds with pearlescent, protruding teeth, oversized for the immature mouth. Henry stood beneath the thick wooden doorjamb. "Get this child out of here!" he shouted.

The innkeeper ran upstairs, puffing when he reached the narrow landing. "Did she say something, sir?" he asked. "How has she offended?"

"I said young," said Henry. "Not infantile."

"What's all the fuss?" asked the Grand Duke Louis, tucking in his shirt as he opened his door. "She's rather a pretty little thing. All she needs is a bath. If you don't want her, I'll take her."

"She's a child, Louis. She should be home with her mother."

The innkeeper stood glowering before the little girl. "The sir says you should be home with your mother. What do you say to that?"

The child glanced up through fluttering eyelashes. "I would rather be here," she whispered, "with them."

"You see, sirs?" asked the innkeeper. He threw up his hands.

"Very well," replied Henry, "but you already have someone in there with you, Louis. Do you think two is prudent?"

"You don't understand, Henry. I can do anything I like so long as I personally do very little. She and my other little friend will do it all, won't you, little angel?"

She looked from one to the other and trembled. Some of her hair had tumbled down her neck. The Grand Duke took her small bony shoulder and led her into his room, closing the heavy oak door behind him.

Henry sat alone on the edge of his bed, noting that the crucifix on the opposite wall was crooked. In a few years, Ena would be the age of the child now most certainly naked and in bed with Louis. His little blonde daughter resembled Beatrice, while Drino looked like his father, Prince Alexander. It had been a year since his father had died. He and Ludwig had placed him into his coffin, surprised to find how light he was. When Henry was a little boy, his father seemed giant, a leviathan in golden epaulets. Henry stood with annoyance to straighten the crucifix, wondering if he now seemed so enormous to Drino and Ena. Plaster fell from the hole in a puff of dust, and the crucifix swung to one side, hanging precariously from the loosened nail.

By the fall, a treaty with Germany had been signed, fixing frontiers in Africa and ceding the island of Heliogland in exchange for Zanzibar. Victoria said it was a bad precedent. "Soon nothing will be secure," she said, "and all our colonies will wish to be free." Cecil Rhodes was made Prime Minister of the Cape Colony, there was a famine in the west of Ireland and a scandalous divorce action in which Captain O'Shea cited Parnell as corespondent, sealing the doom of the Irish statesman.

Beatrice, Louise, and members of the court were rehearsing beneath the vaulted clerestory ceiling of the Waterloo Chamber, on the proscenium stage especially constructed for their theatricals. The vast chamber sparkled from the diamonte gaslit Waterford chandeliers. When Henry walked in, carrying Leopold in his arms, with Drino and Ena running beside him, Louise acknowledged his presence with an incline of her head and a controlled, close-lipped smile one gave from an open carriage.

Leo struggled to get down, and Henry set him on the huge seamless carpet specially made for Victoria in India. The baby crawled onto the stage, teetering back and forth after Drino and Ena, while they slid over the smooth wooden floor, at one time screaming as Drino pointed to the portrait of the Duke of Wellington and shouted, "He's going to get you!"

"You are just in time, Henry," said Beatrice, who had brightened, as she always did in his presence. "You will be in the tableau entitled King Richard and the Saracens. You will be Saladin. The Indian servants will take the part of the Saracens."

There was also to be a three-act French farce that had been censored by Victoria into suitable subject matter and length. Beatrice instructed a claque of the household and servants to clap at the moment anyone forgot his lines, and in the humiliating event that no one on stage knew his lines, the carpenter was to let down the curtain.

They were picking through the trunk of costumes when Leo tumbled off the stage. The fall was not very great, a few steps. The baby began to scream. Later that evening, the blue-purple bruise had spread. Dr. Reid was called. After a quick examination, he took the anxious parents aside. Their youngest son appeared to have hemophilia. Beatrice was numbed. The bleeding sickness, like Leo, Alice's Frittie, Vicky's Waldemar. Dr. Reid gently, patiently, tried to explain that Beatrice, certain of her sisters, and the Queen were most likely the carriers, that hemophilia was understood now as a peculiar family disease; apparently, females were not affected but transmitted it to their male offspring. Something in their blood. Drino? No, they would have had evidence by now, and Ena was a girl. Henry paced, his folded hands behind his back.

"What can we do?"

"Nothing, sir, I'm afraid, except have him watched very carefully, try to prevent him from running about and injuring himself."

"There must be something," Henry said.

Dr. Reid shook his head.

Beatrice was inconsolable. "Not my Leo," she said at first, then, "It's my fault. I'm to blame. I harmed the baby I love the best."

Victoria hitched in to the night nursery, leaning heavily on her walking sticks. She sat before them. "This is a terrible thing," she said. "It is especially terrible for me. I cannot quite comprehend it. Some might say it was a divine visitation, but I find it hard to believe that providence would really select helpless innocent little babies. I will tell you something else. I would do it all again, have all the children I have had, knowing what I know, for if it were not one thing, perhaps it would have been another. Sometimes these things get better. Look at Irene's boy, Waldemar. He has the symptoms, yet his mother tells me they are going away."

Henry agreed that it was best to be optimistic, but Beatrice did not respond, thinking only that her baby would have to live his life like Leopold, for whom he was named, as a cautious, guarded, resentful invalid.

For weeks she and Henry slept side by side, often lying awake without speaking. When he touched her, she turned away, whispering that she did not want any more children. She began to maintain a vigilance over Leo that required running up to the nursery in the middle of meals, dispatches, audiences, sometimes in the middle of the night, to check his activity, his breathing, his safety, his supervision, to scold his nurses or the other children for teasing him, for not giving him what he wanted.

One night, after tossing in the dark, Henry spoke, certain, because of her controlled, shallow breathing, that she, too, was awake. "You have other responsibilities," he said. "You neglect your mother. She is getting older and needs you more than ever. You are not at her side when you are most needed. You neglect the other children. Ena asked me why you are always so cross. She said something poetic, yet frightfully somber for a little girl. She said you make the nursery dark. And you neglect me. Don't you imagine I need some comfort, too? Some tenderness? After all, he is also my son."

It was a long time before she replied. "Perhaps you wish you had married someone else. Someone with whom you could have had a perfect child."

"What nonsense." His fingers found and brushed away a tear. "You sound like my former comrades-in-arms. They talk such rot. Nothing in life is certain, darling; no one in life is warranted." The deep resonating timbre of his voice was like a balm. There was no need to hold back, no enemy to protect against. She let go with choking sobs, a rush of tears, crying all night in his arms.

Leo was soon toddling about, although under restraint, his dimpled smile so engaging it was hard to realize that he was anything but a robust, healthy baby.

Matters pertaining to Eddy and Alicky once again took some of Victoria's attention. First she launched a direct attack on Alicky's infatuation with the Tsarevitch by writing letters of protest to Louis of Hesse and to the Tsarina of Russia. "Ella and Serge do all they can to bring it about," she complained. "Encouraging and even urging Nicky to go ahead with it. Alix heard it from her sister, Minny, the Tsarina herself, who is very much annoyed about it. Louis of Hesse must put his foot down, and there must be no more visits of Alicky to Russia. The state of Russia is so bad, so rotten, and any moment something dreadful might happen."

Next she met with Bertie to consider the situation of Eddy, who had fancied himself in love with Hélène d'Orléans. The marriage, of course, was out of the question, since Eddy would forfeit his right to the throne by marrying a Roman Catholic. Victoria blamed Alexandra for encouraging the match.

"If she does so, Mama," said Bertie, in disfavor again because of a recent moral lapse, a baccarat scandal in which he was required to give testimony in court, "it is because she believes him to be truly in love."

The meeting was interrupted when Miss Phipps came to remind Victoria that Cecil Rhodes was waiting. Henry assisted Victoria from the sofa. "Beatrice will tell you, Bertie, of my concerns."

"What worries Mama," said Beatrice, "is that while the Comte d'Paris broke off the engagement, he gives his daughter permission to write to Eddy. Mama wonders if they are trying to convince Eddy to become a Roman Catholic. Correspondence must come to an end. Otherwise, he is being made a fool of."

"Are those your sentiments on the matter or Henry's?" asked Bertie in icy tones.

"They are the Queen's," said Henry. The doors were closed behind him.

"I'm assuming Mama is meeting with Mr. Rhodes. I saw his carriage. A most admirable man, Henry, unlike you and I, a man of action. What is the meeting about?" asked Bertie. "Can I assume it is a discussion of whether future chartered companies in South Africa originate from royal charter or an act of Parliament?"

"I am not at liberty to say," replied Henry.

"My God, man," said Bertie, "but you are arrogant." He slapped his gloves upon his knee and stood to leave. "You forget yourself and to whom you speak. Do not let your position go to your head. You are the husband of my youngest sister. Nothing more. Somehow you have inveigled yourself into the affections and confidence of my mother, the Queen, like that Hindu fellow that skulks about. I remind you that I am the heir to the throne and that the Queen is over seventy."

Henry swallowed Bertie's hostility as he had swallowed Willy's insults. Since he did not consider the governorship of Carisbrooke Castle a serious pursuit, his resolve was firmer than ever that he find himself useful employment.

When Maurice was born at Balmoral, they waited anxiously watching the dark-haired baby for symptoms of hemophilia and considering as a favorable sign the rapid healing of his navel. Beatrice lay recuperating from her confinement with little to do except read Mr. Kipling's new book and agree with the author's perception of the English gift for shouldering responsibility for uncivilized races. Sometime between chapters, it occurred to her that Mary of Teck's daughter May would make a good wife for Eddy and that the matter, once resolved, would take a great weight from her mother and perhaps, if it became known that she had been instrumental, make Bertie think more kindly of Henry.

"Mary's daughter?" asked Victoria. "She would never do. She is a dear, sweet girl, but she does not have the bearing. Besides, the Cambridge family tends to be a misguided and lighthearted lot."

"Invite her for a visit, Mama, and you will come to see her fine qualities."

May visited Balmoral on approval. Beatrice, still weak and light-headed when she stood, greeted her cousin from a swan-armed chaise longue, wearing a concealing tea gown of gray cashmere with a black velvet medici collar.

Eddy would someday be the King of England, yet it was necessary to know that May wanted that more than she cared that he was not quick. "Are you in love with him?" she asked.

"I am very fond of Eddy."

"That is not the same."

"I feel it is my duty to accept him if he wants me," she replied. "I am afraid, though, that I will not pass muster."

"I have been in your position," said Henry with a smile.

"If you wish to make a good impression on my mother, the Queen," said Beatrice, "read the dailies every morning, keep abreast of what is current, and have something to do at all times, a book, a piece to play on the piano, some needlework, perhaps create an arrangement of wax flowers. You must never be seen unoccupied."

Days later, Victoria paid Beatrice her customary morning visit. She first expressed the wish that Beatrice would stop now after four babies. She mentioned the death of Parnell in Brighton, saying that although she was not in favor of the man, the Irish had lost a great leader. Then a bit of tragic gossip: Crown Prince Rudolph of Austria, whom everyone believed committed suicide with his mistress, Maria Vetsera, was believed to have been murdered, smashed in the head with a bottle. His face, it seemed, had been pieced together and filled in with wax. Last, she pronounced judgement. "May is quiet," she said, "yet cheerful, no frivolous tastes, is fond of Germany, very well informed, always occupied." Weeks later, Eddy proposed, and May accepted.

In January, there was a serious epidemic of influenza, with five hundred deaths in London alone. Henry was off on another excursion, and Beatrice kept the children isolated at Osborne. Princess May and her family went to Sandringham to celebrate Eddy's birthday. The day before his birthday, the Duke of Clarence retired early, saying that he felt wretched. The following day, Dr. Laking diagnosed pneumonia, and a few days after that, delirious and shouting for his regiment, the Queen, and Hélène d'Orléans, he died.

Victoria was grief-stricken. The court immediately went into the deep mourning of hushed hallways, whispered tearful conversations, and black braided camel's hair and crepe. The only pleasant note was the disappearance through fashion dicta of the cumbersome bustle and its wired underpinning. Beatrice, Helena, and Louise attended the funeral. Although a note had been received from Sandringham that said that the ceremony was to be private, they concluded that it did not mean Bertie's sisters. Alexandra watched the ceremony from Katharine of Aragon's closet, while Bertie, below, cried throughout. When Beatrice could not get her pew door opened, a suspiciously long while elapsed before someone was dispatched to assist her. Later, Sir Henry wrote to complain on her behalf to the Prince of Wales. A curt note was received in reply that she had been asked not to come in the first place and if she were angry, she must get over it as she pleased.

The deep mourning was not to lift. In March a telegram announced the death of Louis of Hesse from a stroke.

CHAPTER EIGHTEEN

Months after the wedding of May of Teck to Eddy's younger brother George and the crushing defeat of Gladstone's second Irish home rule bill in the House of Lords, Henry received a telegram saying Sandro, living privately as Count Hartenau, was dangerously ill.

It was arranged that Henry's yacht carry him across the Channel to Cherbourg where he would take the train to Graz. Victoria could not spare Beatrice for a catalog of reasons, including her inability to find glasses to suit her, her constant rheumatic pain and need to be rolled in her chair, and Sir Henry, who could not always be relied upon, as he was becoming forgetful. In addition, there was trouble with the household over the munshi, who had brought over another of his nephews. There were ugly, whispered innuendos that Beatrice was required to dispel.

Henry went alone, occupying a first-class carriage with his equerry and valet, reflecting over clicking wheels that he had last seen his brother six months before in Florence, when Sandro had made him promise that when he died, Henry would see to it that he be buried in Sofia. Henry was met at the station by Austrian aristocrats who were wrapped tightly in capes and cloaks to ward off the bitter November cold. One, with frosted monocle set into his scarred cheek, bowed before him, clicked his heels, and told him that his brother, the Count, died early that morning, that the Countess, who was ill, had eaten nothing all day, and that they were depending on him to help her recover.

Henry stood uncomprehending. He had come to cheer Sandro

back to health, not to comfort his widow. Besides, Sandro was only thirty-six, a year and a half older than he.

Stunned and grieving, Henry was ushered into Sandro's villa and led up the stairs to an immense sky blue apartment with heavy portieres, where Sandro's pale widow, her long dark braid tied in a ribbon, lay in bed propped by mounds of lacy pillows. She took his hand and told him in words barely audible that Sandro had appendicitis, that by the time it was diagnosed, an operation was no longer possible, and that he suffered a painful death. It was the anniversary of his victory against the Russians; he was aware of it. Delirium set in, he thought he was on the battlefield, he gave a word of command, shouted, "Victory, victory," then died.

"Has anything been settled about the funeral?" he asked.

"There is nothing to settle," she replied with dulled, heavy-lidded eyes. "He will be laid to rest in the burial ground of the town church on the third day, as is customary."

"I would like to arrange for Bulgarian officers of the Alexander regiment to stand guard over his coffin."

"I have no objection." Her reply was toneless. She raised her eyes to his. "It was kind of you to come, Henry. You were in his thoughts to the end. He said you live a hard life, more exiled than he."

Henry was not listening. He was thinking that under no circumstances must Sandro be interred in Austria. He excused himself and sent his equerry to telegraph Bulgarian officials about conveying Sandro's body to Sofia. There was serious question as to whether they would want the body at all. Then came Minister Stambuloff's reply. "Bulgaria desires the return of its first Prince."

By evening, an escort of high-ranking Bulgarian officials began to arrive, accompanied by officers wearing the light blue uniforms of the Bulgarian aide-de-camp. A Colonel Grecoff presented himself immediately to Henry. The body of His Highness must be en route to Sofia within twenty-four hours.

Henry found Sandro's widow still in bed in the unaired, overheated boudoir that smelled of geranium. She looked improved, her cheeks pinker, her eyes brighter, a tray over her lap laid with a cup and saucer, pots of jam, and a plate of half-eaten sweet rolls.

"There are Bulgarian officers and ministers in the salon," he began. "Do you know why they are here?"

"To pay homage," she replied, buttering a roll.

"Yes, to pay respects, but they are also here to bring Sandro's body back to Sofia."

She sat upright, clutching tightly at the sheets around her, knocking the tray to the floor. "To Bulgaria? Is that what you are saying? To that ungrateful country from where he had to flee for his life? Are you mad?"

Henry remained firm but spoke softly, signaling the maid to clear the debris of sweet rolls and jam pots, saying it was his sacred duty to fulfill his promise to Sandro. He asked her to consider the departed no longer Count Hartenau but the first Prince of Bulgaria, whom his people desired to have back.

"Then I, too," she said with a jut of her chin, "when my time comes, must be buried in Sofia. Beside him."

He explained that other wives of celebrated men had not been laid beside their husbands, giving as an example Westminster Abbey where there were interred alone many men of note.

In the end, she consented. Henry accompanied the body on a Bulgarian train, with an open, freezing central corridor that whistled as they rode past great herds of buffalo shuffling on treeless hills. Nearing Sofia, with its red-tiled roofs and minarets, the journey became a triumphal procession to the thunder of guns, arriving at the station to an enormous crowd of brown faces in white fur caps, led by the bearded Metropolitan in black robes and high black hat with a long floating lawn veil, a red-turbaned Turkish Mufti, and Stambuloff, the president of the council, in glistening fur cloak.

Stambuloff began to speak as a red-uniformed escort on horseback clattered toward the coffin. "The whole people weeps for its beloved Prince, him to whom Bulgaria owes its independence. Here at last, on our soil, dost thou rest, the soil thou didst love so well, that for its sake thou didst sacrifice all. May his example of self-denial be sacred to us all."

Henry stood silently watching, thinking that his brother had been denied everything, including a hero's death.

He returned to England despondent and vulnerable, wondering what difference it made, the struggling, the passion for Moretta, for Bulgaria. It was over. For nothing. Self-denial. What did it mean? He recalled something Joanna had said. "More exiled than he." Had

Sandro really said that? Had Sandro really thought that? Or was it the actress talking? The inclination to the theatrical.

The reception was almost at an end, the dreary, tedious, endless procession of ladies in three plumed aigrettes and trains spread behind them by pages, waiting, like a flotilla of swans with necks held high and eyes as glittering as their jewels, to be presented to Victoria in the throne room of Buckingham Palace. Victoria, surrounded on the dais by the royal family in full evening dress, had only fallen asleep once, awakened by the snap of Lady Churchill's fan to a debutante whose train of pale blue moiré floated from her shoulders. The girl executed a flawless practiced curtsy, and approached to kiss Victoria's hands. Because she was the daughter of a peer, Victoria leaned forward to kiss her on the cheek.

Then, with assistance from Henry, Victoria stood, followed by Vicky, Beatrice, Lady Churchill, and Louise. Bertie and Alix remained to receive the presentations.

Vicky was distracted by the sight of an old friend, a marchioness who had frequently visited Berlin, and Louise and Henry were left to enter the carriage alone.

"American women cannot curtsy," said Louise, settling her black satin carriage cloak about her. "I think it is a weakness of their limbs, perhaps because they don't ride as we do."

"Perhaps," he replied, in the despondent manner that had become customary since Sandro's death. They rode in silence through St. James's Park, past state coaches waiting with bewigged coachmen and powdered and liveried footmen clinging to embroidered straps.

She spoke first. "I can't believe Sandro is gone," she said. "He reminded me of my father, you know. High principled and handsome." She leaned closer to arrange the black marten trim of her cloak. Her perfume was unfamiliar. "Do you ever wonder why I spend so much time with Mama? Surely you don't imagine I find court life enchanting? Bertie's set has much more fun, I assure you. Don't turn away. They can't hear us on the box. It's simply that I love you and want to be near you. She is not deserving of you. She is too plodding, too unimaginative, too duty bound . . ."

"Don't say anything more about my wife. I will not listen to anything unkind about Beatrice."

"That was thoughtless of me," she said. "Forgive me. It's just that I long for you so."

"And I have tried very hard to stay away from you." He looked out the window. "It can't be what it was. I'm not the same."

"I want whatever you can be. You see how humble I am?"

"Humility doesn't suit you."

"What does?"

"This." He reached across and thrust his gloved hands beneath her cloak, pressing her close, covering her mouth and diamond-chokered neck and soft, uncorseted breasts with hungry kisses that knocked the aigrette from her hair and left her trembling beneath her skirts.

Their meetings were at Frogmore, the little-used mansion on the grounds of Windsor, in the small, cluttered library, which had been closed for renovations. This time it was she who spurred his passion with wild inventions, once handing him silken cords and telling him to bind her to the finials of the daybed. At first, his acquiescence was halfhearted, and the silken cords uncoiled; then the sight of her half-dressed body bound at the wrists and ankles aroused him to volup-tuous heights he would not have thought possible, driving him to a frenzy that helped him to forget, for a time, the torment that had begun to etch itself into his soul.

Beatrice believed Henry was still grieving over Sandro's death, a feeling generated in the way intimates respond to subtle shifts in each other's behavior, that something else was wrong, a nagging thought gathered from the odd moment when she would suddenly catch him gazing into some remote and distant place.

There were problems all around. Victoria required more attention, Leopold, who could not keep from injuring himself and was covered with yellowish purple bruises, had to be carried everywhere, and Vicky's visit, always a disruption in the household, was longer this time than usual.

On the morning Henry had gone to the station to meet Gladstone, Beatrice was describing to her sisters at breakfast a tearful scene with Ena, who, at six, had protested tearfully against the T-shaped back-board she was forced to wear.

"Tell her," said Vicky, her voice dropping so that the footmen could not hear, "it is like a corset, a reminder to its wearer to show self-control, a visible expression of a well-balanced emotional life."

"What nonsense," said Louise. "You probably wear yours even at night."

"That is not the point," replied Vicky, plucking at the enormous puffed sleeves of her yellow pleated silk shirtwaist.

At the sound of a carriage rumbling over the quadrangle, Louise put down her napkin and went to the window. Beatrice also rose to stand in the shadows behind her. Below stood Henry with an equerry and a footman, helping the aged Prime Minister and his wife to alight.

"Bertie says when Gladstone made his last speech in the Commons," said Louise, "he was so blind he stumbled into the speaker's bench."

"He is eighty-four," said Beatrice, "and long past retirement."

Henry handed the Prime Minister's wife down, glanced up, squinted, and smiled at Louise, who was closer to the glass. Then Louise did something strange. She did not wave or smile in return or even nod her head. Instead, she maintained a controlled hauteur and turned from the window.

Beatrice felt her heart drop, a sickening sensation as if a knife had cut the tenuous connections that bound it to her chest. Not again, she pleaded, please not again. She avoided Vicky's prying eyes and went to tell Victoria that Gladstone was on his way, hoping her voice would not betray her to her mother.

Victoria was in her sitting room with Major Bigge and Sir Henry. Since she had begun to complain that the days were so murky, candles burned on the marble mantelpiece and in the crystal chandelier that hung from the ceiling.

"Mr. Gladstone has arrived, Mama, and is waiting in the council chamber."

Victoria looked up. "There is no need to sound as if this were the end of the world, Beatrice. Mr. Gladstone and I are both in favor of his resignation. I do not wish to prolong this any more than I have to, especially since the man is so deaf I will have to shout in his ear." Victoria leaned on Major Bigge, then hobbled to her bath chair where an Indian servant stood waiting.

With hammering heart, Beatrice quickened her steps and found

Henry in the white drawing room with Louise, Vicky, and Mrs. Gladstone, a small, white-haired woman wearing a bonnet of buttercups and green ribbons framing the feathered traceries of her cheeks and brow. The Prime Minister's wife seemed to be waiting for something. They were discussing Eleonora Duse and her performance in *The Lady of the Camellias*. Louise and Henry sat far apart, not once looking in each other's direction, as if to measure a distance between them.

"Duse never seems to feel her scenes," said Vicky. "After her lover's father asks her to sacrifice Armando as an atonement of her past, she stifles all emotion."

"It's a new school of dramatic art," explained Louise. "One must try to appreciate it."

"That may be," said Vicky, "but I don't like it. Sarah Bernhardt melts the whole audience into tears in that scene. What does Duse do? She eliminates the letter writing entirely."

"That's because it's too theatrical," said Louise. She turned to the Prime Minister's wife. "What is your opinion, Mrs. Gladstone?"

Mrs. Gladstone daubed at her eyes, then folded her hands carefully in her lap. Beatrice could hear the ticking of Henry's pocket watch. "Whatever my husband's errors, ma'am, he has always been devoted to the Queen."

The little, thin Tsarevitch came to London when May and George's first baby, Edward, was born. His interest was less in the British line of descent than it was to be with Alicky, who was also visiting Windsor. What was distressing to Victoria was that neither Nicky nor Alicky, who considered themselves engaged, had asked permission of anyone, and neither could be bullied. To dispel any doubt that they were in love and would be married, Alicky was learning Russian and speaking of becoming a member of the Greek Orthodox Church, the mysteries of which she considered closer to God. Nevertheless, Victoria subjected the Tsarevitch to a series of grueling examinations.

The first was during a ride through the home park on the avenue of elms planted by Charles II. "Can you imagine," said Victoria, "Christian wants to have them cut down and Spanish chestnuts planted in their place."

Nicky, in vandyke beard and uniform of the Imperial Hussars, in which his frail body seemed to disappear, strongly resembled his cousin George, the Duke of York, although Victoria privately believed her grandson George to have the firmer chin. "I, too, Your Majesty, like them as they are," he said.

"Alicky has no parents," began Victoria, "and since I am her only grandparent, she is like my own child."

The Tsarevitch cleared his throat. "I recognize that fact, Your Majesty," he said. "I am devoted to Alexandra. She will be my whole life, I can promise you that."

They passed an enclosure of high-backed, russet-colored wild boars. Alicky turned her face from the snorting animals. Her expression beneath her flat hat, piled with silk and velvet fruits, was calm and uninvolved, as if she had no interest in the discussion. She was toying idly with an emerald bracelet, a gift from the Tsarina.

"That is very commendable, Nicky," replied Victoria. "However, my granddaughter will take her place beside you in a country that has no solid foundations, with anarchists lurking in every corner. I would rather you promised me that you will try to influence your father to implement parliamentary institutions. Perhaps when you succeed to power, you will do so yourself. Such institutions are a healthy foundation for a throne."

"Your point is well taken, Your Majesty," he replied, his protuberant eyes apologetic. "But the things you speak of take time. That is not to say they are not worthy of serious consideration." He turned to smile at Alicky and take her hand, afraid to remind Victoria that his liberal grandfather, Alexander II, who had freed the serfs, had been brutally assassinated.

Victoria ended her probe with a reference to the Kaiser, with whom, it was learned, Nicky had begun a correspondence. "I am afraid," she said, "that Willy may go and tell you things against us, just as he does about you to us. If so, Nicky, please tell me openly and confidentially."

Later that evening, Bertie came to discuss the munshi, his concern ostensibly that Indian Hindus might resent a Moslem so close to the Queen. The real issue was the protest of the cabinet ministers that the munshi was privy to their letters. "What do you think of Nicky," began Bertie. "I see him as a young peace missionary, quite different

from his father. He may help to bring about a Russian-English entente."

Victoria did not agree. She concluded that Nicky's character was
weak, because he cleared his throat, acquiesced too easily, and could
not look one in the eye. "I am more fearful of Alicky than ever before.
And be assured before you begin that whatever you have to say about
my faithful munshi, I am going to flatly reject."

During the summer and the months of early fall, when the savage
Matabeles were massing on the banks of the Zambezi against the
volunteer troops of Cecil Rhodes's British South African chartered
company, Beatrice was certain there was something again between
Henry and Louise. This time she decided to say nothing, as she had
about his beard, which was the longest and most unkempt of anyone
in the family. The four children were a consideration in her decision.
More important was the fear that given his present restiveness, forcing his hand might cause him or Louise to do something foolish, like
an open declaration of affection, which would mean virtual banishment from court.

It was a feature of men, like a fondness for uniforms. Beatrice tried
hard to believe this, reminding herself that the idea of absolute fidel-
ity was an impractical notion and that it was childish to feel betrayed.
Whatever Henry's peccadilloes, they were not all consuming. His
interests were also in Africa and on the Impis, who were, in his
opinion, the most warlike tribe in South Africa, similiar to the Zulus
under King Cetewayo. When at a dinner with Lord Wolseley it was
stated that the Impis couldn't fight or shoot, that their aim was poor
and it was only when they got close with short stabbing spears and
knobbed clubs that they were successful, Henry entered the conversation with enthusiasm. "Then we, too," he said, "must learn to fight
with short stabbing spears." Lord Wolseley listened politely, nodded,
then asked him what he knew of the new motorcar, with its internal
combustion engine, that was being produced in France.

In November, Alexander III died, and Nicky became the Tsar of
all the Russias. A week after that, he and Alicky, wearing a diamond
crown and court dress of silver brocade with robe and train of cloth of
gold lined with ermine, were married in St. Petersburg. Victoria's
fears for her granddaughter burgeoned, especially after Nicky was

reported to have said that all parliamentary systems and extension of people's rights were crazy schemes and that he had made up his mind —with Willy's approval and instigation, it was learned—to hold as firmly to the principles of autocracy as his father had.

Victoria at first planned to send Henry and Beatrice to represent her, but Bertie insisted that it was his prerogative as Prince of Wales. Beatrice and Henry remained at Balmoral. While Beatrice read aloud dispatches, Henry and Louise arranged clandestine meetings at the shiel, a small, remote lodge that stood isolated beside a lake. If any of the Highland servants or members of the household had suspicions, not to speak of downright proof, they kept them to themselves or to their diaries. No one wanted to be the one to tell Victoria. First, she would not believe it, and second, her anger would be directed at the bearer of the tale, as it had been to Sir Henry's son Fritz, who had been written off the dinner list after he reported that the munshi was a fake.

While frenetic and often voluptuous, their rendezvous were not always idyllic. Once, after lovemaking in which he had beaten her with a riding crop, he suddenly tossed the counterpane over her half-nude body, then began to dress hurriedly, thrusting his legs into his gleaming boots. "I am beginning to dislike myself very much," he said.

"You enjoyed it while you were doing it," she replied, "and after, as well."

"It sickens me now. Cover yourself, for God's sakes."

"What has happened to make you so prudish? It used to excite you to see the marks you made. Like this one, and this." She folded back the cover.

Henry stopped for a moment, then strode angrily from the room, past Highland servants, who kept their eyes discreetly averted, grabbed the reins from his groom to jump on his horse and gallop headlong and reckless through the firs, whipping the mount as he had the woman, spurring the animal with his heels and the press of his thighs, knocking off low-lying twigs and branches, and passing a clearing in which crofters were dipping sheep in troughs of tobacco and soap.

When he returned to the castle, he found Victoria dictating a refusal to Lord Rosebery's plea for the installation of the new type-writing machine at Balmoral.

Victoria's expression softened at the sight of Henry. "Where were you all afternoon? I am anxious for your opinion. Lord Rosebery suggests I am old-fashioned. Not that he has come out and said it, but he implies it. He asks if my refusal to consider the typewriter stems from the same reasoning that has prompted me to request that no motor-cars be allowed on English roads."

Beatrice noticed that his forehead was scratched and bleeding. She moistened a handkerchief in Apollinaris water and wiped his cuts, while he sat beside Victoria to tell her that she was not the least bit old-fashioned and that any right-thinking person would see that she was as forward as the new century that was almost upon them.

Their nomadic life continued in the same predictable and orderly routine, leavened by an occasional entertainment. At Windsor, Beatrice and Henry went with Helena and Christian to see Oscar Wilde's new play, *The Importance of Being Earnest,* a cynical comedy in which the playwright's scathing wit was unleashed against English manners. "No one can make a joke of respectability," said Helena as they were bundled into their cloaks, "without a flaw in his own morals."

It was bitter cold. As the footman spread fur robes on their laps, Beatrice asked Henry if he agreed with the playwright that twenty years of marriage made a woman a building. "It might have been funny to some," she said, "but I thought it was a dreadful thing to say."

"You have left out the first line," he said. "Without the first line it is not funny at all. You must first say, 'Twenty years of romance make a woman a ruin.' In any case, I thought it was more amusing when Lady Bracknell said that in England education produces no effect whatsoever."

"That is because you are German," snapped Beatrice, who was suddenly for no reason she could think of annoyed. "If you were English, you would not find that funny at all."

He arched his brows in the way he did when he became angry. "You will recall that I am a naturalized Englishman." He turned to trace a clearing on the frosted window with his gloved fingertip.

"You were very wrong," whispered Helena, "to say such a thing. It was quite uncalled for and bound to hurt his feelings and Christian's, as well. And it was an English audience, you may recall, that laughed so hard at that speech the next actor could not be heard."

That evening, when they slipped into sheets warmed with flannel-wrapped bricks, Beatrice apologized for calling Henry a German.

"That is not the point," he said in clipped tones. "I am a German. It is just that you dismissed my opinion as that of a foreigner."

"Forgive me, darling, but you are definitely not treated as a foreigner. Bertie complains all the time that you know more than he does. The Ashanti business, for example," she said, referring to an ultimatum sent to the Ashanti King stating that human sacrifices, failure to keep road open, and slave raids on other tribes would no longer be tolerated.

He was silent; then he spoke in the throaty ebbing voice of one who is falling asleep. "They have certainly kept Africa in a state of war and deprived the colony of its trade," he said. "Although that will end. The King is required to receive a British resident at Kumasi without delay."

"Africa is so far away," she replied. "At the other end of the world."

"The distance doesn't matter. England is bound to her colonies as firmly as you and I to each other."

"Are we?" she asked, rising to rest on her elbow. "Are we firmly bound to one another?"

"How can you ask such a question?"

She lay her head on his shoulder and wondered, as footsteps trampled on the battlements above, what was wrong with her that he did not love her well enough not to seek another.

When Sir Henry suffered a stroke that left him with an impaired memory and a paralyzed arm and leg, Beatrice was wedged into her mother's service more tightly than ever before. Her responsibilities occupied the clerical, homely side of sovereignty, responses to requests, responses to ministers, protocol and arrangements, dedications, investitures, troop reviews, weddings, audiences, and funerals, all of which demanded meticulous planning and impeccable timing. She became as indispensable as Victoria's walking stick, the filter through which Victoria and her subjects were strained. By the time they went to Nice, while Henry set off again on his yacht, this time without a firm itinerary, it was clear to all that Beatrice was the first link in the royal chain of command.

At the time the British East Africa Company left Uganda like a foundling on the doorstep of the government and Oscar Wilde was tried and convicted for homosexual activity with young boys, confirming everyone's suspicions of the relationship between an author's work and his own morality, England was mounting an expeditionary force to restore order to the Ashantis.

One afternoon Beatrice and Henry returned to Balmoral from a ceremony at Edinburgh, where Knights of the Thistle in dark green velvet mantles and white-plumed tudor bonnets had filed solemnly into St. Giles Cathedral to a fanfare of trumpets. Beatrice was expressing her concerns about Drino, who had refused to recopy a soiled page of French verbs in his exercise book. Henry suggested that matter remain in the hands of Drino's new tutor, then said abruptly, "I wish to join the expedition."

At first, she was uncomprehending. Then she realized that he meant the fourteen-hundred-man force being assembled for Africa.

"That's nonsense, Henry. What can you be thinking of? Mama would never allow it."

His words were so low she had to strain to hear. "I am no longer interested in what the Queen will or will not allow. I have abided by her authority for nine years. I can't do it any longer."

"But Africa? It's so far away. There's fever there, and the people are so savage." Her voice began to rise in pitch.

"I am determined."

Later in her dressing room, while one maid unpinned the orders from her corsage and another held a flowing tea gown, her thoughts ranged from panic to despair. Henry would be gone for months. He could get wounded; worse, the unspeakable, the unthinkable, what happened to Eugénie's son, the Prince Imperial, might happen to him. But that was impossible, she reasoned. Henry was the Queen's son-in-law. He would have to be protected. If he were separated from her, he would also be separated from her sister. Perhaps while he was away, he would see how wrong, how foolish he had been. And if his absence was protracted, could it be any worse than his solitary cruises where she never knew where he was unless a gunboat had been dispatched to find him?

They broke the news to Victoria at breakfast. "Henry wants to go to Africa."

"I'll speak for myself," said Henry. "I have advised Lord Wolseley that I am available for the Ashanti expedition."

"But you are not available," protested Victoria. "You are not available at all. I will not even discuss such a thing. How can you even bring it up when you know my leg is so painful I cannot move it. It is a preposterous idea. You are needed at my side. I cannot think of what I would do if you were halfway around the world."

An Indian servant set golden egg cups before them while a Highland servant placed a skillet of sweetbreads on a warmer. "He is quite determined, Mama."

"I can see that," said Victoria. "That doesn't mean that it is not out of the question. Why don't you go on a cruise instead? Perhaps to the west coast of Africa, the Canary Islands?"

Henry tapped the eggshell with the edge of a golden spoon. "I have honored my commitment to you, Mama. And I am not sorry. I would still do it again. But I can no longer sail on pointless cruises. That is not what I was trained for. What I was raised to be. My father, my brother Sandro, were men of action. You offered Louis the captaincy of the royal yacht. He declined, partly to concentrate on the ship already under his command but largely because to accept would have made him a courtier. Which is what I am. Which is what Louis will never be."

"Are you behind him in this decision?" asked Victoria.

"Henry has his heart set on going."

The tartaned gillie moved to serve Victoria the sweetbreads, but the Indian servant took the dish from his hand. "I will ask Dr. Reid to advise us on the dangers of fever. Perhaps when you hear what he has to say, you will change your mind."

"I know of the dangers of malaria," said Henry. "I also know you have serious problems in the colonies which others solve for you while I sit ineffectual and useless. This time I am bound to enlist in your service. Do what I know, lead, fight, win."

"This is cold," said Victoria of the sweetbreads.

"Do you think I have not seen the cartoons that are drawn of me in *Punch?*" asked Henry. "I want to show the people of England that I am ready to take the rough with the smooth. I hope, by volunteering in a national cause, to prove my devotion to my adopted country."

"Your devotion is not in question, but your safety is. You are royalty, Henry."

"Christian and Helena's son is going."

"He is not you, Henry. He is a boy."

"I am nine years his senior, not ninety."

CHAPTER NINETEEN

Henry stood before the oval looking glass with his legs astride, his hands on his hips, as his tailor pinned between the shoulders of his service tunic.

"If Your Royal Highness will allow his arms to drop," suggested the tailor while Drino, Ena, and Leopold sat cross-legged on the Persian carpet, watching their father's valet wrap the dark blue puttees about his calves. Henry handed the pith helmet to the tailor's assistant and tried on the broad-brimmed bush hat, which he angled over his brow, aware that it covered neatly the slight recession of his hairline. "What do you think of my smasher hat, Drino?" he asked.

"I wish that I could go with you, Father," replied the boy.

"When you are grown, Drino, that is certainly a possibility. I would welcome it." He turned to the tailor. "I think it's good." His valet stood from wrapping the puttees and fitted a brown leather harness over Henry's chest to which he attached a holster, pouches for ammunition, compass, binoculars, and a sword. When he adjusted the angle of the sword so that it hung freely, he draped about the Prince's neck a water bottle and a haversack.

"I mean now," said Drino. "I could carry your reserve ammunition."

"There are natives to carry such things for you," said Ena. "Grandmama has said so."

"You don't know anything about battles," said Drino. "The natives carry your food and your sleeping roll. They are not permitted to carry ammunition."

"What is your opinion, Leo?" asked Henry. "Do you think your papa looks like a soldier?"

Leo, in his sailor suit, was still the most beautiful of the children. His expression was sober, thoughtful. "I like your hat best, Father," he said.

"Then you shall try it on." Henry bent to put the felt hat on his younger son's head as Beatrice entered, leading Maurice by the hand. The brim flopped over Leo's face, almost to his nose, prompting an instant response from Drino, who lunged to yank it down even farther.

"Stop," snapped Beatrice in sharp command. "You'll hurt him!" Leo, with a look of resignation of the conscripted invalid, handed back the hat to his father's valet.

Henry's attentions had returned to his own reflection. "What do you think of the fit?" he asked.

Beatrice walked about her husband, restraining Maurice from reaching for the gleaming sword. Henry looked dashing, young, as if the heat of impending danger had melted away the years. "Perhaps the back between the shoulders might be released. It seems pinned too tightly."

"It is not tight at all." He swung his arms. "You see? I am perfectly comfortable."

Tears shimmered in Ena's eyes and spilled down her cheeks, dampening the pale blonde hair that had strayed from its ribbon. "I don't want you to go," she said. "Why must you go?"

Henry knelt beside her on the carpet. "It is Papa's duty to go. But you are not to worry. Papa will not take direct command, nor will he be charged with staff duties. That means that he will be as safe as can be, more like a tourist carrying that new box camera that your mother has."

"Maurice is touching the sword again," said Leo.

Henry left Windsor dressed in the black braided dress uniform of the King's Royal Rifle Corps, on his head a chin-strapped busby adorned with a black egret feather over scarlet vulture plumes. Members of the household, servants, and the children stood shivering in the windy quadrangle. Some of the women held handkerchiefs to their faces as kilted pipers played "Highland Laddie" and Henry and

Beatrice entered their carriage. Victoria stood apart, sheltered in the doorway on the arm of the turbaned munshi, who saluted Henry with his arms crossed over his order-hung, scarlet silken breast.

Pale, brilliant sunshine swept the ground of Aldershot station of its shadows, where Henry and other members of the special force stood smartly at attention, representatives of all the regiments in England, slung with haversacks and backpacks, canteens, and cartridge pouches, as Arthur, the Duke of Connaught, Beatrice's third eldest brother, reviewed them.

There were other women at Aldershot besides Beatrice; mothers, sweethearts, sisters, wives, wrapped tightly against the bitter wind and holding firmly to their wide-brimmed, feather-garnished hats, also come to see their soldiers off, except that they, unlike the Princess, who was forced to publicly control her tears, enjoyed the privacy of anonymity and could weep freely if they chose.

A whistle blew, the military band struck up "Auld Lang Syne," and men began to board the troop train that would take them to the transport and hospital ship *Coromandel.*

"Ena was crying when we left," said Beatrice, thinking that it was an inane thing to say to one's husband as he departed for another continent.

"Tell her I will write from Spain," he replied.

Somehow the milling crowd began to coalesce, gathering more tightly about her, pushing them closer to the train. "Try to walk in the sunlight as much as possible," she said. "There is less fever in the sunlight. And tell your valet to shake your boots. Every morning. Mr. Stanley has said that snakes and scorpions and all sorts of horrid things crawl about inside unless they are shaken."

"You'll be busy," he said. "I'm grateful for that. And don't fret over Drino. You are not used to little boys with unlimited energy. He can't be treated like Leo. Try to remember that it is difficult for him to always be under someone's scrutiny."

"It is just as difficult for Leo," she replied.

"It is not the same. Leo is infirm." He cupped her chin in his black-gloved hand. "I have made you angry. How stupid of me. The last thing I want to do is make you angry."

"I am not angry, Henry."

He dropped his hand and edged closer to the train. She raised her voice, beginning to shout, as were some of the other women. "Tell your valet you want a change of hose twice a day. Your feet can't be damp, and try to rest every afternoon. The sun depletes one." Someone pushed her against his chest. She felt the tug, the trembling weakened knees, the passion she had always felt when close to him, surprised that it could happen there, in the open and at such a time. "I don't think I can say good-bye."

He leaned down to kiss her. "You say it every time I take the *Sheilah* out. This is no different."

"Yes, it is. You were never armed to fight savages. You were never sailing into fever."

"Say instead *auf wiedersehn*, my darling. You will admit that in this case German has the advantage over English." He brought her hands to his lips and looked searchingly into her eyes. "I love you," he said.

"Write, every day, and send telegrams."

"Did you hear what I said? I said, 'I love you.' "

"I heard. I heard." He stepped up into the compartment and closed the narrow door behind him. At first, they stared at one another through the glass, smiling bravely with lips closed tight, then mouthing words that neither understood. Someone on the seat beside him spoke; he turned, and the train pulled away. In a moment he was gone.

Beatrice felt it in her shoulders first. She began to sob.

"Have a nice cry, Your Royal Highness, dear," said a gray-haired woman who had just seen off her son. "He can't see you anymore, and it will do you good."

The birth of two babies, George and May's second son, Prince Albert, and Alicky and Nicky's first daughter, the Grand Duchess Olga, diverted some of Beatrice and Victoria's anxieties. Gradually, mother and daughter accommodated to the idea that Henry's absence would be protracted and that their contact with him would be limited to a handful of sporadic telegrams and letters in a mound of communiqués.

If it was a particularly hectic time, it had its compensations, for Beatrice was never more absorbed. It began with the row over Bertie's dispatch. England and the United States were on the brink of war over the borders between Venezuela and British Guiana. Tensions were heightened by President Cleveland's delivery of a Christmas message to Congress in which he claimed the right to adjudicate the dispute in his capacity as guardian of the Monroe Doctrine. Bertie drafted a conciliatory telegram to be published in the American newspapers and informed the Prime Minister. Salisbury would not hear of its dispatch and refused to sanction any gesture of conciliation. Bertie sent it, anyway, and was called to account by Victoria for his rash action.

Soon after Victoria's stinging rebuke to the Prince of Wales, Beatrice received a telegram from Lord Wolseley that said that Henry was marching with the main column toward Kumasi. They learned that two men had died from heat the first day, eighty had fallen out the second day, that there were cases of fever, among them, the camp commander, Major Ferguson.

Beatrice could not finish her poached turbot and declined the sorbet and the roast mutton that followed despite Victoria's imprecations that she keep up her strength. "Why must they be so thorough?" she asked. "Can't they imagine that I would be wild with worry?"

"The telegram was meant for me," said Victoria, "not for you. I naturally must be apprised of all conditions."

A few days later came the message from Cape Colony that Dr. Jameson, the administrator of Rhodesia, with a few hundred mounted police and a twelve-pounder gun, made a midnight raid into the Transvaal to raise a revolution against President Kruger. Beatrice read aloud from a flurry of dispatches late into that night. The situation in the Transvaal appeared disastrous. Nothing of the aborted and embarrassing mission had gone right; the Boers knew of the insurrection at once. Since plans to cut all telegraph lines never materialized, the expected uprising in Johannesburg fizzled out. Worse and more ignominious, the Boers forced the raiders around the perimeter of the city, surrounded them near the gold mines, and claimed from captured papers a conspiracy to reoccupy the Transvaal involving Cecil Rhodes, the Colonial Office, and Secretary of State Joseph Chamberlain.

In the lavender light of morning, Beatrice eased her aching neck with her fingertips, trying to remember if it were day or night for Henry, while Victoria, clearly at a loss as to what had prompted the raid, was certain only that the Boers were horrid people and that Jameson was an able man.

A cipher from Vicky detailed Willy's intention to declare a protectorate over the Transvaal and send German troops. Lord Salisbury hurried to Osborne to discuss the import of the Dowager Empress's message and to assure Victoria that he and Chamberlain had communicated with foreign cabinets, affirming that Rhodes and Jameson had taken the law into their own hands and that their actions did not reflect the policy of the British Government.

The Prime Minister left for London the same afternoon, just after the delivery of a telegram from the Ashanti expedition saying that Henry had been appointed military secretary and that he was helping to deal with native chiefs who were awed with meeting the great Queen's son-in-law.

Victoria went for her daily carriage ride. Beatrice, wearing a costume of fur-trimmed velvet, her hands thrust into her muff, took the children skating on a pond frozen over with silver-blue ice.

Accompanied by servants who set up a bonfire and a table of hot chocolate and sandwiches, they scored the ice with sharp hissing scratches on blades curved upward like scimitars. Ena, whose eyelashes had been trimmed that morning to make them grow thick, complained that the sun hurt her eyes and that Drino, who was making figure eights, refused to skate with her. When one of the servants brought out a sled made to look like a beautiful white swan, Leo objected to his having to be pushed in the swan with Maurice. Beatrice alone was serene, Henry was safe.

Beatrice's relief at Henry's continued safety was undiminished by her frostbitten fingers or the news later that evening that Willy had sent a message of congratulation to Kruger and that British squadrons were put on a war footing. It was learned that preparations were made in East Africa and on German ships to send expeditionary troops and landing parties to Pretoria. When Lord Salisbury announced that the first German soldier to set foot on Transvaal soil would mean an Anglo-German war, a war that was bound to develop into a world war, as France had already come out on the side of Germany, Beatrice was thinking that when Henry returned, she would try to have another child despite Victoria's admonitions to the contrary. Even while Victoria dictated a letter to Willy, reprimanding her meddling grandson for taking the part of the Boers and for displaying the worst possible good taste, Beatrice's thoughts were on Henry. She wished in particular that she could live over again the moment the train had pulled away. If he would have turned back one final time, perhaps she would have found the courage to send him a kiss with her fingertips.

The news seemed to improve. A few days later, Drino reported Lord Wolseley's latest dispatch all over Osborne. Everyone, even the stableboys washing mud from the carriages, knew that the Ashanti King was prepared to make terms, that Prince Henry was a universal favorite among the men, and that he had jumped into a brawl between native troops and rescued a man from being murdered.

To everyone's surprise, Bertie's apostasy had a salutary effect, his peace message leading to discussions in which an agreement between the United States and Britain was soon to be reached. As Bertie sat through a billowing, fluttering dance recital, waiting without success for kudos from Victoria, Fritz Ponsonby, Sir Henry's son, delivered a telegram that said that Henry had a slight fever, enough to prevent him from going on, and that he would return to Cape Coast the next day with a medical officer and his servant. "Poor Henry," said Bertie. "He will be so angry having to go back to the coast."

Beatrice heard only one word, fever, more malady than symptom, an ailment from open drains and pestilential marshes from which most did not recover. She excused herself before the principal dancer, Miss Ada Thompson, danced the dance of the serpents.

Two days after that, another telegram arrived from Henry saying that thanks to the care of his doctor and valet, he had arrived safely at Cape Coast Castle. Beatrice was consoled that at least he was out of the fighting to come. In the middle of January, they learned that his fever was declining, that he had improved enough to be sent to convalesce in Madeira, although he wanted to stay in Africa until Kumasi was occupied. Against his protests, he was put aboard the H.M.S. *Blonde*. In two days he was expected to be well enough to stroll the decks. Beatrice was given reluctant permission by Victoria to join him.

When a telegram advised them that British forces had arrived at Kumasi and that order had been restored, everyone breathed a sigh of relief. Victoria even began reviewing preparations for her diamond jubilee.

The next morning, Beatrice took breakfast with her silver-moustached brother Arthur and his wife. The Duchess of Connaught was saying how splendid it would be to have Henry back again and that in England, with proper nursing care, he would soon be well. When Major Bigge appeared with a telegram from the H.M.S. *Blonde,* Arthur expressed surprise that the ship had so quickly reached Madeira. Major Bigge handed the telegram to Beatrice. Something in the way he could not look at her made her tear it open. She read that the Colonel His Royal Highness Prince Henry of Battenberg, K.G., had died quietly, off the coast of Sierra Leone. A pulse throbbed in her ear.

Beatrice folded the paper and handed it to Arthur. "The life is gone out of me," she murmured, surprised that her hands did not tremble.

Arthur quickly read the telegram and leaned over to embrace her. "I'm so dreadfully sorry, Benjamina." He stood and dropped his napkin on the table. "I'll tell Mama," he said. "None of us would wish her to hear of it from the household."

Beatrice reached for Arthur's napkin and began to smooth and fold it, deliberately, methodically, edging the creases with her thumbs. The Duchess of Connaught exchanged glances with Major Bigge, then gently took Beatrice's arm and led her to her apartments.

"The children," said Beatrice as they walked past an alcove of waiting pages. "I must see to the children. How dreadful for them. Especially the little ones. They will never really know him."

The Duchess of Connaught assured her that Major Bigge had seen to the children. With the help of a tearful maid, she loosened Beatrice's stays, wrapped her in a lace-trimmed combing sacque, and led her to the sofa.

"But I'm not tired," protested Beatrice. A maid of honor who had just heard the news apologized to the Duchess for her hasty dress and settled a coverlet over the Princess's legs. "I never knew my father, you know," said Beatrice. "The memories are too soft, too vague. They slip from my mind."

The warmth of the coverlet and the possett they gave her to drink made her begin to question what she had read. It was only letters on a piece of paper, transmitted over thousands of miles by someone with a key. The telegrapher's truth, not hers. Soon she began to doubt that she had read it at all. "They make mistakes, you know. Telegraphers. Such things are common."

"Yes, dear," replied her sister-in-law.

Gradually, the disbelief turned to pain, so overwhelming, so wounding, that Beatrice, breathing in short, painful gasps, could only hide. Victoria found her in Henry's dressing room, near a boot stand with boot jacks and boot hooks, smelling his soaps and toilet waters, his lemon-scented moustache wax, and rummaging through his dressing bureau with its razors, shaving brushes, and packs of paper razor wipers.

"I should never have permitted it," said Victoria, seeming smaller, more shrunken.

Beatrice allowed herself to be embraced, ignoring the presence of the Indian servant. "He went out of desperation. He was suffocating and we wouldn't give him air. We are to blame."

"You don't mean what you are saying. You speak from pain that I understand. You are the same age as I when your dear papa was taken from me."

Beatrice stepped back farther into the shadows of the darkened dressing room. "It is I who am bereaved, who must seek my husband's scent in bottles, pluck his hair from combs. It is my grief, my sorrow. Why do you make it yours?"

Victoria leaned more heavily on the arm of her attendant. "You must rest, Baby. The days ahead will be very draining. Believe me. I know. And please remember that I loved him, too."

Servants closed the pianos and drew the draperies, plunging the Battenberg apartments and all of Osborne into a twilight. Louis came from Malta; Bertie, Alix, and the Duke of York came from Sandringham; Louise and Lorne came from London, everyone in deep mourning, the deepest, of course, belonging to Beatrice. Her veil was the longest, her hem the widest, her tight-sleeved gown of clinging, melancholy crepe, unrelieved, as were the gowns of the other women, by any other fabric. Everyone trod softly and spoke in whispers or draped about in poses of regret. Even the children did not have to be reminded to be still. Memorial cards arrived with pictures of broken columns and weeping willows; a supply of black-edged paper and black sealing wax suddenly appeared; and mourning handkerchiefs were given to her hand each time she changed.

Letters began to arrive from officers and men who were with Henry
in Africa, one from an officer aboard the H.M.S. *Blonde* who had
been with Henry when he died. He wrote that His Royal Highness's
last words were that he had come to Africa not to win glory but from
a sense of duty. Tell Her Royal Highness, he had said. She will understand. Beatrice did not understand. Henry joined the expedition because he was restless. Duty was what she did with Victoria, day by
day, hour by hour, month by month, what she had done ever since
she could remember.

Bertie made arrangements for the funeral, attending to all the details, including what regiments should line the route to the church,
what foreign dignitaries would be expected, deciding against mourning coaches with gilt skulls on their doors, not telling Beatrice that he
learned that in order to preserve the body in equatorial heat, crew
members had placed it in a tank made of biscuit tins and filled with
rum.

The royal yacht *Alberta* carried Beatrice, Bertie, Arthur, Helena,
and Louis across the Solent to the *Blenheim* where Henry's body had
been transferred. When Victoria saw the *Alberta* return, she left
Osborne to meet the vessel. It was a still afternoon, and the sun was
going down. A chill gathered from the darkening shadows. After the
booming of the guns and the tolling of the bells on the anchored
naval squadrons, no sound came from the *Alberta* as she glided up to
the pier.

Victoria hitched on the arms of two Indian servants to where the
coffin, covered with a Union Jack, lay between the funnels and the
saloon. Beatrice stood at its head, veiled in black, immobile, staunch,
not at all dissolved in tears, as Victoria had expected she would be.
Victoria stooped with difficulty and laid her wreath, then stood and
looked at Beatrice. Their eyes held. Then Henry's brother Louis came
to take Beatrice's arm.

"We should return to Osborne," he said. "It will soon be dark."

"It is already night," she replied.

The next morning, Beatrice, pale and drawn, returned to the pier
with the children and Arthur to lay an anchor wreath of orchids and
lilies. Crowds swarmed over the quay. In a few moments the knot of
mourners would be observed by thousands of spectators and troops
already lining the route, all keen to witness the funeral, its trappings,

and the state of grief of the principals. Beatrice knelt by the coffin and raised her veil, then pressed her lips to the smooth polished wood, almost as silky as his eyelids, which she always kissed when they used to talk into the night and he fell asleep before her. "All this time," she whispered, "I thought of you as living."

When they stepped onto the wharf, the road to Cowes was already lined with men of the Royal Marine Artillery, the Royal Engineers, the Royal Dublin Fusiliers, the Scottish Rifles, the Scots Guard, Henry's former Gardes du Corps, and the Isle of Wight Volunteer Battalion, all of them, because of the weather, in overcoats. The coffin was borne to a gun carriage, which rolled to the beating of muffled drums and the dirge of a military band. Close behind, led by a groom, was Henry's charger, in black velvet trappings and black plumes, carrying Henry's boots, reversed in the stirrups. Beside the groom walked the captain of the *Sheilah* and Henry's valet. Drino followed next, walking between his uncles, the Prince of Wales and the Duke of Connaught; behind them, other mourners, ambassadors and representatives of foreign royalties, their top hats wound with streaming crepe weeds. Beatrice and the three younger children rode in Victoria's carriage, with mounted equerries on either side.

A church bell began to toll. "It is harder when you don't see a loved one die," said Victoria, nodding to her silent subjects, many of whom were weeping. "That way you are never sure. That way you can't believe. I am thankful that I was there to see Albert breathe his last."

"I am not sorry that Papa died so far away," said Ena fiercely. "This way, in my mind, he will always be standing before the mirror, trying on his uniform."

"Don't look so cross," said Beatrice. "This is your father's funeral. You must appear sad, not angry."

Leo held tightly to Henry's smasher hat, which had been given him that morning, protecting it from the stubby, grasping fingers of Maurice.

Beatrice's disbelief changed to numbness, like frostbite on her fingertips. She heard only the edges of conversation, as when the Duchess of Teck, May's plump, affectionate mother, was suggesting that the ten years of marriage Beatrice shared with handsome, dashing

Henry were the equivalent of another woman's forty with some dull, stuffy husband with an overheated bald head.

Beatrice nodded, wishing everyone would leave her sitting room, including Victoria, whose narrow, anxious eyes never left her face. Louise sniffed behind a handkerchief. "No one is married forty years," she said. "One or the other is bound to die of boredom before long."

Victoria screwed her mouth into a grimace of annoyance and noted that Louise seemed edgy, an odd attitude from a sister offering condolences.

"I have yet to see you cry," said Louise.

Her callous remark stunned everyone into silence. The Duchess of Teck heaved her massive bosom in a startled gasp. Victoria recovered first. "Benjamina is suffering just as any widow who loved her husband deeply," she said, making obvious reference to Louise's estrangement from Lorne. "She doesn't display her feelings as do others. They are more modulated."

"More modulated, Mama? I would say they don't exist at all. Are you suffering?" demanded Louise.

"I don't feel very much of anything," replied Beatrice, "except empty."

"You are contentious, Louise," said Victoria. "I am hard put to know why. We are all grieving deeply."

"I most of all," said Louise.

The Duchess of Teck, so immense that she needed two chairs to sit on, recognized the sound of indelicacy and excused herself, rising to her feet with the aid of a footman and withdrawing from the sitting room.

"It is time you knew," said Louise. "I am lost without Henry."

"We all are," replied Victoria, attempting to check what she feared was inevitable. "It was how I felt when Sir Henry died, but somehow we go on."

Louise was not to be put off. "I am not talking about feelings toward a private secretary. I am talking about the most profound affection a man and woman can share. It is I who should be sitting behind that dark veil. Don't you know that I was Henry's closest confidante? Henry used to tell me everything. I know all about you, both of you, what you said and did, everything."

"I don't believe you," said Victoria.

"It's true." Her sallies became rapid fire and merciless. "We used to laugh at how much alike you sounded. When you thought he was off the coast of Scotland, we were in the Greek isles on the *Sheilah*. Beatrice meant nothing to him."

Beatrice began to cry, weeping softly into her handkerchief.

"Have you lost your mind?" asked Victoria. "What are you saying? I hope you have taken too much sherry, for if you have not, your behavior is inexcusable."

"I am saying, Mama, that we were in love. Beatrice knew it. Ask her. She tried to separate us. I am saying that Henry was miserable with her and happy with me. I am saying he went to his death, because you drove him to it, both of you, Beatrice with her boring, tedious ways and you, Mama, with your constant petty demands."

"I cannot believe a daughter of mine could be so cruel. At such a time. Look at your sister. Look what you have done to her. How can you live with yourself? Did you really expect that we would give you any part of the sympathy that is her due? That this sordid confession would enlist an ounce of pity? What do you know of love? Are you showing love to a sister?" Victoria blinked away her tears. Her voice was tremulous, silvery. "Leave Osborne," she said. "I cannot bear to think that I have borne you."

"I have only said what is so," replied Louise. "I can't help the truth any more than I can help that you never cared about me at all." She stood, kicked her train aside, and strode to the doors. A Highland servant closed them behind her.

Victoria leaned forward to take Beatrice's hand. "Say you did not bear such a terrible burden," she whispered.

"What does it matter?" replied Beatrice. "He's gone. And if I could have him back under the same circumstances, I would accept, gladly, but no one has offered me such terms."

"It's my fault," said Victoria. "I suppose I always knew it and chose to ignore the signs, hoping it would vanish in the way those base liaisons often do. It was another pain, like those in my knee, in my back, that come and go. One stops from being mindful of every single pain, or one cannot go on."

"I don't want to discuss it anymore," said Beatrice.

"I have been thoughtless," said Victoria. "We shall never speak of it again." There was silence. Victoria rang for tea. Within moments, an Indian servant entered with a tray and set it before them, pouring into Victoria's cup and placing the cup firmly in her hand. "I know life is dark and dreadful, yet there is a ray of light. After all, we are together once more, as we used to be, the two of us, like one person, Benjamina, my baby, my dearest companion, my right hand. I will be steadfast at your side while there is strength in my body, to help you just as you helped me through the dark days of my own widowhood. Take sugar, dear, instead of milk. It will give you strength. When you are up to it, you should return to your duties. I won't rush you. But I think it will help you to keep busy. Perhaps at first you will only read aloud."

Beatrice flung the veil back from her face. "I can't breathe behind that thing, and I am tired of the cold. It is making my hands ache. I need the sun. I need to bake out the chill of Osborne. I'm taking the children to Cimiez."

"Dr. Jameson is waiting trial in London," explained Victoria, "and Chamberlain is coming to see me, I imagine about his complicity in the affair. Then there are proposals for the jubilee which must be settled. I can't possibly leave for the Riviera."

"I can," replied Beatrice. "Chamberlain is not coming to see me. And it is not my diamond jubilee."

CHAPTER TWENTY

Despite the protection of a silk parasol and the encumbrance of her mourning garments, Beatrice felt the sun soaking through her gown, her black kid gloves, and her high button shoes radiating away the pains in her hands and in her spirit. She could not get enough.

Cimiez, the hilly suburb of Nice, was bathed in brilliant sunshine. Everywhere were gardens, even now in February, of roses and violets, with crumbling statues and mildewed grottoes hidden among eucalyptus and orange trees and spiraling Lombardy poplars, all to be dusted within weeks by the mistral that would blow from the purple hills and fill the air with a whirlwind.

Below, past the brown-roofed fishing village where donkey carts rattled through narrow streets heaped with oranges, dates, figs, and plums piled up for sale, the deep blue sea washed up among yellow rocks, and boats plied back and forth between the anchored men-of-war and the quay. Every now and then, she caught a whiff of sewage from the sea.

The grief, the emptiness, the awful ache she felt in England, were suspended, transmuted on the warm and fragrant Riviera into a vacuous torpor; her only thoughts were of Leopold, his warmth, his ebullience, the rebelliousness that ultimately caused his death, his attempts to overcome her shyness, so many years ago, before Henry had become her world. Now they were both gone.

As the days turned into weeks, she felt that she could never return to the way things were, not again, the smothering constant attendance, the demanding unbroken docket, complicated by protocol and consanguinity, the complete submersion, like putting one's head under water. Even if she were to resume her duties as before, she could never again take up residence with Victoria. The sea at Osborne, the moors at Balmoral, even Windsor with footsteps tramping on the battlements or echoing beneath the arches of the quadrangle, were laced with too many memories of Henry. She and the children might take a villa nearby; even a cottage would do, like that at Osborne, if there were rooms enough for servants. She might even visit daily at first to make certain things were running smoothly, or twice weekly, if it looked as if they were. It would not be difficult to instruct certain of the maids of honor and perhaps Lady Churchill in most of her responsibilities. She would explain such things as how to best read aloud to Victoria, to make sure one trilled one's "r's," to pause from time to time in case Victoria wanted a note made of a point. She would remind them that when they read from the newspaper, they were to select only items that were humorous and optimistic, to ensure she went to bed content. She would make a list of who was welcome at court and who was not, although, of course, the list would be subject to periodic revisions. She would have to make certain that they knew the signs that told when an application of belladonna to the Queen's tired eyes was warranted or when Victoria simply wanted to take a nap. Then she would try, although she did not expect to be successful, to persuade Victoria to delegate certain matters to Bertie.

While Beatrice warmed herself in the sun and ticked off items to consider, the children went for sedate, strictly supervised excursions with their governess, Leo still clutching Henry's smasher hat. Banned from running, raising voices, and playing, still they were eager to go, seeming not to want to talk of their father and uneasy around their silent, mournful mother. This suited Beatrice. It was painful for her to look at Ena, who reminded her of Henry, and Drino was testy, asking why his father had to wait so long before he could join a campaign. When Beatrice wearily explained that Henry had other duties, Drino seemed to hold her responsible, arguing that none of the duties were military.

There were visitors; Bertie, who had come to Cannes in his yacht, bringing a supply of the special lotion he applied twice daily to his balding scalp; Helena; even a somewhat penitent Louise, all curious and whispering among themselves when or if Beatrice would return to her former duties, saying her flight was understandable, considering the circumstances. Louis, whose ship was offshore, came to persuade her that it was in her best interests to return to Victoria. "My brother would have wanted it," he said.

The only one who applauded her bolt was Eugénie, who drove from her Villa at Cap St. Martin with the Empress Elizabeth of Austria. Both were elderly ladies and therefore experts on death and its aftermath. While Beatrice maintained a stoic reserve before her brothers and sisters, she confided to Eugénie that it was worse in the silent, lonely hours of the night when she would wake with her hand rummaging over the empty pillow beside her. She whispered that sometimes she felt that her marriage had been a dream, that the sun would make her soporific and almost content; then with the chill of the evening and a sickening stab of pain, she would recall that happiness did not lie ahead. It would never lie ahead. It was all behind.

Eugénie said that the pain became easier, although one never forgot. One woke with it in the morning and went to sleep with it at night, although as time went on, the memory became like a soreness that eased up with movement.

Elizabeth disagreed. She said it was with her always, nor would she wish to be rid of it, for if she did, she would lose that loved one more irrevocably than in death. Beatrice recalled that Elizabeth would eat nothing but milk from Schönbrunn cows, which had to be taken abroad when she traveled. Was Elizabeth that way before or after Rudolph's death? Did women get crotchety after the loss of a loved one, or was it age? Would she?

Victoria came to Cimiez at the end of the month with a cavalcade of seventy, including six dressers, a French chef, three cooks, a coachman, an outrider, and a special horsehair mattress with loops that could be loosened in the morning to air the stuffing. In the time Beatrice had been abroad, she had given little thought to who was discharging the services she routinely performed or what the nature of those services was. She felt no remorse, no regret, only firm resolve. Then she saw her mother alight from her carriage, more shrunken, more dependent on the arms of her Highland servant to set her firmly on the ground and seat her carefully in her wheelchair, and when she neared, the milky opacity that was forming over her eyes, diminishing even further her sight. It was when Victoria recognized her and smiled that a pang of guilt as sharp as a knife blade sliced through her.

"You look better, dear," said Victoria in her sweet, silvery voice. "I am glad to see you so improved."

Beatrice edged down a narrow limestone staircase to meet her, grazing the fingertips of her black kid gloves on the rough-hewn balustrade. They sat in the garden on ironwork chairs, surrounded by banks of jasmine, near their feet, a birdbath bearing six winged marble seraphim. Victoria asked for the children, commented on the terrible Armenian massacres in Turkey, then began to talk of the Russian coronation to take place in May.

"Bertie and Alicky," she said, "will bear unsteady crowns."

"You mean Nicky and Alicky, Mama."

"Yes. That is what I said."

She spoke of the series of anti-British articles that had begun to appear in the Russian press, which she fully expected Nicky to repudiate, then changed the topic to the preparations being made for her diamond jubilee. Victoria expressed concern over the stability of the roofs and balconies on the smaller houses south of the Thames, saying she doubted whether the parapets were strong enough to support those who would lean against them. It had been decided, she said, that no other crowned heads of state would be invited, since the protocol involved would be too demanding of her. Then she confided that she regretted this decision because it meant that Fritz couldn't come, and she had great affection for that son-in-law, although not quite so much as what she felt for Henry.

"You mean Willy, Mama."

Victoria looked confused. "If I meant Willy, I would have said Willy."

"Fritz is dead, Mama," said Beatrice softly. "Willy is Emperor."

"Yes," said Victoria sadly, "I had forgotten. Sometimes my thoughts are like a kite. Suddenly I am left holding a broken string."

Beatrice sighed with an exhalation so deep she felt the points of her stays. She made an immediate decision. Her shoulders sagged as if a suit of mail had suddenly been buckled over them.

"I think we should go indoors, Mama, don't you?" she asked. "Then we can plan some sort of schedule while we are on the continent. Perhaps you would even like to dictate a letter to the London County Council requesting that they investigate the parapets."

She signaled to the Highland servant, who took the grips of the wheelchair, while she followed behind, her long black veil fluttering at her knees in the chalky gust.

EPILOGUE

Discarding her deep mourning for the attenuated mourning of white, Beatrice again became Victoria's dedicated companion, more deeply subordinated than ever before, the weight of her responsibilities increasing with Victoria's diminishing capacities. For others, she was often remote and inaccessible, an anchorite amid a population of clergy and librarians, craftsmen and servants, and the fawning, largely female court.

The next five years saw Victoria's diamond jubilee and the outbreak of the Boer conflict. The last of the gentlemen's wars marked a final gasp of empire as well as a change in Victoria's attitude toward the Irish. Because of the gallantry of Irish troops in the South African campaign, she was prompted to visit Ireland for the first time in almost forty years and to decree that henceforth all ranks in Her Majesty's Irish regiment were to wear a sprig of shamrock on St. Patrick's Day.

Beatrice found it increasingly difficult to keep up with the avalanche of state papers that she alone read to Victoria as Victoria's days became naps broken by meals she could not eat. In January 1901, following the death of Lady Jane Churchill, Victoria succumbed with her century, her consciousness ebbing like the tide on the beach below, as Willy cradled her in his arms.

The family and the household tidied up the baggage of succession, swirling around Beatrice like a whirlpool around a pebble. Her dispossession was piecemeal as, her usefulness over, she was relegated to the status of just another unimportant member of a large royal family.

Bertie, now King Edward VII, was determined to sweep aside the sacred cobwebs that Victoria had woven. In addition to smashing statuettes of John Brown, throwing out piles of bric-a-brac, and installing new plumbing, he decided that he could not afford the upkeep of Osborne and donated its stables and surrounding land as a site for a naval college and the great wing as a home for convalescent officers. That Beatrice's home was to be shared with strangers was as insignificant as Victoria's wish that he take the name Albert Edward at the time of his succession.

Events that followed, as in all families, moved between the tragic and the hopeful. Vicky died that summer of cancer of the spine. Two years later, Louis and Victoria's daughter Alice married Prince Andrew of Greece. In 1906, Ena married Alfonso, the King of Spain, the birth of her first son sadly proving her to be a carrier of the dreaded hemophilia.

The First World War was to snap family ties as cousin fought cousin. Beatrice's youngest son Maurice died of battle wounds, as did Vicky's grandson, Maximilian of Hesse, the son of her youngest daughter Mossy. In 1917, George V, now king, announced that all his relations who held German titles should adopt British titles in their place. In this patriotic transliteration, the name of Battenberg was changed to Mountbatten. Several months later, as Willy sought refuge in Holland, Nicky, Alicky, and their five children were executed by Bolsheviks in a cellar at Ekaterinburg.

As curator of Victoria's private journals, Beatrice destroyed nearly half of Victoria's papers. Some historians have labeled this editing of priceless documents an act of vandalism, others have called it a rigid adherence to Victoria's injunction that Beatrice modify any portions that appeared to her unsuitable for permanent preservation. Whichever lent impetus to her zeal can only be surmised. Perhaps, as motivation is seldom unmixed, it was a little of both. Beatrice died in 1944 at the age of eighty-seven, the last surviving child of Queen Victoria.